W9-ACD-772

Praise for Gallagher Gray's first mystery, HUBBERT & LIL: PARTNERS IN CRIME

"Weaves a wondrous web of work relationships shrouded by ghosts of a long-ago scandal . . . In the classic British cozy tradition right down to the body with the antique dagger in its chest."
—*The Drood Review of Mystery*

"One of the most appealing detective stories I have read in a long time."
—*The Virginian-Pilot and The Ledger-Star*

"Gray's writing style is light, interesting, good with characterizations and funny. . . . Delightful."
—Associated Press

"[A] surprise-filled debut . . . [A] superior plot . . . Auntie Lil is delightfully feisty."
—*Publishers Weekly*

Also by Gallagher Gray
Published by Ivy Books:

HUBBERT & LIL: PARTNERS IN CRIME

A CAST OF KILLERS

Gallagher Gray

IVY BOOKS • NEW YORK

Sale of this book without a front cover may be unauthorized. If this book is coverless, it may have been reported to the publisher as "unsold or destroyed" and neither the author nor the publisher may have received payment for it.

Ivy Books
Published by Ballantine Books
Copyright © 1992 by Gallagher Gray

All rights reserved under International and Pan-American Copyright Conventions, including the right of reproduction in whole or in part in any form. Published in the United States by Ballantine Books, a division of Random House, Inc., New York, and distributed in Canada by Random House of Canada Limited, Toronto.

This novel is a work of fiction. Names, characters, places and incidents are either the product of the author's imagination or are used fictitiously. Any resemblance to actual events, locales, organizations or persons, living or dead, is entirely coincidental and beyond the intent of either the author or publisher.

Library of Congress Catalog Card Number: 92-53072

ISBN 0-8041-1146-4

This edition published by arrangement with Donald I. Fine, Inc.

Manufactured in the United States of America

First Ballantine Books Edition: May 1994

10 9 8 7 6 5 4 3 2 1

CHAPTER ONE

1. Naturally, the phone rang just as Tyrone enveloped Camilla in his massive arms and drew her closer to him. T.S. sighed. He had been waiting for this kiss for two weeks now, enduring illegitimate children, plastic surgery, a murder conspiracy, the talking dead and other silly subplots along the way. All for this one single fulfilling moment—a moment now about to be spoiled by a shrill electronic intrusion.

Well, he'd just let the answering machine pick up. He was retired now. He didn't have to answer the phone unless he damn well felt like it.

Unless it was Auntie Lil, of course. Mere machines could not stop her.

It was Auntie Lil. "Theodore!" Her foghorn of a voice, amplified considerably by the answering machine, boomed through his apartment and caused Brenda and Eddie to stir in dreamy feline discomfort.

He ignored her. On screen, Tyrone quivered above Camilla. Their faces wavered closer and closer together, as if controlled by bursts of magnetic force. T.S. had never experienced a kiss like that, but it was just as well. Their necks were weaving from side to side like cobras and he'd no doubt pull a muscle if he tried the same.

"Theodore, I know you're home. And I know you're watching those silly soap operas. You're rotting your brain. Pick up the phone at once or I'm coming over in person. By cab."

T.S. sighed. Auntie Lil would do it, too. She'd be there in twenty minutes and run a white-gloved hand over the television set for signs of heat. Then she'd never let him forget that she'd been right. He picked up the phone reluctantly. Best to stave her off.

1

"I am not watching soap operas," he replied indignantly. "I am trying to read *The New Yorker* without interruption, for a change." He nudged the television's volume down a few notches with his free hand. Auntie Lil was a bit hard of hearing. Chances were good she'd never know for sure.

"Nonsense. I've been calling you every day for two weeks now between noon and 1:00 P.M. and you never pick up the phone. I know quite well that 'Life's Interludes' is on right now. I know what you're up to, Theodore, and frankly I'm a little disappointed in you. Retirement is not a death sentence. There's no reason for you to turn your brain into Jell-O. Thirty-five years of work does not entitle you to fifty more of pure laziness."

He sighed again. There was no arguing with Auntie Lil. His own fifty-five years of humble existence could not begin to match her eighty-four years of self-proclaimed authority.

"What was it you wanted, Aunt Lil?" he asked absently, his attention drawn back to the television. The couple on screen were kissing at last. And last and last and last. T.S. stared. Good Lord, when were they coming up for air? He liked romance as much as the next person, but this really was getting silly. Their lips were being mashed about like silly putty. Surely the show's writers didn't believe that people really enjoyed such fleshy gymnastics. Or did they? T.S. was no authority on romance; he'd devoted his entire adult life to his business career instead. His few brief forays into romance had been, without exception, disastrous and deeply distressing to his personal dignity. As a highly eligible bachelor, he had been subjected to extremely innovative pressure techniques from several otherwise sane middle-aged women. He'd found these experiences humiliating for all concerned.

Auntie Lil's brisk voice cut through his thoughts. "Good. Then it's all settled," she said with great satisfaction. "You'll be glad that you did."

"Glad I did what?" The television set flickered, as if the couple's heat was too much for its cables. And still they kissed on.

Auntie Lil sighed with the patience of a weary martyr. "You're not paying the least bit of attention to what I say, are you?"

"Of course I am . . ." My god—Camilla had pulled away from Tyrone and slapped him across the face. It was a most unexpected plot development. What had Tyrone done to deserve such treatment? T.S. must have missed it. Or was there something going on down there in the waist area, outside of camera range? T.S. leaned forward and scrutinized the screen more carefully, searching for a clue.

"I'm going to march over there right now and rip that television cord out of the wall," Auntie Lil said firmly. "I will not have my favorite nephew turning into some kind of a mesmerized zombie who hums jingles and knows the names of sitcom stars."

The show cut to a commercial, freeing T.S. to respond. "I heard every single word you said," he lied. "And you're right. You're absolutely right." They were Auntie Lil's favorite words to hear and ought to mollify her.

"Good. Then you'll be here in an hour."

Uh, oh. He'd been tricked. He was suddenly quite sure that Auntie Lil had deliberately called him at this time, knowing he'd be preoccupied, and had planned exactly what had just happened. What in the world had he agreed to do now? Well, he would not give her the satisfaction of knowing how well her little scheme had worked. He'd play along and find out the details in his own subtle way.

"What's the address?" he asked casually.

"I knew you weren't paying attention. It's right off the corner of Eighth Avenue and Forty-eighth Street. St. Barnabas Church. Large stone building. The soup kitchen is in the basement. You'll see a long line of people waiting to get in. Hurry. And bring rubber gloves."

Rubber gloves? A soup kitchen? He was in hot water now.

"Theodore," Auntie Lil's voice softened to a suspiciously self-satisfied purr. "Thank you so much for helping out. Two volunteers failed to show. I don't know what we would have done without you."

"Done what?" he finally asked, starting to panic. "What am I doing?"

"You're serving the food. What did you think you'd be doing? I wasn't inviting you over for lunch, you know."

"Serving food at a soup kitchen?" he asked. The show was starting again but Tyrone and Camilla were nowhere to be seen. A silly subplot had taken over the screen.

"Yes," Auntie Lil said firmly. "It's only for today, if it's such an imposition." She stopped, letting her reproachful silence berate him with its own eloquence.

"I thought God helped those who help themselves," T.S. said faintly, knowing that it was a feeble rebuttal.

"How very convenient for those of us who are selfish." There was no sarcasm in Auntie Lil's voice. Sarcasm required subtlety, which was not her strong suit.

"What kind of people eat at this soup kitchen?" he asked. He envisioned an army of dusty, homeless muggers lockstepping toward him with arms outstretched.

"What kind of people do you think?" she snapped. "All kinds of people. Hungry people. Old people. Homeless people. Discouraged people. Mentally ill people. The main thing, Theodore, is that they *are* people. In case you've missed my point."

Miss one of Auntie Lil's points? That was like overlooking a spear sticking in your back. But she had shamed him sufficiently and T.S. knew when he was licked. What was a mere soap opera in the face of starving humanity?

"All right," he agreed grudgingly. "I'll see you in an hour."

"Good. Try to contain your enthusiasm," she ordered, hanging up abruptly.

Maybe she could be sarcastic, after all.

T.S. reluctantly turned off the television and marched back to his meticulously organized closet, swapping his bedroom slippers (thank God she'd not ferreted out that little detail) for a suitably humble pair of shoes from the day-wear rack. Image was important to him. The proper attire said a lot about a man. But in this case, he decided, there was no need to change clothes. He'd be there and back by late afternoon.

2.

He asked his cab driver to detour past the Newsday Building at One Times Square so he could set his watch by the time on their giant electronic clock. T.S. was a precise man and liked to know exactly what time it was. That way he was never, ever late. Except for that one day in 1956 when the subway train he'd been riding on had derailed and made him fifteen minutes late for a dental appointment. The thought still rankled.

They skirted the square traffic and headed across Forty-second Street toward the West Side. His taxi slowed as it started up Eighth Avenue, passing the brightly lit marquees of fast food outlets and even faster sex shops. There were a few hustlers of every breed and brand of business scattered over the dirty sidewalks, but it was relatively deserted in mid-afternoon.

Soon, the business district surrounding the Port Authority gave way to ethnically diverse residential streets, divided by avenue blocks of smaller restaurants, delicatessens and retail shops. It had been several years since T.S. had ventured into the neighborhood that the rest of Manhattan called Hell's Kitchen. A few residents had tried to replace the century-old nickname with the more upscale "Clinton." But—like most of their efforts at gentrification—

the change had not stuck. The area was still Hell's Kitchen and most of its inhabitants were still stubbornly proud of that fact.

Few skyscrapers had invaded the area west of Eighth Avenue. Side street after side street was lined with four- to six-story brownstones in various stages of disrepair and renovation. T.S. peered curiously out the window. Cheerfulness thrived only in very small pockets, but at least it had not given up entirely: streets gleaming with new brick and freshly planted trees were always bordered on either side by streets filled with the gray-stained concrete and crumbling front stoops of poverty.

Hell's Kitchen still had not decided what it wanted to be when it grew up. It was neither a bad neighborhood nor a particularly good one, its varied residents coexisting in a schizophrenic truce that defied description. Hard-working immigrants from every country of the globe peered out of the windows of their small restaurants and shops. Well-dressed businessmen scurried eastward, eager to make their after-lunch appointments. Hordes of preschool-age children swarmed everywhere, held in tow by overweight mothers of all races who shared a single, weary expression. They, in turn, were elbowed aside by fantastically fit actors and actresses, who picked their way through the crowds mumbling lines to themselves and trying on different faces. Attracted by cheap rents and the nearby theater district, they shared apartments in the neighborhood and added to its astounding (even for New York) diversity. T.S. felt that their fresh and hopeful faces only made the reality of the neighborhood that much more depressing.

No matter how hard it tried, he reflected, Hell's Kitchen was still lower middle class with an occasional sprinkling of hopeful yuppies seeking zooming property values. In fact, he passed several of these well-groomed residents as his cab raced uptown. They were tightly gripping their purses and briefcases, as they grimly steered clear of grimy, frantic groups that gathered on certain corners, chattering and pointing with self-importance to nearby windows.

T.S. sighed. That, too, had not changed. Waves of drug dealers and users still washed over the neighborhood's blocks in regular intervals, only to recede a few weeks later, when the cops finally chased them a couple of blocks down the avenue. But never far enough away to matter.

T.S. sighed again. Though the details had changed, the amount of progress was the same. Hell's Kitchen was always getting better, but never, ever quite got there.

He was so absorbed in his thoughts that he did not notice when his driver overshot Forty-eighth Street and pulled up in front of a gleaming, new red-brick skyscraper at Forty-ninth and Eighth. T.S. had heard it was being built, but he had not seen it yet. Its existence was a shock.

"Sorry, buddy." The driver shrugged. It was not his problem. "Con Ed was tearing up the streets back there."

T.S. was too stymied by the new building to reply and simply paid his bill and climbed out to stare. Someone had put a lot of money into this building, and thus into the neighborhood. Perhaps times were changing after all. But it was funny. He was not as happy as he thought he'd be.

The building loomed above him, its upper floors blocked by the brilliant glare of the sunlight high above. It was at least forty stories high on its Eighth Avenue side. T.S. peered around the corner—it stretched down the block all the way to Ninth Avenue, where it tapered down to a more modest six stories in height. Construction was still going on inside the lower floor interiors and torn brown paper ineffectually blocked the internal debris. But outside, brass fixtures and cornices winked in the bright sunlight, beckoning smartly dressed people, who fled from their cabs to step briskly through the building's revolving doors, anxious to trade the grime of the neighborhood for its high-tech, sterile interior.

T.S. paused to read the directory and saw that a major advertising agency had moved into the building. That explained all the slim bodies, deep tans, boxy shoulders, short hairdos and male ponytails flowing past him. Hell's Kitchen would never be the same.

On the other hand, he noticed with surprising satisfaction, the sidewalk surrounding the new edifice was thoroughly splattered with reddish spots. When cleaning the brick and brass for a final time, careless workmen had evidently allowed chemicals to spatter in the wind and fall onto the not-quite-set concrete—giving the new sidewalks a mottled, almost bloodstained, look.

So Hell's Kitchen had not given up without a fight, T.S. decided. And it had drawn the borders right up to the very base of the new intruder.

The thought pleased him and confused him at the same time. Hell's Kitchen always had that effect on his heart. It unsettled T.S., stirring up visions of his poverty-stricken German immigrant ancestors, whose dreams and hard work had helped him escape these very blocks. He experienced the same restless yearnings whenever he examined the hopeful faces that appeared so often in the old photographs showing scores of people crowded on the decks of ocean liners, their faces upturned to gaze at the Statue of Liberty, their dreams worn so nakedly that people a hundred years later could see plainly the longing there. Their ability to believe made T.S. feel lost; their will to succeed made him feel ashamed. His own life had been so much easier.

How could he have been so unwilling to help out at the soup kitchen? If Auntie Lil could do it, so could he. T.S. shook his head, put the familiar guilt behind him, and walked determinedly toward Forty-eighth Street. His destination was obvious. A long line of people stretched around a corner and snaked uptown along the east side of Eighth Avenue. As T.S. drew closer, he saw that the queue led to a small basement entrance tucked under the stoop of a sagging Baroque-style church. City grime stained its sweeping front steps and the main entrance doors were blocked by a massive locked wrought-iron gate. A smaller, collapsible gate prevented anyone from waiting on the steps. Like so many other churches in the city, St. Barnabas could no longer afford to offer sanctuary to the spiritually needy—too many of them also needed an empty pew that they could call home.

The church's side basement entrance was also protected by a locked wrought-iron gate. A large clapboard sign on the sidewalk out front announced: St. Barnabas soup kitchen. 3:00 p.m. All who are hungry are welcome.

There were, apparently, plenty who were hungry. And they were just as Auntie Lil had described them: people of all shapes, sizes, colors and ages. Some were young with ancient faces; they waited in line and looked away when others stared, as if afraid that they could not offer a good enough excuse for their presence. Others were just plain old and stood patiently with the expertise of those who have spent their lives waiting in lines. A number of people were disheveled, dusty and dirty. These mumbled incoherently to themselves and were left unobtrusively alone by the others—who knew better than to make eye contact.

T.S. passed by the line and noticed an oddity. There were a surprising number of elderly ladies: trim, neatly dressed in styles of bygone eras, their hair carefully coiffed in swirls on top of their heads, slightly garish makeup perfectly in place, all of them dignified and quiet. What were they all doing here? One after another, they stood silently in line, staring at the wrought-iron gate that led to the basement soup kitchen. T.S. glanced at his watch:

it was only two-fifteen. Over half an hour before any of them would eat.

He hesitated near the locked basement entrance. A plump woman wrestling with a garbage can on the other side of the gate noticed his discomfort. She paused in her efforts and tucked a frizzy lock of gray hair back behind an ear. She was in her mid-fifties, about thirty pounds overweight, and had attempted to disguise the extra baggage with a broad, khaki-colored skirt of such unrelentingly starched sturdiness that it looked like it could easily withstand a charge of elephants without wrinkling. She wore a short-sleeved, plaid shirt and had a vaguely masculine air about her. T.S. had run into her type before: she was from New England, the outfit declared, and was a capable woman who could take care of herself and was sick and tired of picking up after weak men. In short, she terrified T.S. He stepped back reflexively under the power of her stare as she, in turn, surveyed his own attire. Finally, the woman arrived at a reluctant conclusion, rewarded him with a perfunctory glance and produced a set of keys from her skirt's pockets. She was not the kind of woman to wear a skirt without pockets.

"About time you showed up," she growled through the bars. "Where's the other volunteer?"

She was obviously taking charm lessons from Auntie Lil. "I'm not the regular volunteer," T.S. explained faintly. "My Aunt Lil dragged me down here at the last minute to help out."

"I'm not surprised. Your aunt appears capable of anything." The woman primly unlocked the gate and the crowd moved back obediently, their eyes following T.S. inside. "She's quite the organizer," she added nastily, leaving no doubt that it was the kindest description of Auntie Lil that she could possibly dredge up.

T.S. followed her through a narrow concrete tunnel into a low basement room reminiscent of the barren cafeteria of a poor school on the wrong side of town. The room stretched out with a dreary sameness: a too low ceiling, harsh fluorescent lighting, scuffed linoleum of a vague brownish tint, rows of long, collapsible tables lined with bright aqua plastic chairs that cracked and sagged and were studded with worn black spots.

Dusty plastic flowers in empty glass jars adorned the center of every table. A handful of earnest young people were quickly setting out cutlery and paper napkins. He had entered a time warp. Both male volunteers had long, frizzy ponytails held back with rubber bands and were wearing tie-dyed T-shirts with faded jeans.

The two women wore their long, straight hair parted in the middle in a style not popular since the 1960s. Their long flowered dresses were equally out of date. And, T.S. acknowledged sadly, their concern for the hungry was considered just as old-fashioned by many.

Steam and chatter beckoned him around a far corner where he discovered just how apt the name "Hell's Kitchen" could be. Behind a low counter lined with cafeteria-style rails, Auntie Lil bent over two enormous pots that billowed forth steam above a huge, industrial metal stove. Another woman sniffed at the strange-smelling brew with her. Just then, the grumpy woman who had let T.S. in the gate, elbowed both women aside without apology and withdrew several large pans of corn bread from the oven. It was a domesticated version of the witches' scene from *Macbeth*, made even more bizarre by the imposing figure of a priest who hovered at Auntie Lil's elbow, peering over her shoulder.

Unseen, T.S. advanced to a few feet of the group and watched with familiar amusement. Auntie Lil was making a major production of tasting the bubbling stew, he knew, and the supporting players had taken the stage.

At eighty-four years old, Auntie Lil had the energy and physical presence of a woman thirty years younger. She had never been slim but neither had she ever been fat. Sturdy was the best way to describe her. She was of German stock, as her strong chin, rounded face and large apple cheeks clearly implied. Her bone structure made heavy wrinkling nearly impossible, but her skin, while pink and glowing with good health, was crisscrossed with fine lines over its rosy surface. Her eyes were clear and a steely blue. They did not twinkle with old lady amusement as some people thought at first, but sparkled instead with a stubborn inner fire (as *everyone* soon discovered). Her mind was sharp and her physical abilities still impressive. After more than sixty years of working in the fashion industry, Auntie Lil had acquired an innate nimbleness and confidence of movement that defied old age. She believed in acting first and thinking later. Her hands were large and rawboned, yet still skillful enough to thread a needle on her very first try.

Although Auntie Lil had devised patterns for the world's most expensive dresses, she preferred pants suits above all other forms of attire. Today, she was dressed in bright red knit trousers and a matching tunic. She had wrapped a multicolored jungle print scarf around her thick, white hair. After many years of wearing it long her hair had recently been cut and it escaped from under the scarf in wiry curls to bounce in wild disarray. Brightly painted, carved wooden fish earrings dangled from each ear and her feet were encased in thick white socks and Moroccan leather sandals. As usual, she was a walking United Nations, splashed with enough bright colors to discourage the entire research team of the Eastman Kodak Corporation.

"More chili powder?" the robust priest asked Auntie Lil earnestly. An abundant crop of silver hair curled about his massive head in leonine splendor. His features were strong and authoritative, lacking any hint of meekness or piety, and he was very tall. He was also built like an aging linebacker. His stomach strained out against his priestly garb below a massive bulldoglike chest. He looked like he should have been quaffing quarts of brew in an Irish pub, instead of supervising little old ladies in a New York City soup kitchen. He was a veritable giant of a priest and, T.S. admitted to himself, a good choice for coping with the sometimes physically dangerous demands of running a church in the inner city.

"Perhaps just a touch more chili?" the priest meekly suggested again, when no one bothered to answer him.

Auntie Lil shook her head firmly and raised one arm in an imperious command for silence. She rolled the stew about her tongue and lifted her eyes toward heaven as if seeking divine guidance.

"A touch of cumin?" the priest tried desperately. "Or a little curry, perhaps?"

"Are you insane?" Auntie Lil asked calmly. He was but a mere speck of humanity, her tone implied, attempting to interfere with the divine creation of great cuisine.

"Ah ha!" Auntie Lil smacked the enormous spoon on the stove's metal surface with a bang. Her assistants jumped back in surprise and everyone in the room turned to stare. "More onion!" she declared with celestial inspiration, one finger pointed at the ceiling.

The priest nodded his head in solemn agreement, but the grumpy matron cutting corn bread scowled furiously before banging her knife on the counter with great irritation and pulling several large onions out of a drawer. She plunked them angrily on a cutting surface and began to chop with the homicidal vigor of an ax murderer. T.S. knew at once that she had been the Queen Bee of the kitchen before Auntie Lil had arrived. No wonder she had hated him on sight.

The priest noticed the woman's distress. "Thank you, Fran. As always, you're such a help," he murmured, patting her shoulder with the kind of cautious enthusiasm you'd reserve for an unknown Doberman Pinscher. But the priest's automatic praise was more than enough for grumpy Fran. She turned her face up at the priest and beamed a radiant smile back at him, eyes filled with adoration. Her happy expression transformed her broad face into one that held hints of a former, perhaps even startling, beauty. The priest beamed back at her while the rest of the kitchen staff clanged past without taking any notice.

"Don't just stand there, Theodore," Auntie Lil suddenly commanded T.S. from across the room. "Help me with this chili."

"Nice to see you, too, Aunt Lil," he replied, giving her leathery cheek an affectionate peck. "Don't tell me that Father Whoever is foolish enough to have actually turned you loose in the kitchen? Haven't those poor people outside suffered enough?"

She handed him a potholder. "I'll have you know that this a secret chili recipe brought back to me by a genuine cowboy from Santa Fe in the thirties."

"That's good. All those cowboys waiting outside are going to really love it."

She ignored him. She was good at that. "Father Whoever is Father Stebbins. If you're not going to go to church on a regular basis, at least show it some respect. Perhaps he'll put in a good word for you upstairs."

T.S. tasted the chili and gasped for air. "He'd better make it quick. I think I'm going down." He grabbed his throat and staggered back against a sink already filled with an enormous pile of dirty dishes. Auntie Lil was incapable of entering a kitchen without leaving behind conditions that could qualify for federal disaster aid.

"I suppose you think you're amusing." She handed him a glass of water and stared intently at the pot. "Perhaps I *should* cut it with a few more kidney beans."

He shook his head vigorously. "Why bother? This could solve the mayor's homeless problem in a single afternoon."

"Really, Theodore, I asked you down here to help, not gloat." Auntie Lil handed him another potholder and directed him to move one of the enormous pots to a back burner. He paused in his task to allow the ever-suffering Fran to scrape in her load of massacred onions. Despite himself, his stomach started to rumble. It did smell good, in a kind of diabolic and dangerous way.

Auntie Lil then ordered him to retrieve a huge container of

cooked rice that was stored in a large walk-in freezer at the rear of the kitchen. "Mr. Chang donated it," she explained. "He's got a small takeout joint on the corner."

That was Auntie Lil. Put her in a new neighborhood and she instantly picked up the local slang. T.S. expected her to start talking about a "fast score" at any moment.

For nearly thirty minutes, she dogged him, sending him here and there in search of loaves of bread, pots of beans, more rice and a mountain of grated cheese. "You're looking well, Aunt Lil," T.S. told her when she finally allowed him to stop for breath. "All this ordering me around certainly seems to agree to you."

"Of course I'm looking well. I keep active. You don't see me wasting any of *my* time in front of a television set." She marched across the room and corrected the placement of forks on a nearby table while the other volunteers watched in amusement.

3. The hungry hordes did not stampede in. They shuffled in slowly, almost shyly, the obvious regulars taking the time to show newcomers where to go. The line snaked obediently toward the cafeteria railing while the volunteers took their places behind the counter with practiced competence. T.S. wandered past them, searching for Auntie Lil but, as usual, she managed to outflank him. She gripped his elbow and steered him to a spot behind a huge pot of chili, abandoning him before he could protest. Naturally, it was the hottest spot in the room and it both smelled and felt like his imagined version of the darkest depths of Hell. The odor of fiery chili peppers tickled his nose and made his eyes water as he stepped into place. Fragrant steam instantly assaulted him, fogging up the reading glasses he wore. The very last thing he saw before his temporary blindness was Auntie Lil taking a place at the front of the line.

How typical. While he sweated in Hell, he could listen to her greeting each person as if this were an afternoon tea party and she were the proud hostess. He wiped his glasses with the edge of a potholder and they instantly steamed up again. Only this time— unnoticed by T.S.—a lone kidney bean clung to the exact center of his right lens like a dark and deformed eyeball.

"How nice of you to come today," he heard Auntie Lil tell an unseen person. "Please feel free to eat well. We have plenty." There was a murmuring and she began again with someone new, demonstrating that she had the unerring instincts of a successful dictator—stick to the public relations and let the others do the dirty work.

T.S. could feel his hair begin to curl from the dampness and his stomach took a peculiar dip in response to the spicy aroma. He kept waiting for his glasses to clear but the chili seemed to have taken on a life of its own, spewing up steamy cloud after cloud like an angry volcano about to erupt.

"Excuse me, sir, but I am hungry. Do I get to eat or do I simply stand here and *smell* it?" The new voice was seductively female, full of hidden meaning and ringing with inflection. The enunciation was perfect. Clearly, it was a voice trained for the theater.

T.S. picked the useless glasses from his face, sending the kidney bean flying onto his shoe. He kicked it off with as much dignity as he could muster and folded the glasses into his back pocket, assuring himself that he did not *really* need them. At least not much. In fact, he'd been hoping to keep their recent existence a secret from Aunt Lil anyway (who hid her own behind a cushion on her couch).

His vision cleared. He had expected a young woman, perhaps a beautiful actress down on her luck. He found a frail old lady instead. She was so thin and pale that she gave the impression of being translucent, at first. Blue veins glowed behind parchment-like skin and only her face seemed to be successfully holding back the pulsating emergence of inner organs and blood vessels. And this was only because she wore what looked to be a full pound of makeup, expertly applied but in far too heavy proportions for the daytime. Not to mention the current decade. Her eyebrows had been plucked and were heavily outlined into startling dark thin arches. Her lips were drawn too wide for her frail face and were filled in with a deep scarlet that made her mouth look more like a wound than a feature. Dark eyeliner outlined both the upper and lower lids of small black eyes, and her rouge was applied in tiny crab apples on either side of a patrician nose.

He blinked. She was a vision from a 1940s movie, with the barely contained, too desperate animation of a background extra hoping to catch the audience's eye. Even her seemingly calm waiting was imbued with an overly dramatic patience.

"They each get a ladleful for starters," the young woman serving rice beside him said helpfully. She was holding out a plate of rice and he took it automatically, plopping chili on top before handing it, in turn, to the waiting woman.

"Thank *you*," the old lady murmured. "*So* sorry to have disturbed you." She took her plate and sailed regally down the line toward the basket of corn bred, leaving T.S. to wonder just what her hidden meaning might have been. Sarcasm, he suspected.

"That's Adelle," the rich volunteer informed T.S. "She's sort of the head of the regulars here."

She was also the hungriest, T.S. decided, when he spotted her for what must have been the fourth time in the line. How could she be eating all that chili? My God, the thought was frightening. Until he realized he wasn't seeing Adelle again at all—he was seeing different versions of Adelle. There was an entire team of old ladies, it seemed, who wore heavy, stagelike makeup and dresses that had not been fashionable since the days of Eisenhower. They all spoke in cultured, trained voices and held themselves as tragically erect as queens on their way to the gallows. What in the world was going on?

Two such women stood in line staring at T.S. with blatant curiosity. They looked like seductive grandmothers dressed to kill for a social occasion scheduled many decades ago.

"He looks a bit like John Barrymore in *My Dear Children*, don't you think?" the first one asked her companion.

The companion snorted skeptically and surveyed T.S. "You think *everyone* looks like John Barrymore," she finally said. "It's time you got over that little fling, my dear."

"But he *does* look like him," the first woman replied stubbornly. "Look at that chin."

The companion was still clearly unconvinced. "Let's hope he knows his role a little bit better than our dear Mr. Barrymore," she said archly.

"How dare you say that?" The first woman turned to her friend, blocking all traffic and apparently not giving a hoot. "He was charming in that show. Marvelous, in fact."

"Marvelous?" The second old woman shook her head firmly and looked behind her at a grime-coated bag lady for support, receiving a crazed glare in reply. "The man didn't know his lines," she finally countered. "Only God knew what was going to come out of his mouth each night. He thought he was in a different play every night of the week."

"I am *not* one of the Barrymores," T.S. interrupted firmly, before the argument escalated into hair pulling. "And my role is to serve you lunch." He plopped the chili on their plates and they took his hint with ill-disguised irritation at being rushed in such an unseemly manner.

"You're right," the first old lady sniffed to her friend. "He hasn't got John's dash at all." They moved primly down the line.

T.S. didn't have much time to ponder the insult. Too many people were waiting to eat. He soon got the hang of ladling out chili and, although a few people mentioned that it certainly smelled spicy, there was no one who complained about either its taste or its peculiar dark brown texture. He was just getting into the swing of things—accept plate, plop on chili, turn quickly, hand it over—when his rhythm was interrupted.

"That's Franklin," the rice volunteer told him, pointing out the next person in line. "He gets two big scoops of chili. He needs it."

Franklin certainly did. He was an enormous black man. Not enormous as in big for a human being, but enormous as in big for a bear. He was well over six feet tall, broad faced and broad shouldered, with deep brown skin that exactly matched the mysterious tint of Auntie Lil's chili. He was dressed in overalls that seemed at least as large as a double-bed quilt and he wore a baseball hat turned backwards over a crop of gray-peppered hair. His hands were massive and the size and texture of baseball gloves, but he waited patiently as T.S. piled on the chili, accepting the plate with shy politeness.

"Thank you, sir," he said, nodding his head before rumbling on down the line. The use of "sir," not to mention its second syllable, confirmed Franklin's Southern upbringing. What was he doing in New York City? If not for his size, he'd be eaten alive.

The hungry faces soon stretched back into one long blur of worried brows, tightly knit mouths and murmured automatic thank-yous. Just as T.S. was scraping the bottom of the vat of chili, Father Stebbins appeared toting another one. T.S. was assaulted by a fresh explosion of steam and received, much to his amusement, one of Father Stebbins' parental pats on the back.

"You're doing fine, son. Bless you for helping. God loves a cheerful giver," the priest murmured before moving on to other, more important tasks.

Meanwhile, Auntie Lil was still there at the juncture of the line, handing out trays and welcoming all to what she implied was some sort of marvelously exclusive street soiree. T.S. had to admit she was good at it, she didn't miss a beat. Not even when it came to grasping those hands that were coated with a thick, oily paste of city grime, accumulated through months—and maybe even years—of not bathing. The befuddled and mentally ill bearers of those hands clearly were in no shape to take care of themselves. And yet they wandered the streets. T.S. wondered how they survived.

At last, the final hungry person had been served, and several re-served with what remained. Auntie Lil wandered over to help T.S. dish out the final portions.

"I think my chili was a rousing success, don't you?" she asked T.S. proudly, as usual not shy about fishing for compliments.

"You've found the perfect audience for your culinary talents," T.S. admitted. "Starving, hungry people who haven't had enough to eat to know any better."

He had only been teasing but she looked so disappointed that he immediately amended his remark. "Actually, Aunt Lil, your chili *was* a rousing success. They all look happy and satisfied."

They stared together at the tables crammed with the hungry and the homeless. Heads were bent low over their meals, spoons and bread clutched in hands, bodies protecting the small place that was theirs. Most people had chosen the nearest seat that they could find and there were many unlikely combinations of table companions. But one table hosted no one but Adelle and the rest of the perfectly dressed little old ladies that T.S. had noticed coming through the line. They argued loudly among themselves in vigorous debate, their well-trained voices projecting across the entire room so that all could hear the conversation.

"Leslie Howard brought more vulnerability to the role," one voice proclaimed.

"How can you say that?" another disagreed. "Gielgud was clearly superior."

"You just say that because he complimented you on your hair that one time."

"That is not true. Everyone knows that Leslie Howard did not possess the animal magnetism required to play a proper Hamlet."

"Leslie Howard had plenty of animal magnetism," a third voice interjected hotly. "And I should know. He was a better Hamlet than John Gielgud could ever be. And we all know why?"

"What are you implying? Not even you could have missed the undertones of *Hamlet* for seventy-five years. Gielgud was the perfect man for the part."

A chorus of voices then entered the debate, providing an unlikely backdrop to the dispirited eating going on in the rest of the room.

"I hesitate to ask this," T.S. admitted, hating to let his curiosity get the better of him. "But who are *they*?" He pointed out the table of chattering old ladies with a chili-smeared finger.

"That's Adelle and her crowd," Auntie Lil explained. "They're old actresses who still live in this neighborhood. Most of them have been here for sixty or more years. A few live in tiny rent-controlled apartments nearby. And some live in shelters, I suspect. They meet here every day for lunch. Their government checks barely cover their rent. This may be the only meal they get. They're all quite charming. I recognized a few of their names from when I was a girl and your grandfather would take me to the theater."

Now who was she kidding? Auntie Lil was at least as old as all of them and probably older than most. Not that T.S. felt it necessary to point that out. "They were famous actresses?" he asked politely, instead.

"On no, not famous. None of them were ever famous. They were chorus girls, maybe, or B and C parts at best. An understudy or two for the bigger parts, perhaps. I know a few were Ziegfeld girls. But never, ever famous." Auntie Lil sighed. "Really, I have to admire their dedication to their art."

Maybe. But T.S. mostly admired their dedication to their eats. They held their spoons carefully above their chili, pinkies extended into the air with archaic correctness. But their hands were practically blurs as they quickly and methodically consumed their meals between arguments.

"You might be right about them eating once a day," he observed.

"That's the story for most everyone here," she agreed sadly.

"Lillian!" Father Stebbins' voice boomed in heavy congratulations behind them. T.S. jumped and knocked a chili spoon flying, splattering the weary linoleum with a new layer of gunk. Grumpy Fran was right behind Father Stebbins, tailing him like a faithful dog. She stared first at the spoon and then at T.S.—clearly, he was as troublesome as she had first suspected.

"The chili was a success," Father Stebbins thundered on. "I knew you could do it! Just a smashing success. Why, look at those happy campers!" He threw his arms out in the general direction of the dining room and they stared obediently at the mechanically munching crowd. No one looked particular ecstatic.

"Theodore!" Auntie Lil suddenly clutched his sleeve in fright and pointed across the room. "That woman's in trouble." Another volunteer's scream followed her cry.

A frail old woman, dressed much like the other old actresses, had been sitting at a table away from the main group. She was struggling up from her chair and her face was blue. Her mouth hung open in speechless agony. Her tablemates stared up mutely in mystified astonishment. Her arm jerked suddenly and upended

her plate of chili. It clattered to the floor and slid across the linoleum, leaving a trail of sticky brown goo.

"She's choking!" T.S. cried, sprinting across the room to her,
with Father Stebbins close behind.

Before they could reach her, the old woman clutched at her
heart and fell to the floor, losing consciousness. Her body jerked
slowly, picking up steam until she was shuddering all over in
spasms that came in waves. She gasped for breath desperately,
like a fish gaffed in the gills. She regained consciousness briefly
and turned her face to T.S. Their eyes locked for a single, horrifying second. He saw complete terror trapped beneath the milky
blue of her irises just before she arched and lapsed unconscious
again, her body writhing uncontrollably as her breath returned in
rapid, agonized rasps.

"She's not choking," Auntie Lil said. "I think she's having a
heart attack."

"I'll call an ambulance," one of the young volunteers shouted.
He vaulted over the railing and disappeared toward the back.

"Does anyone know CPR?" Father Stebbins yelled, his head
whipping wildly from side to side as he scanned the stunned diners watching the drama. Adelle and the other little old ladies had
risen as one from their table—they stared, paralyzed with fear.

"Emily!" one of them croaked, a tiny hand fluttering to cover
her mouth as if she had somehow been impolite.

"I know CPR," T.S. remembered. God, it had been years since
he'd had those Red Cross classes. What to do? Breathe in her
mouth? Thump on her chest? She was so frail he'd crack her ribs
if he did it incorrectly, and probably puncture a lung.

Her body had stilled with an ominous suddenness, but he knelt
beside her anyway and lifted one of her hands. It was as thin and
light as a young tree limb dried to a fire-ready tinder. He felt for
a pulse and could find none. Her veins were as thin and spidery
as ink tracings. He reached under her neck, watching as her lips
quivered, then froze. Her breath smelled faintly of alcohol. Her
eyelids ceased fluttering abruptly and opened as her whole face
grew still, eyes slowing to a stop until she stared at T.S. in permanent surprise. Even as he groped for the carotid arteries, hoping for a pulse, T.S. knew the woman was dead. And that
nothing would bring her back. He found his CPR position anyway, and carefully pumped at her chest, stopped, then tasted the
bitter void of her mouth as he tried to breathe life back into her
body. There was no response. He tried for a minute more before
giving up.

"She's beyond CPR," he said out loud. Auntie Lil dropped to her knees beside him and checked for herself. She nodded in agreement and looked up at the crowd.

"I'm afraid she's dead," she announced with just the right mixture of concern and impersonal calm. It was a calm that T.S. knew she did not feel. Auntie Lil was not afraid of much but, he suspected, death headed the list. She was too old not to realize that it lay in wait for her and she shuddered involuntarily whenever its dark breath passed close by. But she was also a woman consumed by common sense and she knew that the last thing they needed was a panicked crowd pressing in around them. So she kept her voice authoritative and confident, taking over the situation with a practiced air. This was fortunate, since Father Stebbins was absorbed in comforting a sobbing Fran—whose aggressive self-confidence had conveniently fled when confronted with the chance to collapse in the handsome priest's arms.

"There's nothing that anyone can do," Auntie Lil announced, rising to her feet and holding up both hands for silence even though no one had said a word. "We've called an ambulance. They should be here any moment. And I suspect the police will arrive as well. Everyone else might as well finish eating."

Now that *was* like Auntie Lil—few things took precedence over eating in her book. When it came to a meal, death could just take a backseat.

Not many other people shared this priority. Some returned to uneasily eating, but others had different ideas. Before either T.S. or Father Stebbins could stop them, a number of diners quietly laid down their spoons and slipped out the door with the elusive grace of shadows. The police were not popular with the homeless. Some avoided the authorities for good reasons, others simply out of habit.

"Do you think the police will want to talk to them?" Auntie Lil asked anxiously as they watched a thin stream of people trickle out.

"Are you kidding?" a young volunteer answered. "An old lady, maybe homeless, dies in a soup kitchen? This one's going in the bottom drawer. Poor old gal."

"I don't think the police will care," T.S. told Auntie Lil, placing a reassuring arm on her elbow. Her mouth started to tremble. It had just sunk in that the dead woman was very close to her own age.

"After all," T.S. added more gently, patting her hand, "people have heart attacks every day. It isn't like she was murdered."

CHAPTER TWO

1. Two ambulance teams from different hospitals arrived at the same time, providing the assembled diners with diversionary entertainment. As a pair of burly paramedics argued at the entrance to the narrow basement door over who would get the job—bumping their big bellies to prevent the other from entering—a tiny female emergency technician wiggled between them and raced over to the dead woman. She knelt beside her and swiftly checked her vital signs, then shook her head and looked back over her shoulder. "Forget it, Bobby!" she hollered at one of the arguing paramedics. "This one's gone, anyway."

"No, I'm not going to forget it," Bobby yelled back. "I'm tired of this guy dogging my ass. It's starting to get personal, know what I mean?" He poked a hammy finger in the chest of the other ambulance attendant, who knocked it away contemptuously and made a sound deep in his throat that effectively combined the growl of a bear with the hiss of an angry snake. Just the kind of guys you'd want to entrust with the lives of your loved ones.

A low murmur rose in the room and Auntie Lil looked up nervously at T.S., but all he could do was shrug. What was he supposed to do about it? Neither paramedic seemed to feel it inappropriate that they were arguing over a dead body in front of four dozen witnesses and it seemed singularly foolish to get on their bad sides. Who would administer to him in case he got beat up breaking them up? It was not that T.S. was a coward. He was simply, physically, very . . . *prudent*.

"I am not forgetting this one," burly Bobby repeated slowly, emphasizing each distinctly uttered word with a poke in the other paramedic's chest.

"Yes, you are going to forget it. Now break it up and beat it." This command was issued by an unseen voice thick with street-

21

wise New York authority. The two men arguing at the door instantly shut their mouths and stepped back silently to let a pair of uniformed NYPD officers enter. The first cop, a petite brunette in a tight uniform, sniffed the odor of Auntie Lil's chili with distaste. The second one zeroed in on the dead body immediately. He was older and his gray hair was cropped in a defiantly out-of-date crew cut. He looked and swaggered like a bad-tempered Marine on the lookout for a fight. His nametag read "King" and he looked like he took it literally.

"Who's in charge here?" he demanded of the room, thumping a large black stick against his palm in a manner that managed to be both bored and threatening at the same time. The assembled group looked up at one another but no one spoke.

"Who's in charge?" Officer King demanded again, pushing the bill of his hat up with a sausagelike finger as he surveyed the room.

This time the crowd turned as one to stare at Father Stebbins. The priest jumped as if someone had goosed him.

"Dear me, I suppose that I am." He stayed well away from the body. "It's a terrible tragedy. Really, very terrible. God has called her home and she has answered."

"Speaking of answers, what happened?" Officer King demanded. His interest in calls was strictly limited to those legally mandated to suspects.

Father Stebbins' hands were shaking and he clutched at his rosary in confusion. "She was eating and, er, she just keeled over. Terrible thing, of course. Though she did depart here in God's house."

The patrolman eyed the priest. "Could you be more specific?" he demanded.

Auntie Lil and the female paramedic decided to butt in at the exact same time.

"She's dead," said the paramedic. "Probably a stroke."

"She's had a heart attack," Auntie Lil declared.

The cop turned his stare to Auntie Lil. Her multicolored head scarf had come partially unwound in the confusion and now trailed behind her like the wimple veil of a princess in a fairy tale. A chili smudge formed a perfect half oval on one of her large apple cheeks. None of this escaped him.

"You a doctor?" he asked Auntie Lil in what was supposed to be a pleasant voice, but instead caused several people to cough in nervous anticipation.

"No, but I—"

"Then get over there with the other old ladies." The cop cocked his head toward Adelle's table and pointed the way with his baton.

Uh, oh. There could be big trouble now. T.S. gripped Auntie Lil's elbow firmly and spirited her to a far corner before she started a riot. "Don't say another word," he warned and she abruptly shut her mouth. But the look she shot Officer King was venomous enough to inspire T.S. to step out of its path.

The first cop was on her radio and the static crackled in the silence of the dining room. Officer King knelt by the dead body and talked quietly to the female paramedic. He nodded his head, then rose and addressed the crowd. "What's her name?" he asked.

No one answered.

"Nobody knows the deceased?" he asked again, loudly. "What's her name?"

Still no one replied, but several pairs of eyes slid over to Adelle's silent table. Officer King, sensing this movement, turned and directly addressed the group of old actresses. "Did any of you ladies happen to know the deceased?" he asked with exaggerated politeness.

"Her name was Emily," one tiny woman finally answered in a tentative voice, her napkin twisted tightly in her hands.

"Emily." The cop nodded thoughtfully. "Well, that clears it all up. Was she related, perhaps, to *Cher*? Or how about *Madonna*?" His unexpected sarcasm welled in the room like a bad smell.

"Her stage named was Emily something or other. We don't know her real name," Adelle finally answered. Her stage voice richened with indignant anger. "And you needn't be so bloody rude," she added. A British accent crept in on "bloody" but fled before the end of the sentence. Adelle was trying on attitudes like clothes, enjoying her brief moment in the spotlight.

Officer King sighed and shook his head, making it clear that few jobs were as annoying as being a patrolman on the streets of the Big Apple. "Okay. Show's over," he said abruptly, wagging his baton toward the door. "Beat it. There's nothing anyone can do. The wagon's on the way."

The wagon? Medieval images of gravediggers collecting dead plague victims and stacking them like firewood on top of carts flashed unwillingly through T.S.'s mind. Auntie Lil stiffened with the tightly coiled anticipation of a hyper bird dog and T.S. was forced to grip her elbow even more firmly. Now was not the time for a voicing of opinion.

"Some of us must remain to wash up," Father Stebbins protested, his hand absently patting one shoulder of Fran's—who remained apparently surgically attached to his side. Her sobbings had stopped magically with the entrance of the police, but she had not, T.S. noticed, stepped away from Father Stebbins.

"Then five of you can stay," Officer King announced arbitrarily. "The rest of you clear out, pronto. This is not a circus."

Auntie Lil glared eloquently, then majestically wrapped her scarf burma-style around her neck as if she were Peter O'Toole in *Lawrence of Arabia*. Most of the other diners fell in obediently behind, shuffling out like an exhausted conga line suddenly weary of the song.

Surprised by Aunt Lil's sudden surrender, T.S. stood staring after the line of slowly departing diners. He had expected her to kick up a fuss, to demand that she be allowed to examine the body. Simply leaving was not in her character at all. Had the lure of a dramatic exit been that much temptation? Somehow he just didn't think so.

"Perhaps you had better go after your aunt," Father Stebbins suggested, plucking at T.S.'s shirt sleeve. "We have enough people to clean up." Fran was marching back into the kitchen, gesturing for the younger volunteers to join her. Having sensed an opportunity to regain supremacy, if only over sinks of dirty pots, she was happy to seize her chance.

More police were arriving and one pair toted a depressingly green canvas stretcher with what looked like a rubber tarp piled on top. T.S. suddenly wanted very much to leave the scene of the death. "Thank you. I'll just make sure Aunt Lil is okay," he told Father Stebbins, his feet skimming across the linoleum in his haste to escape.

The minute he hit the sidewalk he saw the women clustered in a whispering, tightly drawn group a few feet down from the church. Auntie Lil stood at the center, surrounded by Adelle and her followers, and her arms rose and fell dramatically as she addressed the group. Some of the others looked shell-shocked and one or two dabbed at their eyes with hankies. Most stared at Auntie Lil.

T.S.'s stomach tightened a notch. He'd known that something was up when Auntie Lil conceded the battle so quickly. He must have missed a secret signal between the women. You had to watch that Auntie Lil every moment. She was as sneaky as a smart three-year-old. Well, he might as well go ahead and pull her out of trouble one more time.

Unobserved, he sidled over to eavesdrop. It was worse than he'd expected. Auntie Lil was reenacting Emily's death.

"She clutched her throat like this," Auntie Lil insisted, grabbing at her bright scarf. "Her face was blue and her tongue was sticking out like this." She groaned and fell back in exaggerated agony before being caught by a pair of alert old actresses.

"No, no, *no*," Adelle insisted with majestic conviction. "Her tongue was not out, and she did not simply fall back. Nor did she clutch her throat. She did this." Adelle swept an area clear with her arm, held her hands out in supplication, tightened both her face and throat, and began to shudder. The effect was grotesque and startling, but T.S. had to give Adelle credit. The old actress was pretty good. She'd even managed to steal the scene from Auntie Lil.

A few passers-by slowed to eye the scene with concern as Adelle revved up her gyrations. Perhaps it was time to step in.

"Excellent. That was a marvelous reenactment," T.S. told the group grimly, wading in and gripping Auntie Lil's elbow. He would nip this nonsense in the bud. "But what exactly is the point of these macabre charades?"

Auntie Lil shook off his touch like a terrier dropping a snake, and drew herself erect. "We're just verifying that it was a heart attack and not something more sinister." She did not like to be babied in any way, shape or form. Especially in front of other old ladies.

A depressing parade suddenly emerged through the basement entrance. Two bored-looking men in khaki jumpsuits led the way, toting a large heavy plastic bag on the stretcher between them. They were followed by the glowering Officer King, his petite partner and three other uniformed cops. The procession marched glumly over to a blue station wagon and the body was loaded into the back. All five policemen stood near the hood of the car, passing sour expressions between them as if they were searching for the solution to a particularly distasteful dilemma. Just then, Officer King spotted Auntie Lil and the other old ladies. He stared at them for a moment, a curtain of angry wrinkles descending on his furrowed brow. He reached out one hand and very, very slowly crooked his finger, beckoning them forward with unmistakable authority.

"What's *he* want?" someone muttered. "The bully."

"I guess he needs our help after all," Auntie Lil murmured sweetly. She was going to enjoy this as much as she could. Genteel revenge was her speciality.

"Let's make him beg," Adelle suggested, prompting T.S. to grab Auntie Lil by the elbow once again and drag her toward the police.

"This is no time to let our pride get in the way," T.S. suggested pleasantly, though he felt like spanking more than a few of them. The old ladies followed in a tentative bunch, inching forward as suspiciously as a flock of wild ducks confronted with a bread-toting stranger. They approached the small crowd of policemen and the two groups stared silently at one another. T.S. was reminded of the dreary school dances he'd endured as a young lad in Catholic prep school.

"Well?" Officer King demanded after a moment of antagonistic silence had passed.

"Well, what?" T.S. asked back innocently. If he could seize control before Auntie Lil jumped into the fray, there was a chance they could get somewhere.

"No one knew the dead lady?" the cop asked skeptically. "Not one of you? It looks to me like she was part of your club."

"We told you," Adelle said indignantly. "We called her Emily."

Officer King fell silent and his partner stepped forward. "Ma'am," she explained patiently, "one name is not going to get us very far in New York City. Out of all of you, not one of you knew her last name?"

"She liked being called Emily Toujours," a small voice piped up from the center of the pack. "Because she'd been an understudy to Martha Scott in the original *Our Town*. Back in 1938."

"She *said* she'd been an understudy," another voice objected. "*I* never saw her in it."

"Oh, shut up, Eva," someone else suggested. "You're the one who lied about being in *Sailor Beware!* for about thirty years and went around calling herself Eva La Louche until we checked the playbill and found out you'd only been an assistant stage manager." An excited murmur ran through the crowd of old ladies in response to the obvious insult.

"You mean Emily Toujours wasn't even her real name?" Auntie Lil interrupted, ignoring the incipient pandemonium brewing behind her.

"It was real to her," Adelle insisted.

"Perhaps Actors' Equity would have her real name on record," T.S. suggested.

This produced a round of titters from the old women, who giggled at his layman's ignorance until Adelle explained. "She wasn't *in* Equity, love. She hadn't worked in over forty years and none of us can afford the dues."

"It's her own fault for running off and getting married," Eva's persistently dissident voice interjected. "Imagine. Abandoning Broadway in 1945. What a fool she was."

"You haven't worked in that long either," someone pointed out. "And you didn't even get married, Eva."

Another young cop stepped forward into the fray and the old actresses were momentarily distracted as they examined this handsome young personage and admired his uniform. He stood, totally surrounded by them, scratching an ear and trying to decide the best way to deal with a pack of demented old ladies. "It's just that she had no identification on her," he finally explained kindly. "So we have no way of knowing where she lives, or who in her family to contact."

"Hah!" Adelle sputtered. "That's easy enough. She has no family."

"Well, where did she live?" Officer King interrupted brusquely, elbowing the young pup of an upstart patrolman aside. This time, both the assembled old ladies and the other officers glared. Clearly, he was not scoring points on anyone's popularity meter.

"In a shelter, we think," one of the actresses admitted reluctantly. "We're not really sure, because she was rather a private person."

"Definitely a shelter," one old woman confirmed, pushing her way to the front. She was obviously Eva of the discontent voice. She was plumper than the rest and wore her hair in a badly chosen pixie haircut that was dyed jet black and made even wispier by the fact that she was going bald and her pink scalp peeked through. T.S. decided she was stuck in the Audrey Hepburn era, which was unfortunate, since she lacked about three feet of the required height.

"She'd have put on airs, if she had her own apartment," Eva added, crossing her arms defiantly when no one responded.

"Now, Eva, that's just not true," Adelle chided gently. "You really must get over your feud. For heaven's sake, she's dead now. Let it go."

"I should have been the one asked to 20th Century," Eva said sourly, folding her arms even more tightly across her ample chest. "I'm the one that Mr. Zanuck noticed first."

"But nothing came of it," someone in the middle of the pack

protested, voice dripping with exasperation. "It's not like she became a star and you didn't."

"She accused me of being a dime-a-dance girl!" Eva insisted. "When she met her own husband by standing in dark alleys near the USO like some kind of pro—"

"That's enough," Adelle commanded firmly. "Perhaps you should just shut up."

"She was the one who got kicked out of the USO, not me," Eva added sullenly. "And you didn't like her any more than . . ." Her voice trailed off suddenly as she realized the extent of her friend's disapproval.

Officer King was staring at Eva curiously and Adelle hastened to explain. "She's talking about things that happened forty years ago," she told him. "Don't pay any attention to her. She's old and grouchy."

"And you're not?" Eva glared at Adelle angrily.

"Ladies, ladies," T.S. soothed them. "Let's see if we can't put our personal differences behind us. After all, the police need our help."

Officer King grunted, not liking the idea that he needed anyone's help. He started in again: "You're telling me that no one knows her real name? No one knows where she lives? And no one knows if she has family?" The cop stared at them incredulously.

"Why don't you use what little brains you have?" someone in the middle of the pack finally thought to ask. "She had a pocketbook on her. Why didn't you look in there?"

The cops were starting to stare at each other, exchanging distinct but unspoken messages. They were getting bored and had better things to do—like battling packs of drug addicts, a far more rewarding and productive task than battling this gang of old ladies.

"There was no pocketbook on her, ma'am," the young cop explained patiently.

"Certainly there was," Adelle answered stiffly. "She always carried a pocketbook to match her dress. It was a regular fetish with her."

"We searched the room thoroughly," the policewoman replied. "No pocketbook."

"Well, it's no wonder, the way you stood by and let someone steal it," Auntie Lil pointed out, specifically addressing Officer King. "The way you ordered us out of there, you practically handed it to the thief and held the door open for his getaway."

The cop stared back at Auntie Lil for a long moment of silence, then turned his back abruptly and headed for the blue station wagon holding Emily's body. "Okay, let's pack it in," he ordered the other officers. "That's that. We have here Miss Jane Doe, the latest in a continuing series of unidentified Miss Jane Does, laid low by lost dreams and the cruel anonymous indignities of the ever-gracious City of New York."

His blunt and meanly poetic announcement, combined with their rapid departure, had a stunning effect on those left behind. *Was that it?* Was there nothing else they were going to do to help poor Emily? The old ladies exchanged shocked and hurt expressions as the officers and police cars wandered away. One or two started to cry as they watched the blue station wagon peel off from the curb and head down the street.

"What's this?" T.S. asked anxiously, putting an arm awkwardly around one old lady. "Delayed reaction?" His sympathy did not have the desired effect.

"No," the woman sniffed, bursting into full-blown tears. She lay her head on T.S.'s shoulder and sobbed with verve. "But that awful policeman is right. It's anonymous and cruel. We should have known her real name. I feel terrible. They'll just throw her into the river or something." This inaccurate and alarming remark sparked new sets of tears.

"Oh, stop it, Anna, that's really being too dramatic." Adelle spoke with unenthusiastic authority and dabbed at her eyes with a hankie. She, too, was dismayed by the sudden end to events. "Surely, they'll bury her somewhere."

"Yes," someone declared through rising sobs. "In some mass grave in potter's field with homeless drug addicts and abandoned babies and dead convicts that no one wants."

This last statement, topping all others in dramatic impact, opened the emotional floodgates of the assembled old actresses and tears spread contagiously until nearly everyone was sobbing. Even the feuding Eva, her tears fueled by guilt, wept uncontrollably. T.S. and Auntie Lil stared at one another in dismay.

"And I thought you were overly dramatic," he whispered to her.

Auntie Lil did not smile. "I would not like to die unknown, Theodore," she pointed out curtly.

"It could have been any one of us," Adelle declared then, triggering fresh tears.

Nearly a dozen old ladies were sobbing by now and, naturally, people passing by were slowing to get a better look. Clearly, more than a few felt the group had somehow been defrauded by some sort of street con artist. Soon, one well-dressed elderly gentleman stopped and stood fidgeting in anxious sympathy, finally reaching for his wallet. "What's the trouble here?" he asked kindly. "Have you been robbed? Do you need cab fare? Is there some way I could be of help?"

"Help?" an old actress croaked, touching the man's arm with impressive sorrow. "Only if you can stop death, sir, can you be of help to us. We're doomed, I tell you. Doomed."

That must have been beyond his powers, for the elderly gentleman scurried away with sudden haste, looking back only once as he patted his pockets to make sure they had not been picked by what was surely a group of overgrown Fagin-like cohorts.

"There, there," T.S. began to murmur, patting every little old lady that he could reach lightly on the back without any discernible effect. "It's not as bad as that. Perhaps they'll release the body to us."

"We can't bury her without her real name," Adelle declared, nearly howling in her grief and regret. Caught up in steamrolling emotions unleashed by this unexpected chance at the limelight, she had cast decorum to the wind and was now intent on whipping the other old actresses into a frenzy of regret and shamed honor. T.S. and Auntie Lil both knew they had to come up with an idea fast before their sorrow and thwarted theatrical instincts escalated into hysteria.

"I have an idea," Auntie Lil announced suddenly. The women stopped sniffling abruptly and stared at her.

"No, you don't have an idea," T.S. announced just as quickly. He had a sneaking suspicion that he knew just what she was about to offer and an even sneakier one that his services were somehow involved. "There is nothing we can do to help," he answered firmly as Auntie Lil's eyes slid away from his gaze. They both knew that he knew just what she'd been thinking.

It didn't stop Auntie Lil, of course. "We'll find out who she was for you," she offered magnanimously.

"But that's a wonderful idea!" Adelle exclaimed, switching emotions with lightning speed. "You could investigate her identity for us!"

"That's right," another actress agreed. "If you solved all those murders before, you could certainly solve this little mystery."

T.S. stared at his aunt in the expectant silence that followed. She refused to blush and merely gazed straight ahead, sticking her chin out an inch or two farther.

"What *exactly* has my aunt told you?" he asked the group evenly. Auntie Lil inched away from him indignantly, still refusing to meet his eye.

"That she single-handedly solved three murders that had the police utterly baffled," an old lady announced matter-of-factly. "Saving two people's lives in the bargain."

"That's right," her companion agreed. "And got that medal of honor from the chief of detectives. And a letter of commendation from the mayor."

"But they had to keep it hush-hush and out of the papers," another actress reported confidently. "On account of making the NYPD look bad."

"If you could do that," Adelle declared, "you could certainly do this one thing for us."

If Auntie Lil blushed at any of the incredibly exaggerated feats they were repeating, T.S. missed it. He was sure she had not, however, as she was physically, mentally and morally incapable of embarrassment.

"Theodore and I will think about it," Auntie Lil promised graciously, hustling him down the sidewalk before he demanded any details about the medal of honor. "We'll let you know tomorrow if there's anything we can do to help."

"What's the rush?" T.S. protested, looking back at the group that was now staring at them in benign confusion. "I want to hear more about these daring adventures of yours. About how you *single-handedly* solved those three murders. About this medal of honor."

"Oh, shut up, Theodore," she hissed. She had succeeded in dragging him to Broadway and was waving her enormous handbag, trying to signal a cab. Instead, she narrowly missed bashing in several commuter faces by inches. No wonder they all stepped back and let her take the first taxi that screeched to a halt.

T.S. decided to let her suffer in silence, hoping to shame a confession out of her. They rode three blocks without uttering a sound. T.S. pretended he was listening to the cab driver's music, but as he was playing a cassette of some sort of foreign atonal religious chanting, it was difficult to keep up the pretense.

"Oh, all right," Auntie Lil finally admitted. She removed a white handkerchief from her handbag and daintily dabbed at her brow. "Perhaps I did exaggerate our deeds a bit."

"*A bit?*" T.S. asked. "Sounds to me like you've been holding campfires and telling tales all night. Sounds to me like they knew every last detail involved and a good many more that weren't involved."

"They are very dramatic women," Auntie Lil explained stiffly. "They like a good story and they're so appreciative. I simply got a little carried away." She dabbed at her brow again and he saw that she was truly upset. He felt ashamed.

"I'm sorry," he apologized. "Did you know the dead woman well?"

"Emily?" She stared out the window. "Not really. She'd had some long-standing tiff with one of the other ladies and had not been speaking to any of them for several months. But they're right, you know, Theodore. No one—and I mean no one—deserves to die without a name."

Her lower lip quivered and T.S. stared at her in despair. He hoped she would not start to cry. He didn't think he'd ever seen her break down and wasn't sure he could handle it now.

"Now, now, Aunt Lil." He patted her hand sympathetically and her white cotton gloves felt hot to his touch. "Someone will step forward to claim her."

"Oh, isn't that the way of the world?" she asked bitterly. "Always expecting someone else to step forward. No one else will step forward. If we don't do it, we'll never know who she really was." Her lower lip quivered again and it was a little frightening to see her supreme self-control fail.

"This has you really upset," T.S. said quietly. "I hadn't realized quite how much."

"Well, maybe when you get to be my age you'll be able to watch other people drop dead without blinking an eye, but I don't mind telling you that I'm finding it hard."

T.S. blinked. When he hit eighty-four years of age, he was sure he would not even begin to approach Auntie Lil's normal, every-day courage. "You didn't seem so upset before."

"That stupid Officer King had me so angry, that I couldn't be upset. But now I just can't stop thinking of that poor woman lying somewhere dead and no one to even claim her body. Why can't we help them find out who she is? It isn't as if we're sticking our noses into another homicide. This is child's play, really, considering our true capabilities." She turned to him with pleading eyes and he shifted uncomfortably in the seat.

"I just don't see how we could help," he protested faintly.

"We can find out who she is, so her relatives can be notified and she can have a decent burial. And at least be interred under her real name, for God's sake."

"Why us?" T.S. complained. "Let her other friends do it. They ought to know her real name, anyway, if they were the good friends they claim to be. They wept enough tears back there to flood Salt Lake City."

Auntie Lil stared at him without comment for an icy moment, then tapped sharply on the glass divider. "Driver—could you take us to the pier at Forty-fifth and Twelfth Avenue before we go to Queens?"

"You're paying, lady," he answered back, taking a sudden right onto Forty-second Street.

"What now?" T.S. asked. When she didn't answer, he glared out the window. She was punishing him with the silent treatment and he'd be damned if he'd let it get to him.

"Right there is fine," Auntie Lil told the driver as they approached the Hudson. The river sparkled dully in the autumn sunlight, its waves alternating between flat gray and a murky brown. Auntie Lil pointed toward a deserted landfill pier that hosted a small amusement park during the summer months. It was now empty and desolate, no more than a barren stretch of land dotted with an odd patch of dry grass here and there.

"Keep the meter running," she ordered the driver. "You come with me," she ordered T.S.

"You're paying for the cab," T.S. warned her and immediately felt worse. He was behaving like a sullen child. On the other hand, why not? She was treating him like one, wasn't she? And all because he could not go along with her latest cockeyed scheme.

They walked in silence to the end of the landfill, then followed a concrete pier out into the waves. They reached the end and she stopped him beside a set of large pilings and pointed down the river toward the southern tip of Manhattan. "See that shadow there?"

"What shadow? All I see is smog."

"That's the trouble with you, Theodore," she told him. "You're so busy being competent that you're blind. That's the Statue of Liberty." She pointed again.

"I know it's there," he conceded patiently. "You can pretend to see it, if you want to."

She pursed her lips in irritation and stared out over the water. "Your great-grandfather worked these shores," she began. "He came right off a boat, without a dime to his name, and a wife and three children to support." Her gentle tone of voice produced an immediate flush of shame in T.S. She was not the type of woman to talk about the past. In fact, he did not know if he'd ever heard her speak about their ancestors before.

"He worked sixteen, sometimes twenty hours a day," she continued. "And so did your grandfather after him. They endured years of low wages, losing their jobs to the Irish, finding new ones, losing those jobs because they were honest, and getting up at dawn the next day to find new jobs. They worked from sunup to sundown and into the night. Never complaining. Never asking for more."

"That's very admirable," T.S. admitted, trying hard not to let his impatience creep into his voice. He failed.

"This is not a feel-good lecture, Theodore," Auntie Lil told him sharply. "I have a serious point to make."

"Then make it," he suggested. "If you ask me, you're just trying to shame me into doing what you want."

"Not *shame* you, Theodore. I'm trying to *explain* why we should be the ones to help out this poor, dead woman."

"Then explain," T.S. said stubbornly, folding his arms and avoiding her eyes.

"As poor as your family was—and we were very, very poor until a generation ago—a Hubbert has never turned away someone else in need. *Never.* If someone needed help, they got it. It didn't matter if they were Irish or black or even a drunk. Your great-grandmother and her daughters after her never turned away anyone in need. Your mother and I helped your grandmother feed half of upstate New York during the Depression. And it wasn't because we were trying to win our way into heaven, either. We did it because Hubberts have always done it. Because we are blessed. No one has ever lost a baby in childbirth. Damn few of us have died before our time. We have the constitutions of oxen and the good sense to avoid excess in alcohol and religion. And I'm not going to jinx that good fortune now by turning my back on someone in need. So you can help me or you can *not* help me. But I will be very surprised if you really mean 'no,' my dear Theodore. Because if ever there was a Hubbert who has made me proud, it's you. I refuse to believe that you could, in good conscience, walk away from this simple task."

Her lecture finished, she turned abruptly and marched back to the cab. It was the best way to ensure that he would not talk back. But in truth, he had been left speechless. T.S. waited a moment, letting the cool breeze clear his head. He peeked south just as the sun broke out from behind a cloud and did spot a reflected glare in the distance. He sighed. Perhaps Auntie Lil really could see the Statue of Liberty from here. Perhaps he was far too cynical a man.

He shrugged his shoulders in surrender and walked slowly back to the cab, out of habit noting that their small session of family bonding had added a good five dollars to the tab.

"You win," he said simply, shutting the door a second before the impatient driver took off with a roar and cut back east through midtown. "What do you want me to do?"

Auntie Lil's mood change was instantaneous. She immediately stowed her disappointment away in favor of her favorite activity—full-speed-ahead-damn-the-torpedoes-*action*. Within seconds, her handkerchief was tucked back in her handbag and she had pulled out her small notebook. She held a pen poised above its surface and stared dreamily out the window. There was nothing she loved better than a puzzle.

"We just need a good photograph of her," she finally announced. "Then we can show it around the neighborhood. Someone must know her. How can we get one?"

"Beats me. She's dead. No one knows her real name. We don't even know where she lives."

"Why don't you take a picture of her dead?" their cab driver suddenly suggested from the front seat.

Amazing, T.S. thought, he'd been listening to every word they said and had not displayed the slightest emotion. Obviously, he and Auntie Lil did not even begin to approach in strangeness the weirdos this guy was used to transporting.

"Why, that's brilliant!" Auntie Lil exclaimed, leaning forward to tap the seat divider with approval. "You're wasted driving a cab," she declared.

"Yes, back home in my country I was very, very good at tracking down people," the driver answered cryptically. "No one *ever* got away from me," he added, leaving T.S. to imagine himself at the mercy of some sort of escaped death-squad leader.

"Where do they take the bodies?" Auntie Lil asked. She did not really want an answer from the driver. She was merely, as usual, thinking out loud. "The medical examiner's office, that's where. Am I right?"

"Yes, ma'am," the driver assured her. "I saw it on a 'Kojak' re-run."

"How could we get in there?" Her voice trailed off and she stared back over the spires of the Upper East Side with intense concentration. They were passing over the Fifty-ninth Street Bridge and Manhattan lay behind them, its newer buildings shining with bright metallic splendor beneath the sparkling skies of the sunny autumn day. What a shame to die on a day like this, T.S. thought. Even the New York air smelled clean, for a change.

Auntie Lil was silent, searching for a solution. Since T.S. and Auntie Lil had been soul mates for all of his life, he knew what she was thinking at exactly the same time the idea came to her.

"No," he said firmly. "I won't ask her."

"Oh, Theodore." She turned to him and clutched his sleeve, beseeching him for help. He rather enjoyed seeing her beg.

"Lilah knows everyone," Auntie Lil cooed. "And you know how fond of you she is. She's probably been dying for you to telephone her."

"How do you know I haven't been taking her dancing every single night of the week?" he asked grumpily, annoyed at her accurate inference.

Auntie Lil did not bother to answer. They both knew where the truth lay.

T.S. stared out his window and watched a subway train cross the Manhattan Bridge in the distance. Lilah. She moved in a different world, a world of money and meaningless titles and men who owned businesses and women who always looked at least twenty years younger than their age.

He had always been a confident, prepared man in control. But around Lilah, T.S. often felt inexplicably inferior and clumsy. As much as his dreams secretly centered on Lilah, she made his present reality strange and unsettling. He did not like being out of control of his heart, his head or his tongue. So, no, of course he had not been taking Lilah out dancing every night of the week. In fact, he had not seen her at all in months. And Auntie Lil knew it.

Auntie Lil always said that he needed to learn how to live, but just saying so wasn't enough for T.S. Sometimes, he longed for someone to show him how to live. And sometimes he longed for the courage to be different from the stiff and inflexible but capable man that he had been for so many years.

"I could call her," Auntie Lil offered with as much humbleness as she could muster. Even she knew that she was treading on some very thin ice. She liked Lilah almost as much as T.S. liked Lilah, but she had no desire to hurt her beloved nephew.

"No, I'm a big boy. I can certainly call her." There. He'd said it. Now he'd just have to follow through.

"Tonight?" she demanded. Boy, she never knew when to stop pushing her luck. That was probably why she was so damn lucky.

"Okay. Okay. *Tonight.*" He shifted his legs uncomfortably and sighed. Already his palms were starting to sweat.

CHAPTER THREE

1. T.S. spent the early part of the evening devising ways to put off the phone call to Lilah Cheswick. It was amazing how inventive he could be when desperation drove him to it. He began by retracing the steps of his cleaning lady earlier that day, but since she took perverse pleasure in being even cleaner than him (a near impossibility) there was not a single speak of dust to discover throughout his ruthlessly organized and sparsely furnished apartment. Alarmed by his restless activity, Brenda and Eddie followed him the entire time, meowing ceaselessly for more food just in case he suffered a temporary lapse of memory and they got lucky. They didn't—T.S. had put them both on strict diets since they resembled seals more than cats—but they did each nab an anchovy-stuffed olive when T.S. finally decided to tackle the refrigerator.

There wasn't much to do. Like every single one of the rooms in his six-room apartment, the refrigerator was spotless and gleaming clean. He wiped out the butter compartment, just in case the cleaning lady had missed it, then restacked his frozen dinners according to the main entree.

That done, he took a blow dryer to his bedroom slippers to restore the nap then checked all of his paintings and prints with a carpenter's level to ensure they were hanging properly. After all, it had been at least a month since he'd performed these all-important tasks.

Remembering some new purchases from the day before, T.S. then added a few entries to the computerized cross-indexed catalog he maintained on his private music collection, which was heavy on opera and show tunes. There was no point in checking the shelves of hardback books. He'd spent the morning before dusting and organizing those. Paperback's were not allowed in the apartment, at least not after T.S. had eagerly read them. They were spirited down the hall and given to a neighbor so that Auntie Lil would not discover that he read best-selling thrillers and cheap detective novels by the handful each week.

He was finally reduced to killing another hour by rearranging his impeccably organized personal files chronologically instead of alphabetically. Then, realizing the absurdity of such a system, he moved them back as they were. In doing so, a small envelope fluttered to the floor from his *Personal Correspondence, 1942–1955* file. He stared at it. The combination of Auntie Lil's earlier lecture and the letter's familiar handwriting triggered a flood of memories, as well as curiosity about how his past would seem to a stranger. People would find it odd, he supposed, that he had kept a correspondence file beginning with age seven. But then, not many people had been sent to boarding school at such a young age. And even fewer had had their letters to home returned regularly, with grammar and spelling carefully corrected by a well-meaning but rigid schoolteacher mother.

Had T.S. been more sentimental, and less like his mother, it might have hurt his feelings. He had, instead, made a game out of trying to send her letters perfect in every way—thus embarking on a career of perfectionism that, among other compulsions, drove him to save every personal letter he received with the reply date noted on the front of each envelope.

He held the childish letter in his hand. It began with "Dear Mummy and Daddy." How strange. Children never called their mothers "Mummy" anymore, did they? It was hard for him to know for sure. Children were as foreign to T.S. as Zulu warriors, and a great deal more alarming. He noted with satisfaction that his mother had uncovered a mere three mistakes in the letter, and picayune ones at that, at a time when he was only eight years old. Not bad. Of course, by age ten he'd been able to beat her at her own game and had earned brief laudatory replies at the bottom of his own letters in return. It was better than nothing at all and, nearly fifty years later, he still treasured the perfunctory paragraphs of praise from his emotionally distant mother.

Replacing the letter into its proper folder, T.S. ran his fingers over the neat pile of perfectly ordered correspondence. Each letter—with certain rather spectacular exceptions—was very thin and very carefully folded. The exceptions were missives from Auntie Lil, posted from all corners of the world as she trekked here and there, following the fashion designers she served as they searched for new styles and new fabrics. He had awaited each of her letters with an eagerness he felt ashamed to admit to anyone else. No one else at boarding school, he remembered, in all those years away from home, could have claimed more exotic correspondence. Her letters had arrived at his always well-sterilized room with wonderful irregularity, always fat and crammed with clippings, scraps of fabric, photographs of herself with strangers and stacks of postcards she'd meant to send earlier. They literally overflowed with evidence of a world so chaotic it both frightened and excited his prematurely adult mind.

T.S. knew even then how much his mother despised Auntie Lil and her unorthodox, sometime scandalous, ways. But, while struggling to maintain loyalty toward his rigidly conventional mother, T.S. had always been drawn closer to Auntie Lil's warm and loving flame, craving her maternal beacon and carefree, capable spirit. Unlike his mother, who had been "Fondly" for as long as he could remember, Auntie Lil signed her letters to T.S. with "Love Always from Your Most Adoring Aunt." After five decades, he knew she still meant it with all of her heart.

He sighed. Auntie Lil would not be putting off a phone call like a bashful teenager. In fact, she was probably out somewhere right now on one of her many dates eating food of undetermined origin with people whose names were hard to pronounce. Her taste in friends was every bit as exotic as her taste in clothing and correspondence.

He sighed. He owed it to her to call Lilah. And he owed it to her to help her find out Emily's true identity. There had been many times in the past when all that lay between T.S. and a bleak, boring life was his fun-loving Aunt Lil. It was now his turn to pay her back. She wanted so much to embark on a new project. And there was a real need beneath her surface sorrow at the poor woman's death. While his mother was content to spend her days imperiously ordering about the staff of an elderly care facility, Auntie Lil was different. She wanted, T.S. knew, to go down kicking and screaming. And she truly needed new mysteries to survive.

He held a fat and yellowed envelope from her in his hand. Sent from Malaysia in 1954, it still held a sliver of banana frond and a faded newspaper clipping of Auntie Lil flanked by dozens of dark and smiling faces. T.S. ran a finger across the crease of the letter then carefully tucked it back in place. It was time to call Lilah Cheswick.

Lilah was rich enough to afford a houseful of servants, but

hated having them about. T.S. was not surprised when she answered the phone herself on the third ring.

"Hello?" she asked calmly. "Do please hold on." Her smoky voice snaked through the telephone wires, sending a flame shooting down the length of his previously placid fifty-five-year-old body. He was too old for such nonsense, but too young not to want it.

He heard a crinkling sound in the background, then a thump and a muffled ladylike oath followed by more crinkling and an exasperated sigh. Finally, she returned to the phone with apologetic politeness. "So sorry to keep you waiting. Who is this, please?"

"Lilah?" His voice was louder than he'd expected. He calmed down and continued. "Lilah—it's me. I'm T.S." What was he saying? His tongue had a life of its own.

"Theodore!" Only two people in the entire world were allowed to call him by his full name. Lilah Cheswick was one of them.

"Where have you been, Theodore?" Her voice swelled and took on a rich warmth that T.S. was too afraid to even suspect might be for him. Lilah was always a woman to get right to the point. "Why haven't you been calling me?" she demanded in a good-humored tone of voice.

Now that was an excellent question. "I don't know," he confessed. "I thought you'd prefer to be left alone for a while."

"Theodore, you know me too well to really believe that. Robert's been dead for months but, to me, he'd been dead for years."

It was true. T.S. thought back to the murder of Lilah's husband and to her well-balanced sorrow. She and her husband had not had a happy life together and she was not the kind of woman to milk grief for her own benefit. "I don't know why I haven't called," he finally offered. "I thought you'd probably be too busy."

"Too busy? Doing what? My daughters are off at school. I've read every book ever published. My friends bore me and now I can't even get this stupid frozen dinner open, so I'll probably starve to death before they can bore me to death." There was another thump and some more exasperated crinkling.

"Try cutting the plastic with a knife," he suggested. "There's really no other way."

"Theodore, you're a genius. Deirdre's left me for a week and I'm helpless. There!" He heard the thump of a microwave door closing and she was back on the line. "To what do I owe this honor? You have four minutes to explain and then I'm tearing into that dinner with my very well-bred teeth. You don't want to take me out to dinner, I suppose?"

"Yes. Yes, I do." He practically shouted, and didn't even care. Not even he would pass up such an opening. "Let's go to dinner tomorrow night."

"That would be lovely. I think I'll survive until then."

He was so busy admiring her voice and marveling at her calm and apparent disregard of his own nervousness that, at first, he neglected to reply. When he realized he'd been holding the phone silently for nearly half a minute, he panicked and did what he'd always done with women: he blurted out the first thing that crossed his mind.

"Could we stop by the morgue first?" he asked, to his own immediate horror. God, what was he doing? Where was his finesse? He was acting like a teenage moron.

"You're such a romantic, Theodore," Lilah teased, seemingly impervious to any faux pas he might produce. "Have you grown kinky in our months apart?"

"Oh, this is horrible," he forced himself to confess, unleashing a torrent of words. "I'm making an idiot of myself and you must think I'm insane. I've been wanting to call you and I don't know why I haven't. And now I'm calling because I need a favor or, rather, Auntie Lil and I need a favor, but I'm afraid you'll think that's the only reason I'm calling you, so now I feel like a real ass. I think I'd better just hang up."

"Don't hang up, Theodore," Lilah told him cheerfully. "I'll take any phone call I can get from you. On any pretense whatsoever. And if Auntie Lil is involved, then all the better. It tells me that my boredom is at an end. I demand all details immediately."

"A woman died today in a soup kitchen where we work."

"You've been working at a soup kitchen? How wonderful. I'm very proud of you, though I must confess it makes me feel inadequate. I'll have to donate an extra thousand or so tomorrow just to compensate." The good thing about Lilah was that she never flaunted her extreme wealth and, in fact, often made fun of it herself. "But you, Theodore, you back your convictions with actions," she added. "I like that in a man."

"Well, I haven't been working there long," he confessed. He checked his watch. Nine hours, to be exact. No need to get into too many details.

"Anyway, this poor woman died today of a heart attack in front of everyone and no one knows her real name," he continued. "Auntie Lil thinks if we can get a photo of her and show it around the neighborhood, we'll be able to discover who she was and notify her family and then she can be buried under her real name."

"Well, she wasn't murdered, but it is a mystery of sorts. How can I help?"

"Can you find out where they've taken the body and get us in so we can take a photograph?"

"Only if I get to come along. Dinner and the morgue is my idea of the ideal date."

"Are you sure you want to come?"

"I'm sure. At least about the dinner part. I reserve judgment on the morgue. Give me the details, and I'll call you back later tonight."

He quickly filled her in and heard the ding of the microwave just as he finished the story. She assured him again she'd be able to help, then hung up with a cheerful goodbye. That left him with no one but Brenda and Eddie to engage in the all-important rehashing of the conversation. They regarded him with sleepy, yellow eyes and seemed infinitely bored at the possibilities of Lilah Cheswick. They had long since given up on their human being. In their estimation, he was really too dull for words. Brenda yawned and daintily licked at one paw. T.S. was dismissed.

He watched an old Barbara Stanwyck movie while he waited and it was almost as good as having Lilah right there. As promised, she called back several hours later and the deed had been done. Lilah had enough money and enough breeding that no favor asked was too great, and no amount of time too short in which to grant it. The strings had been pulled and the doors were being opened. The dead woman had been taken to the medical examiner's office on the east side of Midtown. They could drop by early tomorrow evening so long as they kept their visit discreet.

"They'll be holding the body there for a week, in case anyone asks about her," Lilah explained. "Then it's potter's field. Do you have a camera?"

"Yes." T.S. kept his camera carefully stored in its original box in the recreation cabinet. He liked it close at hand so that he could film every item he purchased, for insurance purposes. He stored the photographic evidence in a safe-deposit box in the unlikely event a burglar was able to break through the considerable security of his Upper East Side apartment. Few parts of T.S. Hubbert's life went unorganized. He liked life well-ordered and well-mannered.

"Good," Lilah was saying. "Then I'll pick you up tomorrow at six sharp. I can wait outside with my driver while you go in. I'm afraid I'd faint and make a fool of myself. How about you? Are you sure you're ready for this?"

In truth, he already did feel a bit like fainting. But it was at the thought of seeing Lilah again after three months, not a dead body. He had to get a grip on himself. "It won't be my first corpse," he pointed out in what he hoped was a capable and slightly insouciant manner.

"True," she agreed cheerfully. "You do seem to collect dead bodies, actually." Without waiting for his reply, she purred a good night and left him alone with the silence of a single man's apartment and two bored cats for company.

But there was always tomorrow.

2. Tomorrow commenced early with a phone call from a determined Auntie Lil. She was going to the morgue with them and that was that. "I've never seen the inside of the medical examiner's office," she announced. "And I'm not passing up the opportunity to see something new. You needn't worry about me horning in on your little tête-à-tête. I shall discreetly disappear after we take the photographs."

Discreetly disappear? Whether appearing or disappearing, Auntie Lil was about as discreet as a stripper in a monastery. T.S. sighed. He could argue, but what was the point? If he said no, she'd call Lilah who would, of course, urge her to come along for the fun of it. No, there was no way to dissuade Auntie Lil. They'd all just have to troop in like a club of ghoulish thrill seekers. He'd not even be surprised if Aunt Lil brought along a date. There was sure to be someone among her motley collection of admirers who considered the morgue the ultimate good time.

"Now that we've settled that," she decided for them both, "when are you coming down to the soup kitchen to help?"

"I'll be down in a couple of hours," he promised, not even bothering to argue. He thought of his soap operas, but the thrills of Camilla and Tyrone seemed cheap and artificial next to the sudden excitement of his own life. Besides, he was not above having the little old lady actresses flutter around him in gratitude.

Unfortunately, once he arrived at St. Barnabas, it was obvious that the women were overcome with theatrical grief, not gratitude. Neither Emily's death nor Auntie Lil's chili the day before had abated anyone's appetite. The line was as long and patient as ever. T.S. walked by, nodding at those faces he recognized. Nearly every single one of the old actresses was decked out in various styles of mourning wear. From far away, they looked like small black birds scattered among the crowd. Up close, they looked like figures you'd see on the edge of a movie horror scene: frail and cloaked in black, about to fade slowly from view like grim messengers from the beyond. Adelle had apparently dragged out a leftover costume from a stint as Lady Macbeth—she wore a long black gown uniquely inappropriate for the quiet, warm late-September day. But T.S. had to admire her carriage—her proud chin never faltered—and noticed that the other soup kitchen attendees stood at a respectable distance from her regal sorrow. She wore a small triangular hat with a black dotted veil that swept down over her face. Altogether, it was a flawless performance.

Adelle managed a brave smile as T.S. passed by, and he patted her on the back in what he hoped was a consoling manner. Then he spotted plump Eva standing to one side, defiantly dressed in a bright red dress in a ploy to nab the Bette Davis role in the drama. Her arms were crossed firmly across her ample bosom and she appeared ready and raring to fight with anyone who dared question her attire. T.S. wondered how anyone could carry a grudge for nearly half a century. What a waste of energy to be belaboring the past so tortuously. Especially when neither of them had achieved success at the expense of the other. There had to be more to it than what he knew.

He met Auntie Lil just outside the basement door. She was poking around the garbage cans like a hobo, with a rotten banana peel dangling from one hand. "I'm looking to see if Emily's pocketbook was dropped after the thief rifled through it," she announced when she noticed his stare.

"You mean, after the thief took the money and ran."

"No." She daintily lifted the lid off one can and the smell of rotting onions mixed with burnt coffee grounds wafted past. "There was no money for the thief to steal. According to reliable sources, she abhorred cash and rarely carried it on her. Everyone knew it. She always talked about the dangers of carrying money in the neighborhood."

"The thief didn't know it," T.S. commented. "Or he wouldn't have taken the pocketbook." He gently guided her back inside before she started ripping open the sealed plastic bags of wet debris in her search.

"Maybe the thief did know it," she said stubbornly. "And took it anyway."

"What do you mean?"

"Maybe the pocketbook wasn't stolen for the money."

T.S. screeched to a halt and held Auntie Lil firmly in place. "Do not," he said very firmly and distinctly, "go creating a mystery where none exists. We promised to find out the woman's identity. Period. That was our deal. Our sole agreement. Let's not get carried away." Though just warming up, he was interrupted in his lecture by the appearance of the perpetually hearty Father Stebbins and the lampreylike Fran.

"Welcome back, my boy," the massive priest boomed, thumping him on the back so enthusiastically that T.S. was convinced he'd jarred a filling out of one of his back teeth. "I knew you'd be the type who wouldn't get going when the going got tough."

"Where have you been?" Fran asked Auntie Lil rudely. "You left me all alone to skin dozens of cucumbers. I've hardly made a dent."

"You'd better not have made a dent at all," Auntie Lil warned, sailing past the scowling woman with oblivious authority. "If you bruise the flesh, you spoil the entire dish. I can see I'll just have to do this myself."

Lunch proved to be an uneventful affair. No one died, certainly. In fact, no one so much as choked. And much to the chagrin of the ladies in black, few people even seemed to notice their very public attempts at good old-fashioned grieving. But once the meal had been served, Auntie Lil—who was still hot on the trail of the pocketbook thief, despite T.S.'s warning—dragged her nephew over to a table inhabited by Franklin, the enormous black man with the soft Southern accent.

Franklin was sitting with an extremely tall, jaundiced and probably half-demented old man. There was a peculiar gleam in the fellow's rummy eyes and he was as gaunt and intense-looking as a preacher gone brimstone-mad in the pulpit. Everything about him seemed out of place. His clothes hung at odd angles from his skinny body, his hair had been unevenly cut and shaved in one place, plus one foot was missing a sock. Even the white stubble that dotted his chin couldn't get its act together—it was darkly stained in patches from unwashed dirt.

"Listen to what this gentleman just told Franklin," Auntie Lil demanded.

"Come on," T.S. complained. "We had a deal that you wouldn't go and—"

"Tell the man what you just told me," Franklin interrupted, coaxing his grimy dining partner in a gentle voice.

"I seen the eagle lay down with the lamb," the old man declared in a wheezy voice. "He bent over her, I could see he was breathing the evil. Breathed it right in her mouth, he did. That's why she died. He'd been stalking her. I saw him on the streets with the bright-plumed birds of prey. Those birds of a feather, they do flock together."

T.S. stared at him for a few seconds of uncomprehending silence, then turned to Auntie Lil skeptically.

"Tell him the rest," she asked the old man gently.

"I saw him bending under the table while the rest of us was watching the woman die," the old man rumbled, his words punctuated by an occasional juicy cough. "It's bad luck to watch death. So I was watching that man instead, 'cause I'd seen him give her the evil eye and all. I was right wary about the eye turning my way. I saw him reach down and pick something up off the floor. And when they said the coppers were on their way, that man was ready to fly the coop. He was the first one out the door."

"Why didn't you say anything?" Auntie Lil scolded him. "He was stealing her pocketbook. He was picking the bones of a corpse!"

The old man looked a bit taken aback by the sudden intrusion of corpse bones, but he was not fazed by Auntie Lil's dramatic indignation. "Weren't *my* business," he explained patiently. "Weren't my business at all. But look out. There's always trouble when the eagle gets loose among the lambs." He returned to his stew and thoughtfully chewed on a chunk of gray meat, staring up at them impassively with very bright eyes.

"This mysterious man *was* the eagle, not the lamb? Correct?" T.S. asked drily. Much to his chagrin, Auntie Lil brightened up at once, apparently feeling it was an excellent question.

"He was The Eagle, all right," the old fellow announced ominously. He tapped a fist against the biceps of his right arm and nodded sagely. "He was The Eagle."

"The Eagle?" T.S. smiled at him grimly and thanked the old man for his time. Gripping Auntie Lil's elbow, he dragged her firmly away to the privacy of a kitchen corner. "Short of treating me to a real-life cross between Dr. Doolittle and a Charles Dickens character, what was the purpose of that little display?" he asked crossly.

"He saw who stole the pocketbook," Auntie Lil insisted, rubbing her elbow and glaring at him pointedly.

T.S. shook his head and ignored her silent admonishment. Physical containment was the only way to control Auntie Lil. "Auntie Lil," he told her, "as much as I admire your uncompromising honesty, I don't think the police are going to be too interested in trying to prosecute a thief who steals an empty pocketbook from a dead woman that nobody knows." He shrugged. "Let's just clean up, forget about the pocketbook and get ready for what will surely be a lighthearted evening popping in at the morgue in preparation for your latest goose chase."

His nervousness at seeing Lilah Cheswick prompted an enthusiastically sarcastic tone. But the only trouble with being sarcastic when talking to Auntie Lil was that she always cheerfully agreed that it was all too, too true.

3.   By the time T.S. and Auntie Lil had helped the other volunteers scrub down the counters and wash the dishes, it was nearly six o'clock. Lilah was due to arrive any moment and T.S. scurried to the bathroom to do what he could, with what he had left, in the way of physical attributes.

Actually, he didn't look too bad for a man who'd just turned fifty-five. Perhaps the dim bathroom lighting helped, but there were far fewer wrinkles on his strong German face than was the case with many of his friends. In fact, he suspected that a couple of wrinkles had disappeared since he'd retired from his stress-filled job as personnel manager of a Wall Street private bank. He smoothed the skin over his broad cheeks and carefully scrubbed the oil and dirt until he glowed with pink-fleshed health. He did not like to admit it, but he bore a remarkable resemblance to Auntie Lil. In fact, a friend had once correctly commented that Auntie Lil looked exactly like T.S. might look if he were in drag. T.S. had not appreciated the remark.

He'd had the foresight to bring along a clean shirt. Immaculate personal grooming, T.S. believed, was the essential mark of a civilized man. He changed quickly, taking the opportunity to suck in his small gut and compare it in the mirror to what he'd seen a few weeks before. Yes, he was almost certain he'd managed to lose a pound or two. If he held his breath and threw his shoulders back, he looked no worse than he had a decade ago. Of course, he couldn't walk or breathe posed like that, plus his hair had turned an indisputable gray . . . but at least there was plenty of it. He'd taken to wearing it a bit longer now that he no longer had to march in uniformed lockstep with the rest of the Wall Street crowd. Secretly, he believed he looked a bit like an older version of that movie star, Richard Gere, but had yet to summon the courage to ask any friends whether they agreed.

There was a vigorous pounding at the door. "What are you doing in there?" Auntie Lil demanded. "Lilah is waiting for us outside."

"Coming," he called out, quickly tucking in his clean shirt. He didn't look perfect, but it would have to do. Auntie Lil was waiting impatiently. Yet, after making him hurry, she deliberately tarried at the doorway until Fran emerged from a back room. Only then would she leave. Ignoring Auntie Lil, who blocked her nearly every step of the way, Fran followed them out the door and walked briskly to the nearby corner and waited for the traffic light to change. She turned their way only twice—both times to look up at a small window toward the back of the church, no doubt the quarters of Father Stebbins.

In a rare act of imperiousness, Auntie Lil refused to enter the waiting limousine under her own steam. She stood stubbornly at the curb, swatting away help from T.S. until Lilah's driver took the hint. The uniformed man finally looked up from his newspaper, quickly hopped out onto the street and scurried around to open the rear door for them. Auntie Lil gave him a courteous but contained nod, slipped inside the long, dark car and conspicuously bestowed a queenlike departing wave at the far more pedestrian Fran.

Her grand gesture was cut short when T.S.—annoyed at her uncharacteristic pettiness—deliberately hopped in right after her. Besides, it served her right for hogging the seat next to Lilah.

Unlike himself, Lilah *did* look perfect. At least in T.S.'s opinion. She was a tall and athletic woman whose elegant posture was right at home in the back seat of the limousine. Lilah wore a purple crepe dress that highlighted her short white hair and her lovely, outdoor complexion. She shunned hair dye and most other forms of artifice, as if seeking to atone for her great wealth by being scrupulously honest about what money could and could not buy. T.S. admired her healthy beauty and reflected that, had Auntie Lil not been planted firmly between them, he might have gracefully pulled off a suave kiss to Lilah's hand. As it was, he contented himself by craning his neck around Auntie Lil's enormous hat and nodding.

"Hello, there, Theodore," Lilah said with a smile. The combined effect of her voice and face so close to his warmed the temperature of the limousine at least a few degrees.

"Lovely to see you, Lilah," he admitted, grinning like the village idiot and unable to control his facial features long enough to stop. A long green feather swept down from the back of Auntie

Lil's hat *Three Musketeers*–style, then swooped back up just enough to tickle the end of his nose. He sneezed violently and tugged on the end of the feather. "Madam, would you kindly remove your hat?" he asked with a straight face.

Auntie Lil unpinned the contraption and gave it a rumble seat of its own.

"That's a lovely hat, Lillian," Lilah lied smoothly. "Wherever did you get it?"

"My friend, Herbert Wong, brought it back from Pago Pago," she answered.

"*Your* friend Herbert Wong?" T.S. said. "He was my friend first." She was always absconding with his friends. She didn't mean to, she was just so enthusiastic about new companions that, before T.S. knew what was happening, his former buddies would be out getting drunk with Auntie Lil while he stayed home alone and watched television.

"He was your *employee*," Auntie Lil pointed out. "He's my friend."

Lilah winked at T.S. in secret sympathy and he decided that he didn't give a hoot about Herbert Wong one way or the other. "Where is this place?" he asked cheerfully.

"On First Avenue. Grady knows the address." Lilah waved a hand toward the driver. He was a handsome, burly man with the map of Ireland printed all over his broad face. His reddish brown hair topped a massive head and, as they soon discovered, he retained a thick Irish brogue.

"Bit of traffic ahead, ma'am," he called back to Lilah, rather unnecessarily as they had moved ahead little more than three inches in the last half minute. But instead of being annoyed, a curious sensation flowed through T.S. They were stalled near Times Square and all around them, neon lights blinked, it seemed, in time to the music. People flowed around the car, parting and coming back together, trying without luck to peer inside to see if anyone famous rode within. Groups of kids laughed and grabbed at one another, caught up in the joy and sheer energy of New York, while well-dressed adults huddled together in groups, suppressing their childlike merriment at the suspense of waiting for the nightlife to begin. It was an ideal position for someone like T.S.—to be so surrounded by life, yet made invisible and, thus, all-powerful by the anonymous security of the limousine's tinted windows. T.S. suddenly felt like an integral part of this excitement, as if he stood at the center of a large wheel and these lovely people, this wonderful multitude of different faces—all colors and sizes and shapes and expressions included—all belonged to him, every last one of them, and were all a part of him, flowing outward from the center of his benign goodwill like revelers circling a beribboned Maypole.

"Why, Theodore," he heard Lilah say through a cacophony of honking horns, the shouts of religious fanatics and the chatter of at least six different languages. "What an interesting smile just crossed your face. I don't think I've ever actually seen you smile that way before. What in the world were you thinking of just now?"

Glad that Auntie Lil and Grady were occupied in a discussion about whether disco was coming back, T.S. shook his head happily. "I don't really know," he confessed. "I just had the strangest feeling. I really felt alive."

Lilah reached over and patted his hand. Her touch was warm and far too fleeting. "Retirement must agree with you. I've never seen you look so handsome."

Handsome? He preened very casually in the mirrored bar surface. Things were looking up, indeed.

Frustrated by the slow going, Auntie Lil grew increasingly more excited and was bouncing up and down impatiently in her seat by the time they reached the medical examiner's office.

"Have you got the film?" she asked T.S., eyeing his camera dubiously.

"Of course. I'm not an idiot." He checked the back of the camera just in case, though he'd double-checked it twice before leaving the house. He climbed quickly out of the car in response to Auntie Lil's impatient push from behind. "Are you sure you don't want to accompany us?" he asked Lilah politely through her open window, when she made no move to leave the limousine.

"Thank you, I believe I'll just stay here with Grady and come back in for the dinner portion of the evening. Ask for Rodriquez at the door. He knows what to do." Lilah gave a fluttering half-wave just as the tinted window rolled back up, obscuring her face.

Auntie Lil tugged on his arm, admonishing him to hurry. The entrance doors were locked and they rang a bell as instructed. Upon hearing a sharp buzz, they pushed through the front door and found themselves in a dark and empty reception room, the employees having fled hours before. Auntie Lil looked around for an inner door or second buzzer and was just peeking under the front desk when a small, darkish man with thinning hair and suspicious eyes burst through a rear door. He gripped a clipboard against his chest like a shield, stared at Auntie Lil crouched beneath the receptionist's desk, then scrutinized T.S. with almost comical mistrust.

"What do you two want?" he asked, delving right to the heart of the matter.

"You must be Rodriquez," T.S. deflected politely, extending his hand for his heartiest handshake.

Rodriquez ignored the gesture and wrapped his lab coat a little more tightly around his protruding middle. "What if I am?" he demanded truculently.

Auntie Lil rose to her not very impressive height and looked him straight in the eye. "Lilah Cheswick said to ask for you," she explained evenly, a hint of steel underlying her words. "She said it had all been *arranged*," she added with mysterious inflection, managing to make it sound if they were there to rob, not photograph, bodies.

Rodriquez looked at them with even greater distaste. "Oh, yeah. You two are the kooks who want to take a picture of a corpse or something." His expression changed to one of mild interest, as if he'd run up against all kinds of weirdos before and they represented a new, slightly intriguing species.

Good grief, T.S. realized. The creep thought they were on some sort of perverse pleasure trip. Time to nip that notion in the bud. "We're here to photograph a specific woman who died yesterday," T.S. explained with stiff dignity. "We are attempting to secure her true identification from someone in the vicinity of her neighborhood."

"Sure." Rodriquez nodded slowly, unconvinced. But he checked his clipboard and motioned them to follow. "Suit yourself," he said. "It takes all kinds."

Ignoring his jibe, they walked down a long hallway, turned the corner and pushed past a set of swinging doors that led them into a narrow, white hospital-like corridor. Double sets of small square doors about the size and shape of bus terminal lockers lined the walls on each side for as far as they could see. Everything was white. It looked like the storage area of a futuristic stopping point for intergalactic travelers.

"Are all of those full?" Auntie Lil asked spryly. She eyed the doors in great curiosity. "How many of them would you say were victims of violent crime?" she inquired, without waiting for an answer to her first question. "I bet many of them have been shot. Were any of them stabbed?"

"Let's just confine ourselves to one body, shall we?" T.S. suggested, dragging her away from the wall before she started pulling open drawers and examining the bodies for signs of foul play.

"Here she is," Rodriquez announced with a bit of flair. "Number 433."

They gathered around the small door and T.S. could have sworn that Rodriquez deliberately took his time undoing the latch just to heighten the suspense. "Now, don't faint on us, ma'am," he warned Auntie Lil in an experienced voice.

She flapped a gloved hand impatiently and Rodriquez opened the door, smoothly sliding out a gurney on a steel track. It rolled into view and stretched across the breadth of the hallway, gleaming with stainless steel emptiness beneath the glare of the fluorescent lights above.

"There's no one here!" Auntie Lil cried. "What have you done with the poor woman?"

"Done with her? We've done nothing with her at all." Though confused, Rodriquez was still quite capable of automatically heading off blame before it could be assigned to him. He frantically scanned his clipboard list. "You say she died yesterday? West Side. Right?"

"Right," Auntie Lil echoed. "How many old ladies with no known name or address kicked off yesterday afternoon, anyway?"

Rodriquez paused to glare at her briefly, then shook his head and scratched at a small insect bite that had swelled on one of his cheeks. "Hmmm. You wait here."

He turned abruptly and left them staring at the empty locker. But not for long. For different reasons, neither Auntie Lil nor T.S. had any inclination to wait in the hall of the dead while he poked around in search of the missing body. The moment Rodriquez disappeared through another set of swinging doors, both of them went scurrying after him. They were just in time to see him stick his head through a small door set off another, shorter corridor.

With the unerring instincts of a middle linebacker who smells a quarterback sack, Auntie Lil went barreling down the short hall and chose the most efficient route to success. She pushed Rodriquez through the door into the room and crowded in behind him, with T.S. hot on her heels.

They'd found Emily all right. She was lying naked on a smooth steel table that included slanted gutters on all four sides. A thin stream of water tricked through the gutters and ran into a narrow sink that hugged one wall of the room. A tiny man, nearly as gnarled and short as a gnome, was peering intently into Emily's eyes with the aid of a highly focused penlight. His thick eye-

glasses shone eerily with reflected glare and he was issuing a constant patter of noise that sounded—at least from where T.S. and
Auntie Lil stood—like indignant mice arguing among themselves.
A slim Asian woman stared over his shoulder and was listening
raptly to his lecture.

The little man's squeaky voice rose in volume as he reached his
conclusion. "Look again," he commanded. "Notice the breakage
around the cornea. Curiously enough, this is symptomatic of
either . . ." Rodriquez coughed loudly and the little man abruptly
stopped his speech, having finally noticed the company. He was
quite unperturbed.

"Hello, what's this?" he asked cheerfully, eyeing Auntie Lil up
and down with professional detachment. Auntie Lil responded by
straightening her back and opening her eyes wide, as if to prove
that she, thank you, was quite alive.

"These people are here to take a photo of this dead lady,"
Rodriquez explained, cocking his thumb toward the corpse. "I
wouldn't have burst in on you like that, but this old one here, she
pushed me from behind like some kind of maniac." He glared at
Auntie Lil, but she was far too busy staring at Emily to notice his
resentment.

A jagged V-shaped scar tapered down from the dead woman's
shoulders across her breasts, coming together several inches above
the naval before snaking angrily down over the shrunken tissues
and protruding bones of her pelvis. Her skin was puckered and
hairless, the body impossibly small. T.S. stared down at his shoes.
It looked like the freeze-dried body of an eleven-year-old girl.

The tiny doctor scurried to Emily's feet and pulled a white
plastic sheet over her form. "Please excuse the informality. If I'd
known she was having company, I'd have dressed her for the occasion." He cackled at his own joke and T.S. suppressed a groan.
The old man was just the kind of weirdo Auntie Lil loved to collect. No doubt they'd be dining across the table from one another
soon.

"Don't mind my macabre humor," the little man protested,
stopping any potential giggles with an upraised palm, although no
one had either laughed or had the slightest inclination to do so. "I
was simply showing Cheryl here the ins and outs of being a pathologist," he giggled. "Giving her the inside scoop, you might
say." He laughed again with a wheezy kind of snuffling sound and
gestured toward a neat row of glass jars on a nearby shelf.

The jars held floating masses of tissue suspended in clear solution, some pinkish lumps and other grayish slabs. Yellow and

white dangly ropes circled some of the organs, stretching out like tentacles from a body. It was impossible not to stare and still more impossible not to shift that stare to the long scar on the dead woman's torso. The doctor, noting their stunned dismay, rearranged his smile into a more sober expression.

"So sorry. So sorry. I forget that my humor may be a bit much for the layman. You're not relatives, are you?" He gazed anxiously at Auntie Lil. "I thought she was a Jane Doe. I mean, they told me they had no family or name. I was just seizing the rare chance for hands-on education for my new assistant. Not that Cheryl isn't fully qualified, but I have certain procedures that I like followed and . . ."

"Not at all. Not at all," Auntie Lil interrupted. "We're not relatives." She gave a dainty gulp and regained her composure. "My fault entirely for bursting in on you like this. Please carry on as if we weren't even here. We simply want to snap a few photographs to take back to her neighborhood to see if we could find out her true identity."

"How kind of you." His voice sounded as if he meant it, but his look was a bit skeptical.

"Please don't let us intrude," Auntie Lil repeated. "Do carry on with your . . . cutting or whatever." Her curiosity was starting to gain ground. She inched toward the body.

"You don't mean it?" The little doctor was delighted and looked at his assistant euphorically, as if not quite believing his luck. "Don't tell me you're one of the rare human beings who's not been conditioned to blanch at the sight of a little flesh and blood." He rubbed his hands together with anticipatory glee and stared at Emily's body. He looked, T.S. felt strongly, like a rabid raccoon eyeing a disabled fish.

"Well, that depends." Auntie Lil hastened to explain. "To a point, certainly, it can be . . . quite fascinating." T.S., meanwhile, was inching backwards toward the door. He had no desire to do anything but return to the limousine and look at Lilah.

The doctor froze suddenly and stared at them intently. "Say, wait a minute. You're the two people that Lilah Cheswick called me about." He thumped his bald pate in exasperation. "Of course. Now I remember."

T.S. halted his escape and stared back at the doctor. *This* was who Lilah knew at the medical examiner's office? No wonder she'd waited in the car.

"And how is Lilah?" the little doctor asked anxiously. He pushed his glasses up on his nose and peered at Auntie Lil. "I've been meaning to call her ever since my dear wife died. We'd be a perfect pair, what with us both being left so tragically alone. But I've been so wrapped up in my work, I haven't seen her at all. Her phone call was a total surprise. But a welcome one, of course."

"She's fine," Auntie Lil answered carefully. "As lovely and gracious as ever."

The little doctor's face brightened as if he'd forgotten Lilah's beauty. "But, of course. She is *such* a lovely woman." He put a hand on his chin and thought carefully. "Say, would you give her my regards when you see her? Perhaps she could give me a call again? Socially. I'm Dr. Millerton, by the way. Milton Millerton."

"We'd be glad to," Auntie Lil murmured sweetly.

T.S. would be damned if he'd let the little worm at Lilah for one second. In fact, he'd not even mention his silly name and would forbid Auntie Lil to do the same. So the good doctor's wife had died, had she? And just who had done the autopsy on *her*?

"Well, enough of the living," the little doctor decided, rubbing his tiny hands together with great relish. "Let's get back to the dead." He turned to his silent pupil, who was quite nonplussed at her boss's behavior. "You're just in time for the cranial exploration," he called over his shoulder cheerfully. "It's Cheryl's favorite part."

"You mean the skull?" Auntie Lil looked back at T.S. in alarm. "Perhaps we'd better take our photos *first*."

"Good idea," T.S. said. "Then we can leave." Without waiting for permission, he gingerly took one corner of the plastic sheet and peeled it down to Emily's shoulders. Poor woman. Her already frail body had caved in upon death and the skin lay over her facial bones like useless, dried out parchment.

"I've found that 400 film on 60 speed is quite sufficient in this bright light," Dr. Millerton told T.S. helpfully.

T.S. ignored him, but surreptitiously adjusted the speed setting. Old bugger. How would he know? What kind of pictures was he snapping around here, anyway?

The next few minutes were for T.S. perhaps the most annoying of his life. Dr. Millerton issued instructions from his left side while Auntie Lil hovered on the right, ordering him to take a shot of this part of Emily's face, and then the other. Rodriquez and the assistant pathologist retreated to one corner, far from the fray, when Auntie Lil began demanding close-ups of the dead woman's teeth.

"What on earth for?" T.S. asked in irritation, but got no reply.

Auntie Lil was too busy peeking under the plastic sheet that now covered Emily's body.

"What are you doing?" T.S. lowered his camera and stared at his aunt.

"Looking for distinguishing marks," she explained primly. "Haven't you any imagination?"

"Yes. Far too much to be poking around in here much longer."

"No distinguishing marks," the doctor assured her. "The only distinguishing thing Cheryl says she found was a small amount of a brown, muddy substance in her stomach that gave off a very sharp odor. Possibly toxic. It had a caustic effect on the stomach lining. I've recommended she have it analyzed in the lab."

"No need," T.S. said with great satisfaction. "That was Auntie Lil's chili."

"That's nothing to joke about, Theodore," she complained hotly. "My chili was perfectly good and it did not give off a sharp odor. It's probably not even chili."

"One way to find out," the doctor said, holding up a hand as if to ward off an argument between them. There was a distinctly ghoulish twinkle in his myopic eyes. "Cheryl—the specimen jar please." He bowed and held out a hand grandly as if he had just demanded the envelope furnishing the winner's name of a particularly coveted Academy Award.

Cheryl obediently fetched the jar from a small table against the wall and handed it to Dr. Millerton. "Approximately one-third of a cup was present in the stomach proper," she explained in a Yonkers accent that clashed severely with her *Flower Drum Song* exterior. "I removed one-third of that amount for analysis."

"Very good," he assured his pupil. "Now let's see what we have here." He held the jar up to the light and twisted it slowly until he'd examined each angle. He was drawing out the process and clearly enjoying this teasing of Auntie Lil and T.S.. "It does look like chili to me," he finally announced, winking at T.S. "Although it seems a particularly virulent color." He hee-heed loudly and unscrewed the top. "Let's see if it smells like chili."

He made an elaborate show of bending over the jar, still chuckling. Suddenly, he froze. His laughter stopped and he whipped his gnomelike head upright, locking eyes with his assistant.

"What is it, Dr. Millerton?" Cheryl asked anxiously. "Have I erred?" She reached for the jar but the doctor motioned her back, then sniffed deeply in the sudden silence.

"Is there some mistake?" Cheryl asked again, more timidly.

Before the doctor could answer, Auntie Lil's mouth opened in a gasp.

Rodriquez and T.S. turned to her, baffled, while Cheryl stared at Dr. Millerton with a puzzled expression.

When he saw that the others did not understand, the doctor turned to Auntie Lil for confirmation. They stared at one another in astonished enlightenment. Dr. Millerton held out a hand to her, as if asking her to dance, and drew her closer to the jar. Auntie Lil bent over and breathed deeply, then nodded her head. Her action was matched by the satisfied-looking doctor.

T.S. could stand it no longer. "What is it?" he demanded. "What's everyone nodding about?"

Auntie Lil stared at him in uncontained excitement. "Don't you smell that?" she said. "Bitter almonds. Just like I've read." She looked down at the jar, marveling.

"I don't smell anything," T.S. declared. He took a deep breath. Just the same acrid odors as before.

"Not everyone can smell it," Dr. Millerton explained. "Just us lucky ones." He beamed at Auntie Lil fondly.

"But that means . . ." The assistant said hesitantly, then stopped and looked down at the doctor.

"Yes," the tiny doctor agreed, nodding his head sagely and gesturing at Emily with a broad sweep of an arm. "This woman was poisoned by some form of cyanide. I'm absolutely certain of it."

CHAPTER FOUR

1. Auntie Lil did not wait to hear the details, which was just as well since Dr. Millerton immediately became lost in a closer scrutiny of the body. His assistant peered over his shoulder and they conferred together in low tones, not even looking up when Auntie Lil dragged T.S. from the room and hustled him down the corridors toward the exit. Rodriquez pursued them, exclaiming that it was his job to show them out. But Auntie Lil, who remembered each turn with uncanny accuracy, was through with the morgue and its insignificant employees. Greater things lay ahead.

"She was poisoned!" Auntie Lil hollered across the sidewalk in the direction of Lilah's waiting limousine. T.S. scurried after her, smiling thinly at a couple passing by, who stopped and looked at one another, then examined the plaque on the building's door with interest. Mystified, they continued their stroll, dodging Auntie Lil as she darted across the pavement and began to pound on the limo windows. This breach of etiquette did not faze the occupant in the least. The window rolled down slowly, revealing Lilah's expectant face. She held a nearly empty drink in her hand.

"I beg your pardon?" Lilah asked politely. "Did you say what I thought you said?"

"Indeed I did." This time, Auntie Lil did not wait for the chauffeur's help and simply climbed unceremoniously over Lilah to claim her spot in the back seat. She gave a triumphant gasp, produced a white handkerchief from the depths of her cavernous pocketbook and began to fan herself in great excitement.

"This is it," she told Lilah and a blatantly nosy Grady. "I can feel it. Fate has steered us to this puzzle, handed us this predicament. We have been charged with the egregious task of uncovering justice in *her* name." She pointed a finger straight at the

58

roof of the car and smiled mirthlessly. "I'll find them. Just you wait and see."

T.S. was not sure he had ever seen that particular smile cross her face—but he was glad Auntie Lil was not *his* enemy. The smile glittered with a calm rage cooled to concrete by her absolute conviction that justice would be done. He pitied the poor murderer so foolish as to have poisoned an old lady in front of *this* old lady. In fact, he felt compelled to keep a careful eye on her as he snagged the seat next to Lilah.

"She was poisoned?" Lilah asked T.S. breathlessly, leaning so close that he could smell the warm scent of her gardenia perfume.

"That's what the doctor and Aunt Lil say. Me, I'm just along for the ride."

"Not anymore you're not," Auntie Lil promised. "And she was most definitely poisoned. We'll know more when you get us a peek at the autopsy report, Lilah dear."

Lilah nodded calmly. Obtaining an autopsy report was child's play for her. T.S. wondered jealously if the task entailed another call to the gnomish Dr. Millerton.

"I'm sure the police can handle it from here," T.S. tried telling Auntie Lil. He knew protests were useless but felt that decorum called for some sort of halt to arms.

Auntie Lil stared at him. "I'm sure the police won't care a whit."

He sighed. Once she had it in her head that she was locking horns with the New York Police Department, there was no stopping Auntie Lil. She had a point to prove and honor to avenge, thanks to a long-simmering feud between them that had started more than three decades ago when a young patrolman had had the nerve to cite her for running a red light in broad daylight in front of a grammar school. Auntie Lil's defense—that the middle of the block was a stupid place for a red light and no children were around—had not played well in front of the judge. Especially since, in a display of rookie enthusiasm, the patrolman had actually showed up in court, describing Auntie Lil's impulsive behavior and colorful vocabulary with a flair for overacting not seen since the days of silent movies. Auntie Lil had zero tolerance for being imitated and promptly hit him with her pocketbook in front of the judge, thus ensuing an enormous fine and narrowly escaping a token jail term.

Thus had war been declared between Auntie Lil and the police, a feud underscored since by the City's continuous failure to instill its officers with the need for treating law-abiding citizens with a minimum of respect. Ever since the expensive incident, Auntie Lil had relentlessly kept track of her every contact with the NYPD and T.S. had to admit that very few had been pleasant, despite a lack of provocation from Auntie Lil. Even the most innocuous questions, such as asking directions, seemed to irritate the overworked force. And, of course, once Auntie Lil ran up against Lieutenant Abromowitz any residual respect or sympathy for the NYPD went right out the window. But that was another story.

There were more important matters on Auntie Lil's mind now. "Why would anyone kill a harmless old lady?" she asked, enraptured by the intricacies the mystery promised. She stared into space and slowly twirled a white curl absently around a finger.

"Perhaps it was a random killing?" Lilah suggested, impervious to the skeptical expression triggered by her remark. "Some nut case." Her voice slowed and she shivered delicately. "Perhaps they intended to kill someone else."

Now *that* was a good point, T.S. felt.

"No." Auntie Lil shook her head firmly. "She was the only one poisoned. It had to have been added to her portion alone. No one would know it was hers unless it was on her tray. I'm sure it was intended for her. How absolutely efficient they were."

"'Thanks to your chili. The perfect disguise for poison," T.S. added pointedly.

"They'd have gotten her if we'd been serving egg custard," Auntie Lil protested. "And the caustic effect on her stomach lining was caused by the poison, not by my chili. I don't care what you say."

"Caustic effect on her stomach?" Lilah echoed faintly. She finished the rest of her drink in a sudden, unladylike gulp.

Grady rescued her before T.S. had the chance. "Perhaps, madam, you might care for another drink?" he suggested tactfully. Lilah's dismayed face dominated the rearview mirror.

"We haven't got time for that now," Auntie Lil declared. Her brow furrowed as she stared into the depths of her pocketbook for divine guidance. "We've got to come up with a plan at once and move quickly before the police take over everything and ruin it. Dr. Millerton will notify them tomorrow, I'm sure of it. We must have a plan in place by then."

T.S.—who did not share her eminent domain theory when it came to murder cases—patted Lilah's arm reassuringly. "Really, Aunt Lil. Not everyone relishes murder the way you do, you know."

"I'm not relishing *murder*," she protested. "I detest murder. I'm outraged. And I'm also too busy thinking to talk." She bit her lip and decided. "Take me home, Grady. I need to think this over at once."

"Before you commandeer Lilah's car," T.S. suggested tactfully, "perhaps you'd like to confer with us." He kept his voice calm but glared at his aunt. Otherwise, she would have totally missed his point.

The glare had a minimal effect. "Oh, for heaven's sake." She flapped her hankie at them. "Just because I'm going home doesn't mean you have to. We must get those photographs developed at once. Go to that twenty-four-hour place at Times Square. It only takes an hour or so. Then you two can go off and booze it up and whatever it is Theodore has in mind. I'm going to work."

"Boozing it up was not what I had in mind," T.S. protested firmly. "But now that you mention it, I wouldn't turn down a stiff drink in a dark bar."

"Neither would I," Lilah agreed faintly.

"Good. Get rid of me and we'll meet in the morning." Auntie Lil was already scribbling ideas in her small notebook, muttering key points of theories aloud. "Relatives?" she asked herself. "Jealousy? The past?" There was silence. "Love interest?" she shouted triumphantly, jotting it down on a page. "Perhaps corporate espionage? Or drug trafficking? Poison . . . that's a woman's method. Women are poisoners, not men. And what did that old man mean by 'The Eagle' . . . remember? He said he'd seen 'The Eagle' breathe evil into her mouth?"

The air was thick with possible theories as Auntie Lil's disjointed monologue continued while the limousine crawled slowly through the ever-present construction jams that dotted the main roads toward Auntie Lil's Queens apartment house. T.S. did not attempt to translate the obscure and strange collection of possible motives tumbling from Auntie Lil's mouth. There was no talking to her at the moment, T.S. knew. Not when her brain had been seized by such an enticing puzzle. He could practically see the theories zinging wildly from synapse to synapse as Auntie Lil built, pooh-poohed and quickly replaced theories.

He ignored her mutterings and smoothly fixed Lilah a fresh drink from the limo's bar, pouring out a healthy Dewars and soda for himself. It was just as well that Auntie Lil was so preoccupied. He was in no mood to hear what she had to say. He, too, needed time to think. Why *had* someone murdered a harmless old woman? Good Lord, this was much more interesting than those stupid soap operas.

2. While Lilah waited for him in the limousine, T.S. chivalrously escorted Auntie Lil to her door. She scarcely noticed his presence.

"Want me to clear a table for you, so you can work?" he suggested. She nodded absently, too busy wrestling her Jolly Green Giant hat off her head to pay any attention to him.

Auntie Lil's apartment looked like a cyclone had recently blown through and deposited the contents of three other apartments and a museum or two throughout her four small rooms. He picked his way past waist-high stacks of books in the small hallway and managed to unearth a table at one end of the cluttered living room by shoving the bolts of material and magazines covering it onto the carpet where the mess would lie, unnoticed, for perhaps another century or so. He tripped over her bathrobe—which had been hanging from a knob on a china cabinet—when the terrycloth belt became wrapped around one of his pants legs. Untangling it, he noticed that an easel had been set up in the dining room area and that small tubes of acrylic paint cluttered those portions of the mahogany dining table not already covered by unopened Book-of-the-Month Club packages, baskets of letters, empty envelopes, stacks of stationery and a good three dozen pens and pencils. Not to mention the new pair of pink tennis shoes with Auntie Lil's initials etched on the side in gold glitter that protruded from the center of a forgotten bowl of fruit.

It was enough to make him drop to his knees and begin scrubbing, straightening, alphabetizing and bringing order into the utter chaos that was Auntie Lil's home.

Chaos to him, at least. With irritation, he noticed that she sailed directly through the debris to a large cabinet where she quickly found a thick volume with the physician's staff symbol on its spine. "You run along, Theodore," she told him absently, flipping through the pages with purpose. "Have a good time and I'll see you in the morning."

Have a good time? Doing what? Talking about murder? Not his idea of a romantic date. But definitely Auntie Lil's idea of a good time. She was already hard at work, flipping through pages and scribbling theories in her notebook. A pool of light from a nearby lamp cast a halo around her sturdy head, giving her a deceptively angelic look. He gave her an affectionate glance, then shut the door behind him, carefully locking both locks. He'd hate for a burglar to stumble in on Auntie Lil. The poor guy wouldn't stand a chance.

By the time he and Lilah reached Times Square again, it was

past eight o'clock and the well-dressed crowds of theatergoers were safely ensconced in their plush cushioned seats. A momentary lull had descended on the busy streets. Neon lights blinked off and on brightly in the new twilight. The early evening slasher-and-action shows had already started at the many movie theaters nearby. It would be an hour or more before those audiences were disgorged onto the sidewalks, blinking in the artificial glow of New York night and—all pumped up with images of car chases and knife fights—anxious to spill their excitement onto the crowded sidewalks.

"I always find Times Square so overwhelming at night," Lilah admitted.

"I like it best from the back seat of your limo," T.S. replied firmly. They were slowing down in front of the twenty-four-hour photo store and several disreputable characters skulked around the nearby corner, passing off small packages and conferring in their nightly ballet of illicit drugs and small-time scams.

"You wait here. I'll only be a moment." T.S. scurried inside the brightly lit storefront and hurriedly left his order with the bored cashier. After extracting a promise of quick service (at least ninety minutes, never mind the one-hour promise on the sign), he dashed back out to the limo. Already, the hounds were sniffing out the fox. Three young men, nearly identically dressed in absurdly baggy pants, baseball hats and torn T-shirts, were eyeing the rear bumper of the limousine. T.S. saw a "you backed into me and now you're going to pay" scam coming and practically dove into the back seat, slamming the door behind him.

He could have stopped and challenged them, but why show off for Lilah? Restraint *was* the better part of valor.

Grady knew the score and pulled quickly away without incident. Which was exactly what life was like for Lilah—people protected her from the changing state of her world. It would have been a shame not to.

"That's that," T.S. announced. "The photos will be ready in a couple of hours."

"About that drink," Lilah murmured tactfully in reply.

"Yes? Shall we?" T.S. wondered where they might find a cozy spot nearby. He could not go to his usual haunt, Harvey's, because his every move would find its way back to Auntie Lil—courtesy of Frederick, the bartender there.

"I have a suggestion," Grady volunteered. "A friend of mine owns a nice little place over on Tenth Avenue called Robert's."

The limousine glided smoothly over an unexpected area of

newly resurfaced avenues. The streets were the only new things in the whole neighborhood, however. As they drew further west toward the docks, shadows began to step from the darkness in eager anticipation of a wealthy customer. Women of all shapes and colors packed tightly into latex glitter and dirty lace leaned expectantly toward the back seat windows, trying to peer inside the tinted glass. Their faces—garishly attractive at a distance—came into horrifying focus just inches from T.S.'s face. He shrank back reflexively as their cheap glamour revealed itself as nothing more than bad skin, worse teeth, bruises, open sores and sagging flesh. Seductive glances widened into leers and the bright glint of heavily made-up eyes may have been lust—but for drugs, not love, T.S. knew. He shivered and moved away from the window.

"This is like being in a Fellini movie," Lilah declared, while T.S. double-checked the door locks.

"Sorry, ma'am. We're almost there." Grady made a wide turn onto Tenth Avenue and they were momentarily rescued from the onslaught of flesh peddlers.

"There were some awfully young old people back there," T.S. admitted, running a finger under his collar. "It's been a while since I've been here at night."

"Shall I wait?" Grady glided to a stop in front of a tiny but cheerful wood-paneled restaurant nestled between two dark and chained storefronts. Inside, Christmas lights blinked gaily around a single wide window that framed happy couples cozily clustered about small tables scattered over a wooden floor. Red-checked cloths adorned each table and there was not a paper napkin in sight. An old-fashioned oak bar dominated one-third of the room and hosted a handful of relatively respectable patrons relaxing against high-backed bar stools. An older woman, dressed completely in cream silk, furiously worked the keys of a piano backed against one brick wall. As they stepped from the limo, T.S. could detect the strains of a sad jazz tune. His shivers disappeared, as did all remembrance of the sad women behind them. Grady was a genius. He'd discovered an oasis of romantic charm in the heart of a pirate-infested desert.

Lilah peeked in the window. "This is wonderful, Theodore. How quaint." Her genteel enthusiasm made T.S. smile.

"Don't bother waiting for us, Grady," she told the chauffeur. "Just come get us in an hour." She cast a shy glance at T.S. "Better make it two," she decided.

Well. Two hours indeed. T.S. straightened his collar and carefully held the door open for Lilah. He smoothly guided her coat from her shoulders with the élan of forties movie hero, then stashed it on the hook farthest from the door with the prudence of a nineties NYC resident.

Lilah was like a jewel, he decided. One that got more precious and beautiful with age. One that deserved treatment more royal than royalty.

Unfortunately, the establishment was not cooperating. No maître d' appeared nor was there any sign of a waiter. Lilah finally dragged him over to a corner table. "Here," she decided for them. "It's not too close to the piano. So we can talk."

He gulped. Now came the real test. What would they talk about?

That part turned out to be easy. Once a tubby waiter appeared and their drink orders had been taken, Lilah was sufficiently composed to want to talk about murder.

"Auntie Lil will not rest until an answer is found," she warned T.S. "You and I have both seen her this way before." Lilah had a habit of lacing her long, elegant fingers together and resting them on the table while she talked. It made her look a bit like an obedient child. T.S. thought it was a very charming gesture. Of course, Lilah could have whipped off her bra and whirled it above her head while she danced on the bar, and T.S. would have thought that was a charming gesture, too.

"No, she won't give up," T.S. agreed. "I'm not even going to try to stop her."

"Will you help her?" Lilah asked huskily, leaning forward and searching his face in the candlelight. T.S. half expected the piano player to break into "As Time Goes By."

"Someone has to keep her out of trouble," he agreed gallantly, any thought of deserting Auntie Lil now fleeing at the sight of Lilah's expectant face. Their drinks arrived and the woman at the piano began a new tune, filling the bar with another melancholy melody. T.S. took a sip. The Scotch burned a tidy path down his throat and he sighed. Someone dimmed the lights in the bar and he became more aware of the candle flickering between them and the way Lilah's face grew even more radiant in the flattering light. The room's atmosphere thickened with unspoken sentiments as the music wove an air of unexpected intimacy about them. Even the dark oak of the restaurant's wainscotting seemed to deepen with the mood. Other diners around them also grew quiet, drawing their heads together to whisper.

Was this what it was like, T.S. wondered. Was this what he had been missing all those years that he'd buried himself in his books and in his career?

Lilah suddenly stared over his shoulder toward the bar, breaking the mood. "The bartender just made the funniest face."

T.S. turned in time to see the front door bang open with an intrusive thud. An extremely tall woman, lanky and awkward with drink or drugs, tottered in on high spike heels. She was squeezed into a long-sleeved spandex tube dress sprinkled with cheap silver spangles that sparkled against her cocoa-colored skin. A wide run in her silver hose snaked down the length of her long legs like a jagged scar. Dark hair swirled in a tall pile atop her head in a style reminiscent of Motown in the mid-1960s. Garish earrings dangled from extremely prominent ears. She had a tiny round head that topped a long, skinny neck and her pinched face was covered with a heavy coating of cheap makeup. When she blinked her eyes sleepily, her small head arched forward like a turtle's. Her lipstick was a garish silvery pink that glittered in the reflected candlelight. But her fingernails were long and elegantly manicured into blood-red tapers.

The bartender's scowl deepened when the woman approached the bar, waving a dollar bill at him. "Change, sweetie?" she asked the bartender in a throaty whisper.

"Beat it, Leteisha. I told you. You've been eighty-sixed from here. Get lost." A man of few but pointed words, the bartender crossed his beefy arms and nodded grimly toward the door. The woman's expression did not change as she smoothly turned on her high heels and glided as sulkily out the door as she'd entered.

"Just in case you'd forgotten where we were," T.S. noted.

"Now, now, Theodore. Don't be a snob." Lilah's rebuke was real. She was so thoroughly insulated from the crasser elements of society that she did not even understand the concept of being a snob and hated people that were, especially when they fawned all over her trying to sniff out the source of her money.

"I know." T.S. shook his head guiltily. "I've been awful about everything. About coming back to this neighborhood. About helping Aunt Lil in the soup kitchen. I've only been there two days, you know. I'm not the cheerful giver you think I am. And I didn't want to find out who the dead woman was at first. The truth is, I *am* being a snob. I don't want to be back here, traipsing all over these streets. My family lived here, you know. Before my grandparents moved upstate. I'm just two generations removed from Hell's Kitchen myself." There. He had said it. Now she would know he was just another common fortune seeker.

Lilah patted his hand reassuringly. "That only proves you have honest blood. Just because you feel like a snob doesn't mean you have to act like one. We all have our demons to face, remember?" Her own demons, compared to those of many, were quite mild. But they pricked at her conscience nonetheless. "I'm sure you'll be a big help to Auntie Lil. And I hope that you'll let me help you, too. I don't think anyone should be allowed to die that way, Theodore. Murdered and unknown. No matter how poor or old they might be."

She was right, of course. He would help Auntie Lil find the killer. He'd do whatever it took to unlock the secrets behind Emily's death.

Lilah asked him about his family, and the talk of murder passed. Their hours together went by quickly and dinner was forgotten. He would later be unable to really remember what they'd talked about. He would only recall, instead, the soft sound of the piano and the air heavy with cigarette smoke and secrets. He'd remember Lilah's laugh cutting through the surrounding noise, as if it were meant for his ears only, and the quavering high notes of a drunken old lady at the bar who stood up to sing an Irish ballad to herself. He and Lilah joined the rest of the crowd in applause and—if only for a few moments of alcohol and music-inspired togetherness in a lonely city—they were all part of the same family. He would remember the ache that the old woman's voice produced in his heart, and the recurring vision it conjured of sailing ships entering New York Harbor, crowded with people filled with meager hopes and facing a new land. Their dreams did not seem so ridiculous to him anymore.

It was as if he had disembarked in a strange land, where time stood still and strangers welcomed him with open arms. Best of all, he spoke their new language magically, while slipping effortlessly and without fear from one adventure to another. He did not want the feeling to end and was so lost in belonging and warmth for the people around him that he was shocked when Lilah waved at Grady through the window. How had two hours passed so quickly from his grasp? Yet, checking his watch, he discovered that three hours had gone by with Grady waiting tactfully outside for Lilah's discreet signal. It was nearly midnight by the time they were ensconced again in the back seat of the limousine. They pulled away onto the streets of Hell's Kitchen at dark and New York's human nightcrawlers emerged from doorways to watch them glide past. The cozy comfort of Robert's was quickly left behind.

"Where do all these people come from?" he wondered out loud as they cut across Forty-second Street to the photo store. The streets were clogged with hustlers of all colors and ages, eyeing one another for territorial transgressions and scrutinizing each unwary tourist for potential profit. Brightly attired in T-shirts and long shorts that reached to their knees (despite the cool night air), New York's night citizens clustered in ominous groups across from the chaotic entrance to the Forty-second Street Port Authority bus station entrance, laughing and shouting insults as frightened visitors dashed to their cabs. Some hustlers tried to tug at their luggage or hail cabs for them, in hopes of extracting a bribe or two. But most simply watched with smug expressions of streetwise superiority, clutching small brown paper bags containing cans of beer as they waited for something bigger and better to come along.

The limousine crossed Eighth Avenue and made its way toward Broadway through the jangle and noise of the seedy Forty-second Street strip. Boarded-up theaters awaited renovation that would never come, providing dark pools of shadows between the brightly lit storefronts of cheap electronics stores and fried chicken joints. The sidewalks churned with people jostling and seeking a fast score. Hardly anyone noticed or cared that a limousine was passing by—they all had their own sly business to conduct.

"Is it my imagination or does this place look completely different than it did three hours ago?" T.S. asked out loud.

"Is it my imagination or do many of these people look like they ought to be in junior high school, not here?" Lilah answered.

She was right. The night had brought out New York's young runaways. They huddled in empty doorways, wan and unfed, their dark, bright eyes hungrily scrutinizing passers-by with a cynical knowledge far beyond their young years.

Lilah sighed and shook her head. "Thank God my daughters are at college."

The twenty-four-hour photo was, apparently, a bustling center of cheap nightly entertainment. T.S. had to push through a crowd of twenty or more chattering teenagers to reach the front door. They stood clustered in front of the store's picture window watching a small, dark brown man tinker among the automatic photo-developing conveyor belts. The man straightened up wearily and stuck a screwdriver back into his rear pocket.

"Yo, man. It's fixed," someone in the crowd announced with satisfaction. "We gonna get us another peek now."

This crowd must really be bored, T.S. thought as he squeezed in the front door. Surely there were better things to do than watch bad photos of other people's birthday celebrations and vacations crawl by.

The optimistic voice in the crowd had been right. The machinery was fixed. The conveyor belt groaned slowly forward just as T.S. approached the front counter. The bored cashier was gone, replaced by a small Pakistani man who emerged from the elaborate developing contraption holding a wrench in one hand like a weapon.

"I pay much money for this franchise and equipment," he told T.S. "Damn thing breaks down every night. Holy shit."

"What a shame for the neighborhood," T.S. remarked drily as he handed over his receipt. "Looks like this is a real hotspot for cheap entertainment."

The proprietor shrugged philosophically. "Not always. But tonight, some pervert drop off whole roll of pictures of a poor dead woman. As old as my beloved mother. What someone want with such photos, I do not know. This is sick city. Sick city, indeed." He nodded toward the picture window. "The machine jammed in the middle of the order and the crowd that you see gathered. They love death, this bunch. Look at them. They salivate like animals at the kill."

T.S. froze. Outside, the crowd began pushing forward to get a better view. The strip of pictures affixed to the conveyor belt rounded a turn and approached the picture window again. Eyes grew wide and the jokes began, boys nudging their girlfriends and grabbing the back of their necks in hopes of eliciting squeals.

"Oh, dear," T.S. murmured lightly, running a finger under his collar. It did no good. The flush began at the base of his neck and quickly spread across his face. He was humiliated. He was the pervert.

The proprietor had already discovered that fact. He stared at the number on T.S.'s receipt and raised his eyebrows in slow recognition. He surveyed T.S. from head to toe, then peered over his shoulder at the waiting limousine without comment. Then he inched away from T.S., making it plain that he preferred to stand by his conveyor belt rather than be in close proximity to such a clearly debauched human being. Crossing his arms primly, the proprietor took turns staring back and forth between T.S. and the crowd outside while he waited for the morbid photos to make their tortuous way thorough the labyrinth of belts. Some in the crowd got the proprietor's hint and began to eye T.S. with great interest.

T.S. carefully brushed dirt from his shoe, straightened his shirt collar and tried hard to imagine himself somewhere else. When that failed, he thought of the ways he might seek revenge against Auntie Lil for sending him on this mission. After a two-minute wait that seemed more like a two-year prison sentence, his pictures reached the end of their mechanical journey. As the strip of photos neared the automatic cutter, T.S. saw that his exposure settings and framing had, alas for his immediate reputation, been outstanding. The images of a dead Emily were crisp and relentless. At least fifty eyes stared at him intently as the proprietor made a great show of holding up each finished photo before ceremoniously placing it into the order bag.

Once the last damning photo had finally been plucked from the stares of the enraptured crowd, the proprietor marched across the room with the bag pinched between two fingers as if it smelled very bad indeed. He held it out toward T.S. "Twenty dollars," he said primly, holding out an open palm. "You surprise me, sir. Really. I feel compelled to inform you. You really do surprise me."

Humiliated, T.S. paid the hefty tab, suspecting it was at least five dollars over the regular charge. He did not have time to think much about it, however, as his eye had been caught by a small face whose expression was quite different from those surrounding him. A skinny black boy, not more than eleven or twelve years old, stood in the doorway staring at T.S. His eyes were wide and suspicious, his features hardened into a permanent accusatory stare. Yet, T.S. was sure that his unblinking eyes were filling with tears and that the young boy's mouth was trembling. The child stepped back in fright as T.S. opened the door, and he watched T.S. hurry to the limo with undisguised confusion before moving forward as if he had something to to say. T.S. stopped with his hand on the door handle and stared at the child. Why had the photos upset him so much? Everyone else in the crowd loved the macabre real-life postscript to the slasher movies they'd probably just seen.

"Son?" he said to the young boy, who responded by darting forward. T.S. thought he was being attacked but the child veered at the last moment and took off down the block, running as fast as he could. T.S. was so astonished he made no move to get into the limousine until Lilah rolled down the window and called out his name.

"Theodore. We're attracting quite a crowd. Perhaps we should be on our way."

T.S. looked over at the picture window and the crowd of teenagers stared back at him in mystified curiosity and misdirected envy.

"Yo, pops. That's kinky!" someone called out. A few people laughed and that was more than enough for T.S. He quickly hopped into the back seat next to Lilah and thrust the bag of photos into her hands.

"Remind me to kill Auntie Lil in the morning," he told her. "And, Grady, for God's sake, get us out of here."

3. He was awakened early the next morning from a troubled dream in which he lay in a glass coffin, surrounded by leering women in cheap outfits and garish makeup. They leaned over him, grinning suggestively, their pink tongues licking at the glass and their features distorted as they pressed against the sides of the coffin. He woke suddenly, convinced that the tremendous pounding he heard was really his heartbeat, until he finally realized that someone was trying to break down his apartment door. He stumbled to it, still half-asleep, and found an impatient Auntie Lil waiting on the other side. She surveyed his pajamas with energetic disapproval.

"Mahmoud let me in," she explained cheerfully. "I've been up for hours. Here, I've brought you bagels. It's time to get to work."

T.S. made a mental note to cut the doorman's Christmas tip in half. He stared at the clock on the wall. It was barely eight o'clock in the morning.

"You're certainly serious about this thing," he told Auntie Lil grumpily, stepping aside to let her through before he was mowed down. Auntie Lil hated to get out of bed before 10:00 A.M. She claimed the human body had not been made to function before noon and customarily spent her mornings reading tabloids and detective magazines while she drank quarts of black coffee.

"We've got to find out who she was before we can find out who killed her," Auntie Lil announced loudly as she plopped her bag of goodies onto the immaculate surface of his dining room table. T.S. winced. It was the single heirloom he'd taken from his parents' house upstate and in the twenty-five years of his ownership, it had hardly sustained a scratch, despite what he considered flagrant abuse by Auntie Lil.

Brenda and Eddie wandered in belatedly, having to give up

their warm spot at the foot of T.S.'s bed. Letting them sleep there was his sole concession to affection when it came to his pets. They eyed him with suspicious hope. Would they get fed early? Would he come across with the chicken and cheese dinner?

"Feed them so they leave me alone," Auntie Lil ordered. She liked cats about as much as she liked the NYPD.

"I thought you weren't a morning person." The whirr of the can opener whipped Brenda and Eddie into their obese version of a frenzy: their tails switched back and forth, perfectly synchronized, and Brenda let out a ladylike meow.

"This morning, I am a morning person," Auntie Lil replied calmly. "How did the photos turn out? Can you see her face clearly?"

"I'll say. Our little photo exhibit made quite a stir last night. Who says culture is dead in NYC?" He slammed the refrigerator door and felt a little better. There was just enough fresh orange juice left for a single glass.

"Is that orange juice?" Auntie Lil asked with great interest. "If so, I'll take a glass."

"No, you won't." He was being rude, but he didn't care. She knew better than to wake him up. She'd just have to take her lumps.

"If you're going to be so grouchy, why don't you just go back to bed?" She stopped her scolding long enough to discover the package of photos lying on the coffee table next to his precisely aligned rows of *The New Yorker* and *Cat Fancy*. She thumbed through the stack of images with approval. "Say, these are very good, Theodore. You did a wonderful job." She looked at him from over the reading glasses she seldom wore because of her vanity. "I've been thinking about this. Our first step is to find out *who* she was. Then we can find out why she was killed."

"What do you want me to do?" He held up the photos and flipped through them. It would be good to dive into the puzzle and keep his mind off his personal confusion about Lilah.

"I'm going to start canvassing the neighborhood," she told him. "Show the photos around and find out where she lived. Someone has to know, even if she was very, very private. There's nothing else to go on. We need to question Adelle and her friends again, then try to track down the funny old man who saw Emily's pocketbook get stolen the day she died. We know so little about her."

"We know she was an understudy in the original *Our Town*," T.S. pointed out. "And that her stage name was Emily Toujours.

I could go to the Lincoln Center Library and check out the Playbill."

"All right. Of course, we don't know for sure she really was the understudy . . . and that name likely came after the show. But, I suppose we have no other choice. And it will keep you out of my way."

T.S. was slightly offended that she had not grasped the brilliance of his suggestion.

"You go this morning and then we'll meet back at the soup kitchen in the afternoon and compare notes," she decided.

"Do you really think the police will let the kitchen open up today?" T.S. asked incredulously. "After all, someone was poisoned there."

"We don't know that for sure." Auntie Lil's chin jutted out when she was feeling her most stubborn and at the moment it looked like a Grand Canyon cliff. "They'll try to blame it on my chili, but I'm having none of that. Besides, no one died yesterday and people are as hungry as ever. They have to let us open."

T.S. shook his head. "I'd be surprised. But I'll meet you there at one."

4. It felt good to have a mission again. T.S. whistled a Broadway tune as he dressed carefully in slacks, a new plaid shirt he'd prudently purchased on sale and his first sweater of the new fall season. It was the perfect library outfit—a sort of relaxed and quietly intellectual look. He selected a pair of Hush Puppies from his customized shoe rack, and chose socks that were whimsically embroidered with the logo from a Broadway show about tap dancing. He loved Broadway and all there was to do about Broadway. And now he even had a legitimate excuse to hang out at the Performing Arts Library. Why, it was even better than going into the office. In fact, he downright pitied those poor men and women still chained to their desks, marching into work like suited-up zombies each day, squabbling over petty office politics disputes, making minor decisions about unimportant matters, sitting behind their desks and accepting obsequious homage from underlings out to protect their own interests . . . well, he'd better stop thinking about it or he might start to miss it, after all.

By the time he emerged from the subway near Lincoln Center, Auntie Lil was hard at work just twenty blocks due south, the photos of Emily carefully stowed in her enormous handbag. She began with the handful of people already in line for the soup kitchen, but they were not regulars and claimed to never have seen Emily before. Auntie Lil kept a careful eye out for the strange man who had seen "The Eagle" breathe evil into Emily's mouth, but she did not find him or even Franklin, his more coherent tablemate. Using a list she had prepared the night before from a booklet on volunteering, she visited seven separate shelters in the vicinity of St. Barnabas but none of the workers or residents recognized Emily. She even waylaid three postmen and one Federal Express delivery woman, but none of them could help. Being New Yorkers, not a single person so much as blinked at what was clearly a photo of a dead woman.

Because it was mid-morning on a workday, few people occupied the neighborhood stoops. She did show Emily's photo to a family of plump Hispanic women who were fanning themselves with large paper fans while they enjoyed the morning sunshine. They passed the photos eagerly among themselves, then reluctantly confessed that, so far as they were concerned, Emily was a stranger.

Discouraged, Auntie Lil wandered up Forty-sixth Street between Eighth and Ninth Avenues. Called Restaurant Row, the block was home to over a dozen eating establishments, interspersed between largely middle-class apartment brownstones. Restaurant Row was even more deserted than the residential blocks around it. A few deliverymen hurried from their trucks toward restaurants, pushing carts and supplied ahead of them, and a couple of busboys were slowly sweeping their patches of sidewalk clean.

The autumn day was growing warmer by the moment and Auntie Lil began to regret wearing the heavy felt hat she'd purchased on a recent visit to the Austrian Alps. As she neared Eighth Avenue, she spotted a man sitting in a lawn chair in front of a boarded-up hotel. From far away, he looked like just another old soul, slumped and potbellied, tired and discouraged, with nothing better to do but sit and watch life pass him by on a dirty street corner in New York City. His hands were enormous and hung to the sidewalk as he slouched low in the sagging chair. As Auntie Lil grew closer, she perceived an oddity in his profile. His face was unnaturally flattened and the silhouette marred by an enormous lump of a nose that, on even closer inspection, resembled a huge bulb of cauliflower intersected by blood vessels. Above this monstrosity, his milky green eyes were large and placid, and his white hair swept straight back from his broad forehead in carefully combed strands. His clothes were clean and such innocuous shades of brown and beige that he seemed to melt into the dirty concrete wall behind him. Auntie Lil approached him politely and showed him Emily's photos.

"I'm trying to locate a dear old friend of mine," she told the man. He stared at her lips intently as she spoke, then looked back down at the photo and nodded.

"You know her?" Auntie Lil asked in excitement, touching his arm. He looked up and she repeated her question. Again, he stared intently at her lips, then back down at the photo. Slowly, he shook his head and shrugged philosophically.

Auntie Lil could not mask her disappointment. Her shoulders fell and her head sagged along with her hopes, adding a good ten years to her frame. The old man nodded sympathetically and patted her arm in reassurance. Then he smiled and pointed across Eighth Avenue. He was indicating either a boarded-up storefront peppered by half-torn posters and obscene graffiti, or a small delicatessen with a bright yellow awning. The old man pointed again to the deli and made a pushing gesture with his hands.

"I should go there?" Auntie Lil asked. "Will they know her?"

The old man shrugged and spread his hands wide. Maybe. Maybe not. But it was the best answer she'd gotten so far.

Auntie Lil hurried across the avenue, dodging unemployed actors, construction workers in search of coffee, grumpy mothers and squalling children in baby carriages. The deli was cheery and immaculate, its outside walls painted a paler version of the bright yellow splashed across the awning. THE DELICIOUS DELI, promised a sign in the window. YOU WON'T BELIEVE OUR COFFEE. AND OUR HE-MAN HEROES ARE THE BIGGEST BARGAIN IN MANHATTAN.

That decided it for Auntie Lil. She was definitely going in. It was nearly noon, she was famished from walking around and, worst of all, had not been able to enjoy her customary five cups of coffee that morning. Whether they knew Emily there or not, she was paying the Delicious Deli a visit.

A long counter ran down the right half of the small store, stopping just short of the window. Two small cafe tables had been squeezed into the tiny space left over. All were empty, awaiting the lunch rush. Auntie Lil sank gratefully into a small wrought-iron chair and eyed the man behind the counter. He was of medium build, around thirty-five years of age, she judged, with sandy hair and an open, cheery face. He had large round cheeks, wide-set brown eyes and a perfectly chiseled nose. His hair fell across his face and he brushed his unruly bangs aside impatiently.

He was leaning against an enormous coffee machine, carefully hand-lettering the day's special on a portable chalkboard. He wore a short-sleeved white restaurant shirt and an apron smeared with chocolate. His enormous biceps were evidence that he did most of the work around the deli. Indeed, there was no one else in sight.

"Can I get you something, ma'am?" he asked Auntie Lil. The smile that lit up his face was broad and genuine. She knew, at once, that this was his deli and that he had worked very hard to make a go of it.

"You said you had good coffee," she told him, pointing to the sign. "I'll decide for myself, if you don't mind."

"Like the sign says, it's the best in New York." He poured her out a cup and admired her hat. "That's some hat you've got there," he told her cheerfully. "Wait until the ladies get a load of it."

"The ladies?" she asked him. The coffee did smell delicious. Her stomach rumbled with a loud growl.

"How about some cheesecake?" the proprietor offered with a smile as he set her cup down in front of her. "It's on me."

"That sounds wonderful." Auntie Lil rummaged through her enormous handbag in search of her wallet. "I will have a piece. And one of your he-man heros, too. But I've got money to pay for it."

"You're lucky," the young man told her. "A lot of old ladies in this neighborhood don't have two dimes to rub together." He considered his words and blushed.

Auntie Lil laughed at his embarrassment. "It's quite all right, young man. It's no secret that I'm old."

He nodded sheepishly and ducked behind the counter to pile enormous hunks of meat and cheese topped with shredded lettuce and tomato slices on a long hard roll. He had no intention of stiffing any little old lady on the he-man. It was truly of heroic proportions.

"My name's Billy Finnegan." He set the enormous sandwich in front of Auntie Lil and held out a hand roughened by hard work. She gripped it in a firm handshake, pleased at his confidence. It bespoke an honest heart. He was probably someone she could trust.

"Why don't you sit down and take a break? I bet you've never seen anyone as old as me eat a whole hero."

"No way you can eat all that," he told her. "But I'm willing to sit and watch." He pulled out a chair and sighed heavily as he sank into it. "One day I'll be able to afford some help around here."

"Who did you mean by 'the ladies'?" Auntie Lil asked, the hero poised before her open mouth. She surveyed it carefully then decided the best strategy was to simply dive in and put her hearty eating skills to their best use. She took a huge bite and chewed lustily, muttering muffled and barely intelligible compliments to the chef. Billy was too busy staring at her to answer.

She swallowed carefully. "Are you referring by any chance to the actresses who live here and frequent the St. Barnabas soup kitchen?" she asked politely before diving into another bite.

"Sure. You know them? I've never seen you with them before." He forced himself to stop staring at her incredible eating and looked her up and down with a practiced air of evaluation. He was no stranger to the streets and realized that Auntie Lil's clothes were too modern and expensive to place her in the same class as the old actresses who scraped by in the neighborhood.

"I work at the kitchen," Auntie Lil confessed. She was a third of her way through the hero and still going strong. "Don't forget my cheesecake," she reminded him.

Billy got up incredulously and returned with an enormous slice of cheesecake. "Do you always eat like that?" he asked, watching her vacuum down the last half of the sandwich and occasionally checking his watch in astonishment.

"I'm very hungry," she admitted, which was as close as she ever came to apologizing for her eating habits. "Besides, it's delicious."

"I make the secret sauce myself."

"Very good." She nodded and carefully wiped her mouth, pulling the cheesecake over and smelling it with approval. "How well do you know the ladies?"

"Pretty well. I give them credit." He shrugged his shoulders. "Not many stores around here will. But they always pay me back when their checks come the first of the month. And they don't eat much, bless them. I guess they don't have the money."

Auntie Lil slid one of Emily's photos from the packet and pushed it across the table toward him. "Did you know this one?"

Billy picked up the photo and winced. He turned it around several times while he examined it carefully. "That's the Pineapple Lady," he finally said. "She stopped here every morning for a small glass of pineapple juice. I've been wondering where she was." He handed the photo back. "What happened to her?"

"She's dead," Auntie Lil said. She would not mention murder yet. "We're trying to find out where she lived and who she was."

"I don't know her name. Sorry." He shrugged. "She paid cash. Always had exact change, even. Sixty-five cents, right down to the penny. I didn't even know she knew the others. I never saw her with them. But I think that she lived in an apartment building somewhere on Forty-sixth Street."

"An apartment building? Not a shelter?" Auntie Lil asked.

"I think a building. Once I saw her walk by here really late one night. I have to stay open until midnight to catch the theater people coming home from work. It helps me earn enough to cover the rent. She shouldn't have been on the streets so late, and I was surprised to see her out. So I kind of stood in the doorway and watched her walk down Forty-sixth Street to make sure she'd be safe. I saw her turn into some building there in the middle of the block."

"Which building?" Auntie Lil leaned forward eagerly, her cheesecake forgotten.

"I don't remember." He shrugged his apology. "Wish I could help more. But it was over a month ago. I think it was the south side of the street, though."

She was disappointed but not undaunted. It was a start.

The front door bells chimed and three construction workers stepped inside, eager to try the he-man hero and best coffee in New York. Billy scurried back to work behind the counter and Auntie Lil finished her cheesecake while she watched him. He would see a lot, hanging out in the deli all day, just inches from the big picture window. She had to remember that. He probably knew everyone in the neighborhood. It would not be her last visit to the Delicious Deli.

She left her money next to the register, waved goodbye, and headed back to the streets. She had enough time to knock on a few doors before she was to meet T.S. at the soup kitchen. Just then, a patrol car zoomed past and she followed its path up the avenue two blocks to Forty-eighth Street. It turned right and slid in quickly beside the curb, its bumper protruding into the avenue. She hurried up the block and saw two men dressed in dark suits climb out of the back seat of the police car and wave away the uniformed men in the front seat. She reached the corner just in time to see the plain-clothesmen push their way through the waiting crowd and disappear down the steps to the St. Barnabas soup kitchen.

Auntie Lil scurried up the block and cut through the line of waiting patrons, reaching the stairs in time to see Officer King, the bad-tempered patrolman with the Marine haircut letting the two plain-clothesmen in the back gate. It clanked shut just as she reached it. Officer King did not seem to recognize her; he simply turned away and led the other officers through the soup kitchen door.

So, Dr. Millerton had notified the police of Emily's poisoning. That meant there was no sense grasping at straws on Forty-sixth Street, when there might be an entire scarecrow waiting here at St. Barnabas. She waited resolutely at the entrance steps. Someone else would come along soon. And if the police knew anything, she'd soon find out what it was.

CHAPTER FIVE

1. Auntie Lil didn't have long to wait. Father Stebbins arrived at the basement entrance a few moments later, his beefy face an alarming shade of purple. "Terrible news, Lillian, isn't it? It's quite a shock to my system." He shook his head in dismay as he unlocked the back gate.

Typically, Fran hovered a few paces behind. Her beatific expression of obedience faded into a scowl the moment she saw Auntie Lil. "What are you doing here?" she hissed. "Haven't you caused enough trouble?"

"What in the world are you talking about?" Auntie Lil demanded. She drew herself up to her full height, but that wasn't saying much. She still stood nose-to-nose with Fran, whose stouter build gave her a decided advantage.

"Now, now, ladies. Please." Father Stebbins raised two arms in a bishoplike plea for peace. He had probably practiced in front of a mirror. "Let's talk to the police and get it over with. They didn't sound very happy on the phone."

So, Auntie Lil realized, the police had called Father Stebbins and Fran had conveniently been lurking nearby. And both of them thought that Auntie Lil had been telephoned as well. She saw no reason to correct their misconception. It would be so much more convenient for them all, especially her, if she simply weaseled her way inside on their coattails.

"Poisoned," Fran hissed in Auntie Lil's ear as they marched inside the soup kitchen. "That certainly was some *special* chili recipe you used."

Auntie Lil ignored her, yet managed to convey the distinct impression that Fran was too petty to bother with—more important things were going on. The soup kitchen hummed with activity. Several men were going through the cabinets in a mechanical, bored fashion, sniffing condiments, examining the contents of boxes and occasionally placing small samples in labeled plastic bags.

Three uniformed officers sat drinking coffee at an empty table, including Officer King. They flanked the soup kitchen volunteer who had arrived early to find the police waiting to gain entry. She looked frightened and pale, but had joined the waiting patrolmen in observing a cluster of plainclothes detectives gathered around a heavyset man standing at the far side of the cafeteria-style counter. The man was barking out orders in a heavily accented New York voice and gesturing with a hammy hand for emphasis as he spoke. Something about him was tantalizingly familiar to Auntie Lil. She squinted to get a better view. His hair was dark but thinning in back; it glistened greasily under the fluorescent lights. His white shirt was stained under the armpits with sweat, and perspiration poured down the back of his neck. The men around him began to inch back subtly, as if afraid his body heat was contagious. Thanks to the man's authoritative roar, Auntie Lil could hear better than she could see.

"I'm handing you the case, George," the beefy man was yelling, as if sure that George would try to disagree. "But I'll be watching you every step of the way."

A middle-aged Hispanic man with a handsome but bloated face raised his eyebrows in mock appreciation. "Thanks for the confidence, Lieutenant," he said, making no attempt to conceal his sarcasm. "This case is nowhere to start with and you're going to be breathing down my back to boot?" Obviously, neither the detective nor his cohorts were aware yet that civilians were present.

The situation was about to change. Officer King had finished his coffee and had finally noticed the presence of Auntie Lil and her companions. He scrutinized them intently. It took a moment to process the information through his hard head, but belated recall finally transformed his scowling features into an expression of menacing recognition. He stepped up to the unseen lieutenant and whispered in his ear, pointing across the room with an accusatory jab.

The gathered officers looked up in interest and the fat lieutenant whirled around. "Where? Which one was cooking?" he asked, staring intently. His small black eyes focused on them without success. Obviously too vain to wear glasses in public, he took a step closer and stared harder.

"Which one of you was cooking?" he demanded again.

Auntie Lil—who was also too vain to wear her glasses in public—took her own step forward. And froze.

No. It could not be. It was an impossibility. A piece of luck so incredibly bad that it could not have happened to her. Not this time.

But it had. Lt. Manny Abromowitz stood staring back at her. "You?" His voice swelled with warning and his massive chest puffed up, straining against his too-tight shirt. His face flushed deep red and swelled until he resembled a cross between a wart hog and a blow fish about to explode. "What the hell are you doing in the middle of this?"

Even Auntie Lil was cowed by his unleashed anger, never mind the detectives who froze in their tasks to stare curiously at the innocuous little old lady who was giving their pompous lieutenant a heart attack simply by her benign presence.

"I work here," Auntie Lil said calmly, *much* more calmly than she felt. "I cooked the chili the day Emily died."

Fran stepped closer to Father Stebbins. She placed an arm on his elbow and they exchanged open-mouthed glances. Whatever was going to happen to Auntie Lil, clearly it was bad. What in the world did this policeman have against her?

His red face deepened even more, to the mottled scarlet of a radish going bad. "I had hoped that we might never meet again," he announced in a deadly tone of voice. "It was, in fact, my very fondest wish."

"The feeling is mutual, I can assure you," Auntie Lil replied stiffly.

"You think *she* did it?" the detective named George butted in. He stepped between the two of them and gestured toward Auntie Lil. "This lady has a record?"

"I certainly do not," Auntie Lil snapped. "And of course I didn't poison her. If I'd been throwing handfuls of cyanide in the chili, there would be a lot more than one person dead. Any idiot should know that. Even the lieutenant."

"Cyanide?" Lieutenant Abromowitz repeated slowly, giving weight to each of the three syllables. "And just how did you know it was cyanide? Huh? *How?!*"

"I have my ways." She clutched her pocketbook against her chest to calm the beating of her heart. She had thought the lieutenant might be a bit peeved after she solved his last case out from under him, but really . . . this was going too far. The man was positively boorish.

"Well, I suggest you tell George here exactly what ways." The lieutenant gestured toward a chair and cocked his thumb. George took Auntie Lil by the elbow and led her to a table. Lieutenant Abromowitz stood over them, glowering. "Interview this woman very, very thoroughly," he ordered. "I want to know every move she made the day the victim died." Then he whirled on his heels and stomped out the door.

Auntie Lil turned back around for a satisfying peek. He had put on weight since she'd last seen him and his stomach jiggled over the top of his belt as he strode across the room. To top it off, his hair was definitely thinning. Practically gone. But wait—there was a wink of gold on one finger. Oh, dear. Some poor woman had actually married the man and Auntie Lil thought she knew who. He reached the door and slammed it shut behind him.

The resounding crack served as a signal for everyone assembled to turn back and stare at Auntie Lil. Father Stebbins seemed both transfixed and perplexed, while Fran was too baffled to display her usual resentment. Auntie Lil met the gaze of everyone present with a very sweet smile.

"I see the lieutenant hasn't changed a bit," she said. "What a shame for you all."

2. Auntie Lil suspected that her detective, whose full name turned out to be George Santos, didn't like Lieutenant Abromowitz very much. His idea of grilling Auntie Lil was a rather dispirited request to retrace her steps on the day Emily died. This Auntie Lil was able to do in excruciating detail. Her memory was excellent and she had already gone over the scene many times in her own mind, searching for a clue as to how Emily had been poisoned. It took nearly forty-five minutes for poor Santos to take down her full statement. He wrote methodically and without comment, only raising his eyebrows when she mentioned The Eagle and explained their trip to the medical examiner's office. When he was done, he promised to have it typed and to give her a chance to look it over. She nodded, satisfied. She already knew it would do fine. She had even managed to half-heartedly implicate Fran with a vague reference or two to her having disappeared during the cooking (which was true). It would serve as payback for those looks she'd given Auntie Lil earlier.

"So, how do you know the lieutenant?" the detective asked curiously as he tucked his small notebook back into his shirt pocket.

"I had the misfortune of meeting him on a previous case."

"Yes, it's always a misfortune to meet the lieutenant, isn't it?"

Santos patted his pocket and rose to go. "They had to kick him somewhere, I guess. It was just my luck it was Midtown North." He stopped to look Auntie Lil over carefully, then assured her, "The lieutenant may want to suspect you, but you seem like a straight-shooter to me. If we need anything else from you, we'll get in touch."

"Will the kitchen be able to open today?" Auntie Lil asked anxiously. She could see Father Stebbins and Fran being questioned at separate tables by other detectives. Both looked annoyed, worried, anxious and alarmed all at the same time.

"Sure. Business as usual," Santos promised. "We haven't found anything on the premises yet and, like you say, only one person died. And nobody died yesterday, right?" He gave a disinterested laugh. "If she was even poisoned here, which we won't know until they run further tests, it must have been put into her individual serving somehow. That means we're going to want to talk to everyone who was sitting around her at the time."

"These are very transient people," Auntie Lil told him. "I'm not sure you'll be able to find them."

"We're going to try," Santos promised, patting his pocket again. "Starting today. That's why it's business as usual."

They were shaking hands when Officer King ambled up to glare down at Auntie Lil. He *would* be the type who brown-nosed his way into the lieutenant's affections by assuming his every grudge and posture. "Lieutenant says the kitchen can open as always," he announced.

"Thanks, I've already told her that," Santos said calmly. "Don't you have a drug dealer to beat up somewhere, pal?"

Officer King ignored him. "Except for her," he said. He cocked a thumb at Auntie Lil. "The lieutenant says she's not to be allowed back in the kitchen until we find out who did it. He wants to be on the safe side."

The detective looked back and forth between Auntie Lil and the patrolman. "Who are you kidding?" he finally said. "Abromowitz is just being an asshole. There's no reason to keep her from helping out."

"That's what he says. And he's the lieutenant." Officer King shrugged happily and walked away whistling a very bad version of "Jailhouse Rock."

"Sorry," George apologized. "There's nothing I can do."

Auntie Lil rose to make a dignified exit. "That man will never make detective," she declared, nodding toward the departing Officer King.

"What do you mean?"

"Anyone so stupid as to side with Lieutenant Abromowitz on anything deserves to spend their life pounding the pavement." Auntie Lil pinned her hat firmly on and left the befuddled detective behind. She sailed past Fran, who glared at her out of habit, patted Father Stebbins reassuringly on the back, and escaped out the front door.

Well, she'd been kicked out of far worse—and far better—places before. Besides, it had been a real learning experience: it was just as she suspected. The police knew nothing. And with Abromowitz in charge, they never would.

3. T.S. was waiting for her outside. "What's going on?" he demanded. "How come you were inside and they won't let me in?" Other volunteers stood behind him, listening anxiously. Several people in line were eavesdropping as well, their anxious faces lined with both worry and hunger.

"The police wanted to question me about Emily's death," was all Auntie Lil said. "I suggest we go elsewhere to talk."

"Are we going to open up today?" one of the volunteers asked. The early people in line looked at her in alarm, their worried looks deepening.

Auntie Lil nodded. "Yes, but probably late. Better get inside. They're going to need help with the cooking. I was going to make spaghetti. Make sure you use plenty of oregano and garlic and don't let Fran overdo the basil."

The volunteers scurried down the steps and began to call through the gate. Auntie Lil led T.S. quickly away down the block. "Let's get out of here," she said. "Adelle and the ladies will be arriving soon. When they find out Emily was poisoned, there's no telling what will happen. We have more important things to do right now." She dragged him across Eighth Avenue toward Forty-sixth Street, neither one of them noticing that an old actress who had been waiting in line was now scurrying away in the opposite direction.

"Where are we going? What's more important?" T.S. asked. He removed her hand from his arm and carefully brushed the nap of his sweater back into shape.

"Lovely sweater," she said absently. "I gave it to you, didn't I?"

"No. You most certainly did not." She was always trying to take credit for his own good taste.

"I've found out that Emily lived on Forty-sixth Street. We just have to find out which building. And you won't believe this, but Lieutenant Abromowitz is working out of Midtown North now."

T.S. groaned. "Now it really is up to us."

"I'll say. What did you find out at the library?"

"No understudies were listed in the Playbill," T.S. admitted reluctantly. "She might have been in the chorus scene or worked backstage, but that's a lot of people. I wrote them all down. There's no one named Emily at all, except for the main character. I could start tracking the cast members down and asking them if they remember her. If anyone's still alive. But she could have been with the company for only a week, for all we know." They were passing the man with the bulbous nose and Auntie Lil gave him a cherry wave as if he were her very best friend. He nodded back and stared at T.S.

"May as well try," Auntie Lil agreed. "But do it in your spare time. We're more likely to have better luck once we find out where she lived."

"That's true." T.S. scanned the now busy block. "Where do we start?"

Auntie Lil took out the pack of photos from her purse. "I doubt she was able to afford these expensive restaurants," she said, looking up and down the sidewalks. "But we can't afford to skip them. Someone besides Billy has to know her."

"Who's Billy?" He held a photo in his hand and suppressed an involuntary shudder at the sight of the dead Emily.

"Billy owns the Delicious Deli back there," she explained. "He said she lived on this block."

Most of the block was taken up by expensive restaurants either closed or filled with crowds of business people. T.S. had to agree that it was unlikely Emily frequented any of them, but just to be on the safe side Auntie Lil insisted on entering every single establishment and showing Emily's photo to the bartender or host. Flashing photos of a dead old lady in front of waiting patrons did not prove to be a popular task and T.S. began to feel more and more like a pariah as they worked their way down the block.

"Maybe we should come back when they're not so busy," he suggested.

"We have to do it while they're open," Auntie Lil argued reasonably. "Besides, now we're getting somewhere. This is more her style." They had reached the end of the block nearer to Ninth Avenue. Large restaurants gave way to smaller shops and cheaper eating places.

"I'm getting hungry," Auntie Lil declared. "I had a hero earlier, but that must have been three hours ago." She eyed the brightly painted sign of a tiny Jamaican restaurant named Nellie's. "That place looks good."

T.S. peered inside. A small black man sat at a lone table eating a stew of unidentified, grayish origins piled over bright yellow rice. A plump woman the color of toffee was perched on a table behind the counter, staring out at the street with half-closed eyes. She had a beautiful face, broad and polished, that was lightly touched by the fine wrinkles of a satisfied woman in her mid-thirties. Her hair was braided in dozens of tiny plaits with brightly colored beads studding their length. The braids bobbed and swayed as she turned her regal neck, watching people go by.

"It looks like a real popular eating spot," T.S. said sarcastically. Just then, the woman's gaze met his and his words froze in his mouth. Her eyes were dark and sparkling. They seemed to see right through him. Unlike so many eyes in New York City, hers were not cloaked in suspicion but held a sharp intelligence and, yes, maybe even a little bit of kindness. The woman surveyed T.S. with unabashed thoroughness and when she was through, her brightly painted red lips curled back over white teeth in a hint of a grin.

"That woman *smiled* at me," T.S. said incredulously. "Someone just smiled at me right in the middle of New York City."

"I told you it was a good place to eat," Auntie Lil declared. She marched inside and he had no choice but to follow.

"Hello, granny," the woman greeted them in a musical voice full of lilting Caribbean tones. "You in the mood for a little goat curry today? I make it myself."

The small black man eating looked up briefly, dismissed them, and returned to his stew.

"I'm not that hungry," Auntie Lil decided. "Besides, I had it twice last week."

T.S. would have expected this statement to have been received with extreme skepticism, but the woman simply nodded in slow approval. "You more in the mood for a snack, granny?"

"Yes. That's quite right. A snack." Auntie Lil eyed some meat pies with garishly orange crust that were baking beneath a heat light. She gave no sign of objecting to being called "granny." Not that there was a need to object, the title had been uttered in quite respectful tones.

"No, granny. You don't want those pies," the woman told Auntie Lil. She hopped down from her perch and the beaded braids tinkled as they swayed with her every move. "Those are frozen. Cheap for people who don't know any better. You want one of my homemade pies. A dollar more, but worth it." She slid a tray out of a small warming oven against one wall and placed it on the countertop. A spicy aroma filled the tiny shop and, against his will, T.S.'s stomach grumbled. "Maybe your son there like one, too," the woman suggested, her eyes twinkling.

"He's my nephew. But he'll take one." Auntie Lil sniffed deeply. "You made the crust yourself?"

"Of course. That's why it's not that Halloweeny orange."

"In that case, I'll take two."

"Very spicy, granny. Maybe try one, then another."

"Oh, no. I like spicy. Give me two." Auntie Lil accepted the pies wrapped in white paper as if she ate them from a roadside stand every day of her life. She bit into hers with characteristic gusto and groaned in approval.

"Delicious," she said, sputtering a fine spray of crumbs over the front of T.S.'s sweater. "Don't you agree, Theodore?"

He did not. He had discovered a raisin in his pie filling. T.S. loathed, hated, positively despised raisins in any form whatsoever.

"There're raisins in here," he said faintly, holding the offending pie out to his aunt.

"For heaven's sake, Theodore. Aren't you ever going to out-grow that fetish?" Auntie Lil and the woman giggled together. T.S. was just grateful that the small black man didn't join in at laughing at him, the amusing white middle-class male.

"I'll eat it if you don't want it," Auntie Lil finally offered. She placed his pie beside her second one and munched happily on her first. "This is heaven. I've never had better meat pies. Not in Kingston. Or even in Spanish Town."

"You been to Spanish Town?" the woman asked. "My mama came from there."

"I spent several months there one year," Auntie Lil admitted. "We were experimenting with a new kind of batik."

The woman absorbed this information respectfully, but had no curiosity to ask for details. She watched impassively as Auntie Lil polished off her two meat pies and started in on her third. With one hand holding the pie, Auntie Lil pulled the photos from her pocketbook with the other.

"Do you know this lady?" she asked, her mouth full of food as she slid the images of the dead woman across the counter top.

The woman peered down at it. Her face grew very calm and T.S. could almost feel the cooling in the room. Finally, she looked up and shrugged. "All old ladies look alike to me. One granny just like another." Her voice had changed dramatically, its former warmth replaced by suspicion and, perhaps, fear. She crossed her arms and backed away from them, settling on the small table behind the counter again. She stared back out the picture windows, as if they weren't even there.

T.S. knew she was lying. He'd worked with people too long not to know.

"You've never even seen her walking by on the block?" Auntie Lil insisted. She finished off the pie and scrubbed her fingers clean with the edge of her napkin. Small crumbs still clung to her mouth, but she'd soon talk those off.

The woman shook her head firmly, the braids clacking together in terse rhythm. "No, granny. I have not even seen her walking by." Her mouth shut firmly. She was saying no more.

Auntie Lil sighed just as the little black man finished his meal. When he rose to depart, his chair scraped against the tile floor with an angry screech. He stretched leisurely and patted his stomach in approval. "You are a good cook, Nellie," he told the black woman. "You are not such a good liar." He pulled the photos toward him and looked at Auntie Lil from under his bushy eyebrows. His face was small and pinched, and his black eyes glittered deeply from a crevasse of wrinkles like two tiny currants inside a bigger raisin.

His hatred of raisins aside, T.S. decided he was going to like this fellow.

The old man looked T.S. over silently, inspected Auntie Lil once again, then stared down at the photos for a closer look. "You are family?" he asked them.

"Not really. But friends," T.S. said firmly before Auntie Lil could lie.

"She lived next door," the old man said calmly. "I think on the sixth floor." He pushed the photos back toward them. "And now I bid you goodbye."

Nellie shook her head in disapproval, braids bobbing and beads clacking angrily. "You are a good man, Ernest. But not too smart. Some things go on here, better not to get involved. Too many ways to get hurt."

Ernest shrugged and headed for the door. "That may be true, my lovely Nellie, but old Ernest here, he just can't say no. Look again at those photos. That old woman, she did not die in peace. I think it is my choice, not yours, if I get involved." He bowed

and waved a brief goodbye before disappearing through the door
and turning toward Ninth Avenue.

Nellie shrugged. "You heard the man. He say she lived next
door, she lived next door."

T.S. stared at Auntie Lil. They moved as one toward the exit.
The woman called after them just as they reached the sidewalk,
"But remember, old Nellie here, she didn't know a thing."

4. Next door was a small sixth-story brownstone, in cheaply
renovated condition with a new brick facade that was already beginning to crack and crumble. The front door to the foyer was
locked and they peered inside at a row of twelve mailboxes. Six
stories, two small apartments to a floor. Which one belonged to
Emily? The man in Nellie's had said he thought it was the sixth
floor, but hadn't been sure. T.S. could not see a name on either of
the sixth-floor mailboxes. Both occupants labels were blank.

"Someone's coming," T.S. pointed out. He could see a small elevator through the door window, the indicator shining bright green
in the dim hall light. "This place is a real Taj Mahal," he added.
"An elevator and everything."

"Which explains how an old lady could live on the sixth floor.
Who is it?" Auntie Lil asked anxiously, pushing against him and
tramping the back of his heels in an effort to peer through the
window with him.

A young man emerged from the elevator. He was of average
height and very thin, with sharp features and willowy limbs. His
long blond hair was cut in a single length and hung down the
sides of his pointed face in long waves. He looked like an Afghan
hound but moved like a hyperactive Chihuahua. He bent his limbs
with unnatural grace and each step was more a miniature jeté than
a stride.

"A dancer," T.S. predicted. "He'll probably break into a song
from *Oklahoma!*"

Auntie Lil did not appreciate his wit. She was too busy thinking up a good lie.

"Young man," she cried enthusiastically, grasping the fellow's
arm before he could scurry down the steps.

The young man—who, up close, looked more like a forty-five-
year-old who was aging badly and trying to hide it—jumped in
alarm, then patted the sides of his now obviously dyed blond hair
before asking in a high, precisely articulated voice, "Yes? Can I
help you with something? There's no need to get *pushy*, you know."

"I think my sister lives in this building, but I've forgotten the apartment number. I'm from out of town and this street is quite frightening to me. Can you let us in to find her? Her name is Emily."

The man stared at her through suspicious, almond-shaped eyes. "Everyone who lives in this building is in the *business*," he informed her primly. "There's not a soul over thirty, sweetie." he shrugged and whirled gracefully, traipsing lightly down the steps, too quickly to catch Auntie Lil's mumbled retort about him dreaming on if he really thought she believed he was a day under forty.

But T.S. was not ready to give up. "That's a coincidence," T.S. called after him. "I'm a producer myself."

The man stopped in mid-hop and twirled back around, hands on his hips. He surveyed T.S. with a bright smile. "Really? Not the *Chorus Line* road show by any teensyweensy chance . . . I'm just on my way to . . ."

"No, no," T.S. lied smoothly, inspiration flowing through him with genetic enthusiasm. "That's ancient history. I pulled out of that old war-horse years ago. Right now I'm in the process of locating some fresh new talent. We're mounting an Equity showcase of *Peter Pan Grows Up*. It's fascinating really. We've created a whole new chapter in Peter's life."

"You don't say?" the man exclaimed, mouth wide with delight. "Peter Pan is one of my very favorite favorites!"

"Another coincidence," T.S. declared brightly. "See, in my new show, he grows up, marries Wendy and moves back to London. They have children of their own and my show is all about his struggle to mature while still maintaining his childlike wonder. And, of course, Tinkerbell is terribly jealous—she represents the younger woman figure—and all of this threatens his very . . . Peter Panishness. In the end, he comes to realize that his childhood will always live on in the form of his children and grandchildren. So he gives Tinkerbell the boot and he and Wendy retire to Florida and open an alligator farm, a touch of irony you see, and live happily ever after. It's all very, very nineties. A guaranteed smash."

Auntie Lil stared at him in open-mouthed admiration.

The man's eyes had grown wider and wider. "Have you cast the lead yet?" he asked artfully, as if slightly bored, but willing to humor T.S.

T.S. inspected a minute flaw in his sweater. "No. We need a fresh face, a new name, an unknown with tremendous star quality.

But with the maturity to handle sudden fame, of course. It's going to Broadway, you see. After nine months, if the reviews are even lukewarm or better. I consider it a waste of my time to mount anything without a strong future. Of course, the backing is relatively modest."

The man's face fell.

"But I think eleven million will be enough to get us through at least the next year."

The mention of cold cash inspired a playful leap in the man. He cast any pretense of ennui to the wind in favor of appropriately youthful . . . Peter Panishness. "Listen, when you start auditioning, will you give me a call?" he asked gaily, chirping like a member of the Vienna Choir Boys. "If it's a fresh face you need—God knows, I'm fresh!" He twirled violently in a complete circle, dipped down low and extended an arm, his eyes rolling up in the top of his head as he gave T.S. a large wink. He was holding a small white card.

T.S. took it gingerly and examined it. He had created a monster. GREGORY ROGERS, it read, DANCE MASTER EXTRAORDINAIRE. EQUITY & AFTRA. T.S. smiled broadly, "Of course. I see that you have your Equity standing already. Convenient." He placed the card in his wallet, then looked back at the apartment building with a worried frown. "Now, if I could only find my great-aunt. Auntie Lil here is only in town for a few days and anxious to see her sister. I've been so busy with my accountant and all, I haven't really kept up with Aunt Emily . . ."

"Try the sixth floor," the young man offered promptly. "I know everyone on one through five, so if she's here, it's got to be the sixth. Here." He ran lightly up the stairs, bouncing as if he had small springs imbedded in each instep. He unlocked both front doors with a flourish, and scurried back to help Auntie Lil up the outdoor stairs, not noticing her determinedly granite expression. He then bounded to the elevator and pressed the button for them.

"I think we can take it from here," T.S. assured him. Good God. Enough was enough. Any more encouragement and he'd want to carry Auntie Lil over the threshold.

"Call me?" he asked T.S. in a naughty-boy tone, wagging a finger in playful admonishment. He then gave a little half-wave and disappeared down the steps with a stride so determinedly peppy that he kept popping into view above the door glass as if he were on a trampoline.

"Good God," Auntie Lil declared once they were safely in the elevator. "If we had any respect at all for Mary Martin's memory, we'd put that young man out of his misery."

T.S. sighed. "It was kind of a dirty trick to play on him, but I didn't like his attitude."

"And I always thought I was a good liar." She looked at T.S. in keen admiration. "Of course, you inherited your talent from me."

"Probably did." It was one point he would not argue.

They reached the sixth floor and stepped out into a small hallway with cheap blue carpeting. The elevator occupied a corner of the building front. Both apartments' doors opened off the back wall and were situated side by side on the south side of the building. Loud music blared form behind one of the doors, making it impossible to tell whether the second apartment was occupied or not.

"What do we do now?" T.S. whispered, although talking softly was a moot point.

"What do you think we do?" Auntie Lil stepped up to the door of the silent apartment and firmly pressed the bell. No one answered. She pressed it again with equally unsuccessful results.

"No one's home. Time to go," T.S. declared with some relief.

"Don't be daft." Auntie Lil stared at him incredulously. "Of course no one's home. The occupant's dead."

"We don't know for a fact that she really lived here," T.S. reminded her.

"We will in a minute." Auntie Lil surveyed the door carefully. "Good God, it looks like Fort Knox." There were four supplemental locks on the door in addition to the regular deadbolt. Unfazed, Auntie Lil began to rummage through her gigantic pocketbook.

"You must be joking," T.S. said. "You can't pick any of those locks."

She produced a credit card from the depths of her bag. "I can try."

"It's not the right kind of lock," T.S. began, but Auntie Lil would hear none of it. She tried to slip the thin wafer of plastic between the doorjamb and the door, but a heavy metal strip prevented insertion.

"Damn!" Auntie Lil banged a fist against the door and froze. It had yielded an inch. "Theodore!" She pushed it again and it opened further. "It's not even locked. Four locks and not one of them is locked."

"I don't like this," T.S. said. "Isn't there usually a dead body on the other side when this happens in the movies?" He pushed up behind her and they opened the door cautiously, peering around the edge and making their way slowly inside.

There was no dead body inside. Only a dark and deserted studio apartment, devoid of any signs of life at all. The fold-out sofa bed's cushions had been pulled off and left heaped on the floor. Several tables had been swept bare, the contents scattered onto the floor in a jumble of magazines, cracked vases, upturned lamps and three-day-old newspapers.

Several picture frames had been toppled from a window sill and lay facedown on the carpet. Auntie Lil picked them up—the glass was shattered and any photos that had been inside were gone. "Someone had to break these deliberately," she said, pretending to demonstrate. "They'd have had to crack the frames sharply against this edge of the window sill." A small pile of glass lay in a mound, proving her theory. "Why?"

Books were pulled from a small bookshelf against one wall and piled in careless heaps on the floor, pages mashed together or ripped. Even the refrigerator door hung open. The meager contents—a carton of milk, a dish of mold-covered pudding, three eggs and an opened can of now rotting pineapple chunks—no longer smelled fresh.

"It's been searched," T.S. whispered. "At least a couple of days ago. I wonder what they were looking for."

"Shut the front door," Auntie Lil whispered back.

"What?"

"Shut the door. I don't want anyone walking by and seeing us in here."

He obediently shut the door and fumbled for the light switch of a lamp mounted on the wall. Illumination only made the mess that much more depressing.

"The Eagle," T.S. said. "The man sitting beside her. He must have stolen her pocketbook and gotten her keys. The place has been robbed. He knew where she lived."

"It hasn't really been robbed," Auntie Lil said. She picked up a photo frame. "This is sterling silver. Why didn't he take it?" She searched among the piles of possessions strewn across the floor. "No jewelry left. Of course, she might not have had any. But here are some settings of real silver. And the television's still here. Look, here's some sort of handheld video game, still in the box." She held up a crumpled sheet of colorful paper and some ribbon. "It was a present and it's been unwrapped, but the burglar didn't take it. If it was a robber, he wasn't very thorough."

T.S. noticed a small bureau in the minuscule hallway leading to a tiny bathroom. Clothes had been pulled from the drawers and dangled down in multicolored strips. Old lady clothes. Out of style. Smelling musty.

"Here's the closet," Auntie Lil announced in a loud whisper. She poked her head inside and set to work taking inventory. "This is where she lived, all right," she hissed back over her shoulder. "This wardrobe is right out of Central Casting for a proud, retired actress. Besides, I recognize this green suit. Lord & Taylor. Circa 1964. And look at this."

Several stacks of Playbills at the back of the closet had been toppled into disarray. A box of ticket stubs had been opened and dumped on top of the mess. T.S. poked through the small magazines, looking at the titles.

"She's been to just about everything that's hit the stage here in the last few years," he said in admiration. "Talk about supporting the theater."

"Now we know where all her money went," Auntie Lil replied. She picked up a handful of ticket stubs and let them flutter through her fingers. "And why she came back to live in New York. Remember how Eva said she'd left to get married?" She stared at the now empty closet shelves. "Check the hallway bureau. See if there's anything left of a personal nature."

But T.S. did not find any personal possessions in the bureau drawer. And none in the bathroom. And nothing at all in the corner kitchenette. "She didn't eat much," he muttered when he saw the bare cupboards.

"She didn't have much," Auntie Lil replied. "You know what's missing?" she asked her nephew suddenly, as if quizzing a favorite pupil.

"Yes." This was one test he could easily pass. "There's nothing left in the apartment that could identify her. No photos. No personal papers, and here, look at this, even the front page has been torn out of her Bible." He held up a small, leather-bound Bible. The front cover had been bent back and the first page sloppily ripped away. "In fact, it looks like they took out the front page of every book that might have had her name in it." He pushed the piles of books around with his feet. Her clothes were out-of-date, but her books were not. She had the latest volumes of celebrity biographies and several expensive picture books on the Broadway theater.

"What's that red thing dangling down?" Auntie Lie demanded. She pointed to the bible. A thick red ribbon marker several inches wide had been slipped between two pages. "It's a bookmark," he told Auntie Lil. He thumbed through to see what Emily had been reading before she died. "And it looks like she was big into the meek inheriting the earth." He quickly paged through the rest of the Bible. "She's marked a lot of spots about how blessed the children are and stuff like that."

"Give it to me," Auntie Lil asked excitedly. She grabbed the Bible and turned the red marker over, rubbing it between her fingertips. "This bookmark is funny. It's too wide and too thick. There's something between the two layers of ribbon. She pried apart the bottom end of the double ribbon and wiggled two fingers inside. "It's just been tacked shut with rubber cement or something. Look at this." She slid a strip of four dimestore photos out and the huddled under the one lamp left standing to examine it more closely.

Two young boys—one black and one white—stared uneasily into the camera. The white child had jet black hair that hung in greasy strands over his face. The black child had close-cropped hair trimmed flat on top and shaved close to the skull on the sides. Both boys had pinched and suspicious eyes. And both of them looked tired. They had curious expressions on their faces, almost grimaces. Their lips were pulled back unnaturally over dirty teeth and their chins were thrust forward.

"They're trying to smile," Auntie Lil declared. She pressed a hand to her heart. "Bless them. They're trying to smile and I don't think they know *how*."

T.S. examined it more closely. She was right. The boys were trying to smile, despite the dirt and grime and hopelessness revealed by the harsh glare of the cheap photo booth's light. It illuminated them unmercifully, highlighting every bruise and imperfection on their faces. And they each had plenty.

"Those are very old faces for boys so young," T.S. pointed out.

"Yes, they are, aren't they?" Auntie Lil brought the photo up just a few inches from her eyes, then turned the strip over and examined the back. " 'To our Grandma,' " she read out loud. "And they've underlined 'Grandma'." That's it. It doesn't say anything else. No names. Nothing."

"Let me see." T.S. snatched the strip of photos back, turned it over, stared, and flipped it back around to look at their faces again. "How old do you think they are?"

"Not more than eleven or twelve, I'd say. But how can a woman have one completely black and one completely white grandchild?" Auntie Lil asked.

T.S. did not answer. He was too busy staring at their faces. "I know this black kid," he finally said slowly. "At least, I think I do."

"You do?" Auntie Lil stared at him skeptically.

"I think so. But I can't remember where I saw him."

Their whispering was interrupted by a strange sound. The heavy music blaring from next door was not loud enough to mask a newer more disturbing beat. Something was banging against the wall separating the two apartments with an urgent, pounding rhythm. T.S. could hear heavy breathing, occasional deep laughter, and what sounded like small, muffled sobs.

Auntie Lil, who would not admit to slight deafness, apparently could not hear everything. "What's that banging?" she demanded in puzzled irritation. "Do you hear banging?"

"Never mind, Aunt Lil," T.S. assured her. If her hearing spared her the salacious details, he wasn't going to fill her in. "Put those photos in your pocketbook and let's get out of here."

"Wait." She pulled her arm away and gestured toward the apartment's single window. "Look. The window's been left open." They approached it cautiously. It overlooked a small patch of deserted lot squeezed in between the apartment building and the one behind it located on the next block. The window had been left cracked a few inches. They opened it slowly and peeked their heads out. The apartment shared a fire escape with the one next door. T.S.—who was closer to the neighboring apartment—caught a quick glimpse of what the commotion was all about: he saw a bald head gleaming and a stout body bent over someone or something much smaller. T.S. blinked and drew quickly inside.

"Let's go," he said tersely, not wanting to think about what he had just seen.

"Not so fast," Auntie Lil complained, bending back out onto the fire escape. "Don't rush me. I might miss a clue. Like this." She picked up a curl of dark paper and smelled it. "It stinks. What is it?"

"It's the back of a Polaroid photograph," T.S. told her. He scanned the fire escape. "Here's one more."

"Someone was taking photos out on the fire escape. What on earth for?"

T.S. chose to remain silent. "Let's go," he said grimly, grabbing her elbow again. "Someone has already cleaned the place out. We'll tell the police and leave it at that."

"The police?" Auntie Lil asked indignantly. "They don't know her name any better than we do. What good is that going to do?"

"The owner of the building can tell them her name," he explained patiently. They stepped out into the hall and shut the door carefully behind them. "And I think it might be best if you didn't mention our little escapade inside. Let's just say we found out where she lives and leave it at that, shall we?" He jabbed the button of the elevator five times in quick succession, anxious to put distance between himself and what he had seen in the other apartment. They waited a moment without success and he impatiently pushed the button several more times, then stopped abruptly. The loud background music had suddenly ceased. The door to the second apartment opened and a middle-aged man and a young boy stepped out into the hall. The older man had a large bald head that gleamed in the hallway light. A fine sheen of perspiration clung in droplets to the side of his skull. He was red in the face and hurriedly rebuttoning his jacket, taking no notice of the boy behind him.

The boy had light blond, very nearly white, hair that was cut badly in wisps about his face. A small ponytail no bigger than a watercolor brush scraggled down his neck. He wore a black T-shirt emblazoned with jagged strips of silver lightning and the logo of a heavy metal band. His black jeans were so tight T.S. wondered how he could move, but he could—albeit sullenly and without any interest in either the bald man or T.S. or Auntie Lil.

The bald man stopped abruptly when he noticed he had company, stared at the two of them, said nothing, then veered suddenly toward the fire stairs. Without a word, he pushed through the door and disappeared. Auntie Lil took a few steps forward and stared intently after him, puzzled.

The young boy looked up and noticed them for the first time. His eyes were reddened and rimmed with purple shadows underneath. They flickered over T.S. with dulled suspicion, passing by with disinterest until they spotted Auntie Lil. And then the boy literally jumped. Both feet—expensively clad in high-priced athletic shoes—actually left the carpet. His eyes grew wide and he turned even paler than he had been before. Then he slumped against the wall and stared harder at an oblivious Auntie Lil. When she finally turned around and noticed him, the young boy's face cleared and settled back into a dull mask of apathy.

"Son?" T.S. said, sorry to be a middle-aged man at that moment. Even that close a kinship to the thing that had just left them was too close for T.S.

The boy stared again at Auntie Lil. He stopped short of shaking his head, gave T.S. a sharp look and took off running. He pushed past them and fled through the fire door, following the bald man down the steps without a single word.

"What in the world?" Auntie Lil sniffed. The elevator finally arrived and she stepped inside it indignantly. "How very rude."

T.S. didn't think that "rude" even began to describe the boy's behavior. Never mind the sweating man's. But—having seen what the loud music had tried to hide—he did not intend to explain it to Auntie Lil, not even with all her knowledge of people and years of self-professed experience.

There were just some things he'd have to keep to himself.

5. Auntie Lil would not leave the building until they tried to speak to the superintendent about Emily's identity.

"I think we should leave this to the police," T.S. suggested for the third time. "We may be in over our heads." He did not want to say anymore.

"Nonsense. If you don't spoon-feed the police everything, they're no help at all." She pressed the superintendent's bell firmly and did not let up. T.S. was sure that no one was home, but after a good twenty seconds of nonstop buzzing, the door flew open and an irritated round face peeked out.

"What the hell you think you're doing leaning on my buzzer like that?" a small Hispanic woman demanded of Auntie Lil. She was missing a front tooth.

Auntie Lil responded to her rudeness by pushing the door open and peering inside the apartment. Despite the sunny day outside, the drapes were tightly shut and no lights were on. An old air conditioner in one corner of the room hummed loudly, chilling the apartment to near-refrigerator conditions. A tattered red sofa dominated much of the only room that was visible and a short, fat man dressed in a sleeveless undershirt and a dirty pair of pants lay across it. He was ignoring the intrusion and slurping at a beer while he stared at the only light in the room: a television set turned loudly to a game show. Auntie Lil decided to shout above it.

"Where's the super? I want to know the name of the old woman who lives on the sixth floor," she demanded, without any attempt at politeness or a cover story. Auntie Lil had decided that she did not like the events now unfolding.

"I'm the super," the woman who had answered the door replied indignantly. "And take your crabby old hands off my door."

Auntie Lil stepped back and glared at the woman. T.S. moved beside her for support. Together, they stared down the superintendent. She was as short and round as the man on the couch, and her hair had been dyed an unlikely orange. She wore a shapeless shift that was torn under one arm and she, too, held a beer in one hand.

"What is the name of the old woman who lives on the sixth floor?" T.S. asked more politely, though the effort was painful to make.

"There's no old woman living on the sixth floor," the super replied nastily. "No one lives on the sixth floor at all. Go away before I call the police."

T.S. opened his mouth to argue, but before he could get a single word out, the door slammed firmly shut in his face.

"Well, I never," Auntie Lil said. "We are going to the police. I don't like the looks of this at all."

"We're doing more than that," T.S. suddenly decided. He had seen enough to make him very angry. And when he was angry, T.S. could be every bit as determined as his aunt. "I'd like to keep a very close eye on this building. Something is wrong and I don't like it at all.

They hurried out of the claustrophobic hallway and paused on the outside steps.

"Why in the world would that woman lie like that?" Auntie Lil wondered.

T.S. thought of what had been going on in the occupied sixth-floor apartment, and of the disarray in Emily's rooms. "I don't know. But it isn't good."

"Perhaps she got killed for her rent-controlled apartment?" Auntie Lil suggested. "I read about this case in the July *True Detect* . . . well, this periodical I have a subscription to, that told about a woman in—"

"Killed for an apartment?" T.S. interrupted. "That's a bit extreme, even for New York City."

"People get killed for twenty-five cents in this town," Auntie Lil protested.

T.S. thought about it. "You're right. I'll find out who owns the building and we'll go from there."

"We should also start watching the building," Auntie Lil added. "And we need to talk to people at the soup kitchen ourselves."

"Then we need some more help," T.S. said firmly. "That's all there is to it. Whether the police believe us or not, we need someone else to watch this building while we poke around the neighborhood."

Just then, an Asian man passed by. He was wheeling a dolly cart loaded with boxes of fresh produce as he headed toward a corner fruit and vegetable stand. T.S. and Auntie Lil watched his progress down the block, then turned to one another in mutual inspiration.

"Herbert Wong," T.S. said, smiling because—for once—he'd beaten Auntie Lil to the punch.

"Herbert Wong," Auntie Lil agreed with relieved enthusiasm. "Herbert Wong is most definitely our man."

CHAPTER SIX

1. They had gotten no farther than a few feet down the block when a tall black woman sauntered past them. She was dressed in an orange mini-dress that barely covered her butt in the back and was stretched to within a millimeter of popping at the sides. It hugged her ample chest tightly and had long sleeves pulled so far down her shoulders that they resembled matching gloves. Unfortunately, the effect was spoiled by a large rip under one of her arms that exposed a strip of coffee-colored skin and a ragged black-lace bra. The woman wore one dangling fake diamond earring and swung a small black purse in idle circles. Her makeup-smudged eyes were wide and vacant and she took no notice of either Auntie Lil or T.S. Passing them slowly, she promptly bumped into a trash can and careened right off without missing a beat. Her eyes closed a bit as she focused on a nearby building and she began to mutter beneath her breath while swatting at imaginary flies with the pocketbook.

Auntie Lil stared after her. "My goodness. I guess she dresses in the dark."

"She dresses *for* the dark," T.S. corrected her. He stared after the woman's lanky form. "She looks familiar. I think I've seen her before, too."

Auntie Lil surveyed her with distaste. "I can't imagine where," she finally said. "And if you remember, I don't think I even want to know."

T.S. was trying to figure out how someone could move as slowly without freezing into one position. "I think she's on drugs," he told Auntie Lil.

"I should hope so. There must be some excuse for that outfit."

As they watched her curiously, the woman peered up at the numbers of several buildings, then abruptly turned and picked up

101

speed. Eyes fixed on the front door, she wobbled up the front stairs of Emily's apartment building, her body teetering dangerously close to the edge of the top step as she attempted to unlock the front door while balanced on high spike heels. She dropped her keys, bent over to pick them up and managed the task only after hiking her skin-tight dress nearly to her waist.

"She's wearing a girdle," T.S. observed. "Another inch and I'll tell you the brand."

"That despicable overgrown Peter Pan man said there was no one over thirty in the entire building," Auntie Lil said indignantly. "That woman is forty if she's a day."

"And she certainly gives new meaning to his contention that the whole building was in the business," T.S. added. "You wait here."

He crept up behind the woman and caught a whiff of stale liquor mixed with Giorgio perfume. He considered either scent vile in its own right, but the combination was as deadly as mustard gas. He took a step back, which was, unfortunately, downwind, and waited. No wonder she was wobbling, mixing her drink and drugs in the middle of the afternoon like that. She finally succeeded in unlocking the door and lurched inside. T.S. scampered up the stairs and peeked through the front window in an effort to see which floor she called home.

She chose the nearest floor—which just happened to be the entrance hallway—and slumped against a small storage door set into the wall. She closed her eyes as the door slowly opened and the upper half of her body tumbled into the closet, where she promptly fell asleep. Her thighs and legs, encased in torn black stockings and cheap heels, protruded anonymously into the hallway like an updated version of the Wicked Witch of the East in *The Wizard of Oz*. T.S. heard a faint buzz begin. At least she was not dying of an overdose before his eyes, and was still capable of lusty snoring.

He contemplated waiting to see what would happen when the bad-tempered superintendent discovered her tenant sprawled across the carpet. But then T.S. decided he'd had his fill of surly strangers for one day and hurried back to his aunt.

"Which floor?" she asked.

"The front hallway floor. She had just enough steam to get inside and now she's snoring away inside the janitor's closet, near the superintendent's door."

"They're good friends, no doubt." Auntie Lil shook her head

and glanced at her watch. "It's nearly four. I have just enough time to check out the soup kitchen before it closes."

"The soup kitchen? You got tossed out on your ear, remember?"

"I was told I couldn't *work* there anymore," she reminded him. "No one said I couldn't go there for a meal."

T.S. stared at her without comment.

"The sign says that *all* who are hungry are welcome," she insisted petulantly. "Besides, I have to question Adelle and the ladies again."

T.S. sighed. "All right. Give it a whirl. But you're on your own. I'm heading down to Centre Street to see who owns this building and if Abromowitz throws you behind bars, you'll just have to find someone else to bail you out."

"Harvey's at eight?" she asked. "I'll call Herbert and invite him."

"Harvey's at eight." T.S. headed for the subway, thinking longingly of the bar at Harvey's. It would be hushed and dark right now, nearly deserted and at its most inviting. What he really wanted was a good stiff drink and no one to bother him while he drank it. He needed time to explore his memory. Where had he seen that dreadfully attired woman before?

2. Auntie Lil arrived at St. Barnabas just as the last of the hungry in line were entering the basement. She squeezed in behind them and looked around. Fran and Father Stebbins were both busy behind the counter. There were two obviously bored detectives sitting at far tables interviewing people, but Auntie Lil did not recognize any of them. She sniffed the air suspiciously. Yes, just as she had feared. Fran had overspiced the spaghetti sauce and ruined its flavor. Oh, well. After a giant hero sandwich, cheesecake and three meat pies, not even she was hungry again yet.

Just to be safe, she pulled her felt hat down over her face and sidled up to Adelle's table. She knew Fran would not hesitate to take the advantage Lieutenant Abromowitz had handed her and run with it.

"What in the world?" Adelle demanded in a cultured voice. She had decided to be British for the day and her accent was impeccable.

"It's me," Auntie Lil hissed back.

"For heaven's sake, Lillian," Adelle sniffed. "Why the big disguise?"

"I've been thrown out of here," Auntie Lil told the assembled old actresses indignantly. "By the awful lieutenant in charge of investigating Emily's death."

"Can you believe it?" one old lady asked breathlessly. "*Poisoned*. One of us poisoned. But by who? And why?"

"Her secrets caught up with her," Eva declared. "That's what she gets for being so superior."

Adelle sighed. "Sit down, Lillian. Take off that hat and just turn your back to the crowd. They can't tell one old lady from another, believe me."

Auntie Lil did as she suggested. "How was the sauce?" she demanded.

"Overspiced," Adelle answered promptly. "Honestly. That Fran woman doesn't know the meaning of subtle. She's the Marion Davies of the cooking set." Heads bobbed in agreement.

"So you've heard that Emily was poisoned," Auntie Lil said. "It was most astonishing. I helped discover it, you know." The crowd tittered in appreciation, but no one asked for details. They at least pretended to be a well-bred bunch.

"We've been exchanging theories," Adelle confessed. "And we can't come up with a thing."

"Not quite," one old lady ventured. "There is that Arnold Rothstein thing."

Eva sniffed. "It was me, not Emily, that he stood up that night."

"Is that so?" someone asked nastily. "Then you've been lying about your age all these years. Unless you were dating him when you were twelve years old."

"You have a lot of nerve," Eva countered. "You were in theaters before ladies' smoking rooms were." A murmur of approval ran through the crowd. It had been a most worthy insult.

"Oh, come, come." Adelle ordered them. "Her death is not connected to some gangland murder committed sixty years ago." She looked at Auntie Lil and rolled her well-painted eyes. "Eva here has fantasized for over six decades now that she was supposed to go out on a date with Arnold Rothstein the night he was gunned down."

"I was," Eva insisted. "He stood me up."

"You and a dozen others, sweetie," someone said. "He was not the faithful type."

"We thought, briefly, that maybe Emily had set him up somehow," Adelle told Auntie Lil. "And his gang had taken their time on revenge. But I don't see how she could have. She didn't even come to New York until 1937 as near as we can tell."

"She was too plain for him anyway," Eva insisted, patting her absurdly black hair primly into place over her growing bald spot. "I ought to know."

Auntie Lil sighed deeply and drummed the table impatiently with her sturdy fingers. "We need to go about this in an organized fashion," she told the table. "You'll just have to trust me on this. After all, I am a professional, practically, and I'm sure you ladies can appreciate the difference between an amateur and a professional."

"Certainly," Adelle allowed graciously. "The show must go on."

"Exactly. So what I'd like to do is ask you some questions about Emily. I know you don't think you remember much, but you never know when a highly astute question from me can reveal the hidden truth."

No one seemed miffed at Auntie Lil's lack of modesty and they all nodded in agreement.

"If you have anything to add, please speak up," Auntie Lil instructed them. "Otherwise, it might be best to try and remain silent. Opinion is not what we are looking for here, just the facts." It was as diplomatic as Auntie Lil ever got and the old ladies nodded in solemn agreement again.

"My first question is, when did you originally meet Emily?"

"I met her in 1939," Adelle answered promptly. "We were chorus girls in *Hellzapoppin* together. I had a front-row spot and helped her along. She really wasn't a very good dancer, just well endowed."

"I met her right after she came to New York," Eva sniffed. "I think it was late 1938. We shared rooms in the same boarding house on Thirty-sixth Street. She was already putting on airs about *Our Town* and going around calling herself Emily Toujours."

"What about the rest of you?" Auntie Lil asked the remaining actresses scattered around the table. After separating the babble of voices that answered, she determined that a few had known Emily briefly in the early forties and the remainder had not known her at all until the last few years.

"Why did you lose contact with her for so many years?" Auntie Lil asked those who had known Emily many years ago.

"I lost contact with her after the show," Adelle admitted. "We hadn't much in common and when the war started, I got a spot with Al Jolson's revue. We went overseas you know, the man was tireless. How the soldiers loved him. They loved me, too, of course. I was gone for nearly a year and when I returned, we never renewed our friendship. I saw her around town now and then, but that was all."

One of the actresses looked up sharply and stared at Adelle. Auntie Lil did not fail to notice it.

"I kept up with her," Eva volunteered. "Sort of like you'd keep your eye on a snake." She ignored the protests that met this slur. "We were on speaking terms for a few more years, but she moved away from New York in 1944, I believe it was. To marry some sappy officer in the Air Force."

"You don't know the name of the man she married?" Auntie Lil asked.

"No. He was from Kansas or Missouri or Illinois or Ohio or some place like that," Eva said glumly. "I think his first name was Homer or Harold or Horace, or something dreadfully Midwestern."

At least it had been his *real* name, Auntie Lil thought sourly.

"Adelle knew him, didn't you?" an otherwise quiet actress said. They all turned and stared at her, perhaps surprised that she had finally spoken up. "I thought Adelle went out with him first," she exclaimed, feeling a need to defend herself against the stares of her colleagues. "He was quite a handsome man. . . ." Her voice trailed off.

"Perhaps I did." Adelle shrugged. "It's so hard to remember when one has had so very many liaisons through the years." She sighed, as if begrudging the effort those liaisons had required.

"You told me you could learn a script in three readings flat," Auntie Lil pointed out. "And you can't even remember this man's name?"

Adelle was not fazed. "Men were never important to me. Only my characters meant anything."

Auntie Lil sighed. The information wasn't helping her much. "When did you begin to run into Emily again?" she asked the women.

"I recognized her about three years ago at a matinee of *Les Misérables*," Adelle explained. "Or rather, she recognized me. I guess I do look pretty much the same. Emily was much, much older, of course. But she still wore her hair in the same old roll and her cheekbones were unmistakable." She sighed with envy. "She really had the most marvelous cheekbones. She would have looked grand on screen."

"Obviously she didn't," Eva said nastily. "Or Mr. Zanuck would have put her under contract."

"That's right," Adelle admitted, and explained to Auntie Lil. "She was asked to go out to 20th Century in the early forties for a screen test. Right after our show together. They were scouring Broadway night and day for stars back then. But her speaking voice was her weakness."

"She sounded like a mouse," Eva put in. "A *sick* mouse."

"And then, the war interrupted everything just long enough to ruin what little chance she might have had," Adelle continued. "It was just bad timing more than anything else, really. Emily never had my sense of timing, poor thing. She came back to New York for a few more years of trying, not knowing, of course, that the war would throw Hollywood into a golden era. She really should have stayed on in Los Angeles. She was pretty enough. She could easily have been an extra. But by the time she figured it out, I think she had already married this man and moved away. I never saw or heard from her again until that matinee three years ago."

"And over the past three years," Auntie Lil asked, "you've learned nothing more of substance about her private life than that?"

"No," the table chorused in apology.

"She was very private about her life," someone explained. "Secretive, really.

"She didn't want us to know anything about her," another actress added.

"I think it's because she was poor and too proud to let us know," Eva insisted.

Adelle stared at her in warning. "Actually," she said in her even, well-modulated voice, "I think it was because she was rather well-off, compared to us, and didn't want us to know."

Auntie Lil was inclined to agree with Adelle. "I found out where she lived," she told the women, filling in only some of the details. "She had a rather nice little apartment on Forty-sixth Street. It was filled with Playbills and ticket stubs. She certainly had enough money to go to the theater."

"That does take money these days," Adelle said. "Most of us sneak in. We know the usherettes and if there's an empty seat, who gets hurt?"

"But Emily would always buy orchestra seats," another lady remembered suddenly. "Does that help at all?"

"That's true. She was very fond of telling us so," Eva sniffed in disgust. "Of course, she was probably not eating or not buying shoes or something, just so she could lord it over us."

"That's not so," Adelle corrected her gently. "You were the one who always had to pull it out of her. What had she seen? Where had she sat? You were intent on torturing yourself, I believe."

"I'm not quite clear what the problem was between the two of you," Auntie Lil told Eva firmly. "But I think you had better tell me about it."

"That's right," someone else pointed out. "You'd better tell her, Eva. Or else you'll be a suspect."

Several old ladies found the prospect funny. Auntie Lil did not. Eva, in fact, *was* a suspect in her book. And Auntie Lil did not find it amusing to contemplate one old actress killing another. She found it perfectly plausible. Especially by the rather dramatic method of poison in a public place.

Adelle was adept at interpreting expressions and she correctly guessed at Auntie Lil's. "You'd better tell her everything, Eva," she ordered her friend. "It's really not the time to hold back."

Eva looked miserable. "She just never liked me," she admitted finally. "If she had been nice to me, I would have been nice back."

"Of course she didn't like you," someone pointed out. "You were horrid to her."

"She always seemed to get better parts than me," Eva defended herself.

"That wasn't her fault," Adelle interjected.

"Better men, too," Eva added stubbornly. "It was as if God sent her to follow me around and snatch everything I wanted right from my hands just as it was within my grasp."

"Nonsense." The tiny old woman who had crossed Eva before spoke up again. "You just enjoyed suffering so much that every time Emily got something, you convinced yourself that you had wanted it, too. It was you that created those situations, not her. Honestly. Sometimes I think you would have done a better job than Julie Harris in *The Lark*. You've had enough practice being a martyr."

Eva sniffed unhappily. "Maybe. Maybe not. But I did try to be friends with her these last three years. And she'd have nothing to do with me. She liked to have her secrets and she'd never tell me what they were."

"Secrets?" Auntie Lil asked. "Like what?" She saw Fran glancing over the dining room with a proprietary air and quickly bent her face down low. It might be best to remain discreet, considering that being thrown out by Fran was not in her plans at the moment. In fact, she'd rather die than endure the humiliation. Provided it was a peaceful death, of course.

"I don't know what her secrets were," Eva was saying indignantly. "Like I said, she wouldn't tell me."

"What did she tell you exactly?" Auntie Lil asked patiently.

"She said that things around here were not as innocent as they seemed," Eva announced mysteriously. "She said this neighborhood was like quicksand. Smooth on the surface and unholy underneath."

Adelle flapped a hand. "Oh, please. Don't bring that up again."

"What up again?" Auntie Lil stared from one old lady to another.

"She means Fran and Father Stebbins," one actress finally answered. "Though I don't think there's a thing to it."

"Of course not." Adelle dismissed the idea with an elegant flap of her long hands. "Father Stebbins has far too much taste for the likes of her."

Auntie Lil glanced behind the counter. Fran was hovering near Father Stebbins, talking earnestly and getting little reaction from the preoccupied priest.

"I certainly hope you're right," Auntie Lil said.

"Of course I'm right," Adelle insisted. "I admit Father Stebbins is given to clichés, but breaking his vow of celibacy is not one of those clichés."

"She hinted at having younger friends," Eva added. Her brow was wrinkled in thought, an expression that turned her heavily lined eyebrows into twin questions laid on their sides. She really was trying to help Auntie Lil.

"Younger?" Auntie Lil said. "What gave you the impression they were younger.?"

Eva shrugged. "She let it drop that she was bringing a younger man to see *Cats*, I think it was. She said something about hoping she could keep up." Eva glanced around the table, pleased at the effect her pronouncement had on the group. Mouths open wide, they gaped at her, trying to reconcile the image of an aloof Emily dating a younger man.

"Well, you could interpret that many ways," Auntie Lil said.

"That's what I mean," Eva agreed. "She was always hinting at things without ever really saying anything. Just because she knew it drove me crazy."

"It isn't much to go on," Auntie Lil told them. They looked ashamed and she stirred uneasily. "Look here," she added, hoping to brighten their moods. "Did any of you ever see her with anyone else?" They all shook their heads no. She opened her giant pocketbook and rummaged inside, producing the dimestore strip of photos. "How about one of these boys?" she asked, passing the photo around the table.

They took turns scrutinizing it carefully, some of them holding the strip only inches from their eyes, but no one recognized either of the boys.

Auntie Lil sighed and packed the photos back inside her pocketbook. She saw that Fran had finished speaking to Father Stebbins and was eyeing the floor of the dining room as if intending to make a sweep through the tables. The image of Fran grabbing her elbow and marching her out on police orders was not a pleasant one. "I'd better go now," Auntie Lil decided. No sense throwing fuel on Fran's fire. "If you think of anything else, let me know."

"But you haven't told us how we could help," Adelle protested. "She was our friend and we want to help. We want to know where your investigation stands. How will we know what you've found out if we're not involved?"

Auntie Lil did not have time to evaluate the implications of this statement. She was too busy watching Fran approach one of the first tables. Soon, she would be headed their way. "This is serious business," she told the table quickly. "I can't let amateurs gum up the works."

"We are not amateurs," Adelle protested. "My God, we're trained professionals, highly skilled in our craft."

"But in acting, not detecting," Auntie Lil pointed out.

"Same thing," Adelle insisted loftily.

"If I can think of a way you can be of help, I certainly will let you know," Auntie Lil promised. She had to go now or risk ignominious exposure. "I've got to meet Theodore and I'm late," she lied, scurrying out the basement door.

Adelle stared after her. "Well, I never. Talk about poor timing for your exit." She sniffed and the other old actresses nodded their solemn agreement.

3.   As usual, Auntie Lil was getting to do all the fun work while T.S. went off on a futile tangent. But he would still do his best, despite the fact that he wasn't having much luck down at City Hall. First he got lost in the maze of distinguished, Romanesque buildings which looked exactly alike to him and then he crushed in a crowd of early commuters anxious to head home before the five o'clock rush. By the time he found the building holding housing records, it was nearly a quarter to five. Things were not looking good. He rode the elevator to the proper floor in gloomy silence, trying hard to ignore the surreptitious glances of several of his fellow riders. He straightened his shoulders, conscious of their scrutiny. What in the world were they doing staring at him? He was the one properly dressed in stylish clothes. They all had on brown or checked suits at least two decades out of date and had let their bodies go to seed. They looked like a convention of ill-dressed penguins . . . or hair-oil salesmen. As the elevator neared his floor, several of the men drew closer to T.S. The doors opened and one ventured a comment.

"Going to records?" he asked brightly.

"Yes," T.S. replied slowly, noting that a number of heads had turned his way. "I need to find out who the owner of a building is." As he spoke, four men accompanied him out of the elevator and began shouting and pushing to get close to T.S. He stared at them mystified, unable to separate their voices. They waved business cards in his face and babbled. One particularly portly gentleman finally succeeded in elbowing his competitors aside and dragging T.S. a short distance down the hall while the others watched enviously.

"Lenny Melk, real estate consultant," he assured T.S. smoothly. "Don't let those amateurs fool you. What you need is a pro. Someone who knows the lay of the land. Not to mention the clerks and the procedures. Are you aware that you could be lost in these hallways for days, without food or sustenance, seeking knowledge and enlightenment that, for a mere thirty-five dollars, I could obtain in five minutes?"

"What?" T.S. removed his elbow from the man's grasp and drew himself upright, trying not to stare. Lenny Melk was shaped like a middle-aged bear—he was all stomach and sloped shoulders. His gray suit had wide lines of red running through it, except for the three spots where a coffee stain had interrupted the pattern—and his shoulders were peppered with a healthy snowfall of dandruff. In fact, it was a blizzard. His clearly visible scalp shone gray beneath strands of greasy black hair and his doughy face was sprinkled with old acne scars.

"Do you mean to tell me that all of you are nothing but vultures, riding the elevators day after day looking for people to descend on?" T.S. asked.

"Certainly not." Lenny Melk was not the least bit miffed at being labeled a vulture. He thrust a heavily jeweled hand into his greasy hair and combed it back over a large bald spot. "I am an entrepreneur and well worth my modest fee. Of course, if you don't believe me, go right ahead and do it yourself." He waved his hand in the general direction of a large double doorway. T.S. peeked inside. Dozens of people were poring over pages of records at scarred, ancient library tables. Others were engaged in arguments with bored-looking clerks who stood behind a pair of counters at one end of the room. Rows and rows of card catalog drawers lined the walls and the clock on the far wall was ticking ominously closer to five o'clock.

"Better hurry. You got all of five minutes," Lenny Melk assured him smoothly. "These people are civil servants. They're going to start dragging their feet in about five minutes." He checked his watch—a bad Rolex imitation—and began whistling the theme from *Rocky*.

"All right, all right," T.S. agreed. He dug into his pocket for the money. "But I'm waiting here. This is the address I need the info on." He handed the man a handful of bills plus Emily's apartment building number. "I want to know who owns it and if a condominium conversion plan has been filed. And anything else pertinent."

"No sweat," Lenny promised him, pocketing the money with practiced ease. "But I do need two more fivers, on account of the time."

T.S. raised his eyebrows and stared at the man.

"Not for me. For the clerk," Lenny explained defensively.

"Of course," T.S. murmured in resignation. "I forgot for a moment where I was." He handed over two more fives and watched as Lenny practiced his magic. The man was right. He was not an amateur at all. He was truly an entrepreneur. He quickly snatched an oversized bundle of building plans from an abandoned spot on a nearby table and sidled up ahead of several people waiting in line. He held one hammy finger to a spot on the plans and stared at it in mock confusion. Murmuring apologies to those behind him, he bellied up to the front of the counter and snapped his fingers at the clerk. The clerk, a skinny man blessed with the embalmed attitude of all civil servants, turned his way with an astonished glare that quickly changed to a look of barely concealed recognition and what T.S. suspected was a spark of greed. Shielding himself from the view of others with the large building plans, Lenny slipped a five to the clerk and quickly barked out a question. To the chagrin of the entire line, the clerk promptly disappeared in back, behind a stack of drawers that bulged with un-filed papers. Lenny half-turned and gave T.S. a coquettish wave. Feeling foolish, T.S. waved back.

It took several minutes, but when the clerk reappeared, he had a handful of papers that he handed over to Lenny. Lenny stuffed them under his arm and quickly shook the clerk's hand, passing another five to him as he did so. Smiling at the enraged line still waiting, he headed back to T.S., pretending to be unaware of the fact that the clerk was quickly sliding down a wooden barrier and closing his station. "Sorry," the clerk's expression conveyed to the line as he pointed to the clock. "But not really. Better luck next time."

"Let's get out of here before you get lynched," T.S. suggested. A large man, who had been elbowed aside while preoccupied with his official papers, was making a beeline for Lenny. His expression hinted that he was a man of action.

"No problem," Lenny said, glancing over his shoulder. He grabbed T.S.'s elbow and pulled him out into the hallway and into the first open door. It was the ladies' room and, fortunately, it was empty. Pink paint peeled from dingy walls and a cracked mirror had been decorated with a lipstick to read ROSALYN LOVES RANDY FOREVER.

"Here's the story," Lenny announced in a superior tone of voice. He scanned the papers quickly, his expressions ranging from professional boredom to slight interest and back again to boredom. "Looks like the building is owned by some kind of holding company, probably just a dummy corporation, that calls itself Worthy Enterprises, Inc. They've owned it just over two years. They give their address as 1515 Broadway. I never heard of them." He shrugged. "No conversion plan. It's all rental apart-ments." He glanced at the date. "A couple of them go for pretty cheap. Rent control I guess. Real estate taxes are $8,567 a year. Paid on time. Sort of. Anything else you need to know?"

"Anything else you can tell me?" T.S. didn't think it was much to go on.

"Naw." Lenny finished scanning the pages and showed them to T.S. "See for yourself."

It didn't help. He couldn't decipher a thing. He simply verified the address of Worthy Enterprises and thanked Lenny Melk for his help.

"My pleasure," the man replied, giving a portly bow. "Here, please, take my card in case you ever find yourself in need again of real estate consultancy services."

T.S. tucked it in his pocket along with the business card of Gregory Rogers, Dance Master Extraordinaire, and made his getaway. He managed to squeeze into the first elevator that arrived, which put him smack in the middle of an angry crowd of patrons who had not made the five o'clock deadline. Fortunately, no one had connected him with Lenny Melk and he felt relatively safe, with the exception of his wallet, which he discreetly patted periodically. He was, after all, in New York.

As he hurried from the building, he saw the small team of entrepreneurs lurking in the lobby and descending on the dissatisfied crowd, offering their services first thing in the morning. T.S. admired their nerve.

He stopped at the nearest public phone that worked, which turned out to be near Canal Street in the heart of Chinatown. Ignoring the shrieks of bargaining Chinese that whirled around him, he picked his way through the debris of a corner fish store and sought refuge in the gutter. Discarded lettuce lay across his shoe like a deflated balloon and he had to keep one finger firmly plugged in his free ear to hear the operator, but he finally obtained the number to Worthy Enterprises and, ignoring the glare of a waiting Chinese mother and small boy, quickly dialed it, not sure of what he wanted to say.

"Good afternoon," a breathless voice answered. Another Marilyn Monroe wannabe. "This is the office of—" A garbage truck roared past, obliterating the rest of her sentence.

"Hello? Hello?" T.S. shouted. "Is this Worthy Enterprises?"

"Drop dead," the breathy voice replied. It was followed by a click.

4. It was a good thing Auntie Lil failed to warn him that she was also planning to invite Lilah to dinner as well as Herbert Wong. Had he known, T.S. would only have spent a few hours of preparation in being nervous. As it was, he had to endure a few seconds of a humiliating flush that crept up his neck when he spotted her waiting at the bar. Fortunately, Harvey's still believed that ambience required dim lighting and he knew his surprise had been well concealed.

"Got yourself a sunburn, Mr. Hubbert?" Frederick the bartender boomed.

"A sunburn?" he answered. "Why, no. I may have gotten a little more sun than anticipated today. It was quite warm, you know." He kept his eyes firmly away from Lilah.

"The usual?" Frederick asked him. "Auntie Lil has not yet arrived."

"The usual," T.S. confirmed. "My aunt called ahead?"

"No, but this lovely lady let me know the score." Frederick bowed briefly toward Lilah, who flashed T.S. a smile, giving him the opportunity to pretend that he had just spotted her.

"Lilah. What a lovely surprise." He slid onto the stool next to hers and immediately snagged the edge of his sweater on a splinter, pulling out a large loop of yellow yarn that gaped between them like spittle.

"Oh, your beautiful sweater," she fretted, unhooking him from the splinter. "Wait just a moment and I'll fix it." She produced a bobby pin from the depths of her upswept hair, releasing a charming lock of white strands that fell behind one ear. Holding the pin like a tiny sword, she reached one hand under T.S.'s sweater and he breathed in deeply, willing his potbelly to disappear, if only for the next fifteen seconds. She fumbled with the nap, located the offending string and hooked the pin around it, jerking it back through to the inside of his sweater with a quick tug. Holding the side seams tightly between two well-manicured hands, she stretched the nap smooth again. "There," she said, smiling shyly at T.S. "I used to do this for my daughters all the time."

"Not bad," Frederick interrupted from behind the bar. "I could use someone with your skills around my house." He set the Dewars and soda in front of T.S. It didn't stay there long.

"Thirsty?" Lilah inquired. "Have you had a hard day sleuthing?"

"Very hard," T.S. agreed. It seemed incredibly warm in Harvey's. You would think that with all the oak wainscotting and polished wood and brass and hanging plants that it would be at least a little bit cooler than outside. But no, it seemed hotter than a steam room in Hell, at least in his opinion.

"Look. There's Auntie Lil." Lilah turned on her stool and stared at the doorway. So did nearly everyone else in the restaurant. And no wonder. Auntie Lil was wearing a neon green pants suit of diaphanous material. In response to the draft from the front door, it billowed about her like a cloud of poisonous gas. An enormous matching shawl exploding with bright purple flowers trailed off one of her shoulders onto the floor behind her. Suddenly, the front door opened again and a small man hurried inside, hot on the trail of the shawl's tail. Scooping it off the floor, he carefully brushed the dirt from the fabric and tucked it back over Auntie Lil's other shoulder.

"It's Herbert!" Lilah cried it delight.

Herbert Wong blinked his eyes slowly as he adjusted to the dim lighting. He was a petite Asian man of undeterminable age, with a military bearing and a small, rounded belly. His skin gave off a burnished glow and warm age spots dotted his pearlike complexion. Thinning hair was impeccably combed back from a jolly oval face that was dominated by sharply alert eyes. He was wearing a closely cut mustard-colored suit nicely set off by a gray and black diamond-patterned silk shirt. It was snazzy attire that any rock-and-roller would have been proud of, but on Herbert Wong it did not look out of place at all. Its gaudiness was tamed by an inner reserve evident in his regal bearing, and it suited him as appropriately as the colorful plumage of the male peacock. Preening ever so slightly, he scanned the restaurant's interior quickly and his face lit up with undisguised admiration when he spotted T.S. at the bar.

"Mr. Hubbert," he called across the foyer, following this respectful greeting with a tiny bow. Reflexively, T.S. tried to bow back and nearly toppled from his stool, saved only by the quick grasp of Lilah's surprisingly strong fingers. That first gulp of Scotch had gone straight to his head, he'd better slow it down.

Auntie Lil did not call out a greeting. She was too busy tussling with the new maître d', who had obviously not yet had the pleasure of making her acquaintance. If he had, he would not have been wrestling with her or trying to convince her to give the shawl to the coat-check girl. As it was, he held one end of the enormous wrap and was tugging on it firmly while Auntie Lil gripped the other end with no intention of letting go. T.S. slid from his stool to intervene. He wanted the evening to start off smoothly.

"Madam, this is as big as a tablecloth," the maître d' was growling. "I really must insist that you check it." He was a small trim man with a pretentious pencil mustache, squeezed into a too-tight tuxedo. He was obviously single-handedly trying hard to restore 1940s elegance to an unwilling Harvey's Chelsea Restaurant.

"Let go of my clothing, you worm," Auntie Lil said calmly. "This is a Donna Karan original and I'm not giving it up."

"Aunt Lil," T.S. interrupted. "Who would steal it? It screams louder than a burglar alarm. I don't think anyone will even try."

"I don't care. I like my clothing near my body. That is why I *wear* it." She and the maître d' squared off again and pulled, neither of them willing to let go.

Noticing the skirmish, a waiter hurried up, anxious to placate

Auntie Lil. She was a notorious overtipper and thus, a favorite customer. The waiter had wisely decided that it would do no good to antagonize a valuable source of his income.

"Pierre," the waiter cried frantically. "It is no problem. I've plenty of room in my section." Before Pierre—who was more probably named Chip or Bruce—could protest, the waiter led Auntie Lil to her usual table at the rear of the dining room where she had an equally good view of the front door and the huge dessert cart. Herbert darted forward and pulled out her chair for her after cleverly outflanking the overly attentive waiter. The waiter countered by carefully wrapping the shawl around Auntie Lil's chair so many times that it was looking positively upholstered. T.S. contented himself with helping Lilah to her seat and grabbing the spot next to hers.

"A lovely outfit," Lilah murmured Auntie Lil's way.

"Isn't it?" Auntie Lil turned proudly in her seat. "These are the latest colors. A bit bright, so I decided not to wear a hat. It stands on its own, don't you think?"

"Indeed," T.S. affirmed. "I'd say it more likely races." He greeted Herbert politely and, after the usual round of inquiring after everyone's health and settling a few matters of an ingrown toenail here and a vacation to Mexico there, they all settled into ordering a new round of drinks and letting Auntie Lil order everyone's dinner.

"We'll pretend this is a Chinese restaurant," she said. "And we'll sample each other's entrees."

"Excellent idea," Herbert Wong beamed, but he was prone to beaming at anything Auntie Lil suggested. They had become constant companions as both were infused with inexhaustible energy and insatiable appetites for new adventures and friends.

"Don't forget that we are here to work," Auntie Lil reminded them as soon as their appetizers arrived. (Appetizers always arrived shortly after Auntie Lil did.)

Lilah volunteered to begin with a report on the medical examiner's findings. It was brief. Emily had indeed been poisoned. The substance was formally identified as a nitroprusside, a form of cyanide easily accessible to photographers, jewelers, metallurgists and goldsmiths, all of whom relied on it for various chemical synthesis purposes. It could have been put in her food in either powder or liquid form; there had not been enough evidence to support a particular finding either way. Emily had been thin, even considering her age, but not ill-nourished. She had not eaten much that day, which had probably contributed to an almost instantaneous reaction to the minute amount of poison that she had time to consume before her death. Her age was estimated at between seventy and eight-five. It was the assistant medical examiner's opinion (Lilah did not refer to him by name, much to T.S.'s satisfaction) that Emily had borne at least one child in the past and that she had suffered from a slight bone deformity in one leg, which may have helped explain Adelle's belief that she had been a poor dancer. Her teeth were in good shape and indicated regular professional care. She had dyed her hair with a popular silver coloring agent. Finally, she had no tattoos, scars or birthmarks that might help distinguish her from a million other little old ladies. And there was no mention made of her marvelous cheekbones.

They were silent, contemplating the method of murder.

"Women poison," Auntie Lil remarked darkly. "I knew a woman in Montreal once who went through four husbands before they caught her. She even tried to poison the horse of the Royal Canadian Mounted Policeman who finally apprehended her."

"Men poison, too," Herbert politely disagreed. "At home in Singapore, there was a man whose wives always mysteriously died once their bloom of youth had withered. Curiously enough, his mother-in-laws died soon after. We all suspected, but what could we do? One night he drowned off the coast and was eaten by sharks."

Well, good God. There was no way T.S. could top those two when it came to anecdotes about death. He contented himself with a small critical comment instead. "Whether it was a man or a woman, it was a good choice of method. It would almost certainly have gone undetected," he pointed out. "If the coroner had not been training a new assistant, I doubt the poison would have been found. Without an identity, there was no family to insist on an autopsy."

"Indeed," Auntie Lil agreed. "It was ingenious. Right there in a public place, with witnesses present to attest to her heart attack. No identity left on the body. But the killer obviously didn't know that she had friends there who might have been able to provide her name and address. That was a risk. He thought she was a loner."

"Which means the killer had not been stalking her long enough to know that the other actresses were her friends," Herbert added.

"That's right. Probably, he'd known her only in the last few months or so," T.S. decided. "She'd been feuding with the other actresses for about that long. Before then, I'm sure she probably sat at the same table with Adelle and the others. So you're right. He hadn't known her very long."

"He?" Lilah asked and they told her about The Eagle.

"The Eagle?" Herbert Wong repeated thoughtfully. "That's interesting. Did he mean an American Indian?" They stared at him silently and he defended himself. "A wise man covers all possibilities."

"That's right," Auntie Lil agreed, pushing her bowl away. She had already finished her soup and couldn't have done a faster job with a straw. "Which is why we need to cover all the bases in the weeks ahead."

"You have a plan?" Lilah asked, though the others knew this was a rhetorical question. Auntie Lil always had a plan in mind and it usually involved the efforts of others.

"Yes. I've asked Herbert to begin watching the apartment building where she lived. And I'm going to go to the police for help." She added this last sentence as if it were a great sacrifice on her part. "Theodore—did you find out who owned the building?"

He told them what he had learned and it was decided that he would try to track down the person or persons behind the dummy corporation, Worthy Enterprises.

"Excuse me," Herbert Wong then announced politely. They turned to him and waited. "I am most happy to devote all waking hours to my appointed task. But there are times when I must sleep," he admitted reluctantly.

"Of course. You'll have to have help watching the building." Auntie Lil drummed her fingers impatiently and the waiter, misinterpreting her movement, brought them another large basket of bread. She bit absently into a huge breadstick, which immediately crumbled into a small anthill on a spot of the tablecloth directly beneath her chin. She brushed the crumbs idly onto the floor, her brow furrowed in deep thought. "I've got it," she finally said, then swallowed. "Adelle and the other old actresses want to help," she quickly explained. "Herbert, you can supervise them in shifts. We'll watch that building like a hawk, or eagle as it were. There are enough of them to follow anyone who leaves the building. Keep track of their descriptions and the addresses where they go. It won't be easy, but then we won't be doing the work, will we? And it could be most informative." She smiled, extremely pleased at her logic.

That decided, Lilah asked how she might help. Without missing a beat, Auntie Lil explained it was important for her dear Theodore to have someone he could call on night and day for aid.

Her extreme lack of subtlety went unnoticed by everyone but T.S., who was acutely embarrassed by the "night" part. But Lilah was unfazed and happily agreed, pleased to be a part of their plan.

"I'm going to keep interviewing neighborhood people," Auntie Lil assured them. "I'll go back to the Delicious Deli owner first. He mentioned she'd been out quite late at night a month or so ago. It was a change in her pattern and there must have been a reason for that change." She rooted around in her pocketbook while they waited, and finally produced the strip of dimestore photos. "I'm also going to try and find out who these young boys are and what their connection to Emily might be."

T.S. was silent for a moment, but knew that he needed to speak up. He did not want to tell them what he'd seen going on next door to Emily's apartment, but there might be a connection. If so, Auntie Lil needed to be told. The trick would be to do so tactfully. T.S. was a big believer in tact.

He cleared his throat but was saved from immediate action when their entrees arrived. The apportioning, tasting and exclaiming that followed made it easier for him to broach the subject.

"Those young boys," he told his aunt as she shoveled shepherd's pie into her mouth. "I have a feeling about them," T.S. continued. "I think you'll probably find that they live on the streets. And earn their living doing . . . odd jobs and stuff around the neighborhood."

Auntie Lil looked at T.S. as if he were daft. "Odd jobs?" she repeated skeptically. "There are no lawns to mow in Hell's Kitchen."

T.S. sighed. "No. But there are plenty of disgusting and perverted human beings willing to take advantage of starving runaways forced to make a dollar any way they can."

Auntie Lil stopped chewing and stared at him. She swallowed slowly and blinked. "Oh, dear. You don't say."

"I say," T.S. confirmed grimly.

"All right, then. I promise to be careful." Auntie Lil's shoulders slumped a little as she returned to her meal and Lilah gazed anxiously at T.S. Herbert patted Auntie Lil's hand and murmured something soothing. She was not overly fond of children, but Auntie Lil did delight in innocence.

"Perhaps you should try to speak to someone who works with runaways in the area," Herbert suggested diplomatically. "They may know the young boys."

"Brilliant!" Auntie Lil perked back up and patted his tiny hand fondly. "Herbert, you're a man after my own heart."

Carried away by her enthusiasm and praise, Herbert puffed up and made a rash promise. "On my part, I will search without ceasing for this man you call The Eagle," he announced. "I, too, believe he must have given Miss Emily that poison. I will not rest until he has been exposed."

"Then you had better start with trying to find the old man who saw him sitting next to Emily the day she died," Lilah said. She smiled at the group. "See? I have a good idea every now and then, too." Her smile focused on T.S. and he smiled happily back. Lilah was one big good idea, in his book.

By the end of the evening, they'd carefully laid out their plans and each of them had assigned tasks to perform. And although they'd not gotten very far yet, they all felt better knowing that their words would soon become actions.

The only thing left to decide was who would pay the check. After a brief tussle with Auntie Lil and Lilah, T.S. won. Herbert Wong took care of the tip. T.S. was not surprised to notice that it was as excessive as any Auntie Lil had ever left behind.

CHAPTER SEVEN

1. The next morning, T.S. rose early out of long habit. He drank his coffee while staring out over York Avenue, trying to decide how he could track down Worthy Enterprises. Then it came to him in a flash of inspiration, fueled by years as a successful executive. He would get someone else to do it. Best of all, he had just the man for the job.

Each night before going to bed, T.S. emptied his pockets into a silver dish in the top drawer of his dresser. It was easy to find the card. Gregory Rogers, Dance Master Extraordinaire, would not be of much help in this task. But Lenny Melk, Dandruff Master Extraordinaire, just might. He scrutinized the phone number carefully, suspecting the prefix was a public pay phone. Really, what was he doing trusting someone he'd only met the day before? On the other hand, considering the maze of official departments and filings that waited him—who cared?

It rang sixteen rings without an answer, but T.S. was not dissuaded. At this early hour, he had to be home. Sure enough, Lenny Melk finally answered the phone with a sleepy and suspicious growl. "I know, I know, Vinny," he said. "It was the spread that killed me. I'll cover it by the afternoon, I promise."

"It's not Vinny," T.S. replied crisply. Why couldn't people wake up ready and raring to function, their dignity intact? He always did. What the world needed was a little more self-discipline. "This is T.S. Hubbert."

"I'm not buying anything," Melk immediately replied. "So don't waste your time."

"No. It's T.S. Hubbert. We met late yesterday. Around closing time down at 99 Centre. Remember, you helped me out and almost got me lynched?"

There was a silence while this information filtered through

Lenny Melk's besotted brain cells. "Oh, yeah, the real persnickety guy in the yellow sweater," he finally said.

"Yes, that's me," T.S. was forced to reply. He tactfully resisted the impulse to describe Lenny Melk back. "I need your help again. Tracking down who owns Worthy Enterprises."

"Oh, yeah? This sounds interesting. It's gonna cost you. There's a shit storm of corporate filings involved, understand?"

"Of course. How interesting would you say it was?"

"At least two hundred dollars. And another thirty-five in . . . um, personnel expenses."

"Done. Can you have the information by later today?"

"Well . . ." Lenny's voice dropped dubiously. "I suppose so. Since you're getting to be a regular customer and all . . ."

"Fine. Please call me back and leave the information at this number. I trust you will trust me for the payment." There was an astonished silence and T.S. took it for agreement. "I have an answering machine, so leave a message if you need to. It's urgent." T.S. supplied him with the necessary information and rang off. He hated it when other people had answering machines, but he loved his own. Today was not a day to sit at home, waiting for a phone call back. He was meeting Herbert Wong at the soup kitchen just after the noon hour to help coordinate the surveillance of Emily's apartment building. Auntie Lil had prudently decided that she should lie low for a while, at least concerning St. Barnabas.

He checked his watch. It was only eight-thirty and he needed something to do. Now was his chance to show some initiative, come up with some good ideas of his own, stop depending on Auntie Lil for instructions. He began by dressing carefully in a casual yet authoritative sweater-and-flannel-slacks combination, then added a tie. He carefully smoothed his entire outfit twice with a sable clothes brush purchased on a visit to London seven years before. Those British really knew how to take care of their clothes. Decades of butlerism had refined it into an art. He keenly admired their precision.

Properly decked out, T.S. paused in front of the mirror. It was time for action. But no idea came and, in the end, he simply went downstairs to the corner newsstand. He purchased a copy of New York *Newsday* (having read the *Times* hours before) and settled in at a nearby coffee shop. He alternated between flipping through page after page of mayhem, horror, poverty and politics and watching frantic businessmen and grumpy businesswomen rush past the window, headed for a world he was no longer a part of.

It depressed him. He wondered what Lilah was doing today.

She'd said something about helping to make arrangements for a charity auction, which probably involved hobnobbing with retired gentlemen of far greater means than himself. That depressed him even more. He returned to reading the newspaper and discovered, to his irritation, that his favorite local columnist, Margo McGregor, was on vacation. A vacation in September . . . she certainly had her nerve. If she'd worked for him, there'd have been none of that nonsense. He tapped the ink-smudged pages in aggravation, but there was no denying it. He missed the photo they always ran of her, right above her column.

Although well into her thirties, Margo McGregor looked exactly like the little girl that every boy had loved in second grade. At least he knew he would have, if only they'd allowed girls in his prep school class. Margo McGregor was petite, with a small moon face and shiny black hair combed flat against her scalp. The thin glossy strands fell straight down to just above her shoulders where they flipped absurdly up in a single neat wave. She had a pug nose and round, sparkling eyes, and a tiny, pursed mouth that the photographer had captured at the tail end of a sardonic smile. How such a delicate creature could be one of New York's most sarcastic investigative reporters was beyond him, but T.S. loved the unlikely juxtaposition of her physical innocence and extreme cynicism. The paper regularly advertised her as "the wittiest and most insightful columnist in New York." Which was a nice way of saying she was a smartass.

Oh, well, perhaps she would be back in print next week. He flipped the page and read about a snafu at the main post office, then stopped. He'd had an idea. Just like that. Emily must have gotten some sort of Social Security check from the government. Unless she had arranged for direct deposit, damn the convenience. But surely she'd have received a letter or two in her time. Or junk mail. Nothing could stop junk mail. If she'd so much as sneezed, she was on someone's list.

He slid off his stool, left an exactly correct tip—which would certainly not surprise the waitress—and headed for the door. If Auntie Lil could lurk about the streets of Hell's Kitchen, so could he.

2.   Auntie Lil's idea of rising early was rolling out of bed just before the soap operas began. She managed it earlier than usual once again, thanks to an automatic timer on her coffee machine that sent an irresistible aroma throughout her apartment at exactly ten o'clock sharp. Unable to speak without a minimum of caffeine in her system, she downed several cups and dialed Det. George Santos.

Four officers and one public-relations liaison later, she was told that Detective Santos was not in yet and would she care to leave a message?"

"Yes," she announced crisply. "Write this down." Satisfied with the rustling that met her command, she continued. "Lillian Hubbert called to ask, 'Have you found The Eagle?' Also, dead woman lived at 326 West Forty-sixth Street on the sixth floor. Owner of Delicious Deli can confirm. Please investigate immediately." She demanded that her message be read back and, except for the part about whether Detective Santos had found her beagle, the obedient officer had approximated her intent.

Next she called Herbert Wong and Theodore to reiterate instructions. To her intense irritation, neither one was home. They were probably out running wild in the streets, with no regard for her master plan. Another cup of coffee later and Auntie Lil was ready to tackle Father Stebbins.

The priest answered the phone himself, as she'd suspected he would. St. Barnabas could not afford any office help. Father Stebbins was an all-purpose kind of guy.

"St. Barnabas," he boomed into the receiver. "May the Lord's blessings follow you all this fine day."

Fresh out of blessings, she cut to the chase. "Father Stebbins, it's Lillian Hubbert."

"Ah, Lillian . . ."

"I won't take up much of your time," she promised. "I know you're scrambling to make up for the loss of my culinary expertise and that you have more than enough on your plate to handle. I'm sure things have progressed right out of the frying pan and into the fire." He was not the only one who could deal in clichés. At least hers contained apropos allusions. "But I'm not one to sit idly by while others are suffering. I've decided to devote my talents to helping with the young runaways in the neighborhood until we can get this teensy misunderstanding straightened out. Whom do you suggest I call to volunteer my services?"

There was brief silence on the other end. Perhaps he was wondering if she was planning to dish out any more of her special chili to minors. "You might call a fellow named Bob Fleming," he finally said. "He runs a retreat for runaways a few blocks away called Homefront. They're small without a big fund-raising staff and could probably use any help they could get." He paused, contemplating the tact of this last statement. "Not that you aren't a prized volunteer," he finally added. "Why, we're hardly getting by without you."

"I can imagine," Auntie Lil replied confidently. "But I suspect that dear Fran is working night and day to make sure that everyone gets fed."

"She's certainly been a help," he answered promptly. "But she does have problems of her own that sometimes prevent her from devoting her full energies to our own humble hunger-fighting endeavor."

Indeed? But surely a priest would be the last person in the world to gossip . . . still, it was worth a shot. "Problems?" she inquired lightly. "Could I be of help in any way?"

"Oh. No, no, no," Father Stebbins sputtered. "I shouldn't have said as much as I did. She'll be fine. I'm helping her and she's making great progress. I'm sure she'll be fine."

So the conceited old cassock wasn't going to spill the beans. She wouldn't waste any more time with him. "How can I find this Homefront fellow?" she demanded instead.

"I can call him for you right now, if you like."

Auntie Lil checked the clock. "Actually, I've got to run out. I'm meeting a friend at the Delicious Deli. Perhaps I could stop by later and find out when a good time to call him might be?"

There was another tactful silence. "I think it would be easier if you called me back instead of dropping by," the priest suggested diplomatically.

"It's a deal. I'll wait until after the rush."

"And, Lillian," he added in a voice that oozed concern and understanding. "That scene the other day with the authorities . . . I'm not quite sure what your troubles have been—I try not to judge my fellow man—but God forgives everyone. If you ever need a sympathetic shoulder, I'm right here."

Sure. But she'd have to pry Fran off that sympathetic shoulder first. She murmured something neutral and, after receiving another shower of blessings and pietistic clichés, rang off as quickly as decency allowed. My goodness, they all acted like she was some sort of pariah. And Father Stebbins seemed convinced she was on a sure road to Hell. It was no crime being smarter than Lieutenant Abromowitz. If it was, the city jails would be bursting at the bar.

But that was exactly what she was being ostracized for. And it left her no other choice. She'd just have to show Abromowitz up, if it was the last thing she ever did.

3. Waiting for the mailman on the steps of Emily's building seemed foolishly indiscreet, so T.S. searched the streets of Hell's Kitchen for men and women in blue. He soon heard an obnoxious high honking and, following the sound, discovered a slim black mailman impeccably clad in a summer post office uniform of navy shorts and a light blue short-sleeved shirt. Obviously determined to wring the last drop of summer out of the year, he also wore a regulation pith helmet and stalked confidently through the crowd, pushing a wheeled basket of mail while honking an attached bicycle horn incessantly. The horn had inspired a group of hungover winos leaning against a nearby deserted storefront to honk back. They sounded like a flock of inebriated Canada geese.

"Pardon me, do you deliver to Forty-sixth Street?" T.S. asked him politely, ignoring the cacophony of birdcalls behind him.

The mailman paused with one hand poised over the bulb of his bicycle horn. "Why? Who wants to know?"

"I need to find out where someone lives," T.S. explained.

The postman eyed him carefully. Apparently, T.S. didn't look like a serial killer to him, since he then asked, "What's the person's name?"

"I don't know," T.S. explained patiently. "I just know her stage name, Emily Toujours."

"Is this a love thing?" the postman asked. "'Cause if it is, take it from me—those actresses aren't worth the trouble. They're high-maintenance girlfriends. They need a lot of attention. I'd get yourself a nice librarian, if I was you." He honked the horn twice for emphasis and smiled.

Resisting the temptation to grab the horn and beat him over the pith helmet with it, T.S. gritted his teeth and asked patiently, "Do you deliver to Forty-sixth Street or not?"

"Nope." The mailman pointed to a large military green holding box bolted to the sidewalk near the curb. "That would be Beulah. She'll be checking by in about fifteen minutes. Ask her. And good luck, brother. May love shine her blessings upon your brow." He beeped happily and wheeled his cart away, pedestrians parting before his raucous path like a multicolored Red Sea.

Beulah didn't show for a good half-hour and when she did, she wasn't much help. For starters, her feet were killing her and this occupied the first five minutes of their conversation. No, she knew of no one named Emily Toujours or anything else, who lived at 326 West Forty-sixth Street on the sixth floor. "I never delivered no mail to that floor, not never," she insisted. "It's empty. They's probably warehousing."

She was probably being paid off, T.S. decided grumpily. He stomped away without a plan and stood at the corner of Ninth Avenue and Forty-sixth Street, watching the downtown traffic. He heard a voice mumbling urgently behind him. "You can do it," it was saying, "This part is for you. You've got it. You're going to wow them. You were born to play this part. Just get in there and grab it."

T.S. stepped back against a nearby streetlight. The voice belonged to a middle-aged actor, who was mumbling to himself as he waited for the light to change. He clutched the xeroxed pages of a script in one hand and was gesturing into the air with the other. "It's gonna be you," he told himself. "You're gonna knock them dead, Edward, my man. Success is just around the corner."

That did it. T.S. wanted to throw himself in front of one of the many trucks barreling down the avenue. It was all just too depressing. This neighborhood was one big stew of hopeless, naked, walking aspirations.

Except, of course, for the hopeless, naked, stumbling apparitions. Like the rubbery figure lurching up the sidewalk toward him.

It was Emily's building mate, the one who had passed out in the supply closet. She was obviously on her way home after a long hard night that had stretched into the morning. The preposterous wig had slipped to one side and her makeup was badly smeared, but she once again wore the orange mini-dress cut to the crotch and ripped under one arm. No stockings. Just long coffee-colored legs that would have better fit the winner of the fifth race at Belmont. T.S. stepped back and watched her negotiate the corner near Emily's building. What a way to live, he thought sadly. Like a vampire, she was fleeing the light of day and seeking the sanctuary of the dark.

The dark. That's where he had seen her before. She had burst into Robert's during his dinner with Lilah and the bartender had bounced her right back out.

Well, he wasn't doing anything else at the moment. Perhaps it was time to pay Robert's a call.

4.   Thanks to a subway power failure, it was nearly twelve-thirty by the time Auntie Lil reached the Delicious Deli. The owner, Billy, was hustling back and forth handling the small lunch crowd rush of construction workers, taxi drivers and deliverymen.

He recognized Auntie Lil and gave her a wide smile, gesturing toward one of the tiny tables. She sat and, in between sandwich orders, he brought her cappuccino and cheesecake without being asked. The young man certainly had star potential. If justice prevailed, he'd own his own string of franchises one day.

"Nice to see you again. You just sit here and relax," he told her. "Stay a little while and you can meet my daughter."

Auntie Lil nodded back. She was in no mood for children, she never was, but she'd stay. The things she had to endure just to weasel a little information out of people . . .

There was a temporary lull in business and Billy rested his elbows on the counter. "Hey, you remember that old lady you were asking me about?" he said to Auntie Lil.

"Yes. Do you have something new on her?" Her cheesecake was immediately forgotten.

"No. But the cops are in on it now. They got a tip on where she lived."

"What happened?" Auntie Lil asked eagerly.

"My buddy, George, went to check it out personally and it turned out that someone was pulling his leg. Some young blonde actress was living at the address instead. Never heard of the old lady. Said she'd been living there for over three years herself. George was pretty steamed. He doesn't usually follow up on civilian tips, you know. He made an exception because the guy taking the message bungled it, said it was my wife who had called. George was pretty burned about it. Wouldn't even stay for his usual free coffee. Why? What did you find out about her?"

Auntie Lil stared bleakly at her half-eaten cheesecake. "Nothing," she admitted glumly and that was exactly as much as she was going to admit. She didn't believe it. They must have gone to the wrong address. She would call Det. George Santos back. "You know the detective on the case?" she asked Billy.

"Sure, I know everyone. Can you believe someone poisoned that old lady? Who'd do a thing like that?"

"Is this George Santos a good detective?" she asked.

"Well . . . he's a good *guy*." That was as far as Billy would go.

"Does he live in the neighborhood?"

"Sort of. He spends all of his time at the precinct or down at the Westsider."

"Is that a hotel?" Auntie Lil wanted to know. Perhaps she could talk to him there.

Billy laughed. It was not a happy sound. "Some people seem to think it is," he finally said. "Including George. But it's really just a crummy dive bar across from the Forty-fifth Street Pier."

5.   Robert's had a small lunch crowd and a slightly larger group of regular daytime drinkers parked at the bar. T.S. didn't recognize the bartender. He checked out the two waiters carefully. One looked familiar—a finely sculptured, well-built young man with a broad, handsome face and short brown hair cut closely against his head. He was leaning against one end of the bar, morosely staring out the picture window in lieu of staring at his mostly empty tables. He hardly moved when T.S. tapped him on the shoulder. But then, he was probably used to getting tapped on the shoulder by guys at bars. T.S. would set him straight. Quickly.

"Excuse me, I was in here the other night with a lady friend of mine," T.S. began.

"Congratulations," the waiter interrupted, still glumly staring out the window.

"You were here, too," T.S. continued.

The waiter shifted his stare to T.S. "What night?"

"Tuesday. A woman came in for a moment and the bartender bounced her right back out," T.S. explained patiently. "She was very tall. Dark skinned. With high-piled hair and lots of makeup. I'm interested in finding out who she was."

The waiter didn't answer and T.S. was forced to launch into a fashion forecast. "She was wearing spike heels and a silver sequined tube dress with long gloves . . ." His voice trailed off as embarrassment overtook him at last.

"What color?" the waiter inquired.

"What color what?"

"What color were the gloves?" He stared at T.S., waiting for an answer.

"White. What difference does it . . ." T.S. stopped. He was almost certain he was being teased. But in New York City, you never knew for sure. "Do you know who I'm talking about or not?" he demanded with reclaimed dignity.

"Sure, I know who you're talking about. But I'd get a different hobby if I was you."

"I just need her name. Forget the cute stuff." That sounded good. Tough. Very James Cagneyish.

The waiter looked T.S. over with amusement and held out a hand. T.S. sighed and handed him a five-dollar bill. Considering the name could be worthless to their investigation, he thought he was being generous.

"The name's Leteisha Swann," the waiter told him, smiling thinly as if he were enjoying a private joke. "Leteisha Swann is not a welcome person on these premises. She's a little too entrepreneurial for our taste. She was hiding in the bathroom one night. Damn near gave some old guy a heart attack when she jumped out of the shadows and offered to unzip his pants for him." The waiter winked at T.S. "For another ten, I'll get you her phone number."

"No thanks," T.S. replied stiffly. "I can unzip my own pants." Besides, he already knew where she lived. And that her phone number rang on a corner somewhere.

Patience exhausted, he left the sarcastic waiter behind with an overly polite bow.

Leteisha Swann . . . he'd lay ten-to-one odds that the name wasn't real. And the odds on her having known Emily were even less. He sighed and headed for St. Barnabas. No sense in letting Auntie Lil have all the fun.

6. The door chimes tinkled and a miniature lady stepped into the Delicious Deli. There was no other way to describe her as she was far too self-possessed to be called a child. The tiny girl wore a blue and green plaid Catholic-school jumper over a snowy white blouse with an old-fashioned Peter Pan collar. Her straight black hair was cut in a sleek cap around her face and her fine features stood out against a porcelain complexion. Irish beauty at its budding best. The girl was probably no more than six or seven years old, but she had the bearing of a fifty-year-old matriarch.

"Hi, Daddy," she called out to Billy, flipping her hair back with a practiced toss of her head. "I'll take a cappuccino, please."

"Oh, no you won't, Miss Megan Magee. Sit at that table there and I'll bring you a milk." Billy pointed out Auntie Lil and Megan dutifully sat next to her with a slight pout. But the grudge was soon forgotten, thanks to the girl's lively curiosity.

"Who are you?" she asked Auntie Lil, folding her hands primly in front of her and waiting expectantly for the answer. Auntie Lil had the uncomfortable feeling that she was at a tea party.

"I'm Auntie Lil. I'm a friend of your father's."

"You're not *my* aunt," Megan pointed out. "My aunt is young and beautiful and goes dancing every night,"

"I go dancing every night, too," Auntie Lil replied grimly. She was suddenly reminded why she didn't like children.

"Magee, don't talk this nice lady's ear off." Billy set a glass of milk down in front of his daughter and winked at Auntie Lil. "Megan takes after her mother. Where is she, anyway?"

"Two doors down getting carrots. Yuck." Megan wrinkled her nose.

Well, Auntie Lil thought, thank goodness she still harbored some childish traits.

"What can I do for you today?" Billy asked Auntie Lil as he pulled out the chair next to his daughter and sat, wiping his hands on his deli apron. "I've got a couple of minutes before the next rush."

"I wondered if you knew these two young men." Auntie Lil produced the strip of dimestore photos of the two young boys from her pocketbook, all the while keeping a close eye on her plate. Megan was staring at her cheesecake with undisguised interest and Auntie Lil wasn't about to give up the last bite without a fight.

Billy surveyed their faces. "Yeah. I've seen them. They're not allowed in here. They steal. Why are you looking for them?"

She could not think of a single plausible reply, but Megan made one unnecessary. "That's the guy that threw up," she announced proudly. She placed a small finger on the face of the white boy. "Remember, Daddy? You said it looked like he'd been eating pepperoni pizza."

"Megan!" Billy groaned and smiled an apology at Auntie Lil. "Both of these guys hang out around the neighborhood a lot. I think they work out of that run-down sleaze palace at Eighth and Forty-fourth. They've been around here about a year or so. I give them another six months."

Auntie Lil was going to ask why, but the presence of Megan made her hesitate. Besides, she had a sad hunch that she already knew.

Billy was staring at her quietly. "Listen, I'm not quite sure why you're going around and asking a lot of questions," he said carefully. "But you seem like a nice enough lady and I just want to tell you that whatever it is you're doing, I'd stop if I were you."

When Auntie Lil said nothing, he continued. "I was born in this neighborhood. Practically on this block. I grew up here. I've seen it change again and again. I watched the Irish take over from the Puerto Ricans, who took over from the blacks, who got it from the Irish in the first place and around and around and around. Unless you know someone and you've got protection, this is a dangerous place to be messing with. The people you see on the street may seem nice enough, but it's the people you don't see that you have to worry about. I know. I know them. They're not fooling around."

"Has anyone been in here asking about me?" Auntie Lil asked quietly. She did not resent the warning, she just wished she knew whether it was sincere or an attempt to dissuade her from her task.

"No. Not yet. And like I say, I don't know what you're up to and I don't think I want to know what you're up to. Just be careful. Maybe you should find yourself a new way to pass the time." He held up both palms in apology. "Not that it's any of my business."

The door chimes tinkled again and a chubby man entered the deli. He was burly and of just below average height, with a scraggly beard that was beginning to go gray. His long, flowing hair tumbled to his shoulders in brown waves. He was dressed in a flannel shirt and baggy blue jeans. All together, he looked like he belonged on the outskirts of Anchorage, Alaska, rather than in the heart of New York City.

The man quickly scanned the store and his gaze settled on Auntie Lil. "Lillian Hubbert?" he asked politely.

"Yes, that's me. Who are you?"

"I'm Bob Fleming. From Homefront." He glanced at Billy, then looked away with a quick nod.

The deli owner acted swiftly. He took his daughter by the hand and pulled her away from the table toward the door.

"Where are we going?" Megan asked indignantly. "You didn't give me my cake."

"I'm going to watch you walk down the block to meet your mother," Billy answered back grimly. "Now. And don't talk back to me, either."

The atmosphere in the deli instantly chilled. Bob Fleming sat quietly at Auntie Lil's table. They both stared at Billy's broad back as the deli owner stood in the doorway, watching his daughter's progress down the block to where her mother was shopping.

"Careful father," Bob Fleming observed.

"Around here, I guess you have to be."

The man nodded in agreement and stared directly at Auntie Lil. "I've just been by St. Barnabas, dropping off some kids. Father Stebbins said you wanted to help me out, so I thought I'd try and catch you here. We could use some help. But you look kind of old."

"You're certainly direct," Auntie Lil admitted. "But don't worry about me. I'm strong and healthy."

The man nodded. "Sometimes an old lady is good." His voice trailed off. It was plain that Bob Fleming was not a happy man. His shoulders slumped from worry and fatigue. He had not chosen to take an easy path. Runaways in midtown Manhattan could be untrusting, unforgiving and unredeemable. "Old ladies don't usually remind the kids of anyone," he continued. "Except for maybe a long-forgotten grandmother. What can you do?"

"Anything you want me to do." Auntie Lil did not like lying to this man. He worked too hard and spoke too plain to deserve anything but the truth. What she really wanted was to show him the photos of the two young boys. But after Billy's warning, she was reluctant to bring them up again in front of the deli owner. "Can we go somewhere else and talk?" she asked Bob Fleming.

"Sure. We'll go to my office. I don't think that guy likes me very much, anyway." He cocked his head Billy's way and Auntie Lil found it hard to disagree. Billy was leaning against the counter shooting barely disguised glares Bob Fleming's way. He would not meet Auntie Lil's eyes and she finally marched to the counter, money in hand.

"How much?" Auntie Lil inquired politely. She would be back to find out what the trouble was between the two men.

"Three and a quarter," Billy mumbled, taking her money without his usual cheerfulness.

As she left the deli with Bob Fleming, Auntie Lil could feel the owner's gaze following them out the door. And no wonder—Billy stared after them until they were well out of sight.

7.

His thoughts on Leteisha Swann, T.S. was not paying full attention to the Midtown traffic swirling around him. First, he was nearly plowed down by a messenger on a bike—who slowed down just enough to flip an obscene gesture T.S.'s way—and then he took a wrong turn up Ninth Avenue and had to backtrack to St. Barnabas. He was still lost in thought as he ambled up the mottled sidewalk outside the neighborhood's huge new skyscraper. Suddenly, a strong arm gripped his elbow and a body moved in close behind him. T.S. did what any sensible New Yorker would do. He yelled, jumped two feet in the air and clutched the pocket that held his wallet.

"So very sorry, Mr. Hubbert," a distressed voice cried out. "I did not mean to startle you."

"Herbert!" T.S. rubbed his elbow and glared at Herbert Wong. "Why in the world are you skulking around like that?"

"I was not skulking," the retired messenger complained, spreading his arms wide. "I make very much noise. Please accept my deepest apologies." He bowed deeply.

T.S. did not believe him for a minute. Ever since he had, however briefly, questioned Herbert's prowess at martial arts, the elderly Asian man had embarked on a subtle quest to prove T.S. wrong. He was always sneaking up behind him or showing off his strength.

"I am forgiven?" Herbert asked, his face an impassive, dignified mask.

"Of course you're forgiven. I'm just preoccupied or I would have spotted you coming from a mile away." Herbert allowed T.S. this ego-placating fabrication and they walked toward St. Barnabas together, falling into a contemplative silence.

That was another thing T.S. really liked about Herbert Wong. Unlike certain other people, Herbert was perfectly content with quiet. T.S. had discovered this rare trait in Herbert years before, when he had interviewed him for a job at Sterling & Sterling. Herbert had entered the personnel manager's enormous office without a hint of nervousness, sitting down across the desk from T.S. in dignified silence. Nodding, he had waited patiently while T.S. scoured his application with customary suspicion. Unlike most other applicants, he had not blurted out incriminating details during this silence, nor revealed any desperation for a job. At the same time, he had not been secretive and had calmly divulged under questioning that his wife had recently died after a long illness which had stripped him of all his savings. He had sold his small dry-cleaning store as a result. He had no children and the rest of his family lived in Singapore, where he had been raised until he had emigrated to the U.S. as a young man. His only hobbies, it seemed, were traveling and the study of new subjects. He did not enjoy television.

T.S. had instantly felt an affinity with him and tried to steer him toward a more challenging job than the open messenger position. But Herbert had quietly insisted that he had tired of responsibility and that the messenger job was fine. He had put in fifteen good years at Sterling & Sterling before retiring the year before T.S. In those fifteen years, Herbert had never missed a day, never even reported late and had never botched a delivery. In fact, he had once kicked a mugger in the stomach in order to protect nearly one million dollars in bearer bonds for his employer, crippling the would-be thief until police arrived. Then he had insisted on such complete anonymity, for the firm's sake, that T.S. himself, personnel manager of all of Sterling & Sterling, had not heard about it until after his own retirement. Yes, Herbert was a rare man. And T.S. was a little piqued that Auntie Lil had managed to practically steal the retired messenger from him.

Of course, Auntie Lil had never been much concerned with people's official standing in life and, if T.S. were to be completely honest with himself, he'd have to admit that a full friendship between a messenger of Sterling & Sterling and the personnel manager would have been deemed unacceptable by everyone, including himself. But now that he was retired, T.S. reflected, there was no reason why they couldn't be better friends.

"That man is gesturing wildly toward you," Herbert pointed out to T.S., breaking their easy silence. They stood at the corner of Eighth Avenue and Forty-eight Street, waiting for the traffic light to change. Across the busy roadway stood Franklin, the gigantic homeless man with the Southern drawl. His big burly body was still encased in old-fashioned overalls, but he was wearing a clean shirt and a new baseball hat. He was calmly waving at T.S., an action which, in Herbert Wong's book, qualified as wild gesticulation.

"That's Franklin," T.S. explained. "He's a regular at the soup kitchen. He knows Adelle and the other old actresses quite well. I wonder what he wants with me?"

T.S. soon found out. As they approached, Franklin bent over the small laundry cart he used as a portable storage unit and produced an armful of pocketbooks. For one wild moment, T.S. thought he was trying to sell him one.

"I have her pocketbook," Franklin told T.S. "I have been looking for your aunt so that I could give it to her."

T.S. stared blankly at the jumbled assortment of plastic, leather and straw bags. What in the world was he talking about? Auntie Lil's pocketbook was as big as a Buick and even harder to handle. These were wallets compared to her suitcaselike bag.

"Miss Emily's pocketbook," Franklin explained.

"I thought The Eagle had stolen it." T.S. stared at the bags. Which one was supposed to be Emily's?

"He did," Franklin explained. "But like most pocketbook thieves, he dropped it in a trash can when he was done going through it. I have collected these over the past two days. I suspect that Miss Emily's pocketbook is among them."

"There must be seven bags," T.S. pointed out.

Franklin shrugged apologetically. "There are many pocketbooks thrown in the garbage in this neighborhood. But I have developed an eye for these things. I threw away many more than this. Some had identification that made it clear it was not Miss Emily's. I whittled it down as much as I could. None of these have any identification and they are styles that Miss Emily might choose."

T.S. stared at the homeless man. "You have done a superb job," he admitted. "Auntie Lil will be delighted."

"I want to help," Franklin explained. "I have heard that you and your aunt are going to find Miss Emily's killer. I see many things out here on these streets. It is my job. I am always looking, noticing faces. I believe I could be of help."

"You can help me," Herbert Wong butted in. "I'm chief of surveillance. I could use a good pair of eyes."

Franklin nodded almost imperceptibly. "You will not be sorry," he said solemnly.

"What did you mean, it's your job to look?" T.S. wanted to know.

"I am searching for my friend who saw The Eagle breathing evil on Miss Emily. But much more important to me, I am searching for my little brother," Franklin explained. "That's why I'm here in New York City. I have promised my mamma that I will find him and bring him home to South Carolina. So, you see, I am always looking and watching anyway."

T.S. stood in silence. The man's dedication to his mother made him feel ashamed. Here was Franklin, living on the streets, eating handouts, in a city as foreign to him as Moscow, searching seven million faces in hopes of finding the one that would make his mother smile again. While T.S. could hardly stand to visit his mother once a week at the elder care facility.

On the other hand, T.S. reasoned sensibly, Franklin's mother was probably a whole hell of a lot nicer than his own.

"Excuse me, but I see many old ladies looking our way," Herbert interrupted politely. "In front of that church over there. I must surmise that the edifice is St. Barnabas."

T.S. squinted in the bright autumn sun. "You bet. And those old ladies are our other eye. We might as well plunge in before the kitchen opens and we lose them to lunch. You come, too, Franklin. You're part of the team now."

They approached the long line waiting patiently in front of St. Barnabas. T.S. had not wanted to go inside and face questions from Fran or Father Stebbins, so he was perfectly content to plot outside on the sidewalk. He gathered Adelle and the other old actresses together after they had extracted promises that they would be let back in line at their regular spots. Together, he and Herbert Wong explained their task: for lack of a better plan, they were going to watch Emily's building and take turns following everyone who entered or left. Herbert had the master notebook—descriptions and destination addresses would be given to him. In this way, they hoped to determine who was a regular tenant, who was suspicious and who might be able to tell them more about Emily.

"You said you wanted to help," T.S. told the ladies when he and Herbert had finished explaining their plan. "Here's your chance. Can you handle it?"

"Of course! But we must disguise ourselves," Adelle declared.

"Oh, yes!" the other old ladies agreed and began to twitter among themselves. They were smelling the greasepaint and hearing the roar of the crowd once again.

"It's so no one will make us," Adelle insisted when she saw the look that crossed T.S.'s face. She turned to her group and explained, "That means no one will be able to recognize us if we're following them." Her superior air was met with an indignant murmur. Clearly the other actresses knew what "make" meant and who was she to lord it over them? Oh, dear, they had to have a clear leader to nip any mutiny in the bud, T.S. realized.

"*Herbert* will be the head of operations," T.S. emphasized. Another buzz ran through the crowd: how would Adelle deal with this usurping of her power?

She started with a ladylike cough. "I have a great deal of experience handling large group efforts," she began. "I've done some directing, you know."

Herbert watched her quietly. Only his eyes flickered lightly as he surveyed the faces of the assembled group. He was gauging their reactions and loyalty to Adelle. And he was probably doing a damn fine job of it.

"I am sure you would make a fine leader," Herbert assured her in a courtly fashion, throwing in a short bow for effect. "And I am a great admirer of your work. But I find it hard to believe that a superior craftsman such as yourself should be asked to undertake the menial task of mere organization. No, you should be allowed to freely ply your craft, without any administrative cares."

"Franklin has offered to help us, as well," T.S. announced quickly, before Adelle could argue. "Herbert has assigned him to night surveillance. I cannot ask you ladies to roam these streets after midnight. It would put you in too much danger. So Franklin will detail the comings and goings between midnight and seven. He won't be able to follow anyone, but we'll still be able to keep an eye on the building's traffic pattern. Fair enough?"

They all agreed it was a workable plan and began to inch back toward their places in line. Sensing that hunger was taking priority over justice, Herbert and T.S. quickly emphasized the need for discretion, collected the assortment of pocketbooks from Franklin and beat a hasty retreat.

"You are in a hurry?" Herbert asked politely, scurrying to keep pace with T.S.

"You don't want to meet Father Stebbins," T.S. assured his friend. "So far, I have found your English impeccable and cultured. One conversation with Father Stebbins and you'll turn into a walking cliché factory."

Herbert was staring at T.S. strangely.

"What is it?" T.S. demanded, drawing to a stop at the street corner.

The retired messenger bowed deeply and reached for one of the pocketbooks slung over T.S.'s arm. "You must allow me to carry the brown one," he insisted, unsuccessfully hiding the twinkle in his eye. "It clashes with your shoes."

CHAPTER EIGHT

1. Homefront turned out to be a storefront on Tenth Avenue near the Port Authority bus terminal. Bob Fleming unlocked the door and led Auntie Lil inside. The place was deserted and just this side of clean. A circle of empty chairs stood in the front picture window, and there were neatly folded piles of clothing on a table that ran along one side wall. Donated sneakers and shoes of all styles and sizes were heaped beneath the same table. There was a counter running across the front third of the room. It was cluttered with a large coffee urn, soft drinks in a styrofoam cooler, a plate of stale-looking doughnuts and stacks of brochures featuring cover photos of smiling youths. Beyond the counter, a battered wooden desk dominated one corner of the room. Three army cots were lined up neatly against the back wall, beside a stack of extra folding chairs. A number of telephones were mounted against the remaining side wall and penciled numbers were scrawled across the paint above each instrument.

"Home sweet home," Bob Fleming said as he guided Auntie Lil to the rear of the store. "Used to be a dry cleaner's. I kept the twenty-four-hour-service sign in the window. It seemed appropriate."

"You sleep here?" Auntie Lil asked. Army cots were narrow and uncomfortable.

"No. I have a small apartment over on Tenth. This is just for the kids who are too tired to go any further. They can rest here for a couple of hours while I find a place for them in one of the regular city or private facilities. We haven't got enough money to open a bed facility of our own. Yet. Right now, I'm just an outreach and referral program. But that was more than they had. Plenty of people are willing to help runaways, but no one is willing to stand in the open and offer it. It's easy to burn out."

"Why so many telephones?" Auntie Lil nodded toward the row of instruments as she settled into a plastic chair across from his enormous desk.

"That's the one thing I can offer them. A free phone call home. Sometimes that's all it takes. But not very often. We're part of a corporate-sponsored program that pays for toll-free calls anywhere in the U.S. I encourage them to at least touch base with their parents and let them know they're okay."

"What about getting them to go home?" Auntie Lil suggested.

"Home is not such a great place for some of these kids to be." He folded his hands and stared at her. "Frankly, many are better off on their own."

Auntie Lil did not ask him to elaborate. She'd been around the world dozens of times and seen many, many different kinds of homes, including what modern psychologists liked to call dysfunctional ones. She'd seen and heard enough horror stories to last until the day she died.

"So you want to help out?" He was gazing at her strangely.

"Not exactly," she confessed, finding it impossible to lie. Which was a switch. She was usually an outrageous and prolific liar, untouched by pangs of conscience. "Why are you looking at me that way?" she asked defensively.

"Because I knew you were lying earlier when you said you wanted to volunteer," he told her calmly. "Believe me, I've met every kind of liar there is in this world and I can usually spot even the good ones. You're a pretty good one, you know. I bet the little old lady act throws everyone off."

"That's true," Auntie Lil confessed. "Obviously, not you."

"Yes. But you've redeemed yourself by immediately telling me that you are a liar. Why, and what is it that you really want?"

"I'm looking for someone. Three people actually. Do you know them?" She rummaged around in her bag and produced two photographs. The first, of Emily, received only a cursory glance from Bob Fleming.

"Can't help you," he said quietly, handing it back to Auntie Lil. He did not ask how she had obtained the gruesome photo. He stared more closely at the dimestore strip showing two young boys. His eyes flickered across the series of small photos, but his expression was unreadable. "Why do you want to know?" he asked. "Are you a relative?"

"No. Not exactly." She hesitated, unsure of how to proceed. With one woman dead, how could she afford to trust someone she didn't even know?"

"You don't want to tell me," he answered his own question. "Have they done something to you? Snatched your pocketbook? Broken into your apartment? Do you work for the police?"

"The police! Good heavens, no. I'm far too old."

"They used a seventy-nine-year-old woman two years ago to expose nursing home fraud," he pointed out. "And you look just like the type who could handle it."

"You're a very suspicious man." Auntie Lil couldn't decide whether to feel complimented or insulted. "But for your information, there is no love lost between me and the New York Police Department."

"Me, either." He was silent. They stared at one another and just as it looked like it would be a dead end, Bob Fleming sighed and combed his beard absently with roughened fingers. "How about if I lay my cards on the table, then you lay yours beside them?"

She considered his proposition. "All right," she agreed. "But you go first."

"Something funny is going on and I think it has to do with me." His voice was level, but his eyes had narrowed to hard slits. "People who used to talk to me won't talk to me anymore. People I don't even know are giving me the cold shoulder. You saw how that deli owner treated me." He stared at Auntie Lil. "Some woman has been snooping around and asking the kids questions about me. She's middle-aged. Small. Dark hair worn to the shoulders. Who is she? What does she want?"

"I assure you I have no idea," Auntie Lil replied. "I'm here on an entirely different matter. If I wasn't already up to my elbows in a different mystery, I'd try to find out for you."

"Why? Are you a private investigator?" His eyes narrowed even more. He did not like private investigators any more than the public kind.

"No. Sometimes I get involved with . . . puzzles. But I'm not affiliated with any sort of investigative company or bureau at all."

Bob Fleming's eyes darted to the street and he automatically scanned the sidewalks.

"Looks like business is slow," Auntie Lil offered.

"I wish it was. But it's always like this in the middle of the day. But they'll be here. Like vampires. When night falls. That's when they have to face what they've become. That's when they start remembering that they're only twelve or thirteen or ten years old. Night is when they have to stop playing video games and start making money. "It's when childhood starts to look pretty damn good as an alternative to the streets."

"You take it hard," Auntie Lil observed. "You look like you have the weight of the world on your shoulders."

Bob Fleming nodded. "I have a lot of weight on my shoulders. And then some. So I don't need any more. It's your turn. Why do you want to find these boys?"

Having no choice, Auntie Lil told Bob Fleming the story of Emily's death. She omitted the part about breaking into her apartment and simply said that she'd found the strip of photos among her personal belongings. "I just want to find the boys and ask them what they knew about her. Maybe they know her real name. We have to find out who she is before we can find out why she was killed."

"And the police don't care." He was not asking a question. He was stating a fact.

"They don't seem to care very much. I guess she isn't very important in the grand scheme of things." Her tone made it clear that Emily was, at least, important to Auntie Lil's grand scheme of things.

Bob Fleming sighed again. He scrutinized Auntie Lil, seemed to decide she was harmless, then ran a calloused finger down the images. "The white kid is Timmy," he told her. "Only his hair's not black anymore. It's blond. Almost white. He's been working out of this neighborhood for about a year, I think. Been on the streets for around two in all, I'd say. He hangs out with the black kid a lot. That's Little Pete. Timmy's from somewhere in the Midwest or maybe the Southwest. I think Little Pete is from around here. I've gotten them to talk to me a couple of times, but it's no use. They're not ready to give up the game."

Auntie Lil didn't have to ask what game. Despite T.S.'s belief that she be kept innocent, Auntie Lil was well aware of the darker side of life. When you've seen six-year-old prostitutes in Thailand being pushed upon strangers by their mothers, the thirteen-year-old ones in New York can seem pretty tame. "Why is it no use talking to them?" she asked.

"They've got someone taking care of them. A pimp, maybe. A sugar daddy, your generation may have called them. I don't know for sure. But he gives them money. New sneakers. Quarters for the video games. Dollars for the cheap double features. Feeds them junk food, like they like. Forget about broccoli or eating your peas. In return, they keep their mouths shut and do what he wants. They won't give up the game until he pulls the rug out from under them."

"What if he doesn't?"

Bob Fleming laughed bitterly. "The one thing I can absolutely guarantee you is that Big Daddy will pull the rug out from under them. I'm surprised they've lasted this long. They've hardened and it shows on the outside. Look at them—you can see the cracks. Any day now they'll start stealing, or figuring out how they can up their score. They'll start doing drugs, if they're not already. And then they won't be of use to this guy—whoever he is—or any of his friends."

"You don't know who he is?"

Bob Fleming shook his head. "If I did, he wouldn't still be around. I have a policy about people like him. Take them out any way that you can."

"You don't mean that," Auntie Lil protested. "That would make you as bad as them."

Bob Fleming shrugged. "My conscience is clear. And it would still be clear if I personally rid this neighborhood of another scumbag. I have no confidence in the court system to deal with these slime. And I have no trouble helping to hasten their demise."

He was a hard man, but Auntie Lil wasn't going to argue with his position. It probably took a lot more than desire to keep on trying to clean up the streets. Obsession and a fair amount of hatred would be essential, too. "Do you know how I can get in touch with them?" she asked him. "I just want to ask them a few questions about Emily."

He stared at their photos. "I might be able to get Little Pete to talk to you. I doubt Timmy will bite, though. He's cagey and suspicious. Something's going on with him. I don't know what. He got real friendly and now he's been avoiding me. Like a lot of other people I know." He slid the photos back across the desk to Auntie Lil. "I'll see what I can do about Little Pete. How do I get in touch with you?"

Auntie Lil gave him her name and phone number, then T.S.'s number as a back-up. "In a pinch, you can always get word to me through Father Stebbins or some of the soup kitchen regulars," she added.

He nodded. It was early afternoon and he already looked exhausted. "If you really want to volunteer," he said with just the tiniest spark of hope, "I could use some help."

Auntie Lil nodded her head. She didn't like to promise what she couldn't deliver, but she knew the man needed something to go on. "When all this is over," she said, "I'll see what I can do. I assume you'll take either money or time."

"Lady, I will take whatever I can get."

He accompanied Auntie Lil to the door and they shook hands farewell. As she was leaving, she noticed a young girl not more than twelve years old waiting in the shadows of a nearby doorway. Her blond hair was greasy and limp, and her tiny midriff top barely covered a childish chest and an even more childlike rounded tummy. Her hot pants were a wrinkled and grimy lime green. She wore high heels and watched Auntie Lil pass by from under a curtain of dirty bangs. Her eyes were not childish at all.

Auntie Lil walked slowly to the corner before turning around for a peek. The young girl was shyly knocking on the front door of Homefront. Bob Fleming stuck his head out and, for the first time, Auntie Lil saw him smile. His face was transformed, exhaustion giving way to hope. He nodded and gestured for her to come on inside.

Auntie Lil wondered if the young girl would be one of the few who decided to call home.

2.

Like Lemmings, they converged across the street from Emily's building: Auntie Lil, Herbert Wong and T.S. The team of volunteer tails was still at St. Barnabas, consuming their meal of the day.

"Any luck?" T.S. asked Auntie Lil.

"I've got names for the two young boys." She stared at the collection of pocketbooks held by both men. "Not very chic," she admonished them. "One well-matched accessory is usually more than enough."

"Very funny," T.S. acknowledged. "Your pal, Franklin, found these. He thinks one of them might be Emily's."

Auntie Lil's face lit up. "Excellent. I must remember to thank him."

"You'll have plenty of opportunities," T.S. assured her. "Haven't you heard? He's joined the team. Adelle has consented to let him have a bit part."

His little dig at Adelle was lost on Auntie Lil. She had caught sight of Herbert Wong's new tie pin and was busy oohing and aahing over the craftsmanship. T.S., who was not in the mood to hear from what exotic port the pin had hailed, suggested firmly that they adjourn to a more private spot before they began rummaging through the pocketbooks. "Otherwise, we'll look like a gang of thieves," he warned them. "And lord knows Lieutenant Abromowitz would seize on any chance to give us trouble."

The mention of the lieutenant reminded Auntie Lil of her need to talk with Det. George Santos. "Let's go to the Westsider and examine them," she decided for them all. "Detective Santos hangs out there and I need to have a word with him."

She led the way confidently westward, as if she frequently paraded down to the waterfront for a visit to the friendly neighborhood dive bars. Along the way, she explained the mystery of Emily's apartment. Neither T.S. or Herbert could figure it out.

"A young actress said she'd been there for over three years?" T.S. asked.

"According to my reliable source," Auntie Lil confirmed.

T.S. sighed. Auntie Lil never gave away a name when the chance to show off a "reliable source" arose. She had seen *All the President's Men* once too often. But he had no doubt that her source probably was reliable. Which wasn't the same as being infallible. "Maybe they made a mistake," he warned her. "The police might have gone to the wrong apartment."

"That's what I want to check out." She was scanning the signs of the decrepit handful of bars that dotted the Westside Highway. Most were carved out of abandoned warehouses or deserted terminals. "What a colorful neighborhood!" she cried out gaily, but her attempt fell flat. Both T.S. and Herbert were distinctly uneasy. It was as if Hell's Kitchen had abruptly given up its fight for respectability. Only danger, dirt and drunken dreams could be found along this particular stretch of lonely sidewalk.

"Why would someone choose to imbibe at such a place?" Herbert Wong wondered out loud. They had found the Westsider. It was a corner bar with windows thickly coated over with black paint. The sign, faded and dangling from a single chain, slapped against the side of the building with a dull thud every time a truck roared past—which was frequently, since the only barrier between the bar and the Westside Highway was a narrow concrete sidewalk.

Inside the Westsider was even less uplifting. For starters, it smelled sour, and old, like the bottom of a long forgotten keg of beer. The floor was cracked linoleum and coated with a sticky scum that made little sucking noises every time they lifted their feet. A row of torn fake-leather booths lined one wall and the tables between the ripped, overstuffed seats were marred by years of scratched-in initials and vaguely disreputable stains that were clearly visible even given the almost nonexistent lighting. A television at one end blared championship wrestling. The only other patron was a toothless old man perched at one end of a long bar.

He was sucking down a juice glass full of watery draft beer as he watched the televised action. Occasionally, he'd grunt with satisfaction or hoot in glee at a particularly nasty body slam.

The bartender was a barrel-shaped woman clad in a too-tight yellow knit shirt and bright blue polyester pants. She wore black glasses of a cat-eye style popular thirty years before. Her obviously dyed blonde hair swirled above her head like the top of a frozen custard ice cream cone. Some sailor had left her there in 1944, T.S. decided, and never looked back.

Engrossed in the wrestling, the bartender hardly looked up when they entered. Apparently, a little old lady dressed in expensive clothes and accompanied by an impeccably clad Asian gentleman and middle-aged executive type was not an unusual sight around the Westsider. Nor did the bartender seem interested that, between them, they were hauling seven pocketbooks.

"Hear no evil, see no evil," Herbert remarked.

They chose the booth closest to the door where the air was a little bit fresher. T.S. piled the pocketbooks into a heap in the middle of the battle-worn table.

"Drinks?" Auntie Lil suggested brightly.

"Not without an inoculation first," T.S. declared.

"Where do we begin?" Herbert picked up a small green suede bag. "Examine the contents and guess which one is hers?"

"No. We can do better than that," Auntie Lil decided. "The other actresses insist that Emily always carried a matching handbag. She was wearing a light blue dress with black trim that day."

"Are you sure?" T.S. asked. Last time he had seen Emily, she was wearing a rubber sheet and nothing more. Details on her dress had flown right out the window after that.

"It was a Walter Williams original," Auntie Lil announced confidently. "First appearing in his Fall '59 line. Available at Saks and Bergdorf Goodman's in New York. And at selected finer establishments across the country. Retailing at $130, which was not peanuts back then."

Herbert hee-heed quietly as if he had just heard an irresistible joke and T.S. had to be content with rolling his eyes. He should have known better than to question her ability to remember a dress.

"So, it was either this black one here . . ." she placed it to one side and continued, "or this black one. Possibly this brown one, though I would certainly disapprove. The white one is out. She had better sense than that. And this straw bag might have passed . . . but not these." She pushed a purple job and the green suede to one side. "Dig in."

Herbert opened up the straw pocketbook and emptied out the contents in a small heap in front of him, revealing a small rayon wallet, now empty except for a photo of a chubby baby of indeterminate sex. The bag also contained three pencils, a nearly empty purple lipstick, a small compact of garish eyeshadow and a $10 coupon off weekly sessions at a nearby tanning salon. "Not hers," he decided, shaking his head.

Auntie Lil was quick enough to empty out two. But the brown bag held a prophylactic and was ruled out on that basis. The other, a black one, held an address book that inexplicably contained only male names. A matching wallet was crammed with photographs, though no money or credit cards. Most of the photographs were of beefy young men in macho poses. The inscriptions on these photos quickly eliminated the pocketbook as being Emily's, in Auntie Lil's opinion.

"You're sure?" T.S. asked. "After all, this one fellow's written: 'Thanks for an evening I'll never forget.' Maybe she took him to the theater."

"It has to be the one you're hoarding," Auntie Lil insisted. "Empty it before I burst."

T.S. did not answer. He was too busy staring at the clippings he'd pulled from the small black pocketbook.

"What is it?" Herbert asked.

"These clippings," T.S. began. He spread them out across the table top.

"What are they? Just a columnist for one of the local papers if I remember right," Auntie Lil replied. She held one up and examined it. "This one is about corruption in awarding liquor licenses in Manhattan."

"This one is about a schoolteacher who beats children with a paddle," T.S. added. "And this one exposes inferior test scores of Catholic high-school graduates."

"What's so special about that?" Herbert asked. "The author is an investigative reporter, correct?"

"Correct," T.S. replied. "But not *just* an investigative reporter. She's my favorite reporter. Margo McGregor. I was just trying to read her column today, but she's been away on vacation."

"Well, I doubt it's important," Auntie Lil decided, scraping the pile of possessions her way. "There's no way Emily could have had a connection to any of those stories. Perhaps she simply liked to cut and save interesting articles. If this is even her purse." She quickly sorted through the small stack of items. "A tasteful shade of mauve lipstick. Could be Emily's . . . Here's a small pocket Bible, so we're still in the running . . . and . . . bingo! This is her pocketbook. And this is the proof." She spread out an entire handful of theater ticket stubs that had been carefully bound together with a large paper clip. "She was saving them for her collection."

"Notice what's missing," T.S. pointed out. "No wallet, no identification, no address book."

"No way to know who she is or where she lives," Herbert summed up.

"Yes," Auntie Lil agreed. "He stole this to make it harder, if not impossible, for the police to find out who she was."

"That means we're right back where we started," Herbert said sadly.

"Not quite," T.S. broke in. They looked up at him expectantly. "We now know she liked Margo McGregor's writing."

Auntie Lil did not have time to be irritated. The bartender had finally roused herself from her pro wrestling stupor and was standing by their table. "Sorry to keep you waiting," she boomed in a nasal voice. "Most people around here don't exactly expect table service. Which is good since my feet are killing me." She stopped abruptly and stared at the pile of discarded pocketbooks, then looked from T.S. to Auntie Lil to Herbert Wong. A wad of gum worked itself from one cheek, across her tongue, and into the other cheek as she puzzled the situation out. Finally, she shrugged and addressed Auntie Lil. "Now that's a switch," the bartender admitted. "Usually, it's the little old ladies who get their pocketbooks snatched. Not the other way around."

"We didn't steal these," T.S. interrupted firmly. "We found them in the trash and are now trying to determine the owners." It didn't sound very convincing, not even to his own ears. Herbert even winced and T.S. resisted the temptation to ask if he could have done any better on such short notice.

"That so?" The bartender shifted on her aching feet and stifled a yawn. "Takes all kinds, I guess. Now, what d'ya want?" she demanded with a crack of her gum. Then, noticing their expensive attire, a brief smiled curled the corners of her mouth. Perhaps this group had actually heard of a tip before. She'd give it her best shot. "Afternoon special is on," she added politely. "Draft beer's sixty cents."

"Is there a minimum?" Auntie Lil inquired politely.

"Yeah. Two drinks per floor show. And here comes the first show." The bartender's right foot darted out and she crushed a large roach firmly beneath her plastic shoe. It crunched and she whooped at her own joke. When no one else laughed, she coughed, straightened up, and added in a get-tough-quick voice, "People don't get to sit here who don't buy nuthin', if that's what you mean, honey."

"My nephew and I will have the special," Auntie Lil quickly decided. The bartender stared at T.S. like she'd never run across the concept of a nephew before.

Herbert Wong politely ordered a glass of water. The bartender shifted her stare to him, then ambled behind the bar, busied herself over an unseen sink and returned carrying a tray that held three small smudged glasses. Herbert's water was tepid and slightly brownish. In fact, it looked a whole lot like the beer.

"One water for Mr. Rockefeller here," she said, plunking the glass on the table. "And here's a couple of brews for you two mad, mad party people."

"We're looking for a Detective George Santos," Auntie Lil said.

"Yeah? You family? Or planning to confess?" The bartender eyed the pocketbooks again and cackled loudly. "Well, George don't usually come in until five." She snapped her gum and squinted at them to get a better view. "Say, what do folks like you want with a guy named 'Santos'? You don't look like no Spaniards to me." Herbert Wong received a particularly thorough once-over.

"We're friends," T.S. said.

"Georgie's got no friends. Just an ex-wife, a couple of suspects and a lot of acquaintances." The bartender followed this gloomy pronouncement by marching back to the bar and pouring herself a healthy shot of vodka. She slammed it back in one gulp and banged the glass down on the bar.

T.S. watched the bartender's gesture with envy. Such blatant uncouthness! Such freedom! An irresistible urge overcame him. "Allow me," T.S. yelled to her from across the room. He peeled off a few bills from the small wad in his pocket and threw them on the table for effect. "Have another on us. And what the heck— buy the house a round of drinks!" he returned Auntie Lil's stare and confessed in a low whisper, "Sorry. But I've always wanted to do that."

The house—which consisted entirely of the toothless old man—cackled its gleeful approval. He pounded the bar, hooting and grunting with an enthusiasm far surpassing his demonstrated zeal for wrestling.

"You for real?" The bartender eyed the bills as if they might be counterfeit, then shrugged and poured herself another. "Sure you won't join me?"

"No, thank you, madam. This will do us just nicely." T.S. raised his beer glass in salute and nudged Auntie Lil until she did the same.

"Have you lost your mind?" she whispered to her nephew.

"Not at all. You're always telling me to loosen up." T.S. took a deep breath, followed by a tiny sip, which ended up in a fine spray over the pocketbooks. "This beer tastes like it should be tested for steroids," he said, swabbing his mouth out with his handkerchief.

Auntie Lil took his word for it. "Let's come back later," she decided. "I can think of better places to kill a few hours."

"A good idea," Herbert said. "Perhaps by then the rust will have settled to the bottom of my glass of water. I have no doubt it will still be on this table." He led the retreat by hopping up and waving to the bartender. "We shall return," he promised as he bowed his head at her. She bowed hers back, the chain on her cateye glasses jingling as she did so.

"We'd like to surprise Detective Santos," T.S. added, throwing a few more bills onto the pile.

"Sure you would. Wouldn't we all?" She slammed back her second shot of vodka as her cat-eyes followed them out the door.

"I could hardly breathe in there!" Auntie Lil gasped as she gulped in bursts of air that, while not exactly fresh given they were standing by a major highway, were at least foul in a more familiar way.

"They ought to mop the floor once in a while," T.S. observed. "It wouldn't hurt the atmosphere any."

"Your Detective Santos must be one depressed man," Herbert Wong added. "A healthy person would not frequent such an establishment."

"I'll say. I feel like having a few tests run on myself after that visit," T.S. declared.

Auntie Lil just sniffed. She'd seen worse in her day. "I'm coming back early this evening," she announced. "Are you with me or against me?"

"Damn right, I'm with you. You're not prowling around here after dark alone." T.S. looked up and down the deserted sidewalks. Cars whizzed by every few seconds without slowing. It was a lonely place for a bar and a great place for a mugging.

"I must begin the surveillance," Herbert apologized. "I will not be able to join you."

"Then it's just you and me, kid," T.S. told Auntie Lil. "But if we're coming back here, I've got to confess that I definitely need to find a nice bar and have a few drinks first."

Several drinks, several hours and several dinners later, T.S. and Auntie Lil returned to the Westsider. A few hours had made a big difference. Not necessarily a positive difference, but a big one just the same. They could hear the loudest change as they approached. Behind the black-painted windows, jukebox music blared and they were assaulted by a fresh wave of pulsating sound when they pushed open the front door. The female bartender was gone, replaced by two fat balding men in dirty white aprons who scurried back and forth serving the thirsty crowd. Nearly every stool at the bar was taken and many of the booths were occupied as well. The patrons were an odd mixture of construction workers, sanitation and traffic department employees, neighborhood rummies and an occasional waitress still in her uniform. The smell of old beer had been replaced by the odor of bodies packed together après ten hours of manual labor.

They found Detective Santos sitting alone at a booth, staring at a soundless baseball game on the television. Three empty highball glasses sat before him. He held a fourth, filled only with ice, cradled in both hands.

Without asking, Auntie Lil and T.S slid into the seat across from him. He looked up with bleary eyes. "No hope," he told them, shaking his head sadly. "They're twelve games out and only have ten games left. Another magnificent season is at end for the New York Yankees." He raised his glass of ice cubes toward the television set in toast.

"Do you know who we are?" Auntie Lil demanded. She was furious to find her friendly detective replaced by this boozing, discouraged human being.

Detective Santos stared at her, mystified. "Is this a scam?" he asked. He answered his own question by flipping open a small wallet and displaying a gold detective's badge. "If it is, better find a new mark."

"Young man. You're drunk and it's not even eight o'clock." Auntie Lil was truly indignant. She did not believe in getting drunk until ten o'clock, at the earliest.

"I remember you," George Santos said suddenly. He leaned forward and blinked. "You're the lady that Lieutenant Abromowitz hates."

"That's me. And this is my nephew, Theodore. The lieutenant hates him, too," she added helpfully.

"Is that so?" Santos looked T.S. up and down and smiled drunkenly. "In that case, it's a pleasure to meet you."

"The pleasure is all mine," T.S. returned drily.

"Are you on duty?" Auntie Lil demanded.

Santos tilted back his head and stared at her through red-rimmed eyes. "Of course I'm not on duty. I'm piss-ant drunk. Can't you tell?"

"Yes, I can tell," Auntie Lil replied. "And it's a shame, because we wanted to ask you some questions."

"Ask away," the detective told them casually, waving a hand in the general direction of the bar. One of the bartenders scurried over and set a fresh drink in front of him. "Thank you, my good man," Santos told the bartender. "Would any of you lovely people care for a drink or two?"

"No, thanks," T.S. said. "I'll let you have my share."

"Most kind of you," Santos admitted with exaggerated politeness. He belched lightly and covered his mouth, then sighed. His shoulders slumped as if a plug had been pulled and all of his energy drained out at once. "What do you want to know?" he said glumly. "It's about the old lady, right?"

"Right," Auntie Lil answered crisply. "What have you found out?"

"Nothing. Nothing at all." The detective shook his head and murmured into his drink. "Perhaps I should explain," he said.

"Perhaps you should," Auntie Lil pointed out.

He sighed and banged his glass back on the table, sloshing out a small wave of alcohol that emanated an unmistakable odor. Ye gads. The man was drinking straight gin. No wonder he looked and acted like hell. "Your friend was killed two days ago," he began slowly, as if warming up to relate a fairy tale. "And since that time, two more murders have landed on my desk. Murders of people with names and families and addresses. And clues. Which is no small consideration."

"In other words, Emily's death has been put on the back burner," T.S. said.

"I didn't say that." Santos held up a hand as if to stop any protests on their part. "We've sent her fingerprints to Quantico, but nothing will come of it. Not unless she has a record, which is unlikely. I've called every shelter in New York and distributed a Wirephoto of her over police wires. No luck yet, but that's all I can do. Plus, I personally investigated an anonymous tip today. Someone called claiming to have her address."

"That was no anonymous tipster," Auntie Lil said indignantly. "That was me."

"You?" He stared at her closely. "You wasted two hours of my time."

"You went to the wrong address," Auntie Lil stated flatly.

The detective fumbled in his pocket and produced his notebook. "326 West Forty-sixth Street," he read. "Apartment 6-B."

"That's right," T.S. confirmed.

"I went there," he said calmly, sounding more sober than before. "A young girl answered, late twenties. An actress. Said she'd been living there for over three years. There was no little old lady. The apartment looked completely normal. You people are mistaken."

"The place was totally ransacked!" Auntie Lil insisted. "Didn't you see?"

Detective Santos stared at her for a long moment. "How do you know?" he asked evenly.

"Know what?" Auntie Lil demanded.

"That it was ransacked?"

T.S. intervened. "We just heard, that's all. Never mind." He kicked Auntie Lil under the table, not anxious to be booked for breaking and entering by a drunken detective. "Are you sure that the young woman lived there?"

"Look. I talked to the resident. I talked to the super. There's no old lady living there at all. Just some babe with dyed blonde hair and an aerobically fit actress body."

Auntie Lil was angry; T.S. was mystified.

"What about The Eagle?" Auntie Lil demanded. "Have you found him?"

"The Eagle?" Santos shook his head like he thought she was crazy and looked to T.S. for confirmation.

"Don't you look at him like I'm insane," Auntie Lil ordered. "A man swears he saw The Eagle behind Emily that day. He's probably the one who poisoned her."

The detective sighed. "We don't know anything about an eagle. No one we interviewed mentioned an eagle." He was quiet, staring into his drink. "My guess is that you people were given the wrong apartment number. Sounds to me like you went there. I wouldn't want to know if you did." He shrugged. "Maybe it was burglarized, maybe it wasn't. If it was, the woman who lives there doesn't want me to know."

"Why wouldn't she?" T.S. asked.

"You must be joking." The detective took a healthy swig of gin. "It was probably drug-related. What's she going to do? Report ten grams of coke missing?" He laughed as if he'd said something funny, but neither T.S. nor Auntie Lil was amused. He fell silent, staring into the bottom of his drink.

"Can't you tell us anything?" Auntie Lil demanded after a moment of fruitless silence.

Santos jumped, as if he'd forgotten they were there. "I can tell you that if this case had ever mattered in the least, they would not have given it to me." He raised his large brown eyes to them and blinked sadly. "I am not at the bottom of the barrel, you understand. I still manage to stay sober during my shift. But I'm pretty damn close. Everyone knows that I'm a drunk, no one gives me any real work and the only reason I'm probably still on the force is that the lieutenant is too stupid to figure out yet what a loser I am." He shrugged. "And that's nothing but the facts, ma'am."

There was nothing more to say. They left the detective behind and snagged cabs that could take them home and away from the Westsider as quickly as possible.

T.S. was thoroughly depressed by the time he reached his apartment. Brenda and Eddie met him at the door and he was so distracted that he opened two cans of wet cat food and they snagged a bonus feast. But he was immediately cheered by two minor developments. Lenny Melk had called and tracked down the building's real owner. He'd divulge the information the following morning, as soon as T.S. met him with payment in cash. So much for trust. But at least he had the information.

The second message was even more uplifting. Lilah had called to say that her day had been productive but boring, and that she'd missed the chance to detect by his side. It wasn't the same as saying that she'd missed him, technically speaking, but it was enough to inspire him to sing the theme song from *The Impossible Dream* in the shower before he hit the sack.

CHAPTER NINE

1. Lenny Melk's office turned out to be a coffee shop at the corner of Centre and Duane Streets. He was waiting for T.S. out front. "You're the guy, right?" he said, eyeing T.S.'s charcoal gray sweater.

"It's nice to be so unforgettable," T.S. answered drily. "I knew you in a minute."

"I'm kind of a distinctive guy," Lenny admitted, automatically brushing the dandruff flakes off of his shoulders. He wore the same suit he'd worn two days before. It had not been dry-cleaned in the interim.

"Let me buy you a bagel," he offered T.S. "They got great lox here."

Lenny actually did spring for the bagel, but first T.S. had to hand over his cash payment. "I don't like to carry a lot of cash around with me," the entrepreneur confided to T.S. as they waited for their order. "Too dangerous."

"I agree. It's much safer to let your bookie hold it for you."

Lenny stared at T.S. closely and couldn't decide if he'd been joking, so he compromised and ignored the remark. "I've got that information for you," he said, after they had found a spot outside on a nearby low brick wall. "Let's sit here. We can watch all the secretaries going in to work. Take a look at that one, would you?"

T.S. did not indulge in petty ogling of unknown women. He took a look at his bagel instead and then took a bite. Lenny was right. It was excellent. They chewed in silence for a few minutes. Or, at least, T.S. chewed. Lenny Melk went right to the swallow.

"They got a whole string of dummy companies set up," Lenny finally confided, as he licked extra cream cheese from the paper wrapping. "But it's easy to find your way through if you know what you're doing. Like me."

156

"What's the bottom line?" T.S. mumbled through a mouthful of bagel.

"Everything seems to come back to some guy name of Lance Worthington. He runs an outfit called Broadway Backers. Last listed address is 1515 Broadway. Ring a bell?"

T.S. shook his head. "Never heard of the guy."

"Me, either. Must not be any kind of mover or shaker." Lenny bit off a chunk of bagel with gusto. "Speaking of movers and shakers," he sputtered, nodding his head toward a young woman late for work, who had abandoned decorum in favor of speed.

"You find out anything else?" T.S. was nearing the end of his bagel and was ready to move on to more dignified tasks.

"Well, the guy owns a couple of buildings in the neighborhood. One of them is two doors down. The other's on Tenth Avenue." He gave T.S. a crumpled wad of paper. Several addresses were scrawled across the center of the page and the margins were filled with notes like, "19-1/Stormy Spirit: 2nd at Aqueduct."

"Thanks," T.S. told Lenny. "Perhaps we shall meet again one day." He shook the man's hand firmly and ignored the small smear of cream cheese that squeezed between their fingers like putty. It was vastly preferable to watching Lenny Melk wipe his hands on the pants legs of the already well-abused suit.

"A pleasure doing business with you," Lenny declared. By the time T.S. reached the corner and turned toward the subway, the self-proclaimed real estate consultant was already heading for a nearby telephone, optimistically patting the wad of cash in his pocket.

2. Auntie Lil and Herbert Wong were waiting for T.S. at the Delicious Deli. It was obvious from their faces that something big had happened. After introducing him to the deli owner, Auntie Lil pulled T.S. so close that he was practically in her lap, then whispered in his ear. "Be discreet. I'm not sure we can trust him entirely." She nodded toward Billy, who had returned to slicing slabs of roast beef at a rotary cutter located at the far end of the counter. The whirr would have made it impossible for him to eavesdrop.

"Then why are we here?" T.S. asked sensibly. "There are ten coffee shops to every block in this neighborhood.

"Because he knows things," Auntie Lil whispered back. "I can tell. And I want to find out what they are."

T.S. resisted the temptation to roll his eyes. Auntie Lil thrived on adding drama to any situation, even an already dramatic one.

"Listen to what Herbert's got," Auntie Lil told him, forgetting to whisper in her excitement.

Herbert carefully opened a leather-bound notebook. "This is the log," he explained solemnly. "Franklin is an excellent observer. He gave an impeccable report on last night's comings and goings. There is much activity there in the dead of the night. Adelle and her friends added more, but they tend to get caught up in speculative detail. I do not find it necessary to fantasize on the private lives of residents, but they seem to believe the information is important." Translation: he had left them arguing about whether one of the residents was actually an actress or a call girl. "Already, we have spotted several suspicious instances. I will give you the most important ones."

T.S. leaned forward, caught up in the excitement, and tried to see what Herbert had written in the notebook. Herbert picked it up and pressed it closer to his chest. "No sense peeking. I have a special shorthand. I will summarize for you."

The most important events were indeed suspicious. The same man had visited Emily's building three times the previous night. Once at ten o'clock; again at half past one in the morning; and for a final time just after three o'clock. "He was the same man, just kept going in and out with different people."

"How do you know he's the same man?" T.S. asked.

"Descriptions of him match exactly," Herbert said, "once you separate the facts from the fictions perpetuated by the excitable actresses. He is not very tall, short black hair thinning in front, very small ears and he wears a very expensive tan cashmere coat. No hat. Plus, he is chauffeured around in a silver Cadillac, so that makes it easy, too."

"But it's who he was *with* that's suspicious," Auntie Lil butted in, pressing T.S.'s arm in her excitement. "Tell him."

"The first time, he entered with a cheap blonde—that is Miss Adelle's description—very much younger than himself. But when he leaves, he leaves with a young boy who matches the description of the white boy in the small photos found in Emily's apartment. Except that his hair is blond, not black."

"Remember, Bob Fleming told me that the boy had recently dyed his hair," Auntie Lil reminded them. "So, I'm almost sure it's Timmy."

"Shortly after that, a middle-aged man leaves the building in a very big hurry. He had entered it approximately an hour before, but we were not able to ascertain his exact destination there. It is still early when he leaves, so Adelle herself follows him. He stops at Show World—this is a pornographic palace located near the Port Authority—and does not leave there for thirty more minutes. At which point, Adelle loses him in the Port Authority." Herbert bobbed his head in apology. "We cannot all be as skilled as myself in surveillance."

"No, of course not," T.S. murmured. "Go on."

"The second time that the man in the cashmere coat drives up, he is with a tall black man. Very rough-looking."

"Tell him! Tell him!" Auntie Lil commanded, practically bouncing up and down in her seat.

Herbert shrugged. "Maybe this is true. Maybe it is not. Eva, she is one of Adelle's loudest followers—"

"I know who Eva is," T.S. interrupted. "The actress with the bad haircut who had been feuding with Emily."

"That is her," Herbert confirmed. "She says that she saw something funny on the man's arm."

"Which man's arm?" T.S. asked.

"The black man's arm. He was not wearing a coat, despite the slight chill. He was wearing only a short black T-shirt. And beneath one of the sleeves, Eva sees feet."

"Feet?" T.S. was mystified.

"A tattoo of feet," Herbert explained. "Not feet, but more like talons." He curled his hands into claws and illustrated for them. "The feet of an animal with talons, clutching sprigs of branches in them."

"The Eagle!" Auntie Lil explained. Don't you see? He has a huge tattoo of an eagle on his arm. That's why the old man at the soup kitchen kept talking about The Eagle. This is the man who poisoned Emily. Almost certainly."

T.S. was doubtful. For one thing, the information came from Eva. For another, they were guessing at the hidden meaning of words babbled by a probable lunatic. Finally, it had been the middle of the night.

"How could Eva possibly have spotted such a detail?" he demanded to know.

"That is the most clever thing," Herbert said in admiration. "She was right there by the stoop. Not three feet away. They passed right by her and up the stairs."

"That could be dangerous," T.S. said firmly. "I told you to warn them."

"No, not dangerous at all." Herbert broke out in a wide smile.

"She was dressed most convincingly as a bag lady. I did not even recognize her myself. In fact"—he began to laugh, caught his breath and went on—"she is so convincing that the man in the cashmere coat gives her a dollar bill!"

"Okay, okay," T.S. conceded. "Eva makes a great bag lady and she sees the tail end of an eagle tattoo on this man's arm. What next?"

"The man never leaves the building," Herbert explains. "He is still in there."

"Which man?" T.S. asked again.

"The Eagle. The cashmere coat does leave, only this time he is not with a blonde and not with the tall black man. He is with a cheap prostitute. On this point, everyone agrees. She is tall and dresses not very nice."

"Let me fill in the rest," T.S. said. He put his hands against his head and shut his eyes as if he were struggling to foresee the future. "She was wearing a wig, hair piled high. Probably spike heels. She's black and wears mini-dresses that set off the color of her skin. The dresses don't cover very much. She favors torn stockings and long gloves. And she's definitely getting ready to go to work along Tenth Avenue."

"That's right!" Herbert confirmed with keen admiration. "Very good. You have met the lady before?"

"That is no lady. That is Miss Leteisha Swann."

Auntie Lil was staring at him strangely. "How do you know the name of that . . . woman of the night, Theodore?"

He held up a hand and winked. "I can do my own detecting, thank you. How I know is immaterial. That I *do* know is my little secret."

Auntie Lil looked two parts scandalized and one part annoyed. T.S. loved it.

Herbert coughed discreetly and murmured, "If I may continue . . . Mr. Cashmere Coat leaves with Miss Leteisha Swann in his silver car and all is relatively quiet." He paused to consult his notes. "People come and go, but we have ascertained that they live there. Four of the residents have roles in nearby Broadway shows. They arrived in stage makeup at appropriate times on foot. Tonight, we will follow them and confirm."

"More working actors than I thought," T.S. admitted. "When did Cashmere Coat return?"

"Not until three o'clock in the morning. By himself. He enters for a few minutes and when he comes out, he has something like a book in his hand. Franklin has taken over the surveillance and was across the street, so he could not see for sure. Then Franklin breaks the rules."

"Fortunately," Auntie Lil interrupted.

"Yes. Most fortuitous," Herbert agreed. "When Cashmere Coat does not get into the Cadillac and instead starts to walk towards Times Square on foot, Franklin follows him. He knows the man has been in and out all night and sees this as suspicious. The silver car trails the man by half a block and Franklin follows behind the car. Cashmere Coat is walking and looking around, obviously seeking out someone. He stops and has a few words with the cashier of a not-very-nice movie theater at the corner of Forty-fifth Street and Eighth Avenue, then continues on foot. He looks in doorways and down side streets. Finally, he cuts across Shubert Alley and enters a building at 1515 Broadway. He is inside for twenty minutes and when he comes out, he does not have the booklike object with him. He gets in the silver car and it drives away. Franklin returns to his post."

"1515 Broadway?" T.S. said. "That's the same address as the man who owns the building. He has a company there called Broadway Backers."

"Good," Auntie Lil declared firmly. "The game is afoot. You go to 1515 Broadway and I will go find Detective Santos and tell him that The Eagle is in Emily's building."

T.S. looked at her skeptically. "Santos will not be in the mood to hear it."

Auntie Lil shrugged. "What else can we do? We can't let The Eagle get away."

"He won't believe you," T.S. insisted. "He had the apartment checked. Someone else is living there now."

"I'll beg," Auntie Lil conceded.

Herbert cleared his throat gently. "I hesitate to ask, but is it possible you may have made a mistake?"

Auntie Lil straightened her posture indignantly. "Certainly not."

"Just the same, it might be prudent to somehow verify that Emily did live in the building and that a fraud is now being perpetrated."

"How are we going to do that?" T.S. asked. "It was hard enough getting information the first time around. All we had to go on was this guy here, who called her The Pineapple Lady, for God's sake, and some man who liked weird-looking Jamaican stew who *thought* she lived in the building. It's a miracle we found her in the first place. It's not exactly like people are stepping forward by the dozen to verify her residency."

Herbert's burnished face wrinkled in intense concentration. They waited silently and were rewarded when he finally looked up, eyes calm once again. "Then we will work with what we have," he announced.

"Such as?" T.S. wanted to know.

"She liked pineapple," Herbert said simply.

T.S. stared at him, mystified.

"When I resume my shift, I will ask the owner of the Korean fruit stand on the corner if he knows her," Herbert explained.

"He won't tell you a thing," T.S. warned. "I doubt he even speaks English."

"No need to." Herbert modestly brushed dust from his jacket shoulder. "I speak Korean. That is why he will tell me everything. Approach a man in his own language and you are displaying the ultimate respect. It is an irresistible request for help."

"You speak Korean?" T.S. asked, impressed. Herbert was always surprising him.

"Yes. I learned it during the Korean War. Leave it all to me."

"Everything all right here?" Billy interrupted. The deli owner had been standing behind them. All three of the assembled friends wondered for how long.

"We're fine," T.S. assured him. "Just fine." The man moved back behind the counter and began slicing cuts of cheese. "We're meeting somewhere else later," T.S. decided. "I don't trust this guy. Herbert, you're checking with the fruit stand then you're back watching the building, right?"

"Correct. Everyone else will be eating at St. Barnabas for the next few hours, so I must take up the post myself."

"Okay. Auntie Lil—meet me at Mike's American Bar and Grill when you're done at the precinct. It's at Tenth and Forty-fifth."

"Why not Robert's?" she asked. "You keep talking about it. I want to see it."

T.S. was not anxious to become reacquainted with the waiter there. "Let's go to Mike's where we're completely unknown."

They agreed and dispersed towards their tasks.

3.   T.S. could not resist the opportunity to observe Herbert in action. He stood a discreet distance away from the fruit stand watching as Herbert approached a small man in a white apron. He was cutting chunks of fruit from a pile of slightly bruised canta-loupes and pineapples, and was assembling small fruit salads for sale at exorbitant prices to business people too busy to eat any other way but on the run.

Herbert bowed to him from a respectful distance and the man bobbed his head in a terse greeting back. His face was a carefully blank New York mask until Herbert spoke a few words in Korean. Suddenly, the fruit stand owner's face lit up. What followed was a furious conversation involving many smiles, much handshaking and a whole lot more bobbing of heads. After a moment of what seemed to T.S. to be pandemonium but was clearly communication at its finest, the fruit stand owner nodded his head vigorously and took a few steps up Forty-sixth Street. He pointed out Emily's building and nodded again. Herbert beamed and grasped the man's hand in thanks. Bowing, they departed company.

"Well, that certainly worked," T.S. admitted.

"No sweat," Herbert said modestly. "Though if it hadn't worked, I'm quite sure a twenty-dollar bill would have convinced him to talk."

T.S. left the retired messenger to his surveillance and started out for Times Square, where his own task awaited him. That Herbert Wong. He was a most intriguing mixture of old and new.

4. The huge chrome and brick building that was 1515 Broadway stretched many stories skyward. A token desk man sat reading the sports section of a tabloid and did not bother to look up when T.S. passed by.

T.S. quickly found Broadway Backers listed on the seventh floor and took one of the elevators up. The door opened onto a long hall lined with many offices. Broadway Backers was either a sham or not successful enough to merit the entire floor.

He found the right door at the far end of the hall. It had a small plaque and, in a burst of unoriginality, the ubiquitous comic and tragic faces found on green rooms and theater doors all across America. There was no bell, so he simply pushed open the door and entered. A plump redhead—who was unarguably overripe but probably not really a redhead—was talking on the phone, her expression indicating it was a friend (a very close friend) instead of a professional call.

Behind her, in a glassed-in office, a short man dressed in a good suit was waving his arms in front of a well-groomed couple. The couple was as sleek and plump as a pair of otters in the zoo. The short man's mouth opened and shut rapidly while his arms windmilled. None of this seemed to be convincing the couple.

They crossed their arms and rolled their eyes, almost in unison, and then the female half of the couple lit a cigarette and began to speak. The short man never bothered to slow down, so the two of them yammered at each other behind the glass in a furious panto-mime of noncommunication. T.S. was glad the soundproofing spared him the details. He hated it when two people talked at once.

"Here's a big, juicy kiss," the receptionist cooed. T.S. looked up in astonished dread, but she was only bidding a fond farewell to her telephone mate.

"Can I help you?" she asked T.S. in what was her version of the perfect receptionist's voice, gleaned from years of watching television. Her accent was unfortunate. She hailed from the outer boroughs and it showed. If she was working here in hopes of breaking into show business, the accent would have to disappear—or she would.

"I'm looking for Mr. Lance Worthington," T.S. told her. That part was easy. What he intended to do with Lance Worthington af-ter he found him was another matter. T.S. had no idea what he would say. He kept telling himself that all he wanted was a chance to evaluate the man. See if he was on the up and up. After three decades as a personnel manager, T.S. was pretty good at picking out the genuine articles from the phonies.

"Well, Mr. Worthington is in, but he's not available right now." She already had the phone off the receiver and was ready to move on to the next entry in her personal address book.

"That's him?" T.S. nodded toward the glassed-in office.

"That is *he*," she informed him importantly. "And he absolutely positively cannot be disturbed because he is in the middle of hav-ing creative differences with the writers."

"Creative differences?" T.S. asked. No one in the office looked particularly creative and the differences looked more like fatal di-visions.

"That's what producers do," the receptionist told him crossly. "If you were in the business you would know. They have creative differences with the writers."

"Those two are the writers?" It was none of his business, but he couldn't help the question. The couple looked more like they should be wrangling for a better table at Sardi's than writing Broadway shows. The woman was decked out in a fur wrap, for God sake. If they were writing a show, it had to be the sequel to *How To Succeed In Business Without Really Trying*.

"It's a musical about Davy Crockett," the receptionist explained patiently while making it plain that she was being patient. "He writes the book. She writes the music."

Davy Crockett? If those two knew anything about pioneers, T.S. was Ponce de Léon. "I'll come back later," he quickly told the receptionist as he scrutinized Lance Worthington, trying to determine if this was the man who'd been seen at Emily's building three times the night before. He was certainly smarmy enough to fit the description, which had been rather vague. But that was hardly enough for a positive identification. Wait—the man reached up and rubbed his ears, an action T.S. didn't begrudge as the stout woman was still stalking around the office, bellowing. But the short man's ears were very interesting. They were tiny and shaped like cookies. In fact, they looked just like a chimpanzee's ears. Either the man had a habit of pulling at them or he was undergoing aural torture. What was it that Herbert had said? Oh, yes: Mr. Cashmere Coat had very small ears.

The man's next movement confirmed his identity. He shook his head vigorously and looked at his watch, turned his back on the couple and headed for a hook on the back of his office door. Donning a tan cashmere coat, he spoke abruptly to the couple and reached for the doorknob.

"I'll be back," T.S. promised the receptionist, turning abruptly and heading for the hall before he came face to face with Lance Worthington. He wanted to meet him, but not like this. He now had a better plan, a much better plan, in mind.

Turning his back, T.S. paused at the doorway of another office and fumbled in his pockets as if searching for keys. Lance Worthington exited Broadway Backers and passed directly behind him, not more than a foot away. He was humming something T.S. could not recognize. Perhaps the music to his new show. The producer reached the elevator and jabbed the button impatiently. T.S. stared at him out of the corner of one eye. Lance Worthington was a small man, not more than five-eight, with short arms and stubby legs and a rounded head. There was not much of note about him: he moved impatiently with jerky motions, wore expensive shoes, had thinning hair and only a pair of small dark eyes stood out in an otherwise nondescript face. Until he drew attention to those ears. The producer tugged at one, then jabbed the elevator button a few more times for good measure and looked at his watch. If the elevator didn't hurry, T.S. would be left standing in the hall holding a whole lot more than his keys in his hand. Fortunately, a car arrived and Lance Worthington boarded. T.S. caught a final glimpse of his thinning scalp and small round head just as the elevator door shut. Boy, did T.S. hate those ears.

5.

Auntie Lil was steamed. The desk sergeant at Midtown North would not let her past the entrance area.

"I demand to see Detective Santos," she told him for the third time.

"Demand away. The man's not here." The sergeant leaned forward and parked a fist against his chin so he could get a better look at Auntie Lil. He was a budding novelist and was collecting colorful characters for his first book. This old dame was a doozy.

Auntie Lil glared at him. "You certainly take a casual view of your job."

Out of habit, the sergeant checked the position of her pocketbook. It looked big enough to hurt if swung with sufficient force. "Lady, I cannot make a man appear when he is not here. I am an officer of the law, not a magician. Would you like to see anyone else in connection with your problem?"

"No. When do you expect him in?"

"We expected him in this morning," the sergeant replied. "When he actually arrives is anyone's guess. George is that kind of guy."

She did not bother to thank him—what for?—and marched from the precinct angrily, shouldering past a handcuffed suspect and throwing him against a folding chair. The suspect tripped over it and landed on the floor. The arresting officer looked after Auntie Lil in admiration, but she was moving too fast to accept the compliment.

She reached Mike's American Bar and Grill before T.S. It was deserted, except for a woman behind the bar and a handful of Mexican cooks sitting at a table enjoying cigarettes before the lunch rush. For some inexplicable reason, huge clusters of plastic grapes hung from the ceiling in endless waves and fake Grecian columns were parked willy-nilly throughout the interior. Oversized wine glasses served as flowerpots for silk grapevines that cascaded across the center of every table. The bartender, a willowy young woman with straight brown hair and enough black eyeliner to last Cleopatra a lifetime, wore a sheet wrapped over a leotard in an approximation of a toga. She watched Auntie Lil enter with professionally distant interest. In Mike's neighborhood, you never knew what was going to walk in the door. It was always best to reserve judgment until right before you yelled for the bouncer.

"Give me a double Bloody Mary," Auntie Lil ordered. Her fruitless visit to the precinct called for strong measures. She slapped her pocketbook on the bar and scraped a stool up closer to it. "Extra, extra spicy. I'd ask for ouzo, but I hate the stuff."

"Greek is just our theme this week," the bartender assured her. "Next week, we're doing Oktoberfest." If she thought it was unusual for a little old lady to be slamming back a double Bloody Mary in midday, she wasn't going to point that out. "Having a bad day?" she asked.

"Having a bad week," Auntie Lil decided as she sipped at her Bloody Mary.

Since Theodore was certainly taking his sweet time, she decided she might as well get some work done while she waited. There was a pay phone directly behind her, against one wall, and a chair was arranged in front of it. Unfortunately, so was a cook. One look from Auntie Lil however, and he quickly murmured something in Spanish, rang off and hustled back to the safety of the kitchen. He, too, had been working in the neighborhood long enough to know that you never judged a book by its cover, no matter how creased it might be.

Bob Fleming answered the phone on the first ring. "Homefront," he said.

"If you don't sleep there, you might as well," she told him. "This is Lillian Hubbert."

"Of course." He sounded more cheerful than the day before. "I got a good night's sleep in my own bed, actually. Some of my volunteers showed up and we got two kids to call home last night. And one is thinking about entering a resident drug rehab. It looks like it could be a pretty good week after all."

"People still looking at you funny?" she asked.

"Not today. No one's seen me yet. What can I do for you?"

"Did you find Little Pete? Will he talk to me?"

"I think so," he told her. "Stop by later and I'll let you know for sure. I ran into him this morning. He's thinking about it. But he's scared."

"Why is he scared?" Auntie Lil asked.

"He was on the streets a couple of nights ago, three I think, and saw some rich guy in a limo flashing around photos of the old woman, dead. Scared the hell out of him. He said the guy had a mean-looking face, looked like a serial killer or something. Of course, he's a kid and he's got an imagination, so . . . I don't know the connection, but that old lady meant something to Little Pete and he's definitely afraid of the man in the limousine."

"A silver limo?" Auntie Lil asked.

"No. He said it was a black car."

She couldn't figure out how a rich man in a black limo could fit into what they knew. "What about Timmy?" she asked Bob Fleming. "Did you get to talk to him?"

"No. He's still avoiding me. Little Pete doesn't know why. But I found out a bit more about the man who's keeping Timmy. According to Little Pete, Timmy's got a regular job with the guy. It's not a sugar daddy thing. Strictly business. I don't know exactly what that means, but I can guarantee you that it doesn't involve Social Security. Maybe you can find out more."

"I will," Auntie Lil decided firmly. "Thank you. I'll see you this afternoon."

She hung up and nursed another third of her Bloody Mary down the hatch. Things were looking up. Little Pete could tell her something about Emily, she was sure of it. She checked the clock. Where was Theodore? On an impulse, she dialed Midtown North and, to her surprise, was connected to Det. George Santos almost immediately.

"Talk fast," the detective said without waiting to hear who it was. "I've got a stack of messages waist high that I have to return."

"We have located The Eagle for you."

"The man who was sitting next to Emily," Santos repeated, obviously recognizing her voice. He wanted to humor her before she started to fill him in with endless details. He sighed again. "Okay, Miss Hubbert, what's the beef?"

"He entered Emily's apartment building at 1:30 A.M. last night and has not left yet."

"The apartment building where you think she lives," Santos corrected her.

"Regardless of whether Emily lived there or not," Auntie Lil conceded, but only because it suited her current purposes, "reliable sources saw The Eagle enter. And he has not yet come back out."

"Look, Miss Hubbert," the detective said. "I know you're trying to help and I know that you care about the woman who died. But I can't keep running off on wild goose chases. I just don't have the time."

"Please, detective," Auntie Lil pleaded with uncharacteristic mellowness, fueled by the hefty Bloody Mary. "I won't ask you to do anything else. Please just have someone check all the apartments there. I know The Eagle is in there. He's a tall black man with an eagle tattoo on one of his upper arms. If you can find him, I can find the witness who saw him leaning over Emily the day she died. I have people looking for him now."

"You *what*?"

She backpedaled quickly. "I mean, I heard through a friend that they've put the word out at St. Barnabas that the police need to speak to whoever sat near Emily that day."

There was a skeptical silence. "I'll see who's available to re-check the building," he finally promised. "But only because there weren't any new murders waiting on my desk this morning."

"This afternoon," Auntie Lil corrected.

He rang off before she tortured him any more.

6.   Returning from 1515 Broadway, T.S. detoured past St. Barnabas in an attempt to find the funny old man who had first spotted The Eagle. Franklin had not yet been able to find him, but was sure he'd turn up sooner or later. There was a long line waiting for the soup kitchen to open, but no demented old characters with half of their hair shaved away. While he was there searching for familiar faces, Fran walked past him and hurried down the basement steps without giving him even a second glance. She was seriously preoccupied with some problem. And T.S. wanted to know what it was.

He followed her partway down the steps. She unlocked the gate and stepped through, forgetting to lock it again. Before she could unlock the basement door, Father Stebbins opened it for her, greeting her with a wide smile. To T.S.'s complete amazement, Fran brushed past the priest without comment. Father Stebbins stared at her with a worried look on his face, but she marched past him into the kitchen area without so much as a hello.

Now that was something, T.S. thought. But what?

Father Stebbins noticed T.S. standing at the gate. "The kitchen doesn't open until three o'clock," he told him kindly.

Not only had Father Stebbins not recognized him, he'd thought he was a soup kitchen client. So much for T.S.'s theory about the impact of the right attire. On the other hand, he decided, he should be grateful for the anonymity. He slipped back up the stairs while Father Stebbins relocked the gate. The old actresses were not in line yet. They were probably roaming the streets, gathering useless information on innocent people. Well, so long as they were happy doing their jobs, no one was getting hurt.

He cut across Forty-sixth Street to get another look at Emily's building. If Herbert's team was on the job, he didn't see them. But he saw something even more interesting. T.S. spotted a silver limousine approaching the front of the building from the west and hurried to get a better look. He stepped into the doorway across the street and watched as it glided to a stop in front of Emily's building. A tall blonde with lots of hard angles but not much meat on her hopped out of the back seat and ran a few doors down to the corner store, leaving the car door open. A small, round head covered with thin strands of black hair and decorated with two tiny ears emerged from the back seat. It was attached to the tan of an expensive cashmere coat. Lance Worthington marched up the front steps of Emily's building and leaned firmly on a buzzer. T.S. could not see which one. The producer leaned on the buzzer again and turned away impatiently. Halfway down the steps, the front door opened and Leteisha Swann stuck her gawky neck and heavily painted face out the door as she called after Lance Worthington. The look of irritation that crossed his face was clearly apparent, even from T.S.'s viewpoint across the street. The producer shook his head gruffly and climbed into the limo. Undaunted, Leteisha Swann followed him to the car. The door was shut firmly in her face. She glared through the back window, tossed her hair behind her head—a move that nearly dislodged her cheap wig—then turned on her spike heels and sauntered down the block toward Ninth Avenue.

So, Lance Worthington had not been waiting for Leteisha Swann. Who else in the building could it be?

"Got a quarter?" T.S.'s concentration was interrupted by a bedraggled old woman, who stood before him grinning a gap-toothed smile and extending a dirty palm. She looked like someone right out of *Oliver!*"

T.S. fumbled in his pocket for a dollar bill and tossed it her way, returning to his scrutiny of the silver car.

"Thank you, governor. Most kind of you," the old hag cackled in a Cockney accent. "Care for a quick tickle in return?"

T.S. was shocked. He turned to her and prepared to launch into a lecture, but the old bag lady surprised him by bursting into a merry laugh.

"Got you," she said. She lifted the matted hair off of her forehead, rearranged her face and straightened up, grinning at T.S.

"Adelle!" T.S. was not amused. He was appalled. She had

looked exactly like a crazy old woman lost on the streets. A little too much like one, in fact. It frightened him. Were they all that close to the edge?

"Don't let it bother you, guv'," she told him with a bawdy nudge. "I can fool anyone when I put my mind to it." She cackled again and moved down the sidewalk, adding over her shoulder: "You're not the only eyes watching that building, you know."

The encounter was still bothering him when the blonde emerged from the corner store holding a pack of cigarettes and a small brown paper bag. The door to the back seat of the silver car opened and she climbed inside. Just then, the outer door to Emily's building swung open with a bang and a young boy ran down the steps. His blond hair gleamed harshly in the autumn sun and he wore a tight black T-shirt, equally tight black jeans, and brand-new tennis shoes worth about a third of T.S.'s monthly pension check. The boy followed the blonde into the silver car and it pulled swiftly away.

Timmy. The boy in Emily's photos and, most definitely, the boy he'd seen in the apartment next to hers, two days ago with a middle-aged man. Seeing him in person confirmed it and he realized that he should have made the connection before. And he was probably the kid that Herbert had spotted leaving the building the night before.

So Timmy knew Lance Worthington. But what did that mean? And Lance Worthington knew, but did not necessarily like, Leteisha Swann. And none of them looked much like Mother Teresa from T.S.'s vantage point.

He hurried down the block toward his rendezvous with Auntie Lil. As he passed by a large potted fir tree in front of a Brazilian restaurant, he could have sworn he heard his name called out. It was as faint as the wind and just as fleeting.

He stopped abruptly. "What?" he said. A woman passing by glanced at him, stepped up her speed, stared back at him again and accelerated some more.

"What?" T.S. said again.

"Give my regards to Lillian," a muffled voice replied. "The Eagle has not yet flown the coop."

"For God's sake, Herbert." T.S. straightened the hem of his sweater and moved resolutely forward. "Now you're just showing off."

7.   Auntie Lil had not waited for him to begin lunch. The last slurp of Bloody Mary had suddenly convinced her that she needed food—and fast. By the time T.S. arrived, she was halfway through a pork chop practically the size of a manhole. A small pile of bones on her plate signified the recent demise of another, equally enormous chop.

"I'll have what she just vacuumed up," he told the waiter automatically.

"Wise choice," Auntie Lil affirmed, her mouth full of food. "What did you find out?"

He told her the particulars about Lance Worthington and his actions earlier that day, then outlined his plan to find out more about the producer. Her eyes twinkled. Either she approved or she'd had a whopping big drink before he got there. Speaking of which—he ordered himself a Dewars and soda.

"You just want an excuse to see Lilah," she said once she'd swallowed her last chunk of meat. "But I approve heartily. You can get right beside him and see if it's all smoke or a little bit of fire, too. What would he be doing with a street kid?"

"He could be one of Timmy's customers. Or, he could just be there in the building collecting the rent."

They stared at one another, neither of them believing the last theory. "How do we explain the blonde on his arm if Worthington is one of Timmy's customers?" Auntie Lil asked. There went the first theory, too.

"I have even more interesting news," T.S. told her, abandoning their dilemma and savoring the chance to surprise her for a chance.

"What?" she demanded. "You're holding back on me."

He told her about Fran not speaking to Father Stebbins. Her reaction was swift and surprised.

"What could have happened to cause such a thing?" she wondered out loud.

"I don't know." His drink arrived and he refreshed himself, realizing that his encounter with Adelle still rankled. He told Auntie Lil about it. "She was very proud of her disguise, but I was upset."

Auntie Lil reached over and patted his hand. "I know. They live very close to that life and it's frightening to see them go over to the other side. Yet, you have to admire their verve at taking it on, if only as a temporary disguise."

"She said she could fool anyone," T.S. repeated. "And I bet she could."

Auntie Lil was quiet, considering the words. T.S. caught on and fell silent as well.

"She could fool anyone," Auntie Lil admitted. "Perhaps we would do well to remember that."

"Did you get Santos?" he asked. The thought of one little old lady murdering another was depressing, but did nothing to squelch his appetite. His plate arrived and he dived right in. He was hungry. Watching Auntie Lil eat often had that effect.

"He's going to send some men to canvass the apartment building again. This time they'll check every apartment, not just the one we think is Emily's. If The Eagle's there, they'll find him. But I heard something else that's intriguing."

"What?" he asked, hurrying through his pork chops before Auntie Lil decided she was hungry again.

"Bob Fleming of Homefront has obtained information that a sinister, wealthy man in a black limousine was riding around the neighborhood three nights ago, flashing photographs of Emily dead. Where did he get those photos? What is he doing with them? The young black boy in Emily's photos, Little Pete, saw the man. He was frightened and ran away."

T.S. stared at her, mouth open and pork chops forgotten.

"For heaven's sake, Theodore. Close your mouth when you chew."

"Auntie Lil," T.S. said, horrified. "He's talking about *me*." Unwillingly, a flush crept up his neck and across his face. "When I stopped to get the photos developed, I had to do it at Times Square. It was the only place open. A young black kid was in the crowd. He saw me and ran away."

Auntie Lil stared at him. "You might have told me this earlier. Didn't you recognize the child when you saw the photos in Emily's apartment?"

"No, I did not. Remember, I did say I *thought* I'd seen him before." He cut into his pork chop with defensive energy. "Besides, the kid I saw on the street looked a hell of a lot older and wiser than the kid in the photograph."

"It's the same one. I hope to meet and talk with him today."

"Well, then, you'd better keep an eye out," T.S. warned. "So far as I'm concerned neither of these kids is much of a kid. Either one of them, or both of them, might have set Emily up. So watch your step."

It was the most depressing theory yet.

CHAPTER TEN

1. It felt strange to be back in his apartment in the middle of the afternoon. The television stood, dark and cold, in one corner of his living room—now nothing more than a reminder of his past boredom. He passed by it without so much as a glance. It was the telephone he was after. Maybe it was just an excuse to get to see her—and maybe it was a wild goose chase—but if it was a choice between spending time with Lilah and being ordered around by Auntie Lil, he had no trouble reaching a decision.

He reached Lilah on his first attempt and she quickly agreed to clear her schedule and be a part of his plans to learn more about Lance Worthington.

"You are much more than a prop," he assured her formally. "I don't want you to think I'm just using you and your money. Your presence will be essential to my morale."

She laughed merrily, although he had not intended to be funny. He was vaguely embarrassed, but relief took its place when she promised, "I'll be there if you need me."

The next phone call would be harder as it required a host of lies and, despite his Peter Pan performance earlier, T.S. was basically scrupulously honest and thus not a good liar at all.

He located the number easily enough, took a deep breath, told himself he was as good a fabricator as Auntie Lil any day, and dialed. The breathy redhead answered on the first ring. She had been expecting a call from one of her many admirers.

"Broadway Backers," she cooed. "Home of tomorrow's hits. How may I help you?"

"Lance Worthington," T.S. demanded in a deep executive voice. "And hurry. I'm returning his call and I've got another appointment on tap."

"Certainly, sir," she replied promptly. "*Who* may I tell him is calling?"

T.S. winced at her tone. Correct grammar did not excuse an improper voice. But even worse, who the hell *could* she say was calling? He had failed to prepare a cover in advance. So much for being as good a liar as Auntie Lil. He patted his sweater nervously . . . well, what did it matter? No one knew him from Adam and, unlike Auntie Lil, he did not relish skulking around in disguises and playing those types of games. He would give his real name. Besides, he *had* to use Lilah's real name.

"This is Mr. T.S. Hubbert," he told the receptionist. "Private investor."

"Private investigator?" she asked in sudden alarm.

"In-vest-*or*." he repeated imperiously. "And I'm a very busy man."

"Right away, sir," she promised but followed it up by putting him on hold. Less than twenty seconds later, however, a male voice came on the line.

"Lance Worthington here." The producer's tone managed to be unctuous, impatient and suspicious all at the same time.

"T.S. Hubbert," T.S. barked. "I heard you were looking for investors."

Lance Worthington's voice smoothed into a mellow purr. He sounded as if someone had poured a quart of honey down his throat. "We only have a very few spots left," he said. "The new show's getting excellent word-of-mouth. If you want in, the minimum may be a bit steep."

"I can handle it," T.S. assured him. "The main thing is, I want in."

"How did you hear about our new venture?" Worthington asked and T.S. could detect a small note of suspicion creeping back in. Perhaps he was making it too easy.

"My girlfriend told me about it. Lilah Cheswick. Know her? Wealthy widow? Well-built dame? Used to be married to Wall Street's Robert Cheswick." Well-built dame? T.S. almost choked on the words. But it was essential to establish man-to-man contact, and he had a rather heavy-handed idea of what this man-to-man business meant.

As expected, Worthington knew the name Cheswick immediately. Anyone who'd spent time digging around for money couldn't help but know the name. And it did the trick. All suspicion disappeared, to be replaced by ingratiating greed. "Is she interested in investing as well?" Worthington asked. "Like I say, we have a few spots left."

"We'll both have to reserve final judgment until we hear more about the show," T.S. told him. No sense in being too easy to hook. The man's true character would be better revealed if he saw him in full action.

"Let me meet the two of you tonight," the producer suggested. "I don't want to rush you, but we really do need to wrap up the financing and get on with the creative. Timing is everything, you know."

Yeah, T.S. knew that quite well. And timing was particularly important when you thought you had a couple of rich suckers on the line and wanted to reel them in quickly so they could sign on the dotted line.

"I don't know about tonight," T.S. said reluctantly. "I have a business dinner . . ."

"I hate to pressure you," Worthington said smoothly. "But I'm out the rest of the week and I have a couple of other potential investors to talk to who are all very anxious to get a piece of this pie." He let his voice trail off in a small sigh of warning: you're about to lose a big share of profits, it implied.

"Oh, all right." T.S. pretended to suddenly make up his mind. "I'll have my secretary rearrange things. You can't let a good thing go without giving it a chance. Am I right?"

"You're absolutely right. And I'll even make up the lost dinner to you. I'll take you and . . . uh, Ms. Cheswick to dinner while we talk."

Lance Worthington was a particularly greedy man and so, in a flash of perverse justice, particularly easy to gull. Whether or not this got T.S. anywhere was another story. But at least he and Lilah would get a fancy dinner out of their charade.

But even that was not to be. Lance Worthington was not just greedy, he was cheap. He suggested dinner at Sam's, a neighborhood theater bar. It was to give them a flavor of the theatrical life, he said, though T.S. knew the attraction was more likely Sam's low prices. Nonetheless, he agreed to meet the producer there at eight o'clock. The time was perfect, Worthington insisted in an insider voice, explaining that "the annoying pre-theater tourist crowd will have left."

Too bad, T.S. thought to himself. If they decided to stick around, they'd be in for quite a show.

2.   Auntie Lil was perched on a small plastic chair in the outer room of Homefront. She was waiting for Little Pete to show.

Bob Fleming sat at his battered desk in the rear, arguing with someone over the phone about receiving a large share of a city grant. Just as his shouting rose to an angry roar, the front door of the runaway shelter opened and an Irish amazon stepped through. She was a large woman whose height approached six feet and whose weight looked composed entirely of muscle. She wore a pair of tight black leggings, a gray sweatshirt that hung to mid-thigh, thick white socks and sturdy athletic shoes. The no-nonsense outfit only highlighted the woman's incredible physical strength even more. Her leg and thigh muscles were taut and highly developed; her forearms were muscular and firm. But she was not bulky at all. She was sleek and streamlined, moving with the grace of a stalking panther. Her face was broad and burnished by the sun, glowing with a tan the color of honey. Her round cheeks were flushed red in almost comical good health. When she noticed Auntie Lil, the woman's immediate smile was startling— the wide mouth pulled back to reveal large, very white teeth. Above the smile, her eyes glittered with an icy blue that seemed to bore right through Auntie Lil. She stood in the doorway, looking around while she bounced on her insteps and ran impatient fingers through a wavy crop of short brown hair.

Bob Fleming's reaction was enthusiastic. He slammed the phone down the instant he saw her and his scowl was transformed into an unexpected and unabashed grin. He met the enormous woman at the front counter and gave her a quick hug.

"Meet Annie O'Day," he said to Auntie Lil. "Angel of the streets."

"Angel?" the woman repeated in an incredulous voice. She thumped Bob solidly on his biceps with a coiled fist and the burly man cringed in mock pain.

"I'm Lillian Hubbert," Auntie Lil replied, timidly offering a white-gloved hand and fervently hoping it would be returned with all ten fingers intact.

But her hand was not crushed at all. Instead, Annie O'Day tenderly held it between her own massive hands and gently squeezed. "It's a pleasure to meet you, Ms. Hubbert," she said in a soft and calming voice. She continued to hold Auntie Lil's hand while she quietly looked her over, as if absorbing secret signals through the somewhat frail appendage. Auntie Lil changed her mind at once.

This was no wrestling champion at all. This was a nurse, or maybe a doctor.

"Annie is a nurse practitioner," Bob Fleming explained. "She has a mobile medical van and drives around helping out homeless and street people in need of care."

"Oh, my," Auntie Lil replied. She did not know what else to say. A job like that had to be dangerous, tiring and frustrating. There would be an endless supply of ungrateful and uncooperative patients who were in real need of medical care but lacked the mental self-awareness to recognize their own ailments.

"Oh, my, is right," Annie O'Day agreed cheerfully. "That's why I have to look like this." She curled one arm up and one arm down in a mock body builder pose. "You can call me Mrs. T," she added.

Auntie Lil laughed, but her eyes were busy inspecting Bob Flemming's unconscious reaction to Annie. His attention was brightly focused on her and his mouth hovered in a perpetual smile. Yes, it was clear. Bob Fleming had at least one interest outside of runaways. Auntie Lil was glad to see that he had chosen his interest well.

"I must be going," she said tactfully. She was not one to stand in the way of love. Besides, she was wasting her time. "I don't think Little Pete is coming."

"Little Pete?" Annie looked at Bob. "Is she a relative?" she asked skeptically. Auntie Lil was definitely the wrong color.

"I'll explain later," Bob promised, showing Auntie Lil to the door. "What if Little Pete turns up later?" he asked in a voice much more helpful than it had ever been before. Annie O'Day certainly had a positive effect on him.

"I'll probably be at the Delicious Deli," Auntie Lil told him. The man's broad shoulders sagged. She had not meant to remind him of his own troubles. "I could use a coffee or two after my large lunch." The largest thing, of course, being the Bloody Mary.

"I'll send him there if he shows," Bob promised, waving a quick goodbye.

Auntie Lil did not mind being politely hustled out of Homefront. If Bob Fleming and Annie O'Day were as busy as their jobs implied, she did not begrudge them a few minutes alone together in the middle of a quiet afternoon.

She walked toward the Delicious Deli and slowed in front of the Jamaican restaurant. Nellie was inside serving steaming plates of chicken and gravy to a pair of customers. Auntie Lil peered in the spacious window, wondering if she should go inside. She was positive that Nellie knew more than she was saying. What had she seen staring out of her window to make her clam up so thoroughly? Why had she grown so frightened at the sight of Emily?

Nellie noticed her observer right away, and the look she returned was enough to convince Auntie Lil that, perhaps, her time would be better spent somewhere else. Nellie's eyes had narrowed to small, hard orbs, their former openness replaced by tight beams of suspicion.

Auntie Lil quickly hurried on and passed by Emily's building without incident, but had no doubt that Herbert was lurking somewhere nearby. The Delicious Deli was deserted except for Billy and his young daughter, Megan. The two of them were busy piping whipped cream on top of a large pan of rice pudding when Auntie Lil entered.

Billy looked up and his old smile returned. He nodded toward her table and lifted his eyebrows, signaling her to sit. He was well versed in the across-the-room sign language of New York delis.

"Be right there," he promised out loud. "Megan here is our resident whipped cream artist and I promised she could do the pudding today."

Auntie Lil saw that much of the whipped cream was going into the artist's mouth and onto the artist's Catholic school uniform, but uncharacteristically said nothing. She was too busy trying to decide how to approach Billy about the bad feelings he displayed toward Bob Fleming. But she need not have bothered. Billy brought it up himself as soon as he had shooed his daughter into the bathroom to wash the goo off her hands and change her clothes.

"What were you doing with that guy from Homefront?" he asked Auntie Lil, setting a cup of cappuccino in front of her without being asked. "I've been hearing things about him. Things I don't like to hear."

She looked at him, mystified. "He runs a program for young runaways."

"Huh." Billy stared into her coffee, avoiding her face. "Word is he's just as bad as the men he's helping those runaways to escape."

That couldn't be true. She'd had a good feeling about Bob Fleming and she was usually so right about people. "Where did you hear that?" she asked sharply.

"It's going around the streets." Billy shrugged and wiped his hands on his apron, keeping an eye on the bathroom door. He did not want his young daughter overhearing.

"How reliable is street talk?" Auntie Lil asked.

"It's usually pretty good." He stared at her unhappily. "I hate guys like that," he added for good measure. "I think they should be publicly killed."

She shook her head no, unwilling to believe him.

"How's the investigation going?" Billy asked casually.

Auntie Lil looked up at him, surprised. Had she ever said she was investigating . . . perhaps she had.

"I know you're poking into that old lady's death," Billy pointed out. "There are no secrets in Hell's Kitchen. Street talk is pretty accurate, like I say."

Auntie Lil felt there were a good many secrets in Hell's Kitchen. Too many, in fact. And some of them were probably pretty essential to discovering the truth that she sought. She would use an old trick, one that was quite effective when she didn't feel like answering questions: she'd ask the questions instead.

"I know you don't like those young boys in your store," she told Billy. "But I'm trying to talk to one of them. If he shows up here to meet me, will you let him in?"

Billy stared at her again before finally answering. "If you're with him every second and keep him away from the potato-chip rack and the bottles of soda in back."

"That bad?" Auntie Lil asked.

"That bad," he confirmed, then added: "And keep him away from my daughter, too."

3. "Of course I'll join you," Lilah said with enthusiasm. "Who are you going to be? I do hope you gave that awful money-grubbing creature a false name. Otherwise, you'll have to put up with endless annoying phone calls. They're really such a nuisance, these investing types. Never leave you alone until they hear you've gone bankrupt, I suspect. You really have no idea."

He gulped in the silence that followed, then finally admitted in a strangled voice, "Actually, I gave him my real name . . . and your real name, too."

He expected her to shriek in dismay but she laughed instead. "You should be sneakier if you're going to go undercover," she pointed out. "You mean to tell me that after this is over, we're going to have to dodge this producer begging us for money?"

"But you do that already with dozens and dozens of people. I'm sure you've had more experience then me," he pointed out weakly.

"So I have. Well, I suppose the old Cheswick name is essential for hooking our fish," she admitted without a hint of rancor.

"I'm afraid it is," T.S. confessed. "And I hope you'll forgive me one day."

"Well," said Lilah, "that depends."

"Depends on what?"

"Depends on what one day brings."

T.S. was too tongue-tied to manage a reply. She rang off quickly, after promising to pick him up in the limo just before eight.

T.S. sat by the phone enjoying the wave of relief that washed through him. He had actually made a mistake and nothing horrible had happened to him. She had not slammed down the phone. The ceiling had not fallen. The sky had not parted nor had lightning split him in two. True, he had been mildly embarrassed. But that had gone away in an instant. Perhaps he was too hard on himself, he thought vaguely. Perhaps there was such a thing as being too correct. And though he hated to admit it, maybe Auntie Lil was right. He *could* afford to loosen up a little.

4. Billy Finnegan need not have worried about his daughter coming in contact with Little Pete. By the time Little Pete showed up at the Delicious Deli, Auntie Lil had run through two cups of coffee, another cappuccino and a large slice of cheesecake. And Megan had long since been collected by her mother, fed a large meal, scrubbed in a clean bathtub, and dressed in fresh pajamas.

The little boy who stood outside the windows of the deli, peering in through the oncoming twilight, would have found such caring treatment by a mother completely foreign.

He was small, even for his young age, and his skinny frame could not have been even five feet tall. His face was twisted in a hardened imitation of a cynical adult, but a small tremor of fear made his chin wobble a little as he stood beside the door, staring in at Auntie Lil. She knew that, despite his toughness, he was afraid to come inside and risk the rancor of the owner who had no doubt thrown him out many times before. She stared back at him, trying to decide what would be the best thing to do to win his trust. Wait until he gathered his courage and came inside? Or wave him in enthusiastically, as if he really were just a normal little boy coming to meet his grandmother.

But Little Pete was not a normal little boy. That much was clear even in shadow. He stood, pelvis thrust forward, hands curled in fists and arms bent slightly in a menacing pose that belied his familiarity with the streets.

Maybe Auntie Lil had been all wrong when she told T.S. not to worry, that she had seen it all. Because she wasn't sure she had seen this exactly before—this defiant posturing and aggressive adult manner in such a small body. He did not seem to use his small size to his advantage at all. And he could have. It would have provoked pity even in the street. No, this child did not want pity in any form, that much was immediately apparent.

"Think he's coming in?" Billy asked idly. He was leaning against the counter picking his teeth and staring out into the twilight. The deli was quiet and would remain so for much of the night.

"I think he might be afraid of you," Auntie Lil told him, wondering if Little Pete had reasons of his own that she did not know about.

"I can take care of that," Billy decided. He tossed his toothpick into the trash can and flipped up part of the countertop, advancing on the door with a wide smile on his face.

Little Pete coiled, waiting for the verbal lashing that was sure to come. When, instead, Billy motioned him inside, the young boy refused to act surprised. Suspicion had long since replaced surprise in his repertoire of emotions. Instead, he strutted arrogantly past the deli owner as if he owned the place. But he watched Billy out of the corners of his eyes.

"Hello, young man," Auntie Lil called out cheerfully. "I'm the old lady Bob Fleming told you about. My goodness, I've been waiting for hours. I'm starving. Will you join me for dinner?"

Keeping one eye on Billy, Little Pete inched sideways toward Auntie Lil's table. Reluctantly giving up his scrutiny of Billy—who had resumed his stance behind the counter—Little Pete silently gripped the back of a wrought-iron chair at Auntie Lil's table while he looked her over closely.

"You buying me dinner? What for?" he asked in a high voice that tried hard to be gruff, but failed.

Heavens, she realized, his voice had not even changed yet. What kind of family would just let him wander away? And what kind of family was so horrible that the streets of New York seemed a preferable environment? But she could not afford to think about such things now. What she needed was information. And treating him like a child was not the way to go about it.

"I want to ask you some questions," she explained evenly. "That takes up your time. I thought dinner would be a fair payment." She pointed toward the chair he gripped and, slowly, Little Pete pulled it out and perched on the edge of the seat, still half-turned to the door as if he might bolt at any moment.

"Questions about who?" he asked sullenly. His pronunciation was extremely precise, especially for a child who lived on the streets. It told Auntie Lil that he had gone to school at one time, and probably studied hard. And that someone at home had once cared enough about him to provide a good example.

"A friend of yours. Her name was Emily." Auntie Lil answered. "She was an old lady who lived on Forty-sixth Street. She died just a few days ago." Auntie Lil spoke gently but firmly, having decided that the prim schoolteacher mode might serve her best in this situation, so long as she made it clear that she was no sucker and that Little Pete was wasting his time if he thought he could con her.

"Don't know no old lady," he said sullenly. His eyes inched back toward the steam table of hot food at the far end of the deli counter. Billy stood near it, watching his two customers carefully.

"Don't know *any* old lady," she corrected the boy. "And I know that you do. She wagged a playful finger at him. "But why don't we eat first?"

If some sugar daddy was taking care of Little Pete on the streets, he wasn't doing a very good job of feeding him. The child ate two large double cheeseburgers, a mountain of french fries and even a bowl of overcooked green beans when Auntie Lil insisted. To her surprise, while Little Pete was obviously hungry, he did not gobble. In fact, he had nice table manners and kept his napkin nearby so he could frequently scrub his mouth. He even ordered milk, which amused Auntie Lil. That hard outer crust concealed a little gentleman inside.

By the time his plate was empty, some of the hard angles of Little Pete's face had smoothed and he no longer perched on the edge of his chair. He sat back in contentment and the slightly sleepy look that crossed his face made him seem, for just a moment, like the little boy that he was.

"Why you think I know this lady?" he asked Auntie Lil slowly. "I never seen you before. You her sister or something?"

"You've never seen me, but I've seen you," Auntie Lil lied, not answering his other question. Let him think she was Emily's sister. Perhaps he would talk more. "I saw you one night near the twenty-four-hour photo store," she lied. "You were running away. I know why you ran. It was the photos of Emily, wasn't it? The photos of her dead that upset you."

"She was nice lady," he protested. For the briefest of seconds, his lower lip trembled. "I ran because I had to find Timmy. I knew he'd want to know."

"Is Timmy your friend?" she asked gently. "Was Emily Timmy's friend, too?"

"Sure, Timmy's my friend. We're buddies." He stared at her defiantly, as if he expected her to challenge his contention that he had a friend. "And that lady was his grandma."

"His grandmother?" Auntie Lil repeated. "You mean, they were related?"

"Don't know about that." He stared down at his hands, saw they were fists, and self-consciously uncurled them. His fingers began to drum nervously on top of the small glass table. "But he called her grandma," he admitted. "And she was as good as a real one. She let us watch TV at her house when we could sneak away from . . ." He stopped, looked outside as if he were being watched, then continued. "Once she baked us a pineapple upside-down cake and let me and Timmy eat the whole thing."

"You've been in her apartment on Forty-sixty Street? Next to the Jamaican restaurant?"

He nodded and told her more. "Once she brought Timmy to see a play. And she said she could help him, that he wouldn't have to do . . . some things anymore. That maybe she could get him a job somewhere. And then she promised to help me, too. She was going to give us tickets to Los Angeles, she said. We wanted to go where it was warm. She said it was a nice town."

"Los Angeles?" Auntie Lil asked. "Was that your idea or hers?"

"Hers. Timmy kept telling her he was scared because the winter was coming. He hated the cold weather. She said she'd send us to L.A."

"What happened to her?" Auntie Lil asked softly. "Do you know who killed her?"

His lower lip trembled and he shook his head furiously. "Don't know. First time I knew she was dead was when I saw those photos. We was supposed to see her the next day. It was my birthday and she had a present for me. Like she had one for Timmy on his birthday. But I never got the present." He stared into the tabletop. "She was nice to me. Said she could be my grandma, too. That it was okay to call her 'Grandma' like Timmy did. It was out on the streets that she'd been poisoned or something. But I don't know who'd do a thing like that."

"Did she ever tell you anything about herself?" Auntie Lil

asked. "Where she was from? How she knew Timmy? Why she was being so nice?"

"Like what? Why you want to know?" He stared at Auntie Lil. The hard, suspicious expression flickered into view and disappeared. "She was nice to us 'cause she liked us."

"Don't you realize that she was *murdered*?" Auntie Lil asked gently. "Don't you want to find out who did it?"

The hard look came back for good. "I find out who, I'm gonna bust him," Little Pete said angrily. He jabbed with a fist for emphasis, imitating his television heroes and their cartoon courage.

"She never told you about herself?" Auntie Lil persisted. The little boy shook his head. "What about Timmy? Did he talk to her more? Can you get him to talk to me?"

Little Pete considered this. "I don't know. Timmy's scared. First I seen her dead in the photos. And then he seen an old lady coming out of her apartment and this man was with her, he thinks it was a cop. He ran away. Says he's real scared. And he's sad about Grandma dying. Real sad. He says something's going on and he don't understand it. But he won't even tell me what it is, so he ain't gonna talk to you none."

"Isn't going to talk to me at all," Auntie Lil corrected automatically, but her heart wasn't really in it. Little Pete tried on bad grammar like he tried on his street accent—sporadically and not very well. It was posturing and nothing more. Besides, her mind was on more important things. "What do you know about Timmy?" she asked. "Where is he from?"

Little Pete shrugged. He wasn't interested in people's pasts. He had run away to start a new life, not dwell on the old one. And so had his friend, Timmy. "I think he's from Texas," he finally offered. "That's all I know. Says his daddy was mean to him and his momma wouldn't stop it. Ran away. Came here. That's all I know."

"You can't tell me anything else about him?" Auntie Lil demanded.

"Well, he's kind of weird," Little Pete admitted. "Do I get dessert?" he added hopefully.

"Of course you do." She waved Billy over and soon Little Pete was digging into an enormous ice cream sundae, the treat bringing back the little boy in him. "What else do you know about Timmy?" Auntie Lil persisted.

Little Pete shrugged. "He's kind of spooky about religion and stuff like that. He likes to hang out near that church. But he never goes in, he says. Just kind of hangs around outside and looks in when they're praying."

"What church?" Auntie Lil demanded. "You mean the one on Forty-eight Street?"

The boy nodded, his mouth crammed with chocolate syrup and ice cream. "The big one," he muttered through his dessert.

"St. Barnabas? With the soup kitchen? Where Bob Fleming sometimes takes people to eat?"

Little Pete nodded again. "But not Timmy. He won't go inside. Like I say, he just watches through the door sometimes."

Now it was Auntie Lil's turn to drum the glass tabletop with her fingers. "Who would want to kill Emily?" she asked sharply.

Little Pete looked up in mid-bite, startled. "Don't know," he protested. "She was a nice lady. She was gonna give me a present."

Auntie Lil sighed and her mind wandered over what she had learned. Emily had cared about this young boy, Timmy, enough to let him call her "Grandma." And he had hung around St. Barnabas. But, according to Little Pete, never went in.

"How old are you?" she asked Little Pete.

"Now I'm twelve," he answered proudly.

"How old is Timmy?" she continued.

"Timmy's older. He turned fourteen last July. He was born on the fourth of July," he added helpfully.

Auntie Lil sighed. She would have to talk to Timmy herself. "Can you get him to talk to me?" she asked again, letting warmth creep into her voice for the very first time. In fact, she was trying her best to plead—which was distinctly against her nature.

Little Pete shrugged and shook his head. "I can try, but I don't think he'll do it." The boy shrugged again. "Says he's cursed."

"Cursed?"

Little Pete scooped up the rest of his sundae and carefully finished every drop. "Says everyone that tries to be good to him ends up dead." Little Pete looked her right in the eye. "I wouldn't want to help him if I was you."

"What about you?" Auntie Lil pointed out. "You're his friend and you're not dead."

"Me? I'm too little for no one to bother about. Besides, I'm too smart." The little boy finished licking his spoon and let it fall into the dish with a clatter. He winced and looked sideways at Billy, then slowly rose before freezing in indecision.

"It's okay. He knows I'm paying," Auntie Lil assured the boy. "You can go now if you want."

"Man don't like me," Little Pete confided.

"I guess not. You steal his things." Auntie Lil spoke calmly and without judgment. Little Pete shifted uncomfortably from foot to foot and ducked his head. Either he was ashamed or he was trying to say something that was difficult for him to say.

"About the dinner," he finally said in a voice so soft that, even leaning forward, Auntie Lil caught only part of it. "Thanks. But I got to go."

He dashed out the door, blending into the new evening's shadows and reappearing clearly in the illuminated harshness of the occasional streetlight that lit Eighth Avenue at night. Auntie Lil stood in the window, following his small figure through the clusters of theater patrons hurrying toward their shows. The boy walked quickly, head down, minding his own business—the very first rule of life on the street. Halfway down the block, something caught his attention. Perhaps he heard a shouted greeting, or a warning whistle. His head jerked up and he looked furtively around, then turned and raised an arm in greeting. Another small figure hurried across the avenue to Little Pete. They met beneath a streetlight and Auntie Lil saw the glow of a head of nearly white hair. Timmy. Had he been standing on the far corner, waiting for Little Pete? Waiting for a report back on her? The two boys gave each other a high-five hand slap, then turned down Forty-sixth Street and quickly disappeared from view. Just as Auntie Lil was about to return to the table and settle the bill, she saw a by now familiar figure hurrying down the block, right behind the two boys. Or was it simply a coincidence that all were heading down Forty-sixth Street? Whatever the reason, Leteisha Swann, woman of the night, disappeared into the very same darkness that had swallowed Timmy and Little Pete only a few seconds before.

"Find out anything?" Billy asked from behind. She jumped in alarm and he steadied her with a very strong arm. "Sorry. Didn't mean to spook you."

Flustered, she fussed over to her table and hauled her pocketbook onto a chair. "How much do I owe you?" she asked.

"Nothing at all." He began to clear the dishes from the table and ignored her protests. "Listen, lady, whatever it is you're really doing, you got that little monster to act like a human being. So maybe you're not all bad. Forget about the bill. I mean it."

"No, I insist." She held out some bills.

Billy pushed her hand away and sat down across from her.

"What you owe me is to listen to what I have to say," he told her quietly.

She stiffened, but remained silent.

"Around here," he said softly, "people have two faces. The faces everyone in the neighborhood sees. Those are the happy, smiling 'I'm a great guy, let me buy you a drink' faces. And then you have the faces that tell the true story. The faces that come out the second a door is shut and it's okay to let down your guard."

"What do you mean?" Auntie Lil asked, suddenly frightened.

"What I mean is that I can tell you were feeling sorry for that kid. And I got to admit, he acted okay in here tonight. But I've seen him punch old ladies in the stomach for their pocketbooks. I've seen him wave over greasy old men with one hand and pick their pockets with the other. He's an animal and he'll turn on you like one. And he's like just about everyone else in this neighborhood. I know because I grew up here. And the name of the game is survival."

"Even for you?" she asked softly.

"Even for me. If someone or something ever threatened my family, for instance, this nice guy you see here would disappear. Like that." He snapped his fingers and Auntie Lil jumped at the sharp crack. When he saw she had not yet been cowed, he continued. "I'll tell you another story," he said. "Last week a couple of guys came in. They looked kind of familiar to me. We stared at each other for a few seconds—and then we all remembered. We'd gone to Sacred Heart together twenty, twenty-five years ago. Played stickball, ran in the streets when we were bored. Stood around looking at girls walking by. Tried to get beers out of old man Flanagan. Those guys had been my best friends in third and fourth grade. And I'd known them all through high school. And here they were, back bigger than life. Both of them decked out in gold chains and floor-length fur coats. Italian loafers. Hundred-dollar haircuts. Thousand-dollar suits. A tan BMW parked out front. And a wad of cash that would choke one of those horses over in Central Park."

"Mafia?" Auntie Lil asked.

"Doubt it. They're Irish boys. Mafia don't trust them." He leaned forward again. "The point is, after they'd been here about fifteen minutes, they ask me if I'm interested in something very, very special. I say, 'Sure. Why not?' One of the guys goes out to the car, brings back a box, says I'm not going to believe this. 'You'll really get off, Billy,' he tells me and pulls out a stack of magazines."

Billy stopped and his mouth turned down in pain and disgust. "I can't tell you what was in those magazines because it would make you sick. But it could have been my Megan on those pages. Or my son. And it damn sure was somebody's kid. And those guys, those smiling buddies who had been my best friends at one time, had grown up and grown fat and rich on that filth. Those magazines sold for twenty-five dollars apiece. When they saw I wasn't interested, they acted a little hurt that I didn't appreciate the favor, but hey, there were no hard feelings. The Fifty-second Street gang faces came back in an instant. They were the boys again—joking with me, slapping my hands, everything was buddy this, buddy that. Like they'd pulled out *Sports Illustrated* instead. And you know what? I was buddy, buddy back to them."

He looked down at the table, as if ashamed of himself. He shook his head sadly. "Everyone is out for themselves, Miss Hubbert. So be careful. I'm just asking you to be very, very careful. I liked that old lady, Emily. She was a sweetheart. But she obviously put her nose where it didn't belong and now she's lying on a slab in the morgue." He looked up and stared at Auntie Lil.

He had succeeded in thoroughly frightening her, yet she could not quite understand why. She thanked him profusely, assured him she understood and, flustered, hurried out the door. She needed a friend just then and Herbert Wong was the closest one she could definitely trust. This time, he was easy to find along Forty-sixth Street. He was now disguised as a parking attendant and sat on a folding chair in front of a lot that was located a few doors away on the opposite side of the street from Emily's. She mustn't risk blowing his cover.

"Has The Eagle flown the nest?" she asked instead, out of the side of her mouth as she walked briskly past.

"Not yet," came the brief reply.

5. T.S. was startled to see that Lance Worthington had also brought along company. And cheap company at that, not exactly the type of window dressing that T.S. would recommend if he were trying to impress wealthy folk. The producer was ensconced at a table, firmly wedged between a pair of blonde bookends. They perched on each side of him, both staring into their drinks and dragging on cigarettes. The women were thin to the point of emaciation, at least in T.S.'s opinion, and the lack of flesh gave their faces a hard, unpleasant look. The tallest blonde had hair that tumbled wildly down her back in a style far too young for her face and wore a red sequined dress that fit her like a sausage skin. The other blonde, whose hair was cropped short in Louise Brooks–style fashion, wore an equally tight green sheath that shimmered in the restaurant's discreet lighting. Both the red and the green dress were held up by thin straps that threatened to break at any moment.

If Worthington had been dressed in a Santa Claus suit, the scene would have looked a lot like the opening of a poorly plotted porno movie.

"That's him with the oversexed elves," T.S. murmured as he helped Lilah through the entrance.

"I seem to be a bit overdressed," Lilah worried as she and T.S. feigned confused looks and pretended not to know who Lance Worthington was. It was a good effort, but probably not necessary. There were only two other tables with patrons in the entire joint.

"Perhaps you should take off your dress along with your coat and act like you intended to wear your slip all along," T.S. suggested. He was rewarded with a stifled giggle. They stood beside the bar, giving Worthington time to spot them and evaluate his prey. Meanwhile, T.S. was quietly returning the scrutiny.

Up close, he decided, the producer was even more repellent than he had suspected. It wasn't so much the way he looked, it was more the way he moved. His tongue unconsciously licked at his thin lips in greedy, lizardlike darts. His eyes were narrow and glittered unnaturally as they automatically zeroed in on Lilah's large diamond ring, then shifted to her expensive coat and on to her heavy gold necklace. T.S. could practically hear the producer calculating Lilah's net worth. Finished with Lilah, Worthington moved on to evaluate T.S. and it was all he could do to ignore the blatant scrutiny. The whole time he thought he was being subtle, Worthington was tugging unconsciously on his tiny right ear, sometimes stroking it as if for good luck.

T.S. had no desire to get close to the man, but duty called. He might know something about Emily's death. Or why every trace of her had disappeared from one of his apartments. He led Lilah to the edge of the producer's table and the blondes looked up in bored obedience.

"Worthington?" T.S. asked. "I'm T.S. Hubbert. You know Lilah Cheswick, I believe?"

The producer's mouth cracked in a smile that oozed sincerity and he leapt to his feet in fevered gallantry. "I've never actually had the pleasure of meeting Miss Cheswick," he admitted smoothly. "I've heard so much about you, however. What a great pleasure."

He extended a hand to Lilah and she bravely took it, pasting on a smile that was as phony as it was fitting for the bored society matron she had decided to be for the night. It was the first inkling that Lilah was actually going to enjoy their charade and it inspired T.S. himself to new heights. He extended a hand to Worthington and was rewarded with an appropriately manly handshake.

"And who are these charming young ladies?" T.S. asked, injecting an appropriately lascivious tone into his voice. More of that man-to-man stuff.

"This is my good friend, Miss Sally St. Claire," Worthington said enthusiastically. "You may recognize her from the movies." The tall blonde with too much hair nodded primly, then noisily slurped from her drink. T.S. didn't recognize her, but then she did have her clothes on—and he suspected that her movies were hardly late show fare.

"This other beautiful young thing is her good friend, Molly." Molly nodded dully and glanced at the clock above the bar. Her eyes were slightly glazed and T.S. was not at all sure that Molly even knew where she was. Or, possibly, *who* she was.

"Sit down. Do please sit down. Where are my manners?" Worthington actually hurried around the table and escorted Lilah to a seat by his side, booting his "good friend" Sally over one chair. He must really be desperate for money, T.S. thought. Even for a toadying moneygrubber, his obsequiousness was excessive.

"Please excuse me," the blonde named Molly announced suddenly. She stood abruptly and walked toward the back, disappearing inside the ladies' room.

"I'll just be a teensy minute myself," Sally St. Claire added, snatching a small gold pocketbook from the tabletop before hurrying after her friend.

Worthington chuckled as if they had just told a particularly amusing joke. "Girls. What do they do in there? Always got to go in pairs. Makes you kind of wonder, huh?" The guffaw that followed was so incredibly crass and forced that both Lilah and T.S. were thrown for a loop. How were they supposed to behave? Should they laugh along or be above it all? Better get a grip on your character, T.S. told himself. Remember, you've got money. Lots and lots of it.

T.S. compromised and smiled politely. He would be slightly above it all. After all, he was rolling in the dough.

It was the right choice. Within seconds, Worthington was expertly pumping both of them—under the guise of friendly questions—for information on where they lived, how many houses they owned, had they ever been to a particular restaurant in the Hamptons and wasn't the Virginia squire country marvelous in the spring? Didn't they think that the best available property bargains today could be found in the Caribbean? None of his questions were innocuous. They were economic land mines carefully laid in an attempt to strip their net worth bare. T.S. quickly found himself in over his head. He detested name-dropping, whether it was a person or place being dropped, and could not follow the rapid-fire probing. Lilah was good, though, very good. All of the hours spent listening to her boring friends chat on endlessly now paid handsome dividends. By the time the girls returned from the bathroom, Lance Worthington was convinced that both Lilah and T.S. were eager to share their wealth.

What followed was dinner and a painfully detailed description of a musical based on Davy Crockett's life. And damned if Lilah didn't actually convey enthusiasm about such monstrosities as a chorus line of dancing Indians paying homage to the great white pioneer.

During the producer's tedious recounting of the plot, the blondes excused themselves frequently, shunned food of any kind, and spent most of their time in the ladies' room, only to return and sit together giggling inanely over whispered comments that T.S. could not hear. Once they erupted in loud laughter and Worthington leaned over to mutter sharply in Sally St. Claire's ear. She immediately straightened up and her mouth clamped down in a thin line. She shrugged a small apology toward Lilah and T.S., then cast a quick, darting glance at her girlfriend.

Fortunately, the dinner was not quite as bad as the show's concept and T.S. was able to find some solace in the sole *almondine*. He had just worked his way over to the turnip purée when, to his total astonishment, he felt a small foot begin to probe his own. It could not have been Lilah, she was seated across the table next to Worthington, so it had to be the blonde named Molly. It was all T.S. could do to keep from choking and sending flecks of turnip spraying across the tabletop. The small foot had on a remarkably sharp-toed shoe and the hard tip pressed gently on his instep then insinuated its way up his leg. Without even glancing at her, T.S. flushed a deep scarlet and removed his leg from her vicinity. This necessitated sitting practically sideways in his chair, but he had no other ideas on how to repel the attack.

Worthington turned his attention back to a chattering Lilah, who was glibly holding forth on how hard it was to find an investment that gave her a good return on her money these days and how she just hated having everything parked in municipal bonds. She was really pulling out the stops and the level of greed this inspired in Worthington was nearly palpable. T.S. forgot his embarrassment in his admiration for Lilah. By God, now *that* was a woman who had real nerve. She knew how to take on a challenge.

"I've got a great idea," Worthington announced at the next lull in conversation. "I'm having a little get-together tomorrow. For some of the backers and potential investors, the ones who have passed preliminary muster, of course." Good grief, the man had nerve. He actually wanted them to believe that he could afford to be picky about who invested in his show and who was left out in the cold.

"It's at my place," Worthington continued. "I've got a great view of the river. Cocktails, munchies, a little entertainment. What do you say? It's better than those boring charity dinners, I can tell you that." He raised his eyebrows flirtatiously at Lilah and she managed a genteel smile back. T.S. would have rushed to her rescue but the pedicured probe was back at work and he was once again busy defending his personal space at ankle level.

"We'd love to come," Lilah was saying. She smiled sweetly at T.S. but her eyes were full of questions. She was wondering why T.S. was giving her so little help.

"Yes, we'd love to," T.S. quickly agreed. He casually moved his chair a few inches to the left and it scraped across the floor with a piercing shriek. The small foot only inched its way a little closer.

Lilah suddenly looked at the clock, feigning surprise. She must have sensed that something was wrong. "Theodore, darling, shouldn't we be going? You have that appointment with the sultan of . . ." She let her voice trail off discreetly.

"Oh, yes. Of course. I had completely forgotten about the sultan." T.S. leapt to his feet and hurried to help Lilah from her chair, wondering if there even was such a thing as a sultan these days. Apparently, there were plenty of them since no one at the table thought it unusual that they should hurry away. There were no questions about coffee or dessert, and Worthington did not seem concerned. They had promised to attend his party the next night and he was content with what he had accomplished.

After a few halfhearted murmurings about who would pick up the check, Lilah and T.S. managed to escape out the door with all of their jewelry and valuables intact.

Lilah gulped at the fresh air. "My God. The way he was look-ing at my ring I felt compelled to check every three minutes to make sure I still had it on."

"That, that cheap . . ." T.S. struggled for words. "That awful creature next to me was harassing me under the table!" He spotted the limousine parked a few doors down and frantically waved for Grady to hurry. He wanted out of there and away from that ano-rexic ankle assaulter as soon as he could.

Lilah suppressed a smile. "Whatever do you mean, Theodore?"

"That woman was trying to play footsies with me. Right there. Under the table. With you right there!"

"Really, Theodore. Don't take it so hard. What do you think that man was doing to me? I could practically tell you his brand of footwear by now. Why do you think I got us out of there? We'll just have to pump him for information tomorrow. The man was halfway up my shins and I just couldn't take it anymore."

T.S. was incensed. "How utterly despicable. How completely crass. What do they do? Get together and agree on a game plan? Draw straws? Sharpen their toe points? Are they some sort of par-ticularly active foot fetish group? Who did that other blonde get to play footsies with? Maybe the waiter. Did you happen to notice if he was standing next to her a lot?"

"Theodore, Theodore." She stopped his tirade with an upheld hand and ushered him into the limousine's back seat. "Do you think Worthington is harmless?" she asked.

"I think he's a snake," he answered promptly.

"Of course. But I meant, harmless in Emily's death."

"Probably. Why would he bother? But he's certainly up to no good somewhere. I wonder what Auntie Lil found out today."

"In that case," Lilah announced grandly, "let's give her a call." She winked at T.S. and pushed a button on the handrest. A small panel whirred back in the passenger seat door, revealing a com-pact cellular telephone.

"Good heavens," T.S. said, inexplicably annoyed. "It's a good thing they didn't have those contraptions when I was still work-ing. I'd never have gotten any peace or quiet."

"Isn't it just too much?" Lilah agreed. "I've only used it once, to order some Chinese food from the curbside. And that was just for fun. Fun that cost me about three dollars."

T.S. took the phone and suspiciously punched in Auntie Lil's number. He hated machines he did not understand. It would prob-ably cut them off in mid-sentence.

Surprisingly, the connection was quite clear. He could tell that she was tired.

"What's the matter?" he asked Auntie Lil, alarmed. "Are you okay?"

"I'm fine. Just a little discouraged," she admitted. "I didn't find out much today." She filled him in on the details of her meetings with Bob Fleming and Little Pete. But she did not tell him about Billy's advice as she knew this would trigger a fresh round of warnings from him. In return, T.S. told her about their dinner with Lance Worthington.

"He sounds like quite an oily operator," she decided.

"I'm beginning to be sorry I volunteered to find out more about him," T.S. admitted. "The thought of spending another evening with him is repugnant."

"But you also get to spend it with Lilah." Auntie Lil could always point out the good side of a situation. Particularly if it helped her get what she wanted.

"I'm just not convinced that this is getting us anywhere," T.S. said. "Seems to me you're having all the fun."

Auntie Lil sighed. "It is certainly not fun tramping around the streets all day. If you want to be more useful, why don't you go back to the library and check more Playbills. This time, see what you can pick up on any of those old actresses. I'm not sure I trust them. At least, I don't trust some of them."

T.S. agreed only after extracting a promise from Lilah that she would accompany him to Lincoln Center. "Okay," he told Auntie Lil cheerfully. "What are you going to do?"

"I'm going back to St. Barnabas," she said and rang off.

"Do you get the feeling that we're doing all the grunt work?" T.S. asked Lilah. "While she gets to have all the fun?"

"Isn't that the point of this entire episode?" Lilah asked back. "To keep your Auntie Lil happy?" She patted his knee and T.S. was more than pleased to agree.

CHAPTER ELEVEN

1. Auntie Lil had stayed away from the soup kitchen for two whole days, but the strain of controlling her curiosity was starting to get to her. Convinced that they were missing clues that might lead them to Emily's killer, Auntie Lil rose early the next morning and took up a new post near St. Barnabas church. Mindful of Lieutenant Abromowitz's orders to stay away, she stationed herself in the shadows of the deep doorway of a welfare hotel located across the street. She would just watch for a while, she told herself, and see who came in or out. Then maybe, if the coast was clear and that insufferable Fran nowhere to be seen, she'd risk setting foot on the premises. She wanted to talk to Father Stebbins and see what *he* knew about Emily. Perhaps she had been one of his parishioners. After all, what was the worst that could happen? An order from Lieutenant Abromowitz to stay away from the church wasn't exactly the law. Was it?

She had gotten there early and the street still belonged to trickles of commuters that flowed quickly past, heading east and west for their office buildings. They clutched their briefcases tightly in both hands, men and women alike, as they marched determinedly toward more familiar turf. St. Barnabas was on a transient street that belonged to the homeless and hopeless. People came and went, but very few cared to stop. The church itself looked desolate and abandoned in the early morning light. For the first time that year, there was a chill in the air. Auntie Lil wrapped her sweater coat more tightly about her, shivering slightly. At least she was not suffering alone, she told herself. Herbert or Franklin would be just a few blocks away watching Emily's building.

But Herbert was much closer than that. Even as she wondered what progress the watchers might be making, she spotted Herbert near Ninth Avenue, heading east. His path would take him directly in front of her hiding place. As he got nearer, she saw that his face was troubled. Clearly he was preoccupied, yet he did not even blink when she grabbed his elbow and pulled him into the doorway with her.

"Lillian," he said with a polite bow. "It is with much pleasure that I see you so early in the morning. I was just on my way to breakfast. Will you join me?"

"No." She cut right to the point. "You look worried. Why?"

Herbert shook his head. "I've just been by to talk to Franklin. No Eagle yet. It just doesn't make sense. He's been in that building for over two days now. A man cannot simply disappear."

Auntie Lil thought of the back fire escapes and wondered. But why would The Eagle bother to sneak out the back when their surveillance of the building was a secret?

"The police were there yesterday afternoon," Herbert added. Auntie Lil smiled grimly. At least Detective Santos considered her suggestions more seriously than that awful Lieutenant Abromowitz.

"What happened?"

The retired messenger shrugged unhappily. "Two uniformed men entered and stayed several hours. They left alone. It is very puzzling. I stayed quite late last night, watching the building carefully. No sign of The Eagle at all. Franklin is over there now. And who knows how many of those crazy ladies are wandering about beseeching strangers and wearing disguises? Now they've all taken to dressing like bag ladies and popping up just when you least expect them the most. It is like being trapped in an opera out of control."

Auntie Lil had been keeping an eye on the street and spotted the stout figure the instant it emerged into sight, headed for St. Barnabas.

"Get back," she hissed at Herbert, dragging him further into the shadows of the doorway. They peeked across the street together and watched as Fran, her face hidden, pulled a key from her pocketbook and quickly entered through the basement door.

"Don't you think it's a bit early for volunteering?" she asked ominously. "I never arrived until noon." Herbert checked his watch in reply. It was just before ten o'clock in the morning.

"Why do you think she is here so early?" he wondered aloud.

"Now look what's happening," Auntie Lil whispered in excitement.

The main entrance to St. Barnabas opened slowly, the large wooden doors swinging out with medieval ponderousness. Father

Stebbins stepped into a small pool of sunshine that spotlighted the top step. He blinked in the daylight and looked behind him. A small figure stepped into view and stood beside the priest, its nearly white hair gleaming in the autumn sunlight. Together, they searched the sidewalks in both directions, then the priest nodded slowly and unlocked the folding metal gate that blocked the steps from the street. The small figure squeezed through the small opening and took off running lightly, his sneaker-clad feet skimming over the sidewalk with ease.

"That's Timmy!" Auntie Lil hissed. "What's he doing with Father Stebbins?"

Herbert Wong was silent. He was a Buddhist and lacked Auntie Lil's ingrained reverence for Catholic priests. He had plenty of ideas that would account for Timmy's presence. Including none that he cared to share with Auntie Lil.

"I must be going," he told her as they watched Father Stebbins relock the gate. Both noticed that the priest seemed troubled. His face sagged and he was shaking his head sadly as he disappeared back inside the church.

"He did not see Miss Fran," Herbert observed. "I wonder what she is doing down there in the basement all alone?"

"She may not be in the basement," Auntie Lil explained. "There's a door in the basement that opens into the church from the inside. For all we know, they're playing tag up and down the steps right now."

"Not tag," Herbert said solemnly.

"Quite right. The game is much more serious than that."

"I must obtain Franklin's Egg McMuffin and return to my post across from Miss Emily's building," the retired messenger announced. "Franklin is due at the Salvation Army at half past. They have some large clothes in and he would like a new outfit."

"He is a huge man," Auntie Lil admitted. "I dare say his size may come in handy someday."

"Let us hope not," Herbert observed. He left, whistling, and headed down the street toward Times Square. A crisp morning and sudden sunshine often had that effect on Herbert—it warmed his soul and made him happy, regardless of the sad task that occupied him at the moment. Herbert was a philosopher and a man at peace with himself. He did not find happiness and sorrow incompatible at all.

Auntie Lil stayed put. She was stubborn and wildly curious. Not even the thought of black coffee distracted her from her scrutiny. This dedication was rewarded barely a half hour later, when the gate to the basement pushed open and Fran rushed into view. Her face was twisted and small tracks of silver glittered in the emerging sunlight: *tears*. Fran had been crying. To see such a stout and determinedly capable woman in tears was a shock, even to Auntie Lil.

Father Stebbins followed quickly and stood silently on the sidewalk, watching Fran rush down the street. The distraught woman reached Eighth Avenue and turned quickly north, not seeming to care that she rammed into a late commuter and sent him careening off a parked car. His briefcase bounced off the bumper.

Auntie Lil could be discreet and let the drama play out. Or she could be herself and dive in, head first. It wasn't much of a contest.

"Father Stebbins! Father Stebbins!" she called out loudly, scurrying across the street with unseemly haste in an effort to beat out a large bread truck that seemed intent on reaching the next corner in three seconds, even at the price of her life.

The priest looked up, startled. "Lillian! What brings you back here? You must be a sign. In the darkness, yea, I will send thee a sign."

"A sign?" she demanded. "A sign of what?"

"Of divine intervention," he said unhappily, turning away.

The intervention part was certainly right, but not even Auntie Lil considered her role "divine." She fell into step beside Father Stebbins. Together, they descended the steps toward the basement. His worried look had deepened.

"Who was that young boy I saw you with this morning? A new volunteer?" She tried to keep her voice light, but failed. The question sounded like an accusation.

"Young boy?" He stopped and stared at her blankly. "What young boy?"

"On the steps of the church just a little while ago." She should not have asked. A little more finesse was called for. Now she would warn him away.

The priest turned away and unlocked the door. "I'm afraid you're mistaken," he said evenly. "Your eyes must be playing tricks on you. I have been seeing a few special members of my flock who are unable to attend regular confession. That is all. What were you doing? Hiding in the shadows like the enemies of the Church in ancient times?"

She wisely decided to drop the subject. "I came to ask you a few questions," she said instead.

He sighed as eloquently as any martyr the Church had ever immortalized. "What kind of questions? I cannot always supply the answers, you know. A man of the cloth may be as confused as anyone. It seems I lack many answers these days. I have not been of much help to my flock, as it were. Like all others, I am but a man with feet of clay."

"Was Emily one of your parishioners? Did she come attend services here?"

"Mass," he corrected her primly. "No. Although she was a Catholic, I cannot ever recall seeing her at mass at St. Barnabas. She was a private woman and preferred to attend St. Peter's, where none of her friends belonged." He sighed again, distracted, his mind on other topics.

"You seem preoccupied," Auntie Lil said softly. "Is there anything I can do to help?"

His face cleared. "You can cook the meal today," he said hopefully. "I'm afraid Fran has just quit. I don't know what I'm going to do."

"Quit?" Auntie Lil stared at him. "Whatever for?"

Father Stebbins shrugged unhappily. "Sometimes I think that this is a very wicked world indeed." He ignored her question and held the door open as Auntie Lil hurried inside. The basement was dark and smelled faintly of pine.

"The lieutenant ordered me to stay away," she reminded him.

"I'm ordering you to stay and help." The priest wandered back into the kitchen area and opened the pantry door with a heavy sigh. "This world is not fit for the truly good, my dear Lillian," he said. "Too often, what is good only masks evil. And what is evil too often masks still more evil. Nothing is what it seems."

2. Auntie Lil threw together a hasty stew of odds and ends, but no one complained. There was an uneasy air about the soup kitchen that day, brought on by the chill in the weather. Undeniably, winter was coming and, with it, freezing temperatures and the danger of snow. Soon, the streets would not be an option for many of the homeless in line. They were worried. Where would they go? Few wanted to return to the city shelters. One visit had been more than enough for most of those waiting to eat. The shelters were dirty and dangerous and discouraging. At least on the street, they could cling to some measure of privacy, thanks to the anonymity the hurrying crowds bestowed on them.

Adelle arrived with her entourage for their meal a few minutes later than was usual. Though they made excellent bag ladies, their pride would not let them appear at the soup kitchen in full regalia. At St. Barnabas, they had a more important role to play. There, they were the sheltered elite, the crème de la crème of the hungry. Consequently, they were as well groomed and regal as ever by the time they showed for lunch.

"Lillian!" Adelle stared in surprise. "You're back. And just what have you done with Fran? Father Stebbins looks positively naked without his amanuensis."

"She's quit!" Auntie Lil whispered across the serving line, where she had been reduced to dishing out stew due to the lack of able bodies. Fran was not the only volunteer missing. The murder had scared several part-timers away and the kitchen was severely understaffed. "See if you can find out why she quit," she ordered Adelle.

"Certainly. A mere child's play of deduction." Adelle accepted her plate with queenly bearing and led her followers down the line. They had arrived in a single group, making it easy for Auntie Lil to check off each face mechanically. She wondered who was helping Herbert out with his surveillance since they nearly all seemed to be at the kitchen. But wait, one face was missing—and it was hard a face not to miss. Emily's old rival, Eva, was not among the crowd of aged actresses.

No one working at the kitchen had mentioned Fran's disappearance yet, although Auntie Lil caught the other volunteers exchanging silent looks a few times. Father Stebbins remained preoccupied, his mind on more important matters. Once he even disappeared upstairs without warning and did not return for nearly half an hour. This uncharacteristic move—combined with the general air of worry circulating through the crowd—fueled a tense atmosphere at the St. Barnabas soup kitchen that day.

Auntie Lil escaped from behind the pot of stew and headed for Adelle's table. "Where's Eva?" Auntie Lil asked the assembled actresses. They shook their heads collectively.

"Who knows?" Adelle murmured. "She's quite the headstrong lady these days. Has her own theories. Who are we to interfere?"

"She's probably angry at me," a usually quiet old actress admitted. "Now that Emily is dead, I expect I'm on the list as her next great enemy. Eva must always have someone to hate. It's how she gets her energy."

"Why would she hate you, my dear?" Auntie Lil asked quickly when she noticed a subtle but growing movement of glances intended to silence the woman.

"I saw her stop at Emily's table the day she died," the woman explained. "I didn't say anything at first. But after a while, Eva made me positively furious with all of the accusations she was hurling at poor Fran. Fran works very hard here and I think it's ugly of us all to keep guessing at her private life. Much less blame the murder on her."

"Eva stopped at Emily's table right before she died?" Auntie Lil asked.

This time the woman did not answer. Someone's warning kick had gotten to her. Her eyes slid over and met Adelle's, then she looked down and kept silent.

"Eva always stopped to say something to Emily," Adelle explained. "Just to prove that she didn't feel in the least snubbed by Emily's refusal to sit at our table. Though, of course, I believe her feelings were terribly wounded."

"Quite a childish fight they were having," Auntie Lil observed.

Adelle opened her mouth as if to say more, then shut it abruptly without explanation. Her eyes surveyed every woman around the table. No one said a word. They had long ago perfected the art of nonverbal communication—and Auntie Lil was not privy to their code. In fact, she would not even waste time trying. She'd just take another tack.

"Have any of you seen a young boy around here?" she asked hopefully. "About this tall. Very blond hair. The one in the dime-store photographs I showed you?"

They shook their heads solemnly and Auntie Lil sighed. "I'm getting nowhere, it seems," she complained.

"That's all right," Adelle reassured her. "Neither are we."

"How can The Eagle still be inside that building?" Auntie Lil looked around the table. "I'm not criticizing, but are you sure you've been watching carefully?"

"Quite sure," Adelle insisted, her voice rising in incipient indignation. "At least two people at all times. If he had left, we would have seen him."

"Well, I mustn't sit here sulking," Auntie Lil decided. She'd slip away and phone Detective Santos. Perhaps he had found out where The Eagle had gone. Besides, soon it would be time to do the dishes and she had to draw the line somewhere.

The old women watched her go with impassive eyes. They did not speak until she was well out the door.

3.　Auntie Lil had lied. She waited in the doorway opposite to see where the old actresses went. You could never be sure, she reasoned to herself. Better to suspect than to be sorry. It was not difficult for Auntie Lil to follow Adelle's crowd; they were too intent on assuming their disguises to pay her much attention. She trailed along behind them, shamelessly eavesdropping. It appeared that Adelle had a tiny apartment on Fiftieth Street and that the women were headed there to resume their bag lady roles. They chatted like a crowd of showgirls on the way to a performance. It disturbed Auntie Lil that Eva was not among them. She did not trust these streets.

The group headed north up Eighth Avenue and Auntie Lil turned west, satisfied they were doing as they'd promised. She wanted time to think about what she had seen that morning at St. Barnabas. She walked toward the Hudson River, where the huge cruise liners stood berthed at massive docks just a few blocks south from the pier where she had taken Theodore. Not many cargo ships pulled in these days; newer ports on Staten Island and Brooklyn made the trip to midtown Manhattan unnecessary. But the big passenger lines still liked the cachet of boarding their guests in sight of the Manhattan skyline. As Auntie Lil drew nearer, she heard a deep, mournful bellow. One of the passenger ships was pulling free from the dock and sounding its horn in celebration. She was just in time to watch it back slowly into the center of the river and head ponderously down the Hudson toward the Verrazano Narrows Bridge, where it would continue out to sea. The bulk of the boat was incredible. Even the water seemed to strain under its weight.

A cruise leaving in midweek would have few passengers and, indeed, the dock was cleared of any goodbye visitors within minutes. They walked quickly to their cars, anxious to leave the desolate riverfront and get on with their lives. Soon, Auntie Lil was left alone on a small concrete sidewalk that ran between the docks. She stared down at the murky greenish black waters of the Hudson, her mind still on St. Barnabas.

Why would Fran have quit? And did it have anything to do with Timmy's visit to Father Stebbins? Why would the old priest bother to lie about that visit? What could he be hiding? Surely it was no crime to help a young runaway in need of guidance. And the young boy might have nothing to do with Emily's death; their friendship could be a sad coincidence. Just another blow to Timmy's self-esteem.

Her mind wandered to the old actresses. It was a good thing she was allowed back at St. Barnabas, where she could keep a closer eye on the group. Could they know more than they were saying? She would not put it past Adelle to try to solve the murder on her own. Although gracious and charming, the woman clearly hated to share the spotlight with anyone. And wasn't it curious that Eva was missing? Maybe the others had teased her too much at last, or blamed her for Emily's death. Or, conversely, maybe she was just too busy redeeming herself by tailing residents of Emily's building to even stop to eat.

And what about that building? How could any trace of Emily disappear so quickly? Who was living in her apartment now, and why? Was it The Eagle? Did the killer have the audacity to move into his victim's very home? Yet Detective Santos had said that a young blonde woman lived in the apartment. And surely the police would have done a thorough job once they took the trouble to show up. She remembered she had not yet found out the results of the detective's latest search for The Eagle, and made a mental note to call Santos. Was it possible that the entire building was participating in some sort of conspiracy? Surely not. What kind of trouble could an old woman like Emily possibly get into that would drive anyone, much less an entire building, to murder her?

The riverfront was exposed to the wind and, though the day had turned warmer, the breeze and too many unanswered questions conspired to chill her resolve. Auntie Lil shivered and stared down into the nearly black waves. How horrible the gently lapping waters of the Hudson seemed, what terrible secrets they concealed. To drown in the Hudson would be a particularly gruesome fate. One would disappear under that slick surface—mouth choked with unspeakable debris—condemned to death in the unseen depths. Who knew what unknown horrors lived beneath that murky facade?

That did it. She was getting far too morbid. No more visits to the morgue for her. She shook her shoulders briskly and straightened up. It was all very well to stop and reflect, but brooding would not solve Emily's death and feeling sorry for herself would get her nowhere. What she needed was a good strong cup of tea to bring her back. Forget cappuccino, she decided, they always drank strong tea in those old English mysteries and wasn't she practically in the middle of one right now? Billy at the Delicious Deli would be able to help; he kept an excellent supply of teas on hand.

4.   Billy was taking advantage of the lull between lunch and the light dinner crowd. He was leaning over the counter, anxiously scanning an open newspaper. Auntie Lil watched him through the windows of the deli for a moment. Surely, that wide open face was an honest one. She wished she knew for sure.

The bell tinkled and Billy's face fell when he saw that the new visitor was Auntie Lil. "I can't believe it," he said. "I was just thinking of you. It looks like I was right."

"What do you mean?" She followed his stare and glanced at the newspaper. "What are you right about?"

"Bob Fleming," Billy said, somewhat smugly. "Take a look at this." He spun the newspaper around and pushed it across the counter. Without her glasses, Auntie Lil had to lean perilously close. She blinked. The huge headline made it all quite clear: RUN-AWAY SHELTER DIRECTOR CHARGED WITH SEX ABUSE.

"What?" Her voice failed her and she studied the article more closely. It was a column by that female reporter T.S. enjoyed so much. The one with the teasing grin and the sarcastic writing style. Oh, yes—there was her name: Margo McGregor.

"What does it say?" Auntie Lil asked faintly. Damn her vanity. She wanted her glasses *bad*.

"Some kid turned him in. Said he'd been hitting on him at night, taking him home. You know. Stuff like that." Bill's voice trailed off in embarrassment and he released his anger in an effort to regain control. "I told you there was something funny about him. If it was up to me I'd pound him right into the pavement and let those kids take turns walking over his corpse."

"Good heavens," Auntie Lil looked up sharply. "What ever happened to a man being innocent until proven guilty?"

"Charges have been filed against him," Billy said simply. "They expect more kids to step forward as they feel safe."

Kids? They were runaways, miniature savages. God knows what they might say if they thought they could get some attention. She wanted to tell him this, but the words failed her. Such an attitude was not only unfair, but disloyal to Bob Fleming. After all, he had been the one to point out that they were still children; she could not now change her mind and see them as conniving adults. But she could be puzzled and skeptical of the charges. And find out more about them.

"What child made the allegations?" she demanded.

Billy looked at her strangely. "I don't know. They're not going to release the name. He's underage. That's the whole point."

"He?" Auntie Lil stared at Billy intently. "What makes you think it's a 'he'?"

"The articles says so." Billy pointed to the paper and shrugged.

"Listen, I'm sorry if it upsets you, but I told you that street talk was usually right. He's as bad as the men he claims to save those kids from."

"Mind if I borrow this?" Auntie Lil asked rhetorically, since the newspaper was folded and tucked into her enormous handbag before she had finished the request.

"Be my guest," Billy said philosophically. "I don't need a paper to tell me I was right."

He was being a little too smug for her taste. She'd just go find her tea somewhere else. The door bell tinkled angrily behind her.

But the tea was instantly forgotten when a new thought hit her. Suppose it had been Timmy or Little Pete who had accused him? Suppose it was all tied together?

She changed directions and marched resolutely toward Fleming's Homefront office. If anyone was in, she'd try to find out more.

The door was locked and the lights out in the front office. But Auntie Lil could see a figure in the back, head down on a desk. She knocked and when she got no response, she proceeded to try and bang the door down with her pocketbook. After several seconds of ear-deafening assault, the figure rose and drifted her way.

It was Annie O'Day and she had been crying. A lot. The stained cheeks and puffy eyes seemed horribly out of place on her previously cheery and healthy countenance. "You've heard?" she asked glumly as Auntie Lil barged inside.

"I did and I'm having trouble believing it." Auntie Lil looked around to make sure that they were alone. "Lock the doors."

"I just did," Annie mumbled in reply as she led her inside. "Let's sit in back. I'm beginning to like the darkness."

"Is this true?" Auntie Lil demanded, producing the newspaper.

"No, it's not true. But it doesn't matter. Bob is being questioned by the police right now. They wouldn't let me stay with him. It's been at least five hours." The huge Irish woman reached for a tissue and blew her nose with a mighty honk, then tossed the Kleenex into a wastebasket across the narrow space. It banked perfectly and slid inside. "He's ruined whether the allegations turn out to be true or not, I expect. He'll be poison by the time they get through with him. It'll be the end of any grants or donations for Homefront."

"Who says he did this?" Auntie Lil asked, glaring at the newspaper as if it were the columnist's fault that Bob Fleming's character and life had been destroyed.

"Don't you know?" She looked up at Auntie Lil in surprise.

"It's Timmy. Bob told me when he called from the stationhouse. It's the little boy you were looking for. Bob hardly knows him. And then he does this. Why? What did Bob ever do to him?"

Auntie Lil was silent. It had occurred to her at once that Bob Fleming's main contact with Timmy had been on her behalf. What questions had the Homefront director asked on the streets, trying to help her? Was this why he was being attacked?

"Why are you so quiet?" Annie demanded.

"I was wondering if Bob had had any contact with Timmy since I last spoke to him," Auntie Lil said carefully.

Annie shook her head vigorously. "He'd been asking around about Timmy," she explained. "Trying to find out who that guy that keeps him is. Trying to see if Timmy had a last name, or how he was involved with that old lady that was killed. Little Pete wouldn't tell him much, so he had to go to other people on the street. But you know what he was asking about better than I do. He was doing it for you." If it occurred to Annie that Auntie Lil was somehow at fault for what had happened, she did not show it.

"Timmy." Auntie Lil repeated the young boy's name softly and stared thoughtfully at the newspaper. "I want to talk to him."

"You and me and half the police force," Annie replied miserably. "I've been looking for him all day. He's nowhere to be found. And Little Pete has disappeared with him."

"Someone talked to him," Auntie Lil pointed out. She had to bring the newspaper practically to the tip of her nose to be able to read it, but it was a humiliation she was too angry to pay any heed to.

"What do you mean?" Annie stared at the newspaper.

"This woman talked to him." Auntie Lil set the paper back on the desk and placed a strong finger over Margo McGregor's face. "She doesn't use his name, but it sounds like she talked to him for quite a long time. In fact, it sounds like she was the one to break the whole story."

"Let me see that." Annie O'Day slid the paper close and peered at it. "I get the other paper. It was just a small article crammed in at the last minute. I didn't even see this one. God, it takes up half a page. What does it say?" Her voice trailed off and anger settled over her innocent features, lending them a hardened, unpleasant look. She looked up at Auntie Lil. The rage reflected in her ice blue eyes was frightening. "This woman printed every single lie that kid said. That's not fair. That's like trying Bob in the press."

"Perhaps we should have a word with Miss McGregor. I could give her a call," Auntie Lil suggested calmly, hoping to erase the terrible anger that had imbued Annie's face with a suddenly ominous and threatening strength.

"*You* call her," Annie replied defiantly. She threw the newspaper on the floor. "If Margo McGregor can find Timmy, I can find Timmy. And I'm going to, if it's the last thing I do." The article had filled her with fresh resolve and she was up and out the door before Auntie Lil could stop her.

Auntie Lil stood in the back office, wondering what to do next. It was not in her nature to sit and do nothing, but how was she supposed to lock the door behind her if she left? Annie had marched out with the keys. There was nothing she could do but wait until Bob Fleming or Annie returned. She might as well make the best of it. Auntie Lil bolted the door from the inside and crept back into the darker interior. She was not in the mood to deal with any runaways at the moment. There was work to be done.

She gathered the newspaper pages from the floor and put them back together. She did not want to believe Margo McGregor either, but it sounded as if the columnist had done her homework.

Damn. She should have remembered at once. Margo McGregor had cropped up before . . . in Emily's pocketbook, her photo on each of the clippings carefully saved on a variety of subjects. Even worse: Theodore had thought them important. And she had not. She just hated it when she was wrong.

Could Emily have contacted the columnist about Timmy? Was that how the story got started? But there had been no evidence of correspondence with anyone in Emily's apartment, and especially not with Margo McGregor.

There was nothing left to do but go right to the source. She chose a telephone from the many lined up on the wall and began. Pretending to be Margo McGregor's mother, she greased her way through three levels of screening and right to the columnist's desk. Unfortunately, she was not there. A harried and disinterested-sounding colleague took a message and said he'd leave it on her desk. She thought about what to say and decided on: "Have vital information on Emily Toujours' death." That should bring a rapid response. She left the number printed on the phone, hung up and waited confidently.

A half-hour later, it had not brought any sort of response. And she was steamed. She didn't appreciate being trapped in Homefront until Annie O'Day returned while the entire world ignored her phone messages. A whole afternoon of doing nothing would kill her. She'd just have to pester Detective Santos while she waited.

He was in, since there was still another hour before the official cocktail hour began.

"Did you find The Eagle?" she asked anxiously, forgetting to introduce herself.

An introduction was not necessary. "No, we did not find The Eagle," the detective replied crisply. "We thoroughly searched that building, Miss Hubbert, and there is no tall black man living there with an eagle tattoo on his arm. In fact, there is not a single black man living in the entire building at all. Which is unusual in itself but not, so far as we can tell, necessarily illegal."

"But we saw him go in and he never came out."

"Even if that was true—and I have my doubts about it, to be honest with you—there are plenty of ways he could have gone out undetected," Santos explained. "Down the back fire escape, or up to the roof and over onto another building's roof. See what I mean?"

She was silent. He had a point.

"Listen, Miss Hubbert, I know you're trying to help. And I think that I've been a pretty good sport about it. But that was the last time I'll be able to humor you. Two officers spent an entire afternoon checking apartments and questioning people again. With zippo results. I simply can't afford the manpower to go off on any more goose chases. I've got another death on my hands this afternoon, this time a floater with no identification. And there will probably be another murder by morning." He sighed. "Go home and take up knitting or something. Go home and leave us all alone."

The detective hung up gently and Auntie Lil stared out the picture windows of the darkened storefront. A floater. The waters of the Hudson had claimed another victim. She shivered. The secrets of Hell's Kitchen seemed darker than ever.

5. It had been an excellent day for T.S. Such a good day, in fact, that he was halfheartedly considering retiring the tan slacks and black sweater he'd worn to mark his triumph. Why, the sweater still smelled faintly of Lilah's gardenia perfume. And surely there were a few of her silver hairs nestled among its nap. After all, they'd sat side by side for hours in the Performing Arts Library, poring over old Playbills in search of Emily Toujours in cast listings or a glimpse of her face in any photos. Their lack of success at this task had not dimmed the triumphs of the day.

At first, he had felt a bit guilty about St. Barnabas and was unsure if his help had been expected there or not. But he had managed to rationalize that worry away quite nicely by remembering that they had tossed his dear old aunt out on her ear, and that Father Stebbins had failed to even recognize him the day before. So surely his obligations to the soup kitchen could take a back seat to the investigation.

And why should he begrudge himself a cozy lunch with Lilah at a small French bistro off Sixty-second Street? What better way to cap off a morning of careful scrutiny than with exquisite dishes, an excellent dry white, a beautiful woman and a maître d' with enough sense to provide a candlelit atmosphere in the middle of the day. Thus fortified, they had returned to the library and spent a number of happy hours paging through still more Playbills while reminiscing about the many Broadway shows they had seen with other people . . . and the many more they hoped to see together.

Eight hours passed by as quickly as eight minutes, made that much more delicious by the thought that there was still an evening together to come. Who cared if they had to spend that evening in the supercilious company of a cheesy would-be Broadway producer? In fact, who cared that not a trace of Emily Toujours had been found, not even as an extra or in a backstage capacity? He had spotted several of the other old actresses, he thought, in their earlier incarnations, though he could not be positive. The young and painted faces that stared out at him in faded photographs held little relation to the heavily wrinkled versions they now wore.

Except for Adelle. It was true, he discovered, that she did look quite a lot like she had when she was younger. Her broad face and regal neck weathered well. And he found more traces of her career than anyone else's. She appeared to have worked her way up to featured roles by the late forties and early fifties, before disappearing into obscurity again. It was interesting and rather sad from a sociological standpoint, but shed no light on Emily's murder so far as T.S. could determine.

Fortunately, lack of progress made in finding any trace of Emily Toujours was balanced out by progress that had been made in other, quite important areas. Tonight more would be made, T.S. was sure. He searched his closet for evening attire appropriate for a wealthy investor, and settled on his very best suit, custom-made in Hong Kong according to Auntie Lil's strict specifications.

He had a plan: if all went well, he and Lilah would be able to quickly eliminate Lance Worthington as nothing more than a typical Broadway fringe sleaze. Then they could forget about murder for a few minutes and find a small and charming bistro that served drinks.

He hummed as he dressed. He was starting to like retirement; it afforded the luxury of ignoring business as usual. He had risen that morning without even so much as a glance at the newspaper, and now here he was plunging into a world of dim lights, quick looks and shared smiles. A world that would last for as long as he cared it to. There would be no rising early for him tomorrow, no damnable office to sap his energy. He was free. He could be whoever he wanted to be. The emergence of T.S. Hubbert, new man in town, continued on its uncertain course.

He helped it along a bit by selecting a slim, purple tie that shimmered in the right light. Then he turned up the volume on his stereo and blasted show tunes at a volume that astounded his nearest neighbors and sent the cats galloping into the bathroom closet for quiet.

The music was so loud, in fact, that he failed to hear the phone ring. Nor did he notice the message light blinking before he hurried downstairs to meet Lilah. She was waiting in the back seat of the limousine. His highly impressed doorman, Mahmoud, dashed out to open the door for him, bestowing silent and respectful homage on T.S. as a tribute to his excellent taste in women.

If Grady stepped on it, T.S. decided, they would have just enough time for a quiet diner together before Lance Worthington and his party beckoned. There was a small Indian restaurant on the Lower East Side that he thought Lilah would love. It was appropriately exotic and a bit off the beaten path. A good choice, considering the unusual romantic journey (for him, anyway) that he had embarked upon.

6.   T.S. had not talked to Auntie Lil even once that day. Had she known why, it was doubtful that Auntie Lil would have minded a bit. But she *didn't* know why and, consequently, she was steaming. She slammed the phone back in its cradle with childish temper, thinking of how much she loathed answering machines.

Evening had arrived. Auntie Lil sat in the darkness of the Homefront office and glared out onto the crowded street. How dare all those people rush past without a glance, while she was stuck in here? Where was Annie and who the hell had the keys? She ought to just walk out and damn the consequences of an unlocked front door. There was nothing for her here. She was wasting her time.

It occurred to her that Bob Fleming might keep an extra set of keys in his desk. She opened the top drawer and searched through it hopefully, encountering coffee shop packets of sugar, ketchup, jelly and salt; a supply of tattered paper napkins; three cough drops; some loose straws; and an upturned plastic box of paper clips. No keys.

Then it hit her. Good God. She *was* getting old. Why was she sitting here pouting? She was being handed a golden opportunity to rummage through all of Homefront's files. It was nirvana to someone as exquisitely nosy as she: one large desk, two large file cabinets, all kinds of dark corners and countless messy piles of documents. All for the taking. She glanced once more at the front doorway and briskly set to work.

7.

"I thought you'd enjoy a change of pace," T.S. told Lilah.

"It's wonderful here." She patted his hand fondly and he beamed back as if she had just said something enormously clever.

They were sitting in a tiny alcove of a small Indian restaurant, finishing their coconut soup. They were protected from the view of other diners by strategically placed pots of miniature palms and a large and colorful tank of exotic tropical fish. It was a little like being lost on a deserted isle together. Except, of course, for the overly obsequious waiter. Sensing a potentially huge tip from a besotted couple, he hovered about with servile determination. This devotion amused Lilah; the small smile that played about her lips charmed T.S. to distraction.

"Next he'll be offering to eat my soup for me," she decided.

T.S. beamed at her in reply and admired the graceful way she sipped at the remainder of her first course. Early training in a finishing school had left its mark.

"More poori bread, sir?" the Indian waiter inquired, popping out from behind a palm with the sudden efficiency of a Bengal warrior who had spotted a tiger.

"Heavens, no," T.S. replied. The table was littered with plates of untouched poori bread that swelled like small parachutes among the silver.

A few minutes later, a warm breeze of curry mixed with cumin and other fragrant spices announced the return of their attentive waiter. He burst through the palms bearing an enormous tray loaded with plates of steaming food and colorful rice.

"Good heavens." Lilah stared at the feast. "Do we have time to eat all this?" she asked faintly.

T.S. glanced at his watch, annoyed at being reminded of their impending task. He sighed. "We'll just have to be fashionably late," he said firmly. "Lance Worthington will just have to wait."

8. Anyone else would have found it an eerie task to search through the darkened interior of Homefront while unsuspecting passers-by flowed past without a glance. But not Auntie Lil. Her curiosity had consumed her and she was determined to make up for lost time. Blinded by Annie O'Day's charm and Bob Fleming's surface dedication, she had let her heart overrule her head. But now the old Auntie Lil was back in action—and she suspected everyone. She would rummage, uncover, examine and analyze all data. Her mission: to pick apart the life of Bob Fleming and scrutinize the operations of Homefront.

It was slow going because she had to be careful to return everything to its proper place. She would have preferred to flag interesting items, pile them on Bob Fleming's desk and go through them at her leisure. Instead, she examined each item at once and returned it to its proper file, drawer or pile, then carefully jotted down its description and potential importance in her ever-present notebook.

After almost two hours, she had uncovered a number of items that might be of interest, either in investigating Emily's murder or in helping to determine Bob Fleming's character. She carefully listed each item, followed it by a description, and made a note of the questions it triggered, then underlined key points and added her final observations. When finished, Auntie Lil sat down at a desk and reviewed what she had found:

One photo of Bob Fleming: Standing with group of men, all clad in military uniforms. Jungle backdrop. *War photo.* Vietnam? Puts age at 40 to 45. Could work in his favor at trial. Or harm him?

Second photo of Bob Fleming: Has arm around Annie O'Day on a Hudson River pier? Night time. Amusement park and ferris wheel seen in the background. *They are kissing* against a backdrop of colorful lights. Is this how a man who likes boys acts? Could be—*ask Annie questions* to probe if feeling is genuine.

Flyers of missing children: Nearly one hundred xerox bulletins about missing children, with photos and descriptions. From all over U.S.A. Handwritten notes on a few, hard to make out. Looks like dates or NYC locations, followed by question marks. *No one resembling Timmy or Little Pete.*

Separate files on specific children: Maybe 25 in all. Small brown folder assigned to each. Most have only first names listed. Some have photos obviously taken without their knowledge. Attached sheets of paper provide various bits of incomplete information. Notes in different handwriting provide medical diagnosis, i.e. "HIV-neg. Syph. O-N." Why is he building a profile on each of these children? Med notes from Annie? Info for city program? Police? To discover identity? To contact parents? *Other reason?*

File on Timmy: No last name listed. Nicknames: Lightning, Little Big Man, and Zebra. Reference to changing hair color? Other info provided: "Possibly from Texas. Accent. Runs with Little Pete. Age approx 15. Protected. Men only. 8th Ave. between 43rd and 47th." Photo provided: Timmy crossing street with older man, face unseen. Background shows doorway. *Old woman* inside watching? *Emily?* Face out of focus. Group of black and white prostitutes nearby watching Timmy and man. *One may be resident of Emily's building.* Cheaply dressed. *Did Bob tell me everything he knew about Timmy?*

Grant and donation information: Homefront modestly funded, but commitments in place through next year. *Money pressure at a minimum.* No expansion plans found.

City forms: along with more forms. Plus private program forms. *Too many forms in this world.*

Booklets: Misc. on various city and private drug programs, alternative schools, residential options, shelters. Proof Homefront is legitimate? Or only a cover?

Bible: King James version. Small. Cover ripped. Inside worn. No passages underlined. In his favor? Is it his? For children?

Other publications: Misc. Heavy on fishing magazines, camping and other outdoor topics. *New Yorker* magazines that actually look read!(?) *No pornographic material.*

That was all. The sole sum of incriminating or illuminating evidence didn't add up to much in the final analysis.

The phone rang as Auntie Lil was reviewing her list for a second time to make sure that no implications had been missed. "Homefront," she answered automatically, her mind preoccupied with the list.

The frightened voice on the other end brought her immediately back to attention. "Miss Hubbert?" Annie O'Day's tearful voice broke. "Is that you?"

"Yes, it's me. Of course, it's me. I'm the only one you left behind without keys."

"Thank God." The sniffles stopped and Annie gave a frightened laugh. "I must be going crazy," she said weakly.

"I'll say. You left me here without any keys to lock up."

"I'm sorry," Annie explained. "I spent hours looking for Timmy and then met Bob at the station. I got him a lawyer. They're releasing Bob in a few more minutes."

"They're letting him go?" Auntie Lil asked, surprised.

"Just for now. Believe me, they're not dropping anything."

"Why were you crying?" Auntie Lil asked sharply. "You're a big girl. You knew they had charged him. He needs you to be strong."

"I wasn't crying about Bob. I was crying about you."

"Me?" Auntie Lil demanded incredulously. "Why on earth would you cry about me?"

"I was sitting in a chair by the front precinct door," she explained. "This man at a desk across the partition started calling around to other police stations. He kept saying the same thing over and over. They had found a body floating in the Hudson. It was an old lady, did they have any missing person reports that fit? She had not been dead for very many hours. Then he'd describe her. Stoutly built. Broad face. Wearing very young clothes for her age. She didn't have any identification." Annie gulped and continued. "My imagination got carried away. I was afraid it was you. And that it was my fault for leaving you there alone."

"Me? No, it certainly was not me. Stout, indeed. Quite old? Besides, I do not wear clothes that are too young for my age. I simply have a highly developed sense of *joie de vivre*." Auntie Lil stared out the street window. The Hudson River had not claimed her that day, but it had certainly claimed someone who looked a lot like her.

CHAPTER TWELVE

1. Lance Worthington's building was one of those colored-glass and blasted-sand towers that spread like a plague throughout New York City in the 1980s. The newness had worn off quickly and small patches of concrete peeked through the cheap patina of surface beige. Already, the building sagged, as if collapsing from the weight of too high rents and too many tenants struggling to maintain a lifestyle they could no longer afford. It seemed the perfect home for a borderline Broadway producer.

Grady dropped them off in front of the drooping entrance awning with a promise to return every thirty minutes to see if they were ready to escape. Lilah looked around apprehensively. Though on the East Side, the building was located on a somewhat dubious side street that featured frequent and ominous stretches of shadow.

"I'm already depressed," T.S. decided. "How about you?"

"I am now," Lilah replied, staring at the figure of the slumbering doorman. He was a portly soul packed into a too snug uniform with a yellowish stain above the shirt pocket. He was snoring away behind a waist-high counter, with his feet propped up on the top of it and his chair tipped against the wall. This precarious position caused his head to dangle backwards at a preposterous angle, providing guests with an excellent view of his sinus cavities.

"We'll only be a minute," T.S. told the unconscious sentinel. "We're just going to burgle a few apartments and be right out." He glowed warmly at Lilah's appreciative giggle and guided her gallantly into the elevator. He had perfected the art of steering her by the arm, a gesture he felt was nearly as intimate as holding hands yet far less juvenile.

"It was a wonderful dinner," she thanked him again on their

way upstairs. "I haven't eaten so much food in forty years. The most exotic Robert ever got was French."

T.S. was so pleased at how well their dinner had gone that he had no trouble with being reminded of Lilah's deceased husband. He could afford to be magnanimous. After all, it was not as if he were competing with a legend. Good heavens, Robert Cheswick had been a superior horse's ass and, as it turned out, a rather big liar as well.

They reached the appropriate floor and it was immediately apparent where the party was being held. All thoughts of a small tasteful gathering vanished with the first blast of raucous music and the distant roar of drunken shrieks. The apartment door at the end of the hall seemed to nearly pulsate in its effort to contain the bacchanal inside.

"Perhaps we waited a bit too long," T.S. said, slowing down to consider the situation.

"Come on," Lilah urged him, pulling him forward. "We've come this far, we might as well see it through."

T.S. straightened his tie and steeled himself for the coming chaos. After several fruitless moments of pounding on the door, he finally pushed it open and, quite literally, faced the music. He and Lilah stood in the doorway staring at a sunken living room that teemed with an astonishing assortment of human beings in various stages of inebriation. Lance Worthington was nowhere to be seen, but numerous blondes in skintight dresses seemed to be acting as official hostesses or, at least, were being rather athletically friendly to a number of the male guests. There was hardly a man in sight without a blonde draped over his shoulder or sitting upon his knee. A pair descended upon them at once and pulled them into the fray, shrieking welcomes, snatching their coats and guiding them toward a long bar that dominated the one wall with a picture window. Outside, the lights of New York City glowed serenely and T.S. wanted very much to escape back into the night.

Behind the bar stood a dignified, elderly black man dressed in a tuxedo. He looked as if he would rather be enslaved in some pre–Civil War enclave than forced to perform for a party of such obnoxious white heathens. His cool eyes swept over T.S. and Lilah, and his shoulders relaxed. Perhaps here were people who actually had manners, his hopeful expression implied.

"Something from the bar, sir?" the bartender inquired evenly. T.S. had to lean over an ice bucket to catch even a hint of the words. My God, whoever was in charge of the music must be stone deaf. It drowned out even the bartender's deep voice.

T.S. ordered a Dewars and soda for himself while Lilah opted for a white wine spritzer. They clutched their drinks and searched around for a quiet haven. A small alcove that led into the kitchen seemed their best bet. They sought refuge beside a large potted palm (that T.S. suspected was artificial) and surveyed the raucous party.

The sunken living room area was lined on three sides with long black leather couches. A mirrored coffee table dominated the center of the common space and was littered with spilt drinks, metallic pocketbooks and the rather large head of a man who had passed out while sitting on the carpet nearby. The couches were occupied by a half dozen plump middle-aged males, who looked like a contingent of modern gingerbread men, so alike were they in well-tanned coloring, thinning hair and softened body shape. Most of them held a drink in one hand and a giggly blonde in the other.

"I must be seeing double," Lilah murmured.

"I'm seeing quadruple," T.S. decided. "What does he do? Make the girls dye their hair before they get an invitation?"

"Wait. I see a redhead over there." Lilah nodded discreetly toward a short hallway. Sure enough, an extremely tall redhead slouched into view, tugging at her waist in an effort to keep her pantyhose from riding down her long legs. Her face was elongated and drooped with stupor or boredom. She started to the right, stopped abruptly to get her bearings, then lurched to the left and perched on the edge of one of the leather couches where she proceeded to absently ruffle the thinning hair of a tubby businessman. His existing blonde companion looked up indignantly, ready to squawk, but kept silent when she spotted the redhead.

T.S. stared more closely at the balding businessman. His face—red and perspiring from too much drink and too many female hormones hovering nearby—looked oddly familiar. But T.S. could not pinpoint why. Surely they had met previously. Perhaps before T.S. had retired? Or had it been more recently? It was maddening not to be able to recall.

"No one looks very happy at this party," Lilah said suddenly. "Am I right or am I insane?"

"No, you're definitely right," T.S. agreed. "Everyone seems a little bit too desperate for another drink. Even those men on the couch, clutching those women, don't seem particularly thrilled to be here. And the women are clearly bored. They're patting those men on the heads like they're puppies." He searched the interior of the apartment carefully. "I wonder where Lance Worthington is?"

"Lilah Cheswick! What on earth are you doing here?" It was the first cultured voice of the evening and it belonged to an extremely distinguished-looking man who had apparently been hiding out in the kitchen behind them.

"Albert!" Lilah was two parts shocked at seeing someone she recognized and one part embarrassed at being caught at such a freewheeling party. "I'm here with my friend, Theodore. He's looking into backing one of Mr. Worthington's plays. Something about Davy Crockett. What on earth are you doing here?"

Albert shrugged apologetically. "I got roped into backing it, too. I thought I'd better check out what sort of fellow he is. I'm not too impressed, I must say." He sipped at his drink and raised his eyebrows at Lilah in a manner that managed to be superior without being condescending.

T.S. hated the fellow on sight. He pegged him at once as a CEO or president of his own company, one who had started with inherited money but then made a huge success out of—probably doubling or quadrupling—the family fortune. Now he was in his early fifties, all tanned and exercised into good health, probably with one wife behind him and a newer model floating around somewhere. Plus a girlfriend, three secretaries and a legion of toadying employees. T.S. knew the type well. What was he doing at Lance Worthington's party? Surely he had better investments of both time and money to make. Especially if he moved in that world of old money that intimidated T.S. so much—the same world Lilah had grown up in.

It was the one thing, T.S. reflected sadly, that might conspire to keep them apart. All that money. Or a man like Albert. In a sudden flood of insecurity, he silently directed his hostility toward Albert.

If Lilah thought Albert's presence at the party was odd, she tactfully kept silent. But she could sense T.S.'s discomfort and looked so uneasy that T.S. relented. He decided that he would be gracious and attempt small talk after all. "Wonder where our host is?" he asked their new companion.

Albert shrugged, bored, and T.S. took it as a personal insult. "Probably in the back bedroom," Albert finally replied. "He seems to be spending a lot of time there."

As if on cue, Lance Worthington appeared in the back hallway, a familiar blonde on one arm. "There he is," T.S. nodded toward the darkened interior. "And he's got that woman with him. Red dress."

"Sally St. Claire," Lilah murmured. "Although I'm sure that's a *nom de plume* of sorts. It would be the perfect name for the madame of a bordello."

"You know Sally?" Albert inquired a little too casually and T.S. knew at once that he had a more than passing familiarity with Sally St. Claire's more intimate attributes. T.S. had interviewed people for a living for thirty-plus years and picked up a few pointers on the inability of humans to keep silent when it would greatly behoove them to do so.

"We've been spotted," Lilah murmured sweetly. She turned away, but it was much too late. Lance Worthington made a beeline across the apartment, brushing rudely past other guests in his haste to reach what he thought was the wealthiest trio in the room.

"Mr. Hubbert, Ms. Cheswick . . . I'd given up hope!" The producer was maniacally animated, his eyes wide and his lips smacking nervously between sentences. He fidgeted beside them and tugged at his tiny chimpanzee ears. "Silly of me. I thought you'd backed out or something." Unwilling to let anyone answer, he continued with his rapid patter. "I see you've met Mr. Goodwin here. He's one of my most generous backers, aren't you, Al? In for nearly twenty points. We're talking about a healthy six-figure investment, but don't worry." He patted Albert's hand and failed to notice the wincing reaction the gesture provoked. "You'll find it's a good bet, indeed."

The producer turned his attention to Lilah and T.S., darting glances between the two as if not sure which one had the most money and so deserved the most of his attention. "Don't be put off by the . . . uh, exuberance, shall we say, of the party," Worthington ordered with mock seriousness. "We all like to let our hair down now and then." He gave a laugh that sounded far more unpleasant than even he had intended, for he hurried on before anyone else could react. "It's all quite legitimate," he assured them, though no one had suggested otherwise. At least not out loud. "Just take a look at those men in the pit, as I call it. Some of the more respected names in city industry are here." He began to point out each man, citing his position and the amount he was investing in the play. T.S. was appalled at his vulgar breach of etiquette. He also wondered why these otherwise successful men, these "captains of industry" as Lance Worthington declared, would be sinking from $50,000 to $200,000 apiece in something as risky as a musical about Davy Crockett's life? It just didn't add up.

"Enough about that," the producer finally declared, winding up his four-minute speech on the lucrative nature of his show. Mercifully, little of it had been heard by either Lilah or T.S. At least the loud music was good for something. "Let me refresh your drinks," Worthington demanded suddenly. He grabbed the glasses out of their hands and hurried away before they could protest.

"Good grief." T.S. took out a handkerchief and mopped his brow. "That man talks a mile a minute. Is he on some sort of medication?"

Albert stared at him strangely. *"Medication?"* he repeated, casting an amused glance at Lilah, who had the good grace to pretend not to notice.

It incensed T.S. nonetheless. He suddenly wanted to be anywhere but where he was. Lance Worthington was a sleazeball. These people were joy seekers. The women were tramps. And Albert was the worst of them all. He was a supercilious, conceited and pompous jerk. So what if he felt out of his element here? He should be proud he did not fit in. And Auntie Lil could just forget the murder investigation if it meant he had to hang out with this crowd. Lance Worthington was a nasty can of worms, but T.S. saw no connection to Emily's death here and he wasn't going to waste any more time than necessary subjecting himself to aural assault and being humiliated by some wealthy nitwit. As soon as he could swing it, they were leaving.

So indignant were his thoughts that he automatically grabbed the healthy drink offered by a returned Lance Worthington and gulped down a fourth of it.

"I'll leave you to enjoy yourselves," Worthington murmured. He backed away and headed for a plump mogul in a pin-striped suit who was having a little trouble maneuvering up from the deep leather couch. The fact that he was stone cold drunk did not add to his sprightliness.

"Could I speak to you alone?" Albert murmured to Lilah behind T.S.'s back.

T.S. took another gulp of Scotch and turned his head just in time to see Albert grip Lilah's elbow and nod toward the kitchen. T.S. simmered. Should he let this well-bred interloper steal Lilah from his grasp like that? Was he a man or a mouse or what? Would it be totally appalling to punch Albert in the nose? There was, after all, a first time for everything.

Inaction forced the issue. "Theodore," Lilah whispered into his ear. "I need to talk to Albert alone for a moment. Would you excuse me?" She squeezed his arm briefly but did not wait for a reply. Albert guided her smoothly toward the kitchen. T.S. watched as the pair withdrew into a corner by themselves and began to whisper.

Well, he wouldn't dignify such proceedings by standing there and spying. He moved away into the sunken living room and found a seat on the edge of one of the leather couches. A small blonde who was curled up on the floor next to the passed-out man eyed T.S. carefully, then slithered up closer. "Where's your date?" she asked in what she probably thought was a seductive manner but, instead, made T.S. feel as if a snake were crawling up one of his legs.

"If you're asking if I need a date, I can assure you the answer is *no*," T.S. answered firmly. She pouted and withdrew, glaring at him with wounded pride.

My, how time flies when you're having fun, he thought glumly. Already his drink was empty. The thought had scarcely formed in his mind when Lance Worthington popped into view. "New drink!" the producer called out gaily. "Allow me, please." T.S. could hardly protest. He didn't have the time. The glass was jerked from his hand and Worthington gone before he could blink. He waited for the return of his by now necessary anesthetic and surreptitiously stole a glance into the kitchen area. Lilah and Albert were still deep in conversation and whatever Albert was saying, T.S. didn't like it. The man's face had a deep scowl on it and he was gesturing with one hand. Who was he? How did Lilah know him? What was he doing here and who did he think he was to snatch Theodore Hubbert's date right out from under his nose?

Good breeding or not, T.S. had half a mind to go ahead and punch him in the nose after all. In fact, he was seriously contemplating such an action when Lance Worthington appeared with a new drink. "Bottoms up!" he said cheerfully, bestowing the fresh glass on T.S. "Need company? We've plenty to choose from." He let his tiny hands flutter over the living room area. "Live and let live, I always say."

Live and let live unless your name is Albert and you're after Lilah, T.S. thought sourly as he gulped down his new drink. Lance Worthington left him to his misery. Halfway down to the bottom of the new tumbler, T.S. realized he had made a terrible mistake. First there had been wine at what was an enormous and highly spiced dinner, and now he'd topped it off with glasses of Scotch. His stomach lining began to tingle and went numb. While contemplating this, he grew dizzy and was almost certain that he was about to be sick. He was just wondering where the bathroom was when the tall redhead that he had noticed earlier suddenly reappeared. She perched on the edge of the couch near him and leaned forward suggestively, linking one arm through his and pulling him against the straining bodice of her skintight dress. He did not have the strength to protest.

"You look like someone I'd like to know better," she cooed in throaty whisper. She wore so much perfume that T.S. was forced to hold his breath, an act that did not improve his dizziness.

"Don't be shy," the woman ordered breathlessly. Up close, T.S. noted with distaste, it was obvious that she wore what must have been a full inch of pancake makeup. Bad skin lurked beneath and her cheeks were scarlet slashes. Her mouth undulated in front of his eyes in evil, ruby-colored ribbons, like poisonous worms dancing closer and closer.

"I've been watching you," she whispered. Her voice deepened even more and her hot breath brushed against his ear as she insisted with husky conviction, "You've got the heebie-jeebies, haven't you, darling?"

"What?" T.S. asked in sudden alarm. But his tongue was not behaving, it lolled thickly in his mouth and the words came out in a jumble. What had this creature said? That he had the heebie-jeebies?

Something had gone wrong. His tongue would not move at all. The numb feeling in his stomach spread and he felt as if a beach ball were inside his gut, swelling slowly until it could explode.

"You need another drink, darling," the redhead suggested. Her red lips met and a large, hideous tongue flicked out from between them. She dabbed it delicately over her upper lip and T.S. watched in fascination as it moved in slow motion, dragging a small trail of red across the cosmetic landscape. And who had put on a new record? This one was warped. The notes raced and slowed with distracted abandon, tunes tumbling and disappearing, fading in and out. Surely someone would notice it soon. What was worse, someone was spinning the room. What nonsense, he corrected himself. Rooms did not spin. Only, look at those walls. They were turning. Objects and people began to flow together, to blur as if in high speed. He was on a train that was rushing faster and faster and he was unable to tear his eyes from the small window opening in front of him.

"Put him in the back bedroom," T.S. heard a sly voice order. Hands groped under his armpits and he felt himself lifted. The redhead had hold of his body and was urging him forward. She was as strong as a man. T.S.'s near-dead weight did not faze her.

Without warning, Lance Worthington's face popped into view and began to fuzz and bounce in front of T.S.'s own. The producer was laughing and pounding him on his back. T.S. wanted to cough but his mouth would not move.

"I've got a special treat for you," an unctuous voice urged and T.S. realized that it belonged to Worthington. "Just leave it all up to me. Live and let live, I always say." Something had gone wrong with the producer's voice; it sped up to the chatter of a chipmunk then slowed suddenly like a record on the wrong speed.

It was all T.S. could do to open his eyes. When he did, there was the redhead inches away, staring back at him while her red-slashed cheeks danced in the field of his vision. Behind her, silver wallpaper pulsated to the beat of the pounding music. His stomach cramped and T.S. was sure he would vomit.

"Steady there, sir," a deep voice interrupted. "Where are you taking this gentleman? He looks like he needs to go home." Strong arms pulled him away from the talon-adorned hands of the redhead and, suddenly, breaking through the madness, the face of the elderly bartender swam into focus. Coal skin gleaming in silver light; small eyes piercing through his own; lips pressed together, worried and tight: the bartender's face stopped, fixated in perfect clarity before T.S. Behind him, the room spun in circles and the silver wallpaper sent starbursts tumbling across the hallway. How had he gotten so far? What was he doing in the hall?

"Sir? Sir? Shall I fetch the lady?" It was a golden voice, a trustworthy voice, far preferable to the rest. T.S. leaned, seeking the source of that comfort, and managed to drape both arms over the bartender's shoulders. There he clung, unwilling and unable to let go.

An argument ensued but the voices were too jumbled to decipher. It sounded instead as if small animals were quarreling at his feet. T.S. was vaguely aware that they were arguing about him, that the deep-voiced bartender wanted to take him away from the madness. T.S. clung harder, trying to tell the kind man that he was right, that he wanted more than anything to leave. Hands tugged at his jacket and he felt the sharp fingernails of the towering redhead scrape his back through the thin cotton shirt underneath. The bartender's weight shifted as he attempted to fend off the others. Without warning, T.S. lost the strength in his arms and began to slide to the floor.

Just as he was ready to fall asleep, new hands were there, helping him up. Two more pairs of hands: one strong, the other cool and fluttering.

"Theodore? Theodore? What's the matter, Theodore?" Lilah's voice cut through the crashing sounds exploding in his brain. Lilah was there. What was happening to him?

"He's taken sick," the kind voice said from a great, hollow distance. "I'll help you get him into a cab."

"No need," T.S. heard Lilah say. She, too, seemed far, far away. "I've got a car downstairs. Could you help me get him there?" Why did she sound so upset? Where was the problem? He should be helping her, T.S. thought vaguely, not slumped here like a dead man propped for one last good look against the wall.

He was aware that Albert was beside him as well, tugging him forward on one side while the bartender pulled him along on the other. It was hateful to be so helpless and in Albert's power, but there was nothing T.S. could do. His brain still functioned, albeit slowly, but his feet would not work, his arms were as limp as wet noodles and a small fire flared in his stomach. Somehow he was heading toward the door, though his legs dragged behind him like the support poles of a litter. His coat was thrown over his shoulders.

"Hurry! Hurry!" he heard Lilah say. He tried to walk faster and managed to move his legs. He pulled away from Albert before crashing into the door.

He did not remember the elevator ride downstairs, but surely he had taken one. Because the next thing he knew, he was leaning against the cushions in the back seat of Lilah's limo. Ah, safety. He was home free. And away from that whirling crowd, those darting red tongues and those hideous serpentine glances. And here was Lilah, dear, dear Lilah, whispering gently to him as she brushed the hair off his brow.

"Sssh," she was saying, still from a place far, far away. "Don't try to talk." A cool wetness covered his brow, it swept over his face like a balm. Ice. She was patting him with ice. What a wonderful thing a limousine was, he thought thickly. Full of ice and glasses and liquor and . . . *liquor*. Ugh. The very word sickened him. His back stiffened and his stomach began to spasm.

"Grady!" Lilah shouted in sudden alarm. "Pull over. I think you'd better pull over."

What was this? Who was bothering him now? Someone was trying to pull him from the safety of the limo. Strong arms grabbed at his shoulders and he was halfway outside. He fought, pushing away the arms, struggling to be free.

"Just do it," he heard Lilah's sharp voice command. "Throw up, Theodore. Forget that I'm here. Just throw up."

Throw up? How odd. He was dreaming again. Lilah, acting as a cheerleader for him to be sick? He did not have much time to think about the absurdity of it because the nausea finally hit, overwhelming him and stripping him of any strength he had left to resist. He gave up his struggle and stopped fighting the feeling. With a sense of relief, he felt his stomach lurch again and again, jumping beneath his shirt like some sort of small animal trapped inside. I'm sick, T.S. thought vaguely, I'm throwing up in the gutter. People walking by are watching, but what can I do? Another wave of nausea hit and he gave himself up to it.

When he was through, strong arms leaned him back into the car, against the firm leather cushions. The cool balm returned and he could feel the purr of the motor beneath him. With his stomach calm again, Lilah's murmur began to soothe his soul. "They did this to you," she was whispering angrily. "I just know it. Oh, Theodore. What an awful place. What an awful, awful party."

His lips moved. He wanted to speak. Thought formed without sound until finally a half squeak came out. "Albert?" he cried and was silent.

"Albert's not here," Lilah assured him. "Don't worry about Albert. Albert's just a friend. He helped you to the car."

"A friend," T.S. repeated, his head lolling back. The nausea was gone but now a terrible black cloud descended on his head. His temples were pounding and pulsating, and there were needles being jabbed into his eyes.

"My head," he groaned. "Oh, my head."

He felt Lilah's hands on his body, patting him down. What was she doing? Had she turned into one of them? "What?" he asked woodenly. "What are you doing?" His tongue hung to one side like a dead slab of meat. Would none of his body cooperate?

"Your handkerchief is bigger," she explained. "Here it is." She pulled it from his pocket and filled it with ice, fashioning a makeshift pack that she held up to his throbbing temples. He lay back, helpless and unable to respond. The coolness spread across his forehead, distracting him from the pain. He managed to raise an arm and grasped Lilah's hand.

"Lilah," he whispered. His eyes would not open, they were glued down. Still, he could see her sitting beside him. She was so lovely. So pure and graceful and honest and lovely. "Lilah . . ." His voice trailed off. He wanted to collect his thoughts, he felt it was very important that she know how he felt about her before it was too late. But there were so many things he wanted to say and he did not know where to begin.

"You must think I'm awful," he whispered in agony. Now that his physical symptoms were abating some, his pride began to ache from the bruising it had suffered. He was disgraced. He had humiliated Lilah.

"You're not awful," she whispered urgently into his ear. "You're a wonderful, wonderful, wonderful man. Now, stop thinking and talking and just get better."

"You're home," she told him softly a few blocks later. She smoothed his forehead with a practiced hand.

His eyes still would not work properly, but he saw enough to be comforted. They had pulled up in front of his apartment building and there was that splendid fellow, his very own doorman, good old Mahmoud, hurrying to help him inside. The world still washed up and receded with alarming irregularity, but he could hear and feel small snatches of reality as strong arms grabbed him and he was hustled inside.

"I've never seen him like this," Mahmoud said with genuine concern. "What has happened to Mr. Hubbert?"

"Bad business of some sort," the driver, Grady, replied darkly. "Can you help me get him upstairs?"

T.S. saw Lilah in front of him, pressing an elevator button. How lovely. It was *his* elevator button and if he could only walk inside that little door, why he'd soon be looking at *his* walls. And there would be the deep and cool comfort of *his* bed. Sanctuary. Sanctuary was home.

It seemed like a dozen or more arms pulled and pushed him along. Hands fumbled in his pocket, male hands, and he struggled.

"Whoah! Steady as she goes," Grady boomed in his Irish brogue. T.S. fell still and his keys were extracted.

"Save me a trip downstairs," Mahmoud said with relief as he propped T.S. against the doorjamb.

"You'll definitely get a Christmas bonus for this," Lilah told him. They laughed and T.S., thinking they were laughing at him, began to struggle again. He pushed his door open and they tumbled inside.

"Easy! Easy!" Grady's strong arms closed around him and helped him to the couch. He sank back gratefully. "Mighty neat place," T.S. heard Grady say through the fog.

"I'll say," Mahmoud replied. "Mr. Hubbert here is a real stickler for order."

"I'll take it from here," Lilah interrupted the men firmly.

"Grady, please come back for me in the morning. Nine o'clock will be fine."

The men retreated out the apartment door, both looking mildly scandalized. But T.S. and Lilah were too exhausted to notice. She loosened his shirt for him and he breathed in huge, even gulps of air. The room grew still around him. But just when he thought that he was safe at last, a tiny spark of burning sensation flamed into life at the pit of his stomach and spread rapidly through his abdomen.

"Oh, no." He struggled upright and stumbled to his feet. "I think I'm going to be sick again." He staggered down the hall, searching out his bathroom, his lovely, clean bathroom where he could be alone. Lilah gently guided him and watched anxiously as he lurched inside and dropped to his knees, hunched over the toilet bowl.

Gently, she closed the door and stood waiting across the narrow hallway where she could hear him if he cried out. He would be all right now, she thought vaguely, and he would certainly want to be alone.

Only T.S. wasn't alone. As he began to heave and an urgent need to void himself of poison overcame him, two tiny heads poked their way out of the small swinging door that was inset into the larger bathroom closet door. Brenda and Eddie watched cautiously as their master made strange retching sounds into the toilet bowl. They inched forward, tails switching cautiously, and sniffed delicately at his trouser legs. Unsure of their findings, they withdrew in silence to watch. Their creature was very sick indeed.

2. By the time Auntie Lil had been rescued from Homefront by a distracted Annie, it had been too late to track down Herbert for any fresh information. Not even she would tempt the dark city streets at two in the morning. She had, instead, returned home in a glum mood, troubled both by the thought that someone had died in the Hudson River that day and by the many unanswered phone calls she'd made to her nephew. There had to be something else she could do.

She went to bed in a bad mood and rose in a worse one. Half a pot of black coffee did little to improve Auntie Lil's outlook. She sat by the phone, increasingly frustrated, as she dialed without success. Herbert was not home yet—he was probably still overseeing surveillance at Emily's—and Theodore refused to answer his phone. She'd left dozens of unanswered messages and would be damned if she'd leave one more.

She took her anger out on the operator at New York *Newsday*, who kept insisting that Margo McGregor was not in. When Auntie Lil persisted, the canny woman recognized her voice from the day before and launched into an impromptu lecture on how low it was to pretend to be someone's mother.

"Miss McGregor's mother died last year, I'll have you know," the woman informed her importantly. "It was very awkward when I mentioned that you had called."

"I didn't say *where* I was calling from," Auntie Lil pointed out in desperation, but the operator had already cut the connection.

That did it. Another hour like this and the inactivity might actually drive her to start cleaning up the apartment. She dressed and made her way back to Midtown, arriving near Times Square just after ten. If the police couldn't solve the mystery of Emily's building, she had decided, she'd just have to do it herself. After that, she'd return to the soup kitchen and snoop around some more.

If Herbert was on duty, he remained well hidden as she marched firmly up the front steps of Emily's building and peered boldly in the front door. She'd gotten in once before and she could do it again. Unfortunately, mid-morning was a bad time to be lurking around a building full of actors and night people. Everyone was probably still in bed and no one was likely to be coming or going. After five minutes of waiting—a near record for Auntie Lil—she took matters into her own hands. Rummaging through her enormous pocketbook, she found several credit cards jumbled among a tangle of handkerchiefs and loose jewelry at the bottom. She contemplated which one to use and decided to sacrifice her Macy's charge card to the cause.

She wasn't quite sure how to go about it. She checked the street for pedestrians and, other than a pair of figures far up the block, no one was about. She inserted the hard plastic into the doorjamb and began to jimmy it back and forth, hoping to spring the heavy lock. Unaware that such a tactic was useless against a deadbolt, Auntie Lil persisted for several minutes until her card cracked and her temper did the same. She kicked the door in frustration and contemplated her next round of action. She'd fall back on an old favorite. She'd lie.

She pressed four buzzers before she got an answer.

"Who is it?" a sleepy voice mumbled.

"Delivery," Auntie Lil announced in as young a voice as possible. "East Side Floral Arrangements. And hurry, this thing is huge."

She was buzzed in promptly but got no farther than the front hallway before she was spotted. The superintendent was backing out of her apartment with a large wheeled cart piled high with laundry. She maneuvered it toward the front doorway and saw Auntie Lil just as she tried to slip into the stairwell.

Her reaction was instant and curious. Her face drained white and she began babbling so quickly in Spanish that Auntie Lil could not catch a word. The woman made the sign of the cross repeatedly as she spoke, then she took a small crucifix hanging from a chain around her neck. Holding it out in front of her like a talisman, she advanced on Auntie Lil and made a shooing motion with her free hand.

"Out! Out!" she cried at Auntie Lil. "Get out! Get out of my house!"

Auntie Lil opened her mouth to argue but the superintendent was not in a mood to negotiate. Giving up on her crucifix, she dashed to the small hallway closet, grabbed a large push broom and advanced on Auntie Lil with it held in front of her like a sword. "Get out, get out," she warned again. She jabbed at Auntie Lil and narrowly missed poking her in the stomach. That narrow miss was enough.

"I'll be back," Auntie Lil warned, slipping out the front door. "I'll be back."

As she hurried down the front steps, Auntie Lil saw the superintendent slumped against the hallway wall, praying and mumbling in Spanish. Good heavens. You'd think she'd seen a ghost.

Much to her embarrassment, Herbert was sitting with Franklin on the steps of the building across the street from Emily's. They were making little attempt to hide their presence and were sipping fresh cups of coffee while staring glumly at the front steps across from them.

"Not very discreet," Auntie Lil pointed out, sitting gingerly on the cold concrete step beside them. Winter was most definitely coming, that was certain. The stairs still held the cool night air.

"No one alive around here this time of day. Besides, I'm big enough to take care of anyone who gives us trouble," Franklin pointed out. He had received new clothes from the Salvation Army. The overalls had been replaced by deep green pants like those favored by municipal workers. He also wore a bright red sweater over a white shirt and was nothing if not conspicuous.

"And I have discovered that no man is more invisible than a

man of the streets," Herbert replied calmly. "Disguises are super-fluous. New Yorkers supply their own blinders. Besides, did I not just see you walk right down the front steps?"

"Did you see what else happened?" Auntie Lil asked lightly.

"No. Why? You discovered something significant?"

Auntie Lil shrugged. She saw no reason to alert Herbert to the fact that she'd just been chased from the building with a broom. "Any news on your end?"

Herbert shook his head. "Nothing unusual. No Eagle. The regular comings and goings."

"What about the ladies?" Auntie Lil inquired.

"They don't hang out here at night," Franklin pointed out. "We don't let them. Too dangerous, you know."

"Any sign of Eva?"

Herbert shook his head. "Not around here."

"Anywhere else?" She looked at Franklin.

He shrugged. "Haven't seen her for a couple of days," he realized with some surprise. "Come to think of it, she wasn't eating yesterday, now was she?" His brow furrowed as he worked on the puzzle. "She's usually on the block about five or six in the evening. Stays until ten or so. But I didn't see her last night. Did you?" He stared at Herbert, who shook his head apologetically.

"I hope she's not trying anything foolish," Auntie Lil said somewhat pompously for someone who had taken as many chances as she had.

"If anyone was going to try something foolish, that would be Miss Eva," Franklin pointed out. He rose and sighed deeply, then leisurely stretched out to his full height. He looked like a bear emerging from months of hibernation. "Time for bed," he told them good-naturedly. "There's a good doorway down on the highway. Nice view of the river. Gets a good breeze. Some rock and roll doo-wop club. Empty this time of day. Plus a nice warm grate from the laundry next door keeps me warm if I need it. If you'll excuse me," he nodded and ambled off down the block.

"I suppose I should offer him my couch," Auntie Lil said guiltily.

"He won't take it," Herbert told her. "I have tried. He is a man of great independence with a fondness for the river."

"A fondness for the river?" Auntie Lil shivered. "Not me. Did you know that a woman died there yesterday? An old woman. If I didn't know better, I'd have thought it was me from the description."

Herbert looked up slowly. His face grew very still and his eyelids came down ever so slowly until his eyes were nearly obscured. "Description?" he asked softly.

Auntie Lil shrugged. "An old woman. Stout. Wearing too young clothes. That was all I heard."

"Lillian." Herbert's tone was soft and very sad. "Do you not think it a coincidence that one of us is missing? One of us who is stout and old? And prone to wearing clothes that are too young?"

Their eyes met. "How could I have missed it?" she admitted softly.

Herbert's head bowed. "Let us pray that it is not her."

3. It was nearly noon by the time T.S. awoke. The sun streaming in his bedroom window only served to confuse him more. He looked down at himself slowly. He was wearing pajamas. But he could not remember donning them the night before. In fact, he could not remember very much at all of the night before. There had been that party at Lance Worthington's . . . and a man. A man named Albert who knew Lilah.

Lilah. He sat up straight and winced as a spear of pain pierced both temples. The last thing he remembered was watching Lilah huddled in a kitchen corner with that rich jerk, Albert. What in the world had happened after that and how in the hell had he gotten home and into his own bed?

He'd never had a blackout before and, yet, he didn't remember drinking all that much . . . but it hurt his brain to ponder the situation for long. What he needed right now was aspirin.

His body felt like it belonged to someone else. His stomach was tender, and indeed, felt deeply bruised, though no surface scars were evident. His legs were heavy and, when he finally maneuvered them out of the bed, refused to hold his weight at first. He stood, teetering gently, found his balance, then made his way down the hall. Brenda and Eddie emerged from the spare bedroom to watch his progress with reproachful attention and berated him with indignant caterwauling. He had missed their early feeding by hours and hours. Headache and mysteries of the night before momentarily forgotten, T.S. wearily found and opened a tin of chicken-and-cheese bits to still their incessant meowing. It was like having children. Loud and greedy children who could not be ignored.

The kitchen gleamed so brightly that it hurt his eyes. He searched through the cabinets and found the jar of aspirin. A few minutes later he had even managed to pry open the childproof cap. He gulped three of them down then wandered through the living room in his pajamas, sipping at a small glass of warm water. His stomach did not feel as if it would tolerate anything else. Something was not quite right about his apartment. He knew it well and the air held a vaguely foreign scent. Something had disturbed his beloved and rigid routine.

He spotted the coat and froze. A thin black silk evening coat was slung over the entrance chair. Lilah's. But if that was Lilah's coat, where was she? Feeling like one of the three bears, he carefully searched his apartment, discovering fresh evidence of an intrusion in the extra bedroom. The spare bed had been neatly made, but not with his customary precision hospital corners. It was clear that Lilah had slept there last night.

T.S. looked down suddenly at his pajamas . . . but surely not? He blushed deeply and was glad that he was alone. Especially when he discovered his best suit piled in a small heap in one corner of his own bedroom. That confirmed it. He would never, not under any circumstances, simply toss his attire in a pile. Someone else had undressed him last night. But he must have been unconscious, or, at the very least, deeply asleep, to have missed an event as spectacular as Lilah undressing him.

He discovered the note taped to the bathroom mirror. *"Dear Theodore,"* it read. *"I've had an idea. I'm going to check on it and will stop by later. Don't worry about the pajamas. It was imperative that you change clothes. I promise I looked the other way."*

Had it been anyone other than Lilah, T.S. would have been positively scandalized. As it was, it left a warm glow in his stomach, which was a sensation vastly preferable to the one it replaced.

He reread the note. An idea? What idea would be so important that she'd rush out early and forget her evening coat? And why was it imperative that he change clothes?

That puzzle, too, made his brain ache to contemplate. T.S. decided that what he really needed was an ice pack, more aspirin and a few more hours of sleep. On his way to the kitchen he noticed the answering machine. Its light blinked furiously, demanding to be noticed. When he rewound his messages, he discovered six from Auntie Lil, each one more incoherent than the last. She wanted all details, immediately, of the party and of his search at the Performing Arts Library the day before. But he simply did not have the energy to talk to anyone, much less his beloved but demanding aunt.

He erased the taped pleas, turned off the telephone, retrieved the largest cooking pot that he could find, and filled it with ice and water. He returned to the bedroom—followed by a satiated Brenda and Eddie—and drew the curtains tightly. The room grew dark and seemed instantly cooler. It was as peaceful as a church. He took a large towel and dipped it into the icy water, then draped it gratefully around his head.

He lay down stiffly in the center of his bed and arranged the pillow so that it hit just above his shoulders. His head lolled back gently, cradled in a cool balm. If he lay very, very still and pretended he was in the Bahamas, floating on a raft in a clear warm sea, the pounding in his temples actually faded to a dull throb.

With any luck, he'd survive whatever it was that he was going through. At least until Lilah returned to fill him in.

CHAPTER THIRTEEN

1. All it took was three words to the desk sergeant at Midtown North—"jet black hair"—and Detective Santos was out in a flash. He did not look happy. In fact, he did not even look well. His tie was loosely knotted over a crumpled shirt, his eyes were red and bleary and his thick hair stood up in small wispy spikes.

"Not here," he said firmly, leading Auntie Lil toward a small set of stairs nearly hidden against one far wall. They ascended and maneuvered a narrow second-floor hallway that was littered with metal desks stacked at one end. At the very end of the hall, they reached a tiny room containing one small table with a scuffed plastic surface and three beat-up metal chairs. Piles of cleaning supplies dominated an entire wall.

"Charming," Auntie Lil joked but the detective's expression did not change. He was staring at her intently and his mouth was set in a small, unpleasant line.

"It's obvious you know who yesterday's floater was," he said grimly.

Inexplicably, Auntie Lil felt guilty and looked down at her shoes.

"I know who she is, too," the detective continued. "You see, we do some things right around here." He stared harder at Auntie Lil and she looked away. What was he leading up to, anyway?

"I called around the neighborhood shelters," he continued. "To see if anyone was missing. It was the same thing I did when your friend Emily was killed. Only this time I got lucky. I tracked her down to The Dwelling Place on Fortieth Street. The Franciscan sisters there were very worried. One of their residents had not returned the night before and the missing woman was usually very reliable."

"She lived in a shelter?"

"A shelter," he confirmed. "Not a bad one as shelters go, but a shelter just the same."

"Are you sure it was Eva La Louche?" Auntie Lil asked faintly. "I was under the impression the woman I'm seeking had her own apartment."

"It's the same woman," Detective Santos said angrily. "Jet black hair. Only her real name is Eva Stubbs. Which sounds a hell of a lot more believable than Eva La Louche." He would not stop staring at her, not even when he pulled a pack of cigarettes from his shirt pocket and began to smoke in her face. His gaze was relentless.

"Why are you glaring at me?" she finally asked in a voice that sounded remarkably like a little girl's.

"Because Eva Stubbs died with a contusion the size of a softball on her head. And I want to know what she had to do with you. And how you knew it might be her." He ground out his cigarette on the table top, half finished, and promptly lit up a fresh one.

"She was attempting to help in the investigation of Emily's death," Auntie Lil admitted in a feeble voice.

"What? Speak up. You talk louder than an announcer at the ball park. I ought to know. You've been pestering me for a week. So don't pull that little old lady crap on me. Pull yourself together and tell me everything you know." In his anger, all traces of the usual bitter, disillusioned cop had disappeared. Santos was on his home turf and it had been violated and, by God, he was now taking charge.

He was right. She was behaving foolishly. She did have to pull herself together. There was no need for her to feel guilt over Eva's death . . . was there? After all, she had warned the women not to go off on their own. And Theodore had warned them against being on the streets too late at night. Eva had probably disregarded both of their cautions. It was not her fault the woman had died. She straightened her shoulders and began.

"She was a friend of Emily's," she said. "They go back many years. As rivals, more than friends, I would say. I think she had been watching Emily's building and following various people."

"Following people?" The detective's cigarette dangled incredulously from one corner of his mouth, making him look like a Humphrey Bogart character from a forties movie.

"Well, you wouldn't pay any attention when I told you Emily lived in that building," she said defensively. "Someone had to look into the situation."

Santos opened his mouth, changed his mind and shut it abruptly, then stared out a tiny barred window and counted to twelve softly. Only his lips moved. No sound came out—which did nothing for Auntie Lil's nerves. "What else?" he finally asked calmly.

"I don't know anything else," she admitted. "Eva has been missing since yesterday morning, I think. She did not show up for lunch at St. Barnabas. Which was, I gather, unheard of for her."

Detective Santos sighed. "That puts the last time she was seen at about 11:00 A.M.," he thought out loud. "One of the other women at her shelter saw her heading uptown at about that time. Know anything else?"

When Auntie Lil shook her head, he leaned across the table toward her until they were nearly nose to nose. "I'm going to tell you something very important," he began in a deadly calm voice. "And I'm going to be a lot nicer about it than Lieutenant Abromowitz was. Who, by the way, I'm beginning to think may be right about you after all. Two women are now dead. And something tells me that if you had not come on the scene and whipped Emily's friends into a frenzy of righteousness, that this old woman might have been around to enjoy a few more years of her meager but fairly comfortable life."

Now *that* made her mad. "No one forced Eva to do anything," Auntie Lil said defiantly. "And she would rather have died doing something important than to have wasted away bored to tears."

"How about you? How do you want to die?"

"Die?" she repeated faintly, her rebellion dissolving. "That wouldn't be a threat?"

"It's not a threat from me. Have you thought that maybe Eva wasn't the intended victim after all? That maybe it was *you*. There is a great resemblance between you and the latest corpse, wouldn't you say? With the exception of that pathetic dyed black hair, the two of you are remarkably alike in physical characteristics, aren't you?"

For once Auntie Lil was silent. It was an unpleasant but inescapable point.

They heard the sound of muttering and heavy footsteps nearing the room. The approaching male voice sounded artificially firm, infused with booming enthusiasm and phony competence. "We consider the case closed," he was repeating in an overly hearty baritone. "Thanks to our quick work, we feel confident that we've closed the book on yet another disgusting chapter of exploitation of the young." Each time he finished the statement, the unseen man began again, trying on new inflections and tuning up the words here and there.

Santos buried his head in his hands just as Lieutenant Abromowitz poked his head in the room, repeating, ". . . another disgusting case of—" He stopped abruptly when he spotted his detective. "Sorry, George, just getting ready for the press conference on that Fleming pervert. What the hell are you doing way back here?" He noticed Auntie Lil and his face flushed instantly and ominously red. "I've been looking for you," he warned her, stepping toward her and placing his hands on his hips like an angry father about to chew out his wild teenage daughter.

Detective Santos held up a hand. "Please, Lieutenant, I told you I'd take care of it. I've been talking to her. She understands the seriousness of it."

It took all of Auntie Lil's considerable will not to speak up.

"Did you tell her I'd arrest her if she continues to interfere?"

"I was just getting to that part," Santos assured him. "Let me handle it, okay?"

"Arrest me?" Auntie Lil demanded. "I'd like to see you try."

"So would I," Abromowitz agreed, leaning across the table on his knuckles. "Oh, boy, so would I."

2. She was a coward. There was nothing to do but admit it. It had been sweet of Detective Santos to defend her, but it had proved, as always, hopeless to try and change Abromowitz's mind. He was convinced that Auntie Lil was bad news, period. There was no way he would let her help. Following more dire warnings from him that she was to butt out immediately (and her false reassurances that she would) Auntie Lil had returned to St. Barnabas to see how she could help with that day's meal. Her desire was driven partly by a wish to atone for her mistakes and partly by her need to find out more about either Emily or Eva.

Yet, when she passed Adelle and her followers waiting patiently in line, she did not even murmur the faintest detail about poor Eva's fate.

She just couldn't do it. Not yet. Much of what the detectives said had stung its way into her heart. She needed time to think it through. And, besides, the actresses would find out about Eva soon enough and, once they did, would probably be filled with even more resolve to discover both murderers.

Except, of course, that one person was probably responsible for both deaths. Which didn't lessen the danger any. Oh, dear—it was getting rather unpleasant.

The St. Barnabas soup kitchen was equally unsettling. She arrived to find the kitchen at a standstill. Only two volunteers had shown up, Father Stebbins was nowhere to be seen, and long rows of raw chickens stretched out on the steel countertop looking cold and forlorn in the bare room.

"What is going on?" Auntie Lil asked in alarm. "We have to open the gate in less than three hours."

"Volunteers are dropping out like flies because the police keep calling them in for questioning," one of the two women still there reported. "Something else must have happened. And I don't know where Father Stebbins is. He rushed through here about fifteen minutes ago and didn't even say hello."

The trio stared at one another and, most typically, it was Auntie Lil who finally took charge. "You go and beg as much rice as you can from Mr. Chang on the corner," she told one of the volunteers. "If you need help carrying the containers, take Franklin with you. Do you know what he looks like? I think I saw him in line." The woman nodded and hurried off to do her bidding. Auntie Lil turned to the remaining woman. "Do we have any lemons?"

"There's a whole carton in the walk-in," the volunteer replied in a skeptical voice.

"Go get them and slice them. I'll find the tinfoil. We'll have lemon chicken over rice. That only takes an hour. We'll just have to bake portions in shifts. You help me cook. People will have to set their own tables today."

She could have run the U.S. Navy without a hitch.

The enormous task confronting them took all of their energy and, for the next hour, Auntie Lil had little time to contemplate Eva's death or Father Stebbin's inexcusable absence. She had just removed the first batch of chickens from the large ovens when Father Stebbins returned, face flushed and robes in disarray. He hurried down the back stairs from the interior of the church and rushed up to Auntie Lil without any warning, nearly causing her to drop a pan of sizzling food on his feet.

"Lillian," he told her urgently, grabbing her shoulders, "I have to apologize for what I said yesterday. I was wrong. There is wickedness but sometimes it comes in unexpected forms. A terrible injustice has been done and it's partly my fault. I must do what I can to amend the damage I've wrought. I've called Fran, but there's so much more to do."

Mouth hanging open, Auntie Lil stared in astonishment as he hurried away and disappeared through the front basement gate. Then she noticed the clock. They had less than two hours until the gates were scheduled to open and probably eighty more chickens waiting to be cooked. "I think it's only going to get worse," she predicted, returning to her task.

But, thankfully, this time she was wrong. Half an hour later, Fran appeared, calmly walking into the kitchen as if she had merely run out to the corner store for some forgotten spice instead of having been missing for days.

"Hello, Lillian," she told Auntie Lil politely, displaying more manners than she had exhibited in the past two months put together.

"How nice to see you," Auntie Lil stammered back. She wanted to add "Fran," but the name stuck in her throat. After all, she was still her nemesis. Wasn't she? Everything was being turned upside down.

"What do I need to do to help?" Fran asked pleasantly. Auntie Lil, was too surprised to do anything but point toward the remaining chickens lined up in a row. Fran nodded and methodically began preparing them for roasting, without saying so much as one other word and without complaining a whit about the recipe chosen.

It was all too mystifying for Auntie Lil, or at least too mystifying to untangle while juggling a dozen other chores. But the riddle was only compounded further when Annie O'Day arrived at the soup kitchen half an hour before the scheduled mealtime.

"There's an enormous woman yelling for you outside the basement gate," one of the volunteers informed Auntie Lil in a calm voice. Nothing else was likely to happen that day to faze her any more than she already was.

"That's Annie O'Day." Auntie Lil hurried to let the nurse practitioner inside.

"Thank God you're here." Annie grabbed Auntie Lil's hands in her own and, in her urgent excitement, nearly crushed them between her strong fingers. "You've got to come to Homefront right away."

"Now?" Auntie Lil looked over her shoulder. "I can't. Those people outside are hungry."

"You have to. I'll stay here and help."

"Why?"

Annie pulled her into a corner of the dining area and lowered her voice. Fran stood behind a counter and watched them curiously.

"I found Timmy this morning," Annie explained in a rough whisper. "It took a lot of doing, but he admits that he's lying about Bob. But he won't tell me who put him up to it. He said he's afraid of the police but he'll sign a paper admitting that he was lying. He's sitting in Bob's office right now. But he won't talk to anyone but you."

"Me?" Auntie Lil asked in astonishment. "I've never met the young man in my life."

"But you know his friend, Little Pete, and both of the boys think that you are a close friend of Emily's or maybe even her sister."

"Emily? What does Emily have to do with Timmy's allegations?"

"I don't know yet. But I think there's a connection. He won't tell me anything except that he's afraid. He doesn't trust anyone. I think he knows who killed Emily, but he's not sure who else knows. And who may be involved. He knows you're not involved because of some things you said to Little Pete. That's why he wants to talk to you."

"He's at Homefront?" Auntie Lil repeated.

"Yes. And he's alone. We couldn't risk leaving Bob there with him, not after what he told the police and that reporter about Bob. So Bob's at some diner around the corner and Timmy's waiting at Homefront alone. That means he could change his mind at any minute and there's no one there to stop him. Please, you've got to help us."

Auntie Lil was confused, her brain whirling with possible theories, but it did not cause her to hesitate. She had been trying to talk to the young boy ever since Emily died. If he knew the killer, he could very well be in danger. She had to reach him before someone else did.

Grabbing her pocketbook, she rushed out the door at top speed, plowing into a returning Father Stebbins in her haste. His face was cleared of worry and looked more at peace—at least until Auntie Lil crashed into him and sent him tripping over the trash cans in the foyer. The priest stared after her, shaking his head as he watched Auntie Lil scurry away down the sidewalk.

Adelle and her followers also stared after Auntie Lil's retreating figure and whispers passed among them. They looked to Adelle for guidance. Should they follow? She shook her head slightly and they fell back into the line to wait. One thing they all had plenty of was time.

3. T.S. woke again just before three o'clock. The terrible pounding in his head had subsided to a faint buzz, but he still could not recall any details of the night before. The wet towel had soaked through his sheets, but he was too tired to care. His tongue felt like it had been coated with syrup and dipped in fuzz. What in the world had he gone through and where was Lilah? God, what if he had done something to offend her? He reassured himself that the note she'd left had been friendly.

He did not have long to worry. The buzzer rang just as he had managed to pull together a respectable outfit. He was missing his shoes and socks, but bare feet seemed superfluous in light of last night. He padded happily to the buzzer and pushed the okay button without bothering to speak to Mahmoud first. He was not in the mood for any of his doorman's sly comments. At least not until he knew what he was being kidded about. If he hurried, he'd have just enough time to put on a pot of coffee before Lilah found her way to his door.

A brisk, confident knock signaled her arrival. It was one of the things he liked about her. She was a no-nonsense woman. There would be no tentative tap-tapping for Lilah Cheswick.

T.S. flung open the door grandly and gave a courtly bow, a gesture that he immediately regretted. Blood rushed to his head and he grew dizzy. It was a chore to straighten up smoothly, but he did manage a small joke. "Enter my kingdom," he said grandly and beamed a bright smile on his visitor—a smile that froze into a grimace of paralyzed embarrassment.

Lance Worthington and Sally St. Claire stood before him, staring at his bare feet.

"Now this is what I call a real Eastside welcome," Worthington admitted, draping his cashmere coat over T.S.'s outstretched arm. "You must have really enjoyed yourself at the party." He walked to the center of the living room and immediately began to expertly calculate the worth of its furnishings.

"Sorry about your getting sick, sweetie," Sally told him, wiggling in after Worthington with the ease of one experienced at slipping past vigilant doormen. She was wearing a heavy fur wrap, which seemed a bit excessive for the middle of the day in late September in New York City.

"Sick?" T.S. inquired faintly. What had she said about him being sick? He had a vague suspicion that things were turning against him, that his optimistic hopes about the night before were about to evaporate. The trick would be to play it cool, to act as if he knew what he had done.

Sally giggled and covered her mouth with a hand that featured hot pink fingernails as deadly looking as switchblades. T.S. could not take his eyes off them. Surely they were fake. But if they were fake, why in the world would she choose to glue them to her fingers?

"Let's just say that you looked a little *green* to me when you left," she teased T.S., sitting primly on the edge of his sofa. She lit up a cigarette and coyly blew smoke at him. T.S.'s determined smile wavered as the smoke met his stomach, especially when he heard the distinct sounds of casual rummaging behind him.

"This real ivory?" Worthington asked. He was holding up the king from T.S.'s beloved hand-carved chess set and was scratching the bottom with the sharp corner of his heavy gold ring.

"Yes. Do you mind?" T.S. reclaimed his carving and set it gingerly back in place.

"Must be worth a fortune," the producer remarked in admiration. "Nice place you got here. Big for just one guy."

"We tried to call first," Sally St. Claire explained. "No one answered." She crossed a leg and expertly dangled a shoe from one toe as she puffed away on her ultralong cigarette. The shoe had at least a four-inch heel that tapered down to a wicked point. Everywhere you looked, the woman ended in dangerous, jabbing spikes.

That would teach him to turn off the phone.

"How did you know where I lived?" T.S. asked suspiciously.

Worthington stared at him as if he were daft. "You're in the phone book," he explained.

T.S. tried to look casual. Damn. He should have paid that extra fourteen dollars a month for an unlisted number. He recovered his composure as much as he could under the circumstances. "To what do I owe this honor?" he inquired politely. He sat on the edge of a chair and tried hard to pretend that he was not barefoot or that he had any reason to regret his actions of the night before. If only he knew what he had done . . .

"Did you have a good time at my party last night?" Worthington asked suddenly. He had lightly seized one of his tiny, chimpanzeelike ears and was squeezing it methodically as he spoke. He stared at the top tier of T.S.'s curio shelf and a miniature sailor carved out of whalebone caught his attention. He reached for it and hefted it casually in his free hand, still squeezing his tiny ear. T.S. kept a careful eye on the carved treasure; it would fit neatly into the producer's coat pocket. Then he remembered: he'd just been asked a question. Damn those ears. They were positively mesmerizing.

"Well, yes. Of course," T.S. stalled before shifting into full-blown fabrication. "I had a simply marvelous time at your party, in fact." He doubted this was strictly true, but given that his clothes were in a heap in one corner of his bedroom, it was probably a safe bet to assume that he had whooped it up in some manner or other.

"You left so suddenly," Worthington remarked. He was staring out at T.S. from under furry black eyebrows. His eyebrows, T.S. noticed, met in the middle of his forehead like a caterpillar whenever the producer concentrated heavily. "I thought perhaps we had offended you somehow," Worthington added carefully.

"Oh, no. Not at all." T.S. attempted a smile. "When you've got to go, you've got to go," he joked feebly. Where the hell was Lilah? She'd be able to tell him the truth.

The producer's brow smoothed and he relaxed. "Quite so. I always say 'live and let live' myself."

The phrase snagged at his memory with a curious foreboding, but T.S. could not remember where or when he had heard it recently.

"Given any thought to the show?" Worthington asked. "Remember, there are only a couple of investing spots left."

"Well, I haven't had much time to discuss it with Lilah. I mean, Mrs. Cheswick."

"Oh, yes. Ms. Cheswick. Or *Lilah*, as I believe she asked me to call her." Worthington wandered over to the large sliding glass doors that led to the balcony and stood staring intently out over York Avenue. The day had turned cloudy and distinctly gray. It made T.S. sad to think that he had slept the sun away. He was seized with a sudden longing to crawl back into bed, pull the covers over his head and wait for Lilah to arrive.

"She's a very wealthy woman, as I understand it," Worthington added casually. He seemed quite fascinated with the flow of traffic thirty stories below them.

"I'll say," Sally piped up. She stubbed out her cigarette viciously in T.S.'s immaculate teak ashtray and he suppressed a wince. It was not an ashtray intended for actual use. Those were kept locked away in a drawer lined with cedar chips. "Did you see that rock she had on her right hand?" she asked, impressed. "And I bet those earrings were real diamonds, too."

"Sally." Worthington said her name so gently that T.S. nearly missed it, but the effect was not lost on the girl. Her mouth tightened and her shoulders rose defiantly. She shot a quick glance at her boyfriend, then leaned back petulantly against the couch. As she was recrossing her legs and attempting to avoid impaling the footstool with a spike heel, a small furred paw whipped out from beneath the couch and snagged one of her metallic stockings. Her screech brought T.S. to his feet, but Worthington did not even flinch. "There's an animal under the couch!" she squeaked.

"Brenda! Eddie!" T.S. had no choice but to get down on his hands and knees and drag the offender out by the scruff. It was Brenda and she didn't look happy. Her yellow eyes were narrowed to tiny slits and her tail switched ominously back and forth as she regarded Sally St. Claire. "So sorry," T.S. apologized. "I'll just be a minute."

He marched his pet to the back bedroom. Eddie was fast asleep on the bed and T.S. plopped Brenda beside him. "Good work," he whispered to her as he searched beneath the bed for his bedroom slippers. He was stalling for time, hoping to fend off the faint pounding that had returned to his temples.

"Nice bedroom. Big." T.S. whirled around to find that Worthington had followed him down the hall.

"Please. Feel free to look around," T.S. told him sarcastically. But the note of indignation obviously went right by the producer, for he proceeded to do just that, picking up objects on T.S.'s dresser and idly examining the undersides to see who had made them.

"Live alone?" he inquired, his eyes sliding to the open closet door.

"Yes." T.S. sat on the edge of the bed and patted Brenda absently. At the moment, Brenda was his only ally and he'd take any friend he could get. Her tail still switched ominously and her eyes were narrowed. She did not like Worthington any more than his girlfriend.

"Ever married?" Worthington asked. He seemed bored.

"No. How about you?" It was a sore point with T.S. He had never learned to tolerate the undertones that crept into people's voices when they inevitably asked the infernal question.

"Me? Once was enough. Got taken to the cleaners. I learned my lesson."

His lessons had done nothing for his taste in women, T.S. thought grimly. The producer was giving him the willies. He was too smooth, too calm, too bored. Like a rattlesnake pretending to be asleep. Get to the point, man, T.S. wanted to shout, so I can go back to bed. He wondered vaguely if this had been the plan, to separate him from Sally. Was she robbing his silverware drawer even as he sat there?

"About Lilah," Worthington began carefully, immediately grabbing T.S.'s attention. "She's a very nice woman. Cultured. Refined. But she seems to have a bit of a problem loosening up." He replaced a silver clothes brush on the dresser top and switched to fiddling with the blinds. "I see that a lot in older women. I like watching people. I'm a connoisseur, you might say, of human behavior." He turned suddenly and stared at T.S. "I saw that nothing caught your fancy at last night's party." He watched T.S. intently, searching for a reaction.

"Not my style," T.S. hedged, confident that whether he remembered the party or not, it was an entirely appropriate remark.

"That's what I thought. But I want you to be happy. I really do." Worthington's smile was reptilian: the lips slid back silently and T.S. half expected a small, forked tongue to dart out. "I like my investors to be happy," the producer added.

"*If* I invest," T.S. pointed out. It was clear that playing hard to get was the way to hook Lance Worthington.

"I feel confident that you'll come on board," the producer replied. "It's just too good an opportunity to pass up." T.S. shrugged and Worthington continued. "Tell you what, I've got a treat in mind for you. Something that I think you'll find very interesting. It was a bit hard to set up, but for you, I made the extra effort." He smiled again and handed T.S. a small envelope that was in his pocket. "Be at this address tonight at nine. If you've got other plans, cancel them. Because I think you'll be very, very pleasantly surprised. Then call me tomorrow morning and we'll talk."

T.S. took the envelope automatically, then shook the outstretched hand offered to him by Worthington. He would play along for now, then call Auntie Lil and see what she thought he should do next. He was not in the mood to waste any more time with this sleazy pair. He had a feeling that if he didn't cut off contact with Lance Worthington soon, he'd end up on a suckers list for the rest of his life and spend his retirement years fending off endless schemers searching for a gullible investor.

"Don't worry about seeing us out," Worthington told him smoothly. "I've got another appointment and I'm a few minutes late."

But T.S. was not about to let them get out the door without a good look at what they held in their hands. He stuffed the envelope in his pocket and followed Worthington back into the living room, retrieving his cashmere coat for him. The silence was a curious one, as if words were being understood without being said. Worthington was smiling as if he had discovered a great secret, and Sally was a little too casually examining the small run that Brenda had left in her stocking.

"Sorry about that," T.S. managed, his innate good manners taking over. But he'd be damned if he'd offer to replace the tawdry things. Sally shrugged her shoulders prettily, he was to pay the matter no mind. T.S. understood then that some sort of a signal had been given and received; Worthington had trained her well.

"Like I say, I'm a connoisseur of human behavior. 'Live and let live,' I always say," Worthington repeated as he hurried out the door.

What was that supposed to mean? T.S. stood in the doorway as the pair made their way to the elevator. What in the world were they up to and what did it have to do with him?

He had plenty of time to think it through before nine that night, but first things first. T.S. returned to the kitchen and checked his silverware; it was all there as far as he could tell. He took a quick inventory of his most precious possessions, not doubting for an instant that it was a normal reaction to having those two in one's home.

Nothing was missing, yet he had a curious sensation that something had been taken. They had seemed so satisfied.

He turned the phone back on and dialed Auntie Lil's number. No answer. She was probably out minding the business of New York's other seven million inhabitants. All at one time. There was nothing to do but wait until Lilah returned from her errand. She, at least, could fill him in on the details of last night.

Restless, he fetched more aspirin and a cup of coffee, then dragged a chair in front of the sliding glass doors where he did his best thinking. The rest of the world was so tiny from this vantage point, and it made him seem more powerful. He sipped at the scalding liquid, then—remembering what Worthington had slipped him in the bedroom—he carefully opened the envelope stored in his pocket.

It held two keys taped to a small piece of paper. Emily's address was neatly printed beneath them.

4. It was not until she was a block away from Homefront that a sudden thought struck Auntie Lil. It emerged with frightening clarity: she could be walking into a trap. What if *this* was what had happened to Eva?

Auntie Lil hesitated, unsure of who she could turn to for help. Certainly not Detective Santos. He had threatened her with everything short of the electric chair if she continued to interfere. Herbert was probably back on the street by now. She'd just have to try Theodore again. She fumbled for a quarter in the depths of her enormous pocketbook and dialed her nephew. The answering machine picked up again. Where was he and what in the world was he up to? Her message reflected her annoyance.

She couldn't afford to speculate. She'd miss meeting Timmy. She hung up and pressed on toward Homefront. A block away, she slowed and began checking the windows of the nearby diners and delis. When she caught sight of Bob Fleming sitting all alone in one of them, staring into his coffee cup, she relaxed. If he was in there, that meant he wasn't waiting behind a door to knock her over the head and toss her into the Hudson to follow poor Eva down the river.

Of course, Annie O'Day was nobody's weakling. And who was to say that she had stayed behind at St. Barnabas? She could just as easily be waiting behind a door at Homefront. As could anyone else who was in on the scheme. And suppose Bob was nothing more than a ruse to relax her and lure her into the trap?

Suppose, suppose and suppose. She was sick of supposing. Auntie Lil shook her head resolutely and headed toward Homefront. At some point you just had to stop supposing and get on with life.

Homefront was empty: there was no one waiting behind the unlocked front door to hit her over the head, or anywhere else for that matter. Auntie Lil even checked behind Bob Fleming's desk, but the frustrating truth was all too clear—Timmy had fled. For whatever reason, he had changed his mind about retracting and taken to the streets again, leaving the director of Homefront to grapple with the charges against him as before.

"He's gone, isn't he?" The deep voice startled her and she jumped, knocking the receiver of a telephone off the wall. Bob Fleming was too distraught to care. He just brushed past her and sat down at the desk, head in hands. "I knew he wouldn't stick around. He was too scared. I'm surprised he even came here in the first place." The big man sighed. "I'm not surprised Annie could talk him into telling the truth, but I'm even less surprised that they got to him again."

"They?" Auntie Lil stared at Fleming. His despair was genuine and so, she thought, was his innocence. "Who's 'they'?"

He shook his head. "I don't know. It could be anyone. I step on a lot of toes if I do my job right. When I take kids off the street, I'm taking money out of someone's pocket. It could be a lot of people. But if I knew . . ." His voice trailed off and he stared out the window at the empty sidewalk. "He won't be back."

His hand flashed down with one swift, sudden slap and a small container of paper clips shattered into plastic shards. Bob Fleming took no notice.

Auntie Lil did. Whether Bob Fleming was innocent or not, she became acutely aware that she was alone with him in a small room with an exit that was easily blocked and a storefront that was too far west to attract much traffic this time of day. She edged toward the door, clucking sympathetically. Two more steps and she was only an arms' length away from the opening.

"Where are you going?" Fleming asked her suddenly. She took another step toward the door and he watched her with an absent, perplexed scrutiny as he played with the paper clips scattered across his desk.

"I've got to get back to St. Barnabas," she said as calmly as she could, confused by the sudden fright washing over her. "They are terribly shorthanded and need help serving."

Bob Fleming stared out the window. "Annie's there."

"Yes, she is. But I'm sure she needs help." Auntie Lil backed up carefully, feeling the doorjamb behind her. One more step and she'd be home free.

"Perhaps I should go with you. I might as well help out." Bob Fleming stood abruptly but she was already out the door, pretending not to have heard. Without looking back, she waved a cheerful goodbye over one shoulder and walked rapidly east. His brooding preoccupation disturbed her. He looked as if, beneath the surface, emotions were simmering at dangerous levels; when he finally cracked, the explosion would be considerable.

She headed toward Emily's street, thinking of her next step. She had told Bob Fleming the truth; her final destination was St. Barnabas. But first she needed to talk to Herbert Wong.

When Auntie Lil walked past the Jamaican restaurant, Nellie was back on her table perch, surveying the streets. Their eyes locked briefly but Nellie's face showed no signs of recognition. Perhaps she had truly forgotten who Auntie Lil was. Or perhaps she was just a very good actress.

Herbert was once again ensconced in the parking lot across

from Emily's house. This time no attendant was in sight and his only companion was a large, mangy-looking dog that slept quietly at his feet.

Herbert rose and bowed respectfully. "The attendant and I agreed that so long as I was here, I might as well help him out. Therefore, he is in a bar nearby enjoying his newfound freedom and I, being a scrupulously honest man, collect the tolls for him. It gives my pose much legitimacy."

"I thought disguises were superfluous and New Yorkers supplied their own blinders," she pointed out somewhat archly.

"Forgive me." Herbert bowed again. "I was in a distraught state when you found me. Tired and depressed from a night of fruitless work. Besides, if I help out the parking lot attendant, he will tell me what goes on in Miss Emily's building when I am not here."

"Where's Franklin?"

"He is seeking the man who first spotted The Eagle. He was seen near Madison Square Garden early this afternoon, so Franklin is down there now."

"At last." Auntie Lil stared at the facade of Emily's apartment building. "Anything unusual happen today?"

"No. Except that The Eagle has still not yet left the building and that the police claim he is not inside, everything here appears to be normal."

Auntie Lil sighed and her face sagged. It was time to break the bad news to him.

"You have found out the whereabouts of Miss Eva," Herbert Wong said sadly as he searched her face. Herbert often communicated on a deeper, unsaid level.

"Yes. It was her."

Herbert's face fell in dignified sadness. "I do not believe that it could be thought of as your fault," he said quietly. "I hope you are not blaming yourself."

"Well, of course I am." Auntie Lil stared dejectedly at Emily's building. "If not for me, they wouldn't have been parading around the streets. In fact, it might be because of me specifically that she was killed."

"You must explain," he said gently, guiding her to his chair.

"The police, or at least Detective Santos, think it likely that the killer was after me. We are very alike in physical characteristics, except for our hair."

"Perhaps." Herbert allowed a tiny shrug, as if humoring the police. "However, perhaps not. She may have brought it upon herself through her own actions."

"Maybe." Auntie Lil felt silent.

"And you cannot bring yourself to inform the other ladies at St. Barnabas?"

"Correct. You may call me a coward, if you wish."

"You are a brave and honest woman, Lillian," he replied. "But this is not a task that you should handle. I shall tell the ladies the bad news myself. We are due to assemble in a few hours. Instead of the usual warning, I shall tell them of Eva's death." He paused briefly. "I will also tell them that they must not pretend anymore. That they must stay at home where it is safe and leave the rest of the investigation up to the police." He stared steadily at Auntie Lil and she did not respond. It was one of the few times he had ever tried to impose his will on her and she sensed that arguing with him would not be a wise course to choose. Besides, he was right.

It still hurt to admit it. "You're right," she finally said, rising with a sigh, telling him of the dire warnings she had received from Detective Santos and Lieutenant Abromowitz. "It is too dangerous. We must give up the game."

"Regrettably," Herbert added.

"And so it must be done." She managed a small wave and continued her trek to the church, passing a familiar old man in another lawn chair at the far end of the block. His nose was as bulbous as a cauliflower; his clothes were as drab and tan as the building behind him. He recognized Auntie Lil, but she was too preoccupied to notice that her progress up Eighth Avenue was being carefully observed.

It was back to the soup kitchen, she thought glumly, back to being nothing more than a bored old lady whose mind was sharper than her body and who harbored illusions that she could, with all her frailties, be the one capable of bringing justice to the mean streets of Hell's Kitchen.

Stop whining, she commanded herself suddenly. There was still an ace card she could play. She stopped at three pay phones until she found one that worked, then dialed Margo McGregor's number. The columnist still was not in and the busy reporter who answered took her latest message with bored efficiency.

Auntie Lil hung up glumly. She had to get through to Margo McGregor for help. Because her only hope now was publicity. Maybe then, public pressure would force Lieutenant Abromowitz to put more men on the job.

CHAPTER FOURTEEN

1. As soon as she saw the long line still snaking down the sidewalk toward St. Barnabas, she realized that they were in deep trouble and hurried inside. Nearly everyone should have been fed by now.

To her surprise, Bob Fleming had kept his word. Despite his own miseries, he was there behind the counter handing plates of hot food across to hungry patrons. Father Stebbins was back at work beside him, looking uncharacteristically subdued. Annie O'Day was sweating over one of the big industrial stoves in back, while the remaining volunteers fought valiantly to maintain order.

She saw at once where the confusion began. Auntie Lil appointed herself guardian of the silverware and napkins, then began to hand out trays. The logjam in the line cleared quickly and the flow of hungry people picked up their pace.

Thank God Adelle and her followers had already been through the line. Auntie Lil did not think that she could look them in the eye knowing that Eva was dead and that they were all about to be pulled off their unofficial positions on the case. Herbert was right. This was a job for him. He handled the dirty work so well.

Auntie Lil took advantage of a lull in the crowd to speak to Bob Fleming. She felt guilty for having been afraid of him at Homefront. "I must salute you," she began. "Being able to put your own troub—" She stopped. Bob Fleming had turned pale and was not listening. He was staring at the door behind her.

She whirled around. Little Pete was heading straight for them and his face was streaked with tears. Gone was the tough little man of the streets. He was a terrified child crying for help. At first she could not understand his words, he was emitting such an hysterical mixture of cries and bellowings. Bob Fleming was better at the translation.

"What?" He jumped over the counter and pushed a hungry customer aside. "What did you say?" he demanded of the terrified boy. Father Stebbins hurried around the counter and joined the tableau.

"He's dead," Little Pete shouted, tears streaking down his face. "I think he's dead. The man said to go get him at Homefront and bring him to this old building but when we got there, Rodney started beating up on Timmy. You should have heard the sound. I had to run away. He was too big." The boy held his hands over his ears and shut his eyes to erase the memory. "I didn't know where else to go. You wasn't at Homefront so I thought of here."

"Where is Timmy now?" Fleming shouted, pulling on Little Pete's arms. He screamed over his shoulder for Annie O'Day. Auntie Lil knelt down and drew the sobbing boy close. She was vaguely aware that a crowd had gathered around them, and that Adelle and her followers hovered on the outer perimeter watching and exchanging horrified glances.

"Where is he now?" Bob Fleming insisted again, before he was pushed aside by an efficient Annie O'Day.

"Pete, Pete, Pete," she repeated over and over until the boy calmed down. "Maybe Timmy isn't dead. Maybe he's just hurt. I want you to bring me to him. Okay? I'll come with you now and you show me where he is. Where the man left him. I'm a nurse. Maybe I can help Timmy." She spoke slowly and calmly until the small boy stopped trembling. The rest of the room waited quietly. She knew what she was doing.

"He's in that old piano warehouse along Eleventh Avenue," Little Pete sobbed in a tiny voice. He gulped. "There's a way to sneak in the back."

"He's talking about the building at Eleventh and Forty-sixth," Annie told Bob Fleming sharply. "Call an ambulance and have them meet me there." She turned back to Little Pete and her voice softened to that of a mother crooning a child to sleep. "Can you take me there?" she asked gently. "I'll bring my bag and we'll see what we can do."

Pete nodded and waited while Annie grabbed her bag from a shelf in the kitchen, then took her outstretched hand. They walked calmly out of the basement and the crowd parted before them without comment. Even the most deranged of the kitchen's customers sensed that something terrible had just happened and that, whatever it was, it was bad enough without their help.

As soon as Annie and Little Pete hit the steps, they began to run.

Auntie Lil stared after them, only dimly aware that Bob Fleming had dashed upstairs in search of a telephone. She was startled back to reality by a terrible choking sound. Father Stebbins had turned pale blue white and was slumped against the counter with his hand on his throat, coughing violently. The cough turned into a rasping wheeze.

Oh, God, Auntie Lil thought. Not another.

"Asthma," Father Stebbins wheezed helplessly. "Medicine upstairs." Fran took off running up the steps without being asked, while Auntie Lil loosened his collar. He bent at the waist, trying to breathe. The mixture of choked air and garbled words was as terrifying as Little Pete's pronouncement had been. The priest sounded as if he were being strangled into silence.

"My fault," he whistled between whooping intakes of breath. "This is all my fault."

"Don't talk," Auntie Lil commanded, shooing the curious back. She exchanged a glance with Adelle and the elderly actress majestically wound her way through the crowd toward Auntie Lil.

"Help him," Auntie Lil said simply. "Fran is coming with medication." Without waiting for the reply, she turned and walked briskly out the door. She would see for herself what they had done to Timmy.

A block away, a running figure brushed past her. She stared after broad shoulders in a plaid lumberjack shirt. Bob Fleming was heading for the warehouse, too. He would get there well before she would. But she was hurrying as fast as she could.

When she finally reached the intersection of Eleventh and Forty-sixth, it was marked by two huge abandoned buildings. She had no way of knowing which one was the right one until Bob Fleming burst out onto the sidewalk through the twin door of one of them, his shoulder tearing off the padlock from the inside like a battering ram. He had climbed in the back and blasted his way out of the front to create a clearer path for the medics.

"Stand there and wave down the ambulance," he commanded Auntie Lil. "I have to help Annie bring the kid down the steps."

Auntie Lil obeyed. The sound of sirens was still far away, wailing impatiently in short bursts of indignant bleating. The ambulance had gotten trapped in the heavier afternoon traffic along the West Side arteries and selfish drivers were blocking its path. Auntie Lil began to curse, unaware that Little Pete had returned to stand by her side. Then a small hand slipped into hers. It was trembling.

"Annie says he's alive," the small boy stammered. "Annie says he's alive."

"Of course he's alive," Auntie Lil told him crisply, though she was weak with relief at his words. "We aren't going to let Timmy die. And we aren't going to let you get hurt anymore, either."

The sounds of sirens grew louder, accompanied by flashing red lights and the sound of an angry man on a bullhorn.

"Clear the lane," a deep voice boomed. "Clear the lane immediately."

"Cops!" Little Pete shouted. It was a single but powerful word, and it triggered an automatic reaction in him. He jerked his hand from Auntie Lil. Before she could stop him, he darted across the packed lanes of traffic. She watched helplessly as the small figure ran down the opposite sidewalk. He turned up toward Tenth Avenue and was gone.

The door clanged open behind her again and Bob Fleming reemerged, holding a small bundle of blood, flesh and ripped clothing in his hands. Annie O'Day walked calmly beside the human catastrophe, holding an I.V. drip bag in one hand. It was attached to a small, clear tube that snaked down into the gore. "Where is it?" she asked angrily when she saw no ambulance waiting.

"It's here!" Auntie Lil shouted as she stood on her tiptoes and waved her pocketbook frantically, putting her legendary cab-hailing skills to good use. Her gesture was answered by the stepped-up volume of a siren and, suddenly, the ambulance dispensed with the traffic jam altogether. It hopped the curb and came tearing down the sidewalk toward them, followed by two patrol cars.

The attendant was out of the passenger seat before the vehicle had stopped. Another pair of medics popped from the back with a stretcher. The small figure in Bob Fleming's arms was swiftly transferred to a stretcher and lifted into the back of the ambulance.

"What is it?" a burly paramedic asked quietly.

"It's a small boy," replied Annie O'Day.

2.   Despite a cup of coffee and his resolve to puzzle out Worthington's motives, T.S. had not been able to stay awake long enough to get anywhere. His body had cried out for still more sleep and he had barely been able to make it to the living room couch before he was out again. He awoke hours later to the rude sensation of having his face scraped with sandpaper. He opened an eye and an enormous yellow orb stared down at him. Worse, something was nibbling at his toes.

He groaned and struggled to sit up. What was he doing asleep on his own couch? The murky light outside indicated that it was early evening; the behavior of his hungry cats confirmed it. He padded into the kitchen and fed Brenda and Eddie an entire can of cat food each. After scratching Sally St. Claire, they deserved it.

He checked the answering machine. There was a message from Auntie Lil, but the street noises behind her made it difficult for him to understand. The gist of the message seemed to be that she loathed his answering machine. He sighed and tried to reach her at home without any luck. She must still be busy at the soup kitchen, he reasoned. Perhaps he should stop by to see.

Lilah's coat still hung, untouched, over a chair. Where was she? What was taking her so long?

He made himself some plain egg noodles and nibbled at them tentatively. They went down smoothly and stayed there. In fact, he felt almost human again. He pulled out the envelope that Worthington had given him and reexamined the address and apartment number. It was not Emily's, after all, but the unit next door on the same floor. Why would Lance Worthington invite him to that particular apartment? What could be waiting for him there?

Of course. T.S. suddenly remembered the sounds he had overheard and the shadows he had seen the day that he and Auntie Lil had searched Emily's apartment. A young boy had run past them, followed by a red-faced man trying to hide his identity.

But surely Worthington didn't believe that *he* was one of those sweaty middle-aged men who—T.S.'s spoon clanked abruptly into the bowl.

Of course Worthington thought he was into young boys. The man's mind was in the gutter. In such a disgusting context, the producer's entire cryptic conversation that afternoon made perfect sense.

T.S. knew exactly what would happen. He would walk into the apartment and a young boy would be waiting for him. One of those tough, overused hardened street kids with a heart made of leather. In fact, the young boy could very well be Timmy. If so, it was the perfect opportunity for T.S. to speak to him alone. They'd been trying to contact the boy for a week to determine how and what he knew about Emily.

Even more significantly, Auntie Lil had failed utterly at this task. Finally, it was his turn to get there first.

Except that he wasn't going to be stupid about it. Being alone in a room with an underage boy who specialized in middle-aged men was far too indiscreet an act to attempt without a witness. And who could guarantee the boy would be alone? He needed a hidden observer, someone to protect his own reputation. It had to be a person who could be counted on to remain discreetly in the background shadows. Someone who would not try to butt in at a delicate moment and wrestle the conversation away from T.S. Which absolutely ruled out Auntie Lil. But left Herbert Wong. Herbert was agile enough to climb a fire escape, smart enough to stay hidden and easy to contact.

T.S. checked his watch. It was nearly eight o'clock, which meant that Herbert was conveniently at his post across from Emily's building already. Unless he was getting carried away again with his potted plant disguises, T.S. would have no trouble spotting him and enlisting him in the plan.

Four aspirins and another shower later, T.S. was on his way back to Hell's Kitchen.

3. Herbert Wong had heard about Timmy's injuries from Adelle and her followers at their afternoon meeting. He, in turn, had broken the sad news about Eva's death. Their reactions had, surprisingly, been muted. Until he realized that many of the old actresses may have been in shock. The more shaken women quickly returned to their tiny apartments or group homes where they felt safe. Three of the hardier ones, including Adelle, elected to accompany Herbert to Roosevelt Hospital where, they assured him, Timmy would have been taken. Herbert wanted to see if Auntie Lil needed him.

Their presence complicated an already chaotic scene. Timmy had been whisked immediately into the emergency room entrance, but the waiting area outside was jam-packed with the poor of the neighborhood, who considered the emergency room to be a de facto doctor's office. This annoyed the overburdened nurses and aides, who were forced to make such patients wait and wait while the more drastically injured were attended to. The medium-sized room was clogged with clusters of rejected and weary mothers holding ragged children whose running noses and frequent coughs rendered a diagnosis redundant. Interspersed among these contagious hopefuls were pockets of the more befuddled homeless, who came to Roosevelt for a kind word and, perhaps, the chance of being treated as a human being by an understanding doctor or nurse. They were also there for the warmth. The night outside had grown chilly and the waiting room cozy from the heat of many bodies. In short, it was a clean, well-lighted place.

Here and there among this noisy, angry crowd were real emergency-room candidates. They were in pain and outnumbered. A young man in athletic sweats slumped in a chair, his face contorted in pain and one ankle propped on a nearby coffee table. His girlfriend fussed around him, rubbing the injured joint and glaring at an oblivious nurse's aide. A basketball had rolled under his chair, forgotten by all but a young boy sniffling nearby, who eyed it with longing and hope. Against the far wall of the waiting room, a very young and very drunk Danish sailor, on leave from his ship berthed nearby, clutched a hand that dripped steady drops of blood onto his white uniform. The scarlet stain spread across his chest as if he had been pierced in the heart. But the nurses—who had already confirmed that it was a minor cut hand inflicted by a broken beer bottle—had decided that he deserved to wait.

The only respite from the madness of this hopeless system was a small cluster of waiting figures anchored by a waving Auntie Lil. They had pulled their chairs in a broad semicircle in front of the double-wide doors that led to the treatment rooms of the emergency facility. Every time anyone entered or exited the inner sanctum, Auntie Lil was able to peek inside and demand updates from whatever hounded medical professional had failed to move quickly enough to avoid her. One dashed successfully past just as Herbert, Adelle and her two consorts joined the group.

"Sir!" Auntie Lil demanded of the already departed doctor. He left a faint whiff of antiseptic behind.

"How is he?" Herbert asked Auntie Lil quietly. "Miss Adelle filled me in on what happened."

"He's alive. That's all I know," she replied miserably. She lifted her brows slightly and slid her eyes quietly to the right. Father Stebbins sat crouched in a chair beside her, a rosary clutched in his hands. His lips moved silently as he prayed and his eyes glistened with tears. He alone among the suffering had managed, at least in mind, to escape the stuffy waiting room. Fran sat next to him, tightlipped and silent, her hand resting lightly on the priest's arm.

"What happened?" Herbert asked Auntie Lil quietly, aware that Adelle was listening in. "I heard very few details. Only that the young boy's friend ran into St. Barnabas shouting that Timmy was dead."

"We don't know yet," Auntie Lil told him. "He was lured to an abandoned building and beaten almost to death. Little Pete escaped unharmed, but he ran away before he would say who was responsible."

From long habit, Herbert's eyes slid from face to face in the dreary room. "That's the Homefront man," he confirmed in a low voice, indicating Bob Fleming.

Auntie Lil nodded. They watched the Homefront director quietly argue with a nurse at the admitting desk. He was obviously a veteran at negotiating quick settlements in the overcrowded, overworked atmosphere. He spoke quickly and firmly, but in a low voice, his finger frequently hitting the countertop for emphasis. Each time the nurse's face appeared about to cross over to anger, he would lean close and whisper something that triggered a quick smile.

"He knows what he's doing," Herbert confirmed.

"Let's hope so. He signed a stack of papers two feet high." Auntie Lil nodded toward the cold steel doors. "They let Annie inside. They seem to know her well here."

Herbert nodded and gently took Auntie Lil's hand. "Not your fault," he said simply and she replied with a weak smile.

"Miss Hubbert." Bob Fleming stood before them, looking tired but hopeful. "I guess they don't have time to read the newspapers around here. They don't seem to know I'm a pariah. They've agreed to admit him if Homefront guarantees the bill. I'm going to go down to the precinct now and talk to the detectives who questioned me about Timmy's allegations yesterday."

"Now?" Auntie Lil asked in surprise.

Fleming shrugged. "There's nothing more I can do here and I might as well volunteer for questions before they come and drag me down there. This way, it will look a whole lot better. I'm sure I'm the number one suspect in their book."

"I can certainly vouch for your whereabouts when this happened," Fran spoke up. Her voice was firm and calm; she remained in complete control. Father Stebbins, on the other hand, appeared not to have heard. He was still lost in prayer and worry.

Fleming nodded his thanks. "Good. You'll have to. But it's still better this way. Annie will be out in a minute with a progress report. They say he's not as bad as he looked, but . . ." He shrugged and headed for the door, leaving them to the same, dismal shared thought: the boy had looked dead. "Better" could still mean pretty awful.

They sat in silence, staring at the double doors, until a sudden moan from Father Stebbins made them all jump.

"My fault," he said distinctly, before lapsing back into prayer. Fran patted his arm.

The others were not reassured. Auntie Lil met Herbert's gaze, their look interrupted by a quiet hiss from Adelle. The elderly actress rolled her eyes with exaggerated drama and motioned for them to join her in a far corner, where they were forced to evict a nearly incoherent homeless man in order to preserve their privacy. The odor he left behind mingled with the strong smell of hospital ammonia. Auntie Lil felt faint and wavered.

"You okay?" Herbert asked solicitously as he gripped her elbow tightly, ready to steady her in case of a fall.

She shook him off with a dignity and strength that she did not, in truth, feel. "Of course. It's just that . . . things seem to have gotten out of hand."

Adelle and her followers put their heads together closely, exchanging a private look. "One of my girls saw Father Stebbins with Timmy this morning," Adelle whispered ominously. "And look at him now, blubbering into his rosary."

They turned as one and stared at the distraught priest. Fran stared back at them without emotion.

"Discreet, discreet," Herbert muttered with a sigh. "Please, ladies. We must be more discreet."

"I saw him with Timmy the other morning, too," Auntie Lil admitted. "But he is a priest. Perhaps he was hearing his confession or offering guidance."

Auntie Lil and Adelle exchanged an even glance. Both had noticed that Father Stebbins had disappeared for long stretches of time. "Not enough time to run up Tenth Avenue and beat up a small boy and get back in time to pass the lemon sauce," Adelle finally admitted aloud, somewhat dejectedly.

"But enough time to tell someone else to do it," Auntie Lil pointed out. Despite Herbert's warning, they turned again as one and stared at the priest.

"Ladies, *please*." Herbert was clearly annoyed at their lack of self-control. "You cannot be good at this unless you can control your curiosity." He steered Auntie Lil firmly back to her seat.

"How much longer do we have to wait?" Auntie Lil complained, settling back into the uncomfortable hard plastic. It was just like the chairs at St. Barnabas.

A few minutes later, the swinging doors opened and Annie O'Day appeared. Blood had dried all over the front of her gray sweat suit, but her face and hands had been scrubbed clean. Even exhausted, her pink cheeks glowed with health.

"How is he?" they asked in near unison.

"His condition has stabilized. They're admitting him now. We're in luck. One of their better doctors took an interest." She pushed her short hair off her face with a weary gesture.

"I must see the boy," Father Stebbins insisted in an abruptly commanding voice. He stood and rushed for the door.

"You can't." Annie blocked him with one quick movement, her shoulder bouncing him into a nearby wall.

The priest stared at her, dazed, and rubbed his shoulder almost petulantly. "I have to talk to him alone," he contended. "Please. I'm his priest."

Auntie Lil popped up from her chair in a sudden burst of panic and stared between Father Stebbins and Annie. "No one sees him alone," she blurted out.

Annie nodded her agreement, crossing her arms firmly as she barricaded the swinging doors. Their eyes met and both Auntie Lil and Annie O'Day nodded: they understood exactly what the other was thinking.

4. St. Barnabas was dark and barren, the basement darkest of all. It looked as if no one had set foot inside for years. Both safety gates were firmly padlocked. Clearly, Auntie Lil was not inside.

T.S. stood on the sidewalk, his light coat wrapped tightly against the early autumn chill. He was wondering what he should do next. It was nearly nine o'clock. He would be secure with Herbert backing him up, but—on the off chance that Worthington was somehow involved with Emily's death—if something happened to both him and Herbert, no one would ever know who was responsible. He ought to get word to Auntie Lil. Or he'd end up like Emily.

He tried Auntie Lil again at home without success, dialed again out of pure stubbornness and listened to fifteen empty shrill rings before finally relinquishing the phone to an impatient teenager. The gaunt young man was hopping lightly from foot to foot as he tried to intimidate T.S. with a stern stare. T.S. ignored it, though he was shocked to see that the kid wore an electronic beeper strapped to his belt. Great, thought T.S. grimly, as he headed uptown one block, we're making progress with our young after all. We've introduced them to the miracles of science. A new age of technologically advanced drug dealing is dawning.

T.S. was stalling for time and he knew it. He was heading uptown because he had a vague idea that his great-grandparents had once lived on the site of the old Madison Square Garden. The lot where the towering new skyscraper now stood. He felt alone and abandoned, and he needed their comfort before embarking on his uncertain task.

The streets of Hell's Kitchen were curiously deserted in the post-twilight hours between curtain rise and curtain fall on nearby Broadway. It was not late enough for the sleaze merchants to be peddling their wares; it was too early for the nightcrawlers to have yet emerged. There was an uneasy peace about the neighborhood, giving it more of an air of a destination, rather than just a stop along the way. Gradually, T.S. became aware that the sensation was not unpleasant. He felt at home.

He reached his block and stood in the shadows of the huge sky-scraper at Forty-ninth and Eighth, looking up at the sky. The big building was nearly dark at this time of night, only the lower res-idential towers displayed the occasional light. But across the street, a long row of older apartment houses bravely fighting di-lapidation blazed defiantly at the steel and concrete intruder. The shabby exteriors proudly housed vibrant interiors: the street twin-kled with the lights of many filled rooms.

This was the real heart of Hell's Kitchen, T.S. thought. He had been mistaken when he believed the neighborhood was losing its fight against change. It knew just what it was doing. The lifeline of Hell's Kitchen had not changed one iota since the days of his great-grandfather. It still drew its extraordinary energy from the thousands of lives hidden behind worn doors and thin walls. And not even the drug dealers or prostitutes could vanquish the spirit of the families and people who hung on here. They were tough, he realized, much tougher than he was. They avoided disappoint-ment by not expecting too much of their neighborhood. And they had learned to recognize what was most important to them: a safe place called home, never mind the surrounding streets. Plus a job. Friends and family. Neighbors to nod to on the street. They had no patience or time for anything else. He would do well to re-member their lessons.

His first stop was the Delicious Deli. He saw by the clock in the brightly lit but nearly empty restaurant that he would be a few minutes late for his appointment at Emily's building. No matter. He was mere seconds away.

"Help you with anything?" the proprietor asked. T.S. could not remember his name, it was something fairly common. Phil . . . Willy. No—Bill. Or, rather, Billy.

"I want to leave a message for my aunt," T.S. told him. Perhaps Auntie Lil would stop by here before she went home.

"That's real considerate of you. But this ain't a post office," Billy replied good-naturedly. "I can't guarantee she'll get it."

"It's my Aunt Lil. An elderly lady."

"Oh, *her*." Billy's eyes rolled back in his head and he sighed. "What's the message? She'll no doubt be snooping back around here soon enough."

"Tell her I went to *the* building. That I was invited."

Billy stared at T.S. "You went to the building invited," he repeated.

"No. *The* building."

This time Billy got the inflection right.

As T.S. stepped out again into the night, Billy watched him for a few seconds, then reached for the telephone.

T.S. had expected to see a few of the older actresses disguised as bag ladies scattered around, but Forty-sixth Street was nearly empty. The long row of restaurants stretched in front of him quietly, seeming to breathe deeply in the break between pretheater *prix fixe* and posttheater suppers. There was one old man parked in a lawn chair on the corner. T.S. checked out his enormous nose surreptitiously. Good heavens. What had happened to the poor fellow? He looked like he'd lost a fight with a meat grinder. T.S. continued down the block, still surprised at the lack of activity. Where was Herbert? Where was Adelle? Or even Franklin? What was this about a blanket of surveillance?

He walked all the way to the end of the block, passing the Jamaican restaurant where they had first discovered a clue about Emily. He reached Ninth Avenue without seeing anyone he knew. No one. Just a few strangers brushing past. He went back up the block and this time drew a curious glance from Nellie, the proprietor of the Jamaican restaurant. She was perched on her customary table, staring blankly out into the night and bobbing her many braids to some unheard rhythm. Her eyes took in T.S.'s returning figure without emotion, but T.S. had no doubt that she had recognized who he was.

One door down, he reached Emily's apartment house again. Still no sign of the ever-vigilant Herbert Wong. He stood at the front door, holding the key. Quite frankly, he was afraid to go in. He did not know if he was being foolish or brave.

A figure was hurrying up the block toward him. At last, he thought, one of the bag ladies. Probably Adelle. She was that tall. But he was very much mistaken. The willowy figure passed through a pool of light and he saw that it was Leteisha Swann, ubiquitous woman of the night. He remembered the morning she had stumbled into this very building and passed out in the closet. Oh, dear, she was no doubt headed home for a breather. And he was in no mood for witnesses. He was about to turn his back to the door when she breezed right past the building, her steady gait showing no sign of inebriation. She was heading quickly toward Eighth Avenue, her tall figure squeezed into a long-sleeved silver dress. She negotiated the spike heels like the pro that she was. Within a half-minute, she had disappeared into the shadows at the upper end of the block.

T.S. still lingered at the front door. He wondered briefly what Auntie Lil would do in such a situation, found his answer, and quickly inserted one of the keys. It fit. The tiny downstairs hall was deserted and smelled of sour cooking oil with a faint underfragrance of cheap wine. He hurried into the elevator and pushed the sixth-floor button, looking nervously around to see if he was being observed. He felt slightly ridiculous, huddled in the tiny elevator, his hands clutched tightly in the pockets of his trench coat. Who was he expecting, anyway? Peter Lorre?

The elevator car creaked and groaned its way to the top floor. That hallway, too, was deserted. He would use his wits well, he decided firmly. If he was taking a big chance, he'd best eliminate as many little ones as he could. He checked the stairway door. It opened easily, onto winding stairs and landings that, as far as he could see, were deserted and, thankfully, well lit. He inspected every corner of the hall and tried Emily's door. It was securely locked. That left only one thing to do.

He put an ear to the door of the apartment next to Emily's. There was a faint sound inside. A vacant hiss of static and garbled voices. Someone was watching television. Surely, murderers didn't sit and watch television while they waited for their victims? He inserted the key in the lock and turned it lightly. The bolts opened with a loud click. Immediately the television went silent. T.S. took a deep breath and slowly swung the door open all the way to the wall. If someone was hiding behind it, he wanted to know.

The inside of the one-room apartment was dimly lit by a single lamp that cast a pool of light across a cheap rug. In the center of the room stood a small black boy, hands jammed in his pockets. His head was ducked slightly and he stared up at the door with a furtive unease that exploded into fright once he recognized T.S. "You!" the boy shouted, dashing for the door.

T.S. responded automatically. He slammed the door shut behind him and stood against it, preventing the boy's escape. "What about me?" T.S. shouted back. This did nothing for the young boy's panic.

The kid backed away, eyes wide and voice trembling. "Stay away from me," he ordered in a trembling voice. A small hand darted into a jacket pocket and he pulled out a knife. It clicked open and gleamed in the dull light. It was a ridiculously small blade. On the other hand, no blade was ridiculous, T.S. reminded himself.

"Look, son, I'm not here to hurt you," he reassured the boy in as calm a voice as he could manage. "You have no reason to be frightened of me. No reason at all. What do you think I am? I'm as confused as you are about this."

"I'm not confused. I know who you are," the boy spit back angrily. He took a step backwards and looked behind him. He was checking out the fire escape, T.S. realized.

"It won't do you any good," T.S. lied. "I have a friend on the fire escape." Sure, some friend. Herbert was probably at home in bed asleep, leaving T.S. to deal with this pint-sized homicidal maniac.

"Don't come near me," the boy warned T.S., moving back and forth in a semicircle with the blade extended in front of him.

"Son, please." T.S. held a hand up. "You've seen *West Side Story* one too many times. Put the knife away and tell me who you think I am."

The boy did not put the knife away, but he did lower it. He eyed T.S. suspiciously. "You're the man who had dead pictures of Timmy's grandmother," he said bitterly. "I saw you pick them up from the photo store. You were practically drooling over them. You're the man who killed her."

"Me?" T.S. stared at him incredulously, remembering the frightened child who had darted toward him before veering off into the shadows. He certainly looked a hell of a lot more grown up standing four feet away with a knife in his hand. "No, no, no, no," T.S. told him. "A thousand times no. I am definitely not the person who killed Emily. I took those pictures of her at the morgue, after she was dead. I'm trying to find out who killed her. Don't you remember the background of those photos? White. Like a hospital."

The boy's eyes narrowed. He was, at least, considering believing T.S. "How do I know you're not lying?" he finally allowed.

T.S. remembered that the boy had talked to Auntie Lil. "Look, I'll prove it to you. Your name is Little Pete, right?"

The boy stared at him. "Maybe. So what?"

"I know all about you. You're Timmy's friend. You called Emily 'Grandmother,' too. She bought you presents on your birthday. You have nice table manners. You eat your green beans last. How am I doing?"

"How do you know those things?" Little Pete asked sullenly.

"You had dinner with my aunt. Auntie Lil. The old lady who bought you dinner at the Delicious Deli a couple nights ago."

"You're lying," Little Pete said. "That was Emily's sister."

"No, no. She was just a friend of Emily's. And she is my aunt. Here, look." He thrust his face into the light and Little Pete stared at it blankly. "See," T.S. said. "We've got the same nose. Big. Look at this." He turned his head so Little Pete could see his profile. "And check out these cheeks. They're exactly the same. And the hair. Face it. We're practically twins." He was desperate and sounded like a babbling fool, but it was better than grappling with a knife-wielding teenager.

Besides, it worked. Little Pete relaxed and folded the knife away. "You sure do look like her," he admitted grudgingly. "What are you doing here? You'd better leave. I'm waiting for somebody."

"You're waiting for me," T.S. explained. The look this statement inspired in Little Pete instantly shamed him. "But not for the reason you think," T.S. added quickly.

"The man is not going to like this at all," Little Pete answered. He moved to a large, sagging bed that dominated the bare room and sat on it dejectedly. "He'll beat me to death like Timmy."

"What?" T.S. moved toward him. "What did you say?" He knelt beside the boy and Little Pete buried his face in his hands. T.S. patted his back and the fatherly gesture summoned what was left of the little boy in Little Pete. The child began to sob and talk at the same time, his garbled explanation discernible only in bits and pieces. It took ten minutes for T.S. to figure out what had happened. And he finally had an idea of where Auntie Lil might be.

Timmy had been beaten up, Little Pete explained. On the orders of a man who used to be nice to Timmy and Little Pete. Because Timmy had done something wrong. At first, everything had been going well. The man had gotten them customers, clean ones. And paid them plenty of money. Given them clothes and shoes. Food. Then, a couple of days ago he told Timmy he had to do him a favor. Timmy never told Little Pete what the favor was, but it had something to do with a priest. Timmy didn't want to talk about it.

He'd done what the man asked, but then he'd started to feel bad about it. So Timmy had changed his mind, Little Pete explained, and the man had sent someone after him. Little Pete was sure that Timmy had been beaten up to teach them both a lesson about crossing the man. They'd come and taken Timmy to the hospital and Little Pete didn't even know if he was still alive or not. Little Pete figured he'd been spared his own beating only because he had this job to do tonight. The man in charge had told him to come here and take Timmy's place. But now Little Pete was frightened. He'd been thinking about it. He was sure that once tonight's job was over, the man would send Rodney after him, too.

"Rodney?" T.S. asked, "Who's this Rodney guy?"

"He works for the man in charge sometimes. Tall dude. Skinny, but strong. He has an eagle tattooed on one arm."

The Eagle. He did exist. At last they had a name for The Eagle.

"Who's the man in charge?" T.S. asked him. "Who pays you and Timmy to come to this apartment?"

Little Pete shrugged. His tears had slowed to a trickle and T.S. saw with some dismay that the tough little street survivor was about to take over again. "I can't tell you. If I tell you, he'll have me killed."

"You told me about Rodney," T.S. pointed out.

"I don't care about no Rodney anymore." The boy looked up and fierce hatred twisted his face. "I'm getting me a piece from a friend. After tonight, the dude will be dead."

If it was true, T.S. would have to do something to stop him. But for now, he needed more information. T.S. knew that he'd never convince the boy to tell him who the top man was, so he tried another approach. "Look, if you won't tell me who the man is who hired Rodney, at least tell me why he has you and Timmy come to this room?"

"Why?" Little Pete spat the word out like T.S. was too stupid to live. "Why do you think?"

"No, I know that . . ." T.S.'s words trailed off and his face flushed pink. Then he swallowed and continued, reminding himself that the new T.S. was in control. "I know about that part. But why does this man want to make the men you see happy?"

Little Pete shrugged. "Guess they pay him money. They sure don't pay me. The big man pays me, through Timmy."

T.S. thought hard. Hustling two boys didn't seem like a profitable enough venture to merit renting an apartment like this. "What does this man tell you to do with the men?" T.S. was fishing and he knew it.

"Whatever they want. Look, you sure you know what goes on up here?" Little Pete's distress had turned to incredulity. Who was this pathetically uninformed old geezer? Did he know nothing about real life?

T.S. surveyed the room. There had to be another reason why everything took place here. Yet it seemed an ordinary, if drab, apartment. There was a chair, a bed, a coffee table, small refrigerator and a makeshift bar in the room. The door to a small, empty bathroom stood open. And there was a single large cabinet against one wall with an old black-and-white television perched on top of it. Not a very nice place for an assignation. But not very nice assignations, either.

"Where does all your, um ... action take place?" T.S. asked.

"We do it here, in the room," Little Pete pointed out patiently.

"Where in the room?" T.S. stood in the middle, turning in slow circles. It was as bare as a prison cell and not nearly as charming. Why did the meetings take place here, instead of the homes of the men? Or a hotel? And why was the cabinet here? It was tall and a rather nice piece of work. It gleamed with a black enamel finish.

"Here on the bed," Little Pete answered slowly, as if talking to a particularly stupid individual. This old dude was hopelessly out of step.

"Always on the bed?" T.S. confirmed.

"That's what the man says. Says he doesn't want his apartment trashed. Keep it on the bed, boys, he says," the kid answered sullenly.

Trash this place? T.S. stood by the bed next to Little Pete. The cabinet was lined up directly against the far wall. There were two sets of double doors on the cabinet, one on top and one below.

"I heard music coming from this apartment one time," T.S. told Little Pete.

"Sure. Stereo's in the bottom of the cabinet there. We're always supposed to turn on the music and say it's because of the neighbors. We turn on the music and the lights."

"The lights?" T.S. stared up at a large fixture hanging from the center of the room.

"Yeah. They get off on it," Little Pete answered dully. "Like to see what's going on, the man explained. The lights come on with the music."

What? T.S. winced at Little Pete's matter-of-fact explanation of what went on in the room, but at the moment he was more interested in why the lights went on with the music. There had to be more to it than giving perverts an eyeful of their perversion. Why always music? And why was the stereo in the bottom of the cabinet, instead of the top?

Maybe the men who hurried up to this room for their fun were too blinded by lust to consider the odd setup, but T.S. was clearly not sidetracked and knew that something odd was taking place.

"Turn on the music," he told Little Pete.

The boy stood suddenly and stared at him. "Hey, man, you said that . . ."

T.S. was appalled. "I don't care about anything but the music," T.S. quickly assured him. "I would never lay a hand on you, son." He felt a little sick to his stomach. What kind of world did he live in, where trust was so hard to maintain?

Little Pete clicked open the bottom doors of the cabinet and pressed a button. Loud music filled the room and the light above came on, illuminating the room with an even glow that was somewhat discreet, but nonetheless very thorough.

"Can you turn that music down?" T.S. asked, wincing at the pounding beat. "And what's in the upper cabinet?"

Little Pete shrugged, twisting the volume dial. "Don't know. It's locked."

T.S. examined the wooden front. Though the bottom doors were secured with magnetic latches, the upper ones had not one, but two large traditional keyholes. And the upper keyhole had lost its center bolt. He looked at it closely. Of course. It concealed a camera lens. "Let me have your knife," he told Little Pete. Dumbfounded, the boy handed it over.

It took several minutes and, by the time he had finished, the front of the cabinet was splintered and ruined. Little Pete was moaning about what the man would do to him as T.S. finally pried the upper doors open.

The device was surprisingly simple. Anyone with the money for a smaller lens could have set it up. The cabinet housed a video camera and the red light showed that the unit was busy recording. T.S. was sure it had been turned on as soon as Little Pete had flipped the music switch. Other equipment was stored in the locked cabinet—including an enlarger, chemicals and darkroom supplies—indicating that other photographic activity went on in the apartment. And there had been those strips of Polaroid paper on the fire escape shared with Emily's apartment, T.S. remembered.

Little Pete was staring at the camera. "It's on," he said, genuinely enraged. "The man's going to see you talking to me." He reached for the tape.

T.S. stopped him. "It's all right, son. He'll never know. We'll make it look like someone broke in and stole the tapes. He'll never even find out." T.S. was desperate, lying, promising anything he could. Because he knew that he needed that camera on. It had occurred to him that it was a very good time to have Little Pete go over what he would reveal about The Eagle. On tape. In case the kid decided to pull another disappearing act.

Besides, it was also a good way to preserve his own integrity.

CHAPTER FIFTEEN

1. There was nothing to do but to wait, surrounded by the misery of the overcrowded emergency waiting room. It was nearly ten o'clock and they had been at the hospital for over five hours. Stubbornly, they still sat there, thinking of the young boy upstairs, old far beyond his years, without friends or family.

It was an assorted group that kept vigil. Each of them was determined not to budge for his or her own reasons. Auntie Lil wanted to keep an eye on Father Stebbins and, yes, she admitted it, Annie O'Day. Herbert stayed put in case Auntie Lil needed his services, but also because it would be unthinkable of him not to contribute what goodwill he could in such a sad situation. Adelle refused to budge, waiting out of curiosity and a desire to help. Her two followers would stay as long as Adelle. Fran waited because Father Stebbins had helped her so much in the past, and now he truly needed her. And Father Stebbins, well, he waited for reasons unknown to most of the others, overcome with guilt, fingering his rosary as he prayed over and over.

They were there for so long, hoping for more news of Timmy, that even the elderly couple had been administered to and the young boy with the basketball injury bandaged. Others had limped and coughed their way inside to take their place by the time Annie O'Day reappeared.

"He's going to be sleeping through the night," Annie told the group. "There's nothing more that we can do."

The cumulative effect of her words, their growing hunger and the increasingly crowded conditions in the waiting room finally convinced them all that it was time to move on.

"There's nothing you can do tonight," Fran repeated to a distraught Father Stebbins. "Let me make you a strong cup of tea before you go to bed. It will do you good."

The big priest rose numbly. "It's all my fault," he repeated. "I tried to do the right thing. He trusted me and look what I did to him." He shook his head and allowed himself to be guided by Fran toward the exit door. "Texas," he mumbled on his way out. "I should have called Texas. And damn the seal."

"Well, that's it for the Father," Adelle remarked crisply. "He's blathering on about Texas and seals." Her followers murmured in appreciation of her observation, but Auntie Lil was annoyed. She did not approve of witty remarks that were made at the expense of common sense. Of course he was blathering about seals, she thought to herself. The confessional seal. Not the kind that balanced balls on their noses.

Auntie Lil was suddenly very tired and hungry and ready to be away from this all. "I could use a cup of coffee myself," she announced abruptly.

"I could use a gallon," Annie added. She took Auntie Lil's arm as if to help her to the door but, in truth, it was Annie that needed the support. "I'm exhausted," the big woman admitted.

Auntie Lil patted her arm in reassurance. "You were magnificent tonight," she told her. "You saved the boy's life." Annie nodded weakly, and Auntie Lil was alarmed by her sudden lack of vigor. Perhaps she, too, had not eaten all day. "Let's stop by the deli for a bite," Auntie Lil decided for them both. "If I know you, you're planning to go by the police station and see Bob. You can't do that without proper nourishment."

"Coffee?" Adelle said scornfully, a bit miffed at being left out. "I believe a good stiff drink is in order." She looked hopefully around at her followers, then settled her gaze on Herbert Wong. Her entire face rearranged itself: eyes widened, her eyebrows rose and her lips pursed in an inviting smile. She looked as if she were preparing for a screen test. "Herbert," she cooed prettily, "regrettably, it appears as if our adventure is at an end. What say we toast to auld lang syne before resuming our humdrum lives?" She placed a tentative hand on his arm and cocked her eyebrows higher. "We really should raise a toast to Eva."

Herbert's face brightened. He was not averse to either drinks or escorting three lovely ladies. Nonetheless, he glanced at Auntie Lil first.

"Go on, I don't mind a bit," Auntie Lil told him with exaggerated dignity. Mustering an air of superiority, she declared, "I don't feel the need to depend on alcohol at the moment, anyway."

Herbert bowed politely to Lillian, then escorted Adelle and her followers out the door.

"Wait until he finds out he has to pay," Auntie Lil muttered under her breath.

"We could join them," Annie offered, but her heart wasn't in it.

"No. You need something hot," Auntie Lil decided. "And so do I." They negotiated their way around a tramp who had made his home across the entrance ramp, then turned south on Ninth Avenue. Behind them, heading north, Herbert and the elderly actresses chatted together eagerly. Adelle laughed loudly at something Herbert said; Auntie Lil gritted her teeth and ignored them.

"Look—there's Fran and Father Stebbins." Annie pointed out two figures half a block ahead of them, making their way down the darkened sidewalk, heads bent low together as they talked.

"I'd give anything to know what's going on with those two," Auntie Lil remarked wistfully. "It seems I haven't cracked a single secret yet."

"Let's slow down and follow them," Annie suggested. "Maybe we'll learn something along the way." They matched their pace to the couple ahead of them.

Thus, a strange parade formed. At the front ambled a distraught Father Stebbins and a preoccupied Fran. They walked, unseeing, past busy stores and crowded restaurants, their minds focused on distant problems. Behind them, Annie and Auntie Lil walked slowly.

They were all too distraught or so busy scrutinizing their own prey that they failed to notice those who, in turn, were watching them.

2.

"She's going up to his room," Annie predicted. They stood across the street, watching in the shadows, as Father Stebbins fumbled with the key to the massive padlock that secured the front gate. Fran waited quietly, as if she knew the routine. The pair disappeared inside the church and a series of lights flickering on charted their progress to the upstairs back room. Annie was right. But what did it prove?

"I don't think waiting here any longer will do us much good," Auntie Lil decided reluctantly. "Besides, I'm getting a chill. I'm sorry I didn't bring that nice shawl I bought in Devonshire last year."

"Coffee, then," Annie said. "Good and hot." They headed for the cheerily lit windows of the Delicious Deli. They could see Billy inside, busily wiping down the counter and arranging the desserts in preparation for the after-theater crowd. Auntie Lil and Annie were his only customers. He looked up briefly, spotted the blood on Annie's sweat shirt and did a double take. Adding Auntie Lil into the equation called for yet a third look at them.

"That your blood or her blood?" he asked evenly, nodding at the mess.

"I've got to get home and change," Annie admitted. "Someone beat up a street kid, Timmy. The one that ran with Little Pete. Know him?"

Not a muscle twitched, not an eyelid flickered. The proprietor's face was perfectly still. Finally he shrugged and gave a heavy sigh. "Yeah, I know him. He was just a boy. A kind of well-educated boy, if you know what I mean, but it doesn't seem quite fair that an adult would beat him up like that."

"She didn't say an adult beat him up," Auntie Lil said sharply. There was a silence and they looked at one another.

"I just assumed," Billy said evenly. He pointed to Annie's sweat shirt. "Looks like he took it pretty bad. I figured the other guy had to be bigger."

Either Billy had known the beating was coming or he had grown so weary of the neighborhood's sad lessons that he was adopting a fatalistic calm in response.

"Can I get a black coffee and a hero?" Annie asked. She laid her head briefly on the upper counter. "And no cracks about Bob, please. He didn't do what they said in the papers and I'm tired of people thinking he did."

Billy looked away quickly and filled her cup without comment. He turned to Auntie Lil as a sudden thought struck him. "I have a message for you," he told her. "People seem to think I'm some kind of a post office."

"A message?" she repeated. Perhaps Little Pete wanted to see her again.

"Yeah. From some guy claiming to be your nephew."

"That was my nephew, Theodore," Auntie Lil told him crisply, her coffee order forgotten. "What did he say?"

"He said to tell you that he'd had an invitation to go to *the* building."

Auntie Lil stared out the window and thought hard. Who had invited Theodore to Emily's building and why? How annoying that he had found something out without her. "What time was that?" she asked Billy, acutely aware that Annie was listening carefully.

"About an hour ago. You want anything or do you just want to leave another message back?" He raised his eyebrows sarcastically and slapped meat and cheese on a hard roll for Annie.

"I'll be back in a minute," Auntie Lil decided. "Wait here for me, Annie. We may need your help."

Before the younger woman could protest, Auntie Lil was heading out the door. She planned to pass by Emily's building and see if she could get in the building somehow. Listening in at doors might have been beneath her, but she was not above being petty. She might hear something useful, and if she heard anything that indicated Theodore was in trouble, she'd be able to go for help.

As Auntie Lil left the deli, the door of a car parked nearby opened. A lanky figure cut across to the avenue opposite Auntie Lil and stepped into a doorway. The remaining occupants stayed put, peering into the deli to watch as Annie O'Day chatted with Billy.

The nearby Broadway theaters had emptied their audiences almost simultaneously and noisy groups of people were making a beeline to Eighth Avenue from the east, hoping to snag a cab uptown. The women were snugly wrapped in furs and the men were taking this early opportunity to show off their new fall coats. The chattering crowd shoved past Auntie Lil, oblivious to her age. They wanted only to be the first to reach the street with an outstretched hand. The avenue grew quite crowded and, though preoccupied with her plans, Auntie Lil was highly annoyed. She elbowed her way across the street, then stepped to one side for a breather. A vacant storefront at the corner of Forty-sixth and Eighth afforded her more room, although the small pool of darkness cast by the decrepit awning and deep doorway probably housed a wino or two.

Or something much worse. A big woman dressed in a strapless gown and wearing a long blonde wig stepped out from the darkness and gripped Auntie Lil's left elbow. An even stronger hand grabbed her from the right and twisted her arm sharply. "Don't say a word," a gruff voice ordered. "Just start walking and look straight ahead. Go straight down Forty-sixth Street."

Stunned, Auntie Lil obeyed their order. Her feet moved of their own accord, though her stomach sank in complete terror. A small pricking sensation in her side told her that the woman on the right held a small knife and would use it to goad her if she had to. Auntie Lil slid her eyes to the right and caught a glimpse of black hair piled high above silver spangles. The hand gripping her elbow wore gloves.

They moved swiftly down the sidewalk, passing the man with

the huge bulbous nose who liked to hang out near the corner. He was sitting in his usual spot in a lawn chair, blending into the building behind him. They passed by and Auntie Lil did not dare turn her head, but he saw her and stared after them, his sleepy eyes regarding the unusual trio with careful disinterest. He turned back and stared across Eighth Avenue at the bright lights of the Delicious Deli.

"Who are you?" Auntie Lil asked her captors helplessly. The pair of women steered her quickly around the many crowds of chattering friends trying to decide which restaurant they should patronize. She was being borne through the crowd as easily as a child between her parents. No one noticed and no one cared.

They passed by a man and woman arguing fiercely; they were attracting more attention than she was. She should try making a noise, like screaming bloody murder. Surely that would attract someone's notice.

But when she opened her mouth to scream, the tiny pinprick at her side turned into a sharp stab. Something warm welled through her thin pants suit. She realized what and felt weak.

"Don't say a word, don't open your mouth," the cruel woman on the right ordered. "We just want to ask you some questions and then we're going to let you go. But if you make a scene, I'll stab you right now. You'll be dead before you hit the ground."

Auntie Lil knew from the calm tone of her voice that the woman meant just what she said. She contorted her face instead, trying to attract someone's attention. Wedged between the two gaudily dressed prostitutes, she would have made a ridiculous sight anywhere else but New York. But packed among the crowd of theatergoers, they only blended in with the chaos and elicited not a single glance.

Where were they taking her and why? There was something familiar about the woman. Especially her long gloves . . . Of course, it was that woman that T.S. seemed so fascinated with. What was her name? All Auntie Lil could think of was a bird. Why a bird?

"Who are you?" Auntie Lil asked again. The sharp stab answered back.

"Shut up," Leteisha Swann ordered calmly.

They were already halfway down Forty-sixth Street, heading west rapidly. They passed a bar just as the door opened wide. Sounds of Dixieland jazz drifted out across their path, then faded behind them with a sweet finality. Auntie Lil strained her ears, hoping for more. The music had somehow been reassuring.

But up ahead, barely visible a few blocks away, the Hudson

River gleamed, its waves dully reflecting the light of the full moon above. Auntie Lil stiffened and dug her feet in automatically. But the strength of her two captors prevailed and they only lifted her from the sidewalk, carrying her inexorably forward. They were the strongest women she had ever known, hardened by street combat and the drive to survive. Maybe even stronger than Annie O'Day. Damn. Why had she left Annie behind?

They passed Emily's apartment building on the other side of the street. Auntie Lil looked upward. A light gleamed on the sixth floor. Was Theodore there? Would this be the last time she was near him?

Then it hit her. This was what had happened to Eva.

It was as if the woman in silver spangles could read her thoughts. "If you're quiet, we'll let you go. We just want to find out what you know. We're taking you somewhere private to talk. We don't plan to hurt you."

The docks. She knew with certainty, now, that they were hustling her over to the deserted docks near the Westside Highway. Should she struggle? She shifted an arm and prepared to fight back.

"If you don't come along," Leteisha Swann repeated patiently, "I'll stick you right here and leave. You'll bleed to death in the middle of the sidewalk and no one will ever know we did it. It's your choice. Die now or take a chance we'll let you go."

The finality and calm confidence of the prostitute filled Auntie Lil with complete despair. The woman was a professional, unfazed by abducting her in public and under the noses of hundreds of other New Yorkers. She knew just what to do, and, most probably, meant exactly what she said. She'd know right where to stab her, too. There was nothing to do but go along. Perhaps they did only want to talk to her. Perhaps Eva had been stubborn again and that was why she died.

They passed the Jamaican restaurant at the corner of Ninth. Nellie, the owner, sat perched on her customary table. Auntie Lil turned her head slightly and their eyes locked. Auntie Lil's were wide with terror, but Nellie's remained as dark and impassive as ever. In fact, Nellie's braids barely clicked as she turned her head so smoothly to watch the unusual trio crossing the avenue. They were heading straight west toward Tenth Avenue. Nellie hesitated, then her eyes clouded over. She looked as if she had reached a decision, but just then the front bell tinkled and a rare pair of customers entered the shop. Relieved at the momentary distraction, Nellie hopped from the table and set to work filling their order.

But her eyes still stared out into the darkness that yawned on the other side of Ninth Avenue.

Forty-sixth Street between Tenth and Eleventh Avenues was deserted. They were too far from the theater to attract restaurant-goers so the block was completely residential. Now it would do her no good to scream. A trickle of warmth ran down her right side and dripped onto her shoe. Just as she'd thought, the cruel woman on the right had drawn blood with her earlier jab. As sturdily built as she was, Auntie Lil was eighty-four years old and had not eaten dinner. She did not know how long she could last without fainting.

"This is a quiet block," she suggested helplessly. "We could talk here."

They ignored her and continued to pull her forward. Up ahead a ragged figure rummaged in a pile of garbage sacks. They drew closer and Auntie Lil could spot a decrepit old woman with frazzled hair and filthy clothes hanging from a gaunt frame.

Adelle, she thought triumphantly. Or one of the other retired actresses.

The old woman reached into a bag of garbage and pulled out a discarded container of Chinese food. She stuck two grimy fingers inside and scooped out the gummy contents, sniffed it then nodded and took a tentative bite. Auntie Lil's hopes fell. The poor woman would be of no help to her.

Soon, they reached Tenth Avenue and there to the left, Auntie Lil could see the neon lights in the windows of Mike's American Bar and Grill winking in the near darkness. It seemed like years ago, instead of days, that she had met Theodore there for lunch. What she wouldn't give for the chance to sit at the bar there again, sipping a Bloody Mary.

A crowd of men joking and drinking beer on the corner stepped aside to let them pass.

"Help," Auntie Lil cried out weakly, but a shrill laugh from the woman on her left masked the sound.

"Hola!" the prostitute sang out to the men. "Don't go anywhere. I'll be back!"

"Hola!" one of the men called after them. "You girls working with your granny these days?" The crowd laughed but their merriment quickly faded behind them as the two women stepped up their speed, nearly dragging Auntie Lil between them. Only a deserted street littered with the shadows of huge trucks and empty garages stood between them and the piers of the Hudson.

"Just a block more to go," Leteisha Swann announced calmly. "Then we shall see what we shall see."

3.
"Don't you know Rodney's last name?" T.S. asked Little Pete once again.

The kid shrugged. "He's weird. Comes and goes. Disappears all the time. No one knows where he lives, man. I don't like him. Never did. Since way before he beat up Timmy, I knew he was bad news. He's real mean, you know. Real mean and real calm. Won't say nothing and then, bam, you're down on the sidewalk. Cold. He's a cold man. Real cold. Makes me shiver just thinking about him. I'm going to bust him good."

"No, you're not. You're going to tell this to the police and let them bust him," T.S. said firmly. He switched off the tape and slipped the cassette into his jacket pocket.

"The police?" The boy's voice trembled. He was still unconvinced, though T.S. had spent the better part of a half hour pleading with him to at least tell the cops about Rodney. And the rest helping him trash the apartment in what T.S. knew to be a futile attempt to make it look as if it had been robbed.

"It's all right, son. I'll stay beside you every minute. They won't ever have you alone." Both T.S. and Little Pete took reassurance in his repeated use of the word "son." And both needed reassurance at that moment.

"We won't mention the man at all," T.S. promised. "Just Rodney. Don't you want to see him punished for what he did to Timmy?" Little Pete nodded glumly and they left the apartment. T.S. didn't think they'd get very far before he bolted.

"What are you going to do with that?" the small boy asked as they waited for the elevator. He stared at the videocassette.

T.S. patted it. "Let Detective Santos take a look." Especially if you take off running down the street like I think you're going to do, he thought to himself.

"The cops." Little Pete's back stiffened and he repeated the word several times, as if not quite believing that he was going to take a stand on the same side as his old enemies. "What if Rodney finds out it was me who told on him? He'll get out and kill me."

"No, he won't," T.S. said calmly. "They'll put him away somewhere where he won't be able to get to anyone ever again."

"For beating up a kid?" The little boy gave an ugly, adult-sounding laugh. "That's a joke. You don't know nothing, man."

"He killed Emily," T.S. said simply. "He killed Timmy's grand-mother and we're going to get him." There. Maybe that would keep the kid in tow.

Little Pete's eyes grew wide and his mouth shut abruptly. He stood only inches from T.S. in the elevator car, craving the comfort of his solid presence like a chick seeks the shelter of his mother's wings. They rode down in silence, T.S. sometimes absently patting the boy's head.

The street was crowded with theatergoers and they had to push through a batch of plump and bejeweled ladies to reach the street. Sure enough, as T.S. had suspected, Little Pete began to drag his feet.

"You go without me, man," the boy started to say, but an indignant buzz cut him off. Shouts rang out on the other side of the street.

"What's up?" Little Pete asked, standing on his tiptoes. T.S. unashamedly followed suit. Someone was pushing through the throng of restaurantgoers. A whole line of pushing people, in fact. They burst into a patch of deserted sidewalk and, in that instant, fifty-five years of constant connection to another human being culminated in a certainty that, somehow, Auntie Lil was in danger. He knew it the second he recognized the figure plowing through the crowd at the head of the pack.

Annie O'Day was barreling down the sidewalk and Billy of the Delicious Deli was a few feet behind. Inexplicably, they were being followed by a funny old man with a huge bulbous nose and an impressive ability to run like a younger man.

"What is it?!" T.S. cried out as they passed by.

"Your aunt!" the deli owner yelled back when he recognized T.S.

Heart thumping, T.S. joined the procession, bringing up the rear. They pushed through the disgruntled crowd without apology, enduring thrown elbows and sharp shoves. His heart pounded so loudly that, for a moment, T.S. was afraid he would not be able to keep up. But once he got going, he hit his rhythm. Plus fear and pride gave him energy. By God, but that funny old man was fast. But wait—here came someone even faster. Little Pete passed him on the left as they neared Ninth Avenue.

"What are we doing?" the boy shouted at T.S. as he fled past. He was ready to be in on the action.

"Follow them!" T.S. shouted back. "Or better yet, call the cops." The small boy screeched to a halt on the far side of the avenue and dashed to the nearest pay phone. T.S. kept running. Annie's light-colored sweat shirt bobbed in front of him like a beacon in the darkness. It was followed by a patch of white from the deli owner's apron. T.S. prayed fervently that whatever was wrong, those two were on the side of the angels.

The lead runners crossed Ninth Avenue and hesitated, unsure of where to go next. T.S. slowed with them and scanned the sidewalk. There was no sign of Auntie Lil. Should they go west or head up or downtown?

Suddenly, someone crashed into his left side. T.S. was momentarily thrown off his stride but recovered in time to continue the chase. A large black woman dashed ahead of him, eating up the distance between T.S. and the old man with the funny nose.

"Straight ahead!" she was shouting. "And hurry! Hurry!" Her beaded braids bobbed wildly as she raced along. Mesmerized, T.S. increased his speed.

4. The Westside Highway teemed with intermittent life, then fell back into loneliness. They were in an area of seldom used side streets, but as stoplights several blocks away on either side disgorged waiting cars, long lines of autos would periodically zoom past. No one slowed as they passed. People picked the highway because they were in a hurry and it would take more than a little old lady flanked by prostitutes to merit a second glance.

Only a few streetlights still worked on the deserted stretch of sidewalk where they waited in a pool of darkness for a chance to cross the road. A few blocks farther downtown, Auntie Lil could see the enormous bulk of the *Intrepid*, a huge aircraft carrier that had been converted into a floating museum. Now closed for the season, its shadow dominated several blocks of the river. Across from it, the lights of The Westsider bar blinked steadily.

She wondered if Detective Santos was slumped at his table, empty glasses of gin scattered before him. Would he ever guess that she had been brought just a few blocks from him before her death?

Auntie Lil could not stop the unhappy thought. Because she was certain now that they meant to kill her. Otherwise, they would have stopped in the last block where there wasn't a human being to be found. There was little she could have told them, but she would have tried. Now, with the deserted pier just a few lanes of traffic away, she saw that she had been more than foolish. It would have been better to have risked a stabbing in a crowd than certain death in the oily waters of the Hudson.

Ahead of them stretched a length of sidewalk along the river that was topped with the abandoned girding of an old highway. Unused now, its only purpose was to house the makeshift cardboard shacks of the homeless. Its structure cast deep shadows on the nearby piers, creating an area of virtual darkness next to the water. There was a lull in traffic and the two women quickly dragged her across the highway. They obviously had a destination in mind, no doubt because they had been there before.

They pulled her to a corner of the pier near the sidewalk, completely shaded by the darkness. Helplessly, Auntie Lil watched as lines of cars zipped past. No one could see them where they were.

"She's bleeding," the woman on the left complained. "Why'd you have to go and cut her? She would have talked to you."

"Talk to me?" Leteisha Swann gave an ugly laugh. "Don't be stupid. I don't care what this old lady has to say. She can tell it to the fishes. If you can find any in there."

"Hey, you said you weren't going to hurt her," the blonde protested. "People saw us back there. If this gets in the papers as a killing, they'll remember. Maybe they didn't say anything at the time, but they saw us."

"Doesn't matter to me," Leteisha Swann said calmly. "After this, babe, I'm going to disappear." She snapped her fingers. "I disappear like that. It's much simpler than you think."

The other prostitute stared at them in the darkness, her doubt obvious in her uncertain, husky voice. "I don't know, Leteisha. We don't have to hurt this old lady. I know I'm not getting enough money for that. You probably aren't, either. Let's just see what she knows and let her go."

Leteisha Swann. Auntie Lil remembered. That was the woman's name. T.S. had been right all along—she was part of what was going on.

"I'm not doing it for the money," Leteisha explained to her friend. "I'm doing it for the fun." She smiled. Her teeth gleamed against the darkness of her face.

The blonde prostitute stepped back, horrified. "That's rank, Lettie. You and me both got mothers, you know."

"Is this how you people live?" Auntie Lil demanded. "Discarding people like they were garbage, dumping them to the bottom of the river like trash?"

"People *are* garbage, grandma," Leteisha said calmly. "And taking out the trash happens to be my speciality."

Auntie Lil had heard enough. She kicked Leteisha in the shins and elicited a reaction. It was not what she had hoped. The woman cursed and pulled Auntie Lil closer to her chest, her elbow hooked around Auntie Lil's throat. Her arm was like a vise, cutting off any chance of escape or even any hope of being able to make noise. Auntie Lil knew she'd never be able to wiggle her way out.

"I'll hold her and you cut her throat," Leteisha ordered her companion.

The other woman stared back in disgust. "No way, Leteisha. I'm not cutting her throat. You needed help getting her here, I helped," the blonde insisted. "I've done my part. Now I'm out of here. I'm not cutting anyone's throat." The woman turned to go but a hiss from Leteisha stopped her.

"You help me now or you'll be next," Leteisha ordered. "So help me God, you won't be able to walk these streets without wondering when your turn will come."

Auntie Lil was furious, frightened and indignant. They were arguing over her as if she were the last piece of bait in some fisherman's pail. She tried to struggle but the grip of the arm only tightened. If she moved again, all air would be cut off.

"Screw you. I'm leaving," the blonde decided. She turned to go and Leteisha gave a low growl. There was no other way to describe the ugly sound that emanated from between her tightly clenched teeth. It was a *growl* and even Auntie Lil, who thought she was as frightened as a person could be, felt fresh terror at the unnatural sound.

"You're going to be—" Leteisha's threat was cut off by the sounds of distant yelling. Startled, she fell silent and pulled Auntie Lil further into the shadows. The blonde took a panicked step forward.

"Don't move," Leteisha ordered in a deadly voice. Auntie Lil could not have moved had she wanted to. But she listened carefully and realized that the sounds were coming closer. People were yelling, several people. What was it they were yelling? Was that her own name?

"Aunt Lil!" she heard a female voice bellow. Others shouted as well.

It was now or never, Auntie Lil thought to herself. Do something—anything—or you're going to die. She twisted with all her might and croaked, "The police!" before Leteisha's arm cut off any other hope of sound.

It had been enough. The skittish blonde panicked and ran south along the pier.

"Stop!" Leteisha ordered, but it was too late. The blonde

reached the end of the shadows and fled across a pool of street-light, heading for the huge battleship a few blocks farther south.

"Over there!" a female voice bellowed again. "There's some-one." Auntie Lil felt faint, more from frustration than physical deprivation. She was acutely conscious that, with help only a few feet away, she could still easily die if Leteisha chose.

The shouting grew louder and, suddenly, an odd parade was running across the highway. Cars honked and brakes screeched. Auntie Lil stared at the figure in the lead. It looked like Annie O'Day but, my God, what a frightening figure she made—all muscle and anger and noise. She held a scalpel straight out in front of her like a spear and was screaming, "Let her go! Back off! Let her go!" Her eyes scanned the shadows of the docks in front of her. She was still uncertain as to exactly where Auntie Lil was being held.

Not surprisingly, given the determined figure and the out-stretched scalpel, Leteisha chose to do just as Annie suggested. Cursing, she flung the knife into the black waters of the Hudson, pushed Auntie Lil to the pavement and began to run furiously south. Kicking off her heels as she fled, she dug into the sidewalk with astonishing speed and took off after the blonde. Auntie Lil fell against the rough surface, scraping her elbow and one cheek. She lay flat against the concrete, gasping for breath. Annie O'Day bent over her, the scalpel held high in the air. It gleamed in a patch of moonlight.

"Are you all right?" Annie asked anxiously, holding up Auntie Lil's head and checking for cuts or bruises.

Auntie Lil managed a small nod, and saw that others were heading her way. "Go get her," she told Annie weakly, pointing south after Leteisha Swann.

Annie took off running into the darkness, the pounding of her sneakers on the sidewalk echoing eerily in the silence between groups of cars. The shouting had stopped and there was only the sounds of heaving breathing and other footsteps approaching the dark corner of the pier. Auntie Lil wanted to meet them with head held high, but she felt so weak . . . the closeness of the scare had drained her of her remaining strength. She was scared, damn it, scared and angry at herself and ashamed . . . and discouraged that her body had proved so frail. The effort was too much and, dazed, she lay her head back down on the concrete. She'd just rest for a teensy moment.

Someone was panting heavily just inches from her ear. "Oh God," she heard the gasping voice say. "Aunt Lil? Aunt Lil?"

"She's dead!" the voice shouted in sudden panic.

"Certainly not!" she replied weakly. "I absolutely refuse to die like this." Her head felt a bit better and she opened her eyes. It was Theodore, her own dear Theodore.

"Stop fussing, Theodore," she ordered weakly. "I'm fine. It's just that . . . just that . . ." She could not finish the sentence. She forgot what she was about to say. She was lost in the bliss of believing that, finally, she was safe. If Theodore was there, that meant she was safe. Struggling to sit, she curled up and leaned against him. He held her close and patted her wiry curls.

"It's okay," he said reassuringly. "They've called the cops and an ambulance. You're with me now. You're safe."

She wanted to thank him, but the relief was too much. Just then, a competent hand took hold of her arm and checked her pulse. "You're okay, granny," a melodious voice assured her. She opened her eyes again to find Nellie, the woman who owned the Jamaican restaurant on Forty-sixth Street.

"You saw me," Auntie Lil said simply. "I thought you were going to ignore it."

"I saw you. And I should have done something right away. I'm ashamed of myself. Trying to look the other way." Nellie glanced at T.S. "Her pulse is good. She's been nicked a little in the side and there's blood, but I think that she's mostly scared."

"I thought you said all little old ladies looked alike," Auntie Lil joked feebly.

"Not all little old ladies eat three of my meat pies." Nellie waved two waiting figures over. The funny old man with the bulbous nose stepped from the darkness and looked down at Auntie Lil with deep concern.

"You saw me, too?" she asked in deep wonder. He nodded solemnly and gave her a small smile.

"Tommy saved your life. He came running into the deli," Billy explained, patting the old man on the back. "It took us a minute to figure out what he meant. Old Tommy here doesn't talk."

The man nodded again, smiling more widely this time.

A small bouncing figure darted out from behind the old man. "You okay?" Little Pete asked breathlessly. "I called the cops. They're on their way."

As if on cue, a squad car pulled up by the sidewalk, siren off. But the lights flashed furiously, casting multicolored shadows for blocks down the road. Two uniformed officers stepped from the cars and approached the group cautiously, their faces obscured by shadows. Seconds later, an ambulance came shrieking up and two paramedics hopped out with a stretcher, looked around and, seeing no one obviously injured, stood to one side and waited for orders.

Just then, amid much scrambling, deep cursing and heavy breathing, Annie O'Day appeared from the south. All that weight lifting and soccer and running and bicycling had paid off. She had Leteisha Swann firmly by the neck with one hand, while the other twisted Leteisha's arm tightly behind her back in an upward grasp.

"Let me go, you big amazon," the prostitute was arguing fiercely, her whole body trembling. But when she saw the two officers—one male, one female—she relaxed and her complaining attitude evaporated instantly. "Officers, these people are harassing me," she said in a plaintively indignant voice. "On account of my profession. This wild woman here is assaulting my person."

"Why, you liar!" Anger gave Auntie Lil strength. She struggled to her feet and leaned forward, eyes blazing. "How dare you add lying to attempted murder, you killer . . . you, you thief!"

"Let her go," the male officer ordered, ignoring Auntie Lil. Annie reluctantly relinquished her grip on Leteisha. The policewoman backed into position behind Annie, as if she were the troublemaker.

Leteisha took a long time before she spoke, first primping her hair, dress and gloves carefully back into place. Auntie Lil was not fooled: she was stalling for time to think up a story. Oh, how dangerous and cunning this woman was. One minute she was the quintessential cold-blooded killer and the next she could be a flustered, slightly dumb, poor little streetwalker victim of society. One who was obviously friendly with the cops on the beat.

"Like I say," Leteisha began in a polite, throaty voice. "This old lady approached me on the street and asked me for directions to the—"

"You're a damn liar!" Auntie Lil shouted as she darted forward and flailed at the woman. She had just been pushed too far. Her punches bounced off the woman's arms—she seemed made of steel. Before the policeman could interfere or his partner could get around Annie, Leteisha Swann shoved Auntie Lil and sent her flying against the concrete wall of the pier front. The fight only took a few seconds. Auntie Lil bounced off the wall and fell to the ground, groaning at the shock.

For T.S., it was the breaking point. Fifty-five years of well-bred behavior disappeared in a single enraging moment. He felt like he was underwater, swimming up for air. The breath exploded in his lungs; his ears began to ring. Red spots swam before his

eyes and power surged through his body, energizing him with un-
believable fury.

"Don't you ever touch my aunt again," he announced just before he drew back a fist and sent it crashing into the center of the
prostitute's face. He heard a crack as his knuckles went numb.
Leteisha Swann flew backwards, where she hit the pier railing and
crumpled to a silver heap on the sidewalk.

Officer King grabbed T.S. from behind, locking his arms firmly
at his side. The assembled crowd stared at the still figure of the
prostitute in amazement, then turned and gawked at T.S.

The policewoman calmly helped Auntie Lil to her feet, then
bent down to take a look at Leteisha Swann.

"Help her up, too," the male officer ordered his partner. The
policewoman grabbed the prostitute by both arms and hoisted her
upright.

Annie O'Day peered at Leteisha Swann's face closely. "You
broke her nose," she pointed out to T.S. with undisguised approval.

The policeman released T.S. and took a closer look. "That's
assault and battery," he warned T.S. darkly.

"There's something funny about her," Auntie Lil declared, glaring at Leteisha as she struggled to catch her breath.

The prostitute groaned and her head bobbed groggily. Her hair
had slipped wildly to one side.

"That's a wig," Nellie announced darkly. "Not a good one, either. If you ask me."

Little Pete was staring at Leteisha Swann.

"What's the matter, son?" Nellie asked him kindly. She put her
hand on the young boy's arm. "You're trembling. What is it? Tell
us."

Little Pete could not speak. He just stared at Leteisha, then
looked to T.S. for help. In a single glance, T.S. understood.

Darting forward before the officers could stop him, T.S.
grabbed at Leteisha's hair. The wig ripped off with a sticky sound
like a zipper, to reveal a smooth brown scalp beneath. Her head
was completely shaved.

Even the jaded officers looked stunned at the development.

"It's a wig all right," Billy agreed.

"It's a man!" Nellie corrected.

"It's Rodney!" Little Pete announced loudest of all, fear discarded in favor of anger. He stared Leteisha in the face. "It's Rodney. The man who beat up Timmy."

The cops stared at one another, uncertain what to do. Auntie Lil took advantage of their inaction.

"Rodney?" she asked, turning to T.S. for guidance.

He nodded grimly, sucking at his injured knuckles. "You know him all right," he told Auntie Lil. He gripped the long glove that adorned Leteisha's right hand and peeled it back to her wrist—revealing a large eagle tattoo adorning the prostitute's lower bicep. The eagle clutched branches in his talons as he swooped downward in fierce supremacy.

"I give you The Eagle," T.S. told the assembled group, sweeping his injured hand out like a magician's. "Behold the disappearing man."

"He is real," Auntie Lil whispered, flushing as the closeness of her own death was reinforced.

"Damn right I'm real," Leteisha shot back, struggling to stand upright. Her voice deepened and she grew more defiant as she gingerly touched her bleeding nose. The game wasn't over yet and so far as she was concerned, her name was still Leteisha Swann. "So maybe I was assaulting this lady," she told the officers. "But I was just trying to get her pocketbook. And I have no idea of who this Rodney guy is."

This unleashed another round of protests from the group until the policewoman blew her whistle for silence. Confused, but still determined to maintain his authority, the male officer addressed Leteisha Swann. "Robbery is a serious crime," he began.

"Not as serious as murder," a confident voice interrupted. The small crowd parted automatically at the sound of this new voice and Detective Santos stepped through into the clearing.

"What are you doing here?" the male officer demanded grumpily. He didn't like someone else taking over on his home turf.

"I was up the street," Santos explained tersely, nodding toward The Westsider. "I saw the flashing lights."

"I called you twice at the precinct like you asked," Billy spoke up angrily. "Fat lot of good it did her." He nodded toward Auntie Lil's bleeding leg, but Detective Santos ignored the jibe. His conscience was clear—he had warned Auntie Lil.

Santos stared at Auntie Lil then squinted at Leteisha Swann's eagle tattoo.

"He beat up Timmy," Little Pete piped up bravely. Nellie patted his shoulder in reassurance.

"That so?" Santos said softly. He scrutinized Leteisha as carefully as an exhibit in a museum. "Interesting tattoo. I believe we may have to make that charge murder."

"You've got no witness," Leteisha challenged him. But clad so absurdly in women's clothing, the revealed killer was suddenly more pathetic than frightening. His defiant posture and threatening tone seemed silly and out of place.

"We'll find a witness, don't you worry." A polite, deep voice tinged with a heavy Southern drawl floated out from the shadows behind them. Franklin stepped into view, his massive body clad once again in his customary overalls. Behind him, movement rippled in the darkness. An unseen crowd had gathered. The homeless who had declared the abandoned upper roadway their home had been drawn to the pier by the flashing lights and the unusual sounds.

Franklin twisted his hat in his hands and stared steadily at the killer, his natural diffidence nowhere in evidence. "I've spent all week looking and I don't plan to quit now. I'll find the man that saw you. Just you wait and see."

"Franklin!" T.S. stepped up to shake his hand. "Where have you been?"

"Been looking, that's where I've been." His head nodded toward the unseen homeless gathered in the darkness on the fringes of the pier. "I'm getting close. Met a man up here tonight who knows the old fellow who was sitting next to Emily the day she died. I'm on my way down to the Bowery for him now."

"He's our witness," Auntie Lil announced in triumph. "Franklin will find him."

"Met another man up there who saw you with Miss Eva the other day," Franklin continued softly to Leteisha. "Course, you looked a little different than you did that day at the soup kitchen." He pretended to look Leteisha over carefully. "More like you look right now, I'd say. With the wig back on, of course. *Ma'am*."

Detective Santos had been watching this exchange with a patience quite unlike him. Now he turned back to the waiting officers. "Take him in," he ordered tersely, pointing at Leteisha. "I'll meet you there in half an hour."

"Just him?" the policeman protested. He looked at Auntie Lil pointedly, then back at the detective.

"That's what I said," Santos explained tersely. "And no one talks to him until I get there. Understood? No one, not even the lieutenant."

"What about her?" the male officer asked again. He pointed his baton at Auntie Lil.

"Miss Hubbert and I will be there shortly," the detective answered smoothly. "After we get this little nick here checked out."

He took Auntie Lil's arm tenderly and patted her hand as if she were a rare jewel. "I owe you an apology, Miss Hubbert. That and a return favor. We'll stop by the hospital first." He broke into a big smile. "You'll get good service, I guarantee it. I plan to escort you there myself."

Auntie Lil tried to smile back but found herself bursting into fervent tears. T.S. took her firmly by the shoulders and made her sit on the curb. There—surrounded by her new friends—she cried until she could cry no more. Detective Santos and the ambulance crew waited patiently for her to finish.

CHAPTER SIXTEEN

1. Detective Santos kept his word. Auntie Lil and T.S. were quickly ushered in back past the hospital waiting room crowd. No questions asked and no questions answered. Within half an hour, the hospital was behind them and an unmarked car was waiting at the curb. Auntie Lil climbed in front with the driver without a word, leaving the back seat to Santos and T.S. The men exchanged glances and both understood that she was still shaken up by her ordeal. Santos had spent much of the time in the hospital questioning them about their actions in the previous days. Reviewing the events had made it all too clear to Auntie Lil that she had no one but herself to blame for her near-miss with death.

"Billy tried to warn me," she said suddenly as they pulled away from the hospital and headed for the precinct. "Every time I went into his deli, he tried to warn me."

"Billy's a good guy," Santos agreed. "I told him to keep an eye out for you two. He called me twice tonight to say you were still snooping around. Unfortunately, I've just picked up the evening shift and was out on my dinner break."

It was Auntie Lil's turn to be tactfully silent. Anyone who would take their dinner break at the Westsider was not exactly nutritionally minded.

The driver gunned the motor and they were thrown back in their seats as he maneuvered skillfully past a line of taxis jockeying for lane supremacy. It shook Auntie Lil out of her momentary reverie. She shivered slightly and turned to Santos and T.S. "Leteisha must have been following me the whole time," she told the two men. "I had dinner with Little Pete right in the middle of that picture window. It was stupid of me. Very stupid." Auntie Lil's sigh lingered in the quiet of the car and Detective Santos changed the subject to one nearer his own heart.

"So you think the big man is Worthington?" he asked T.S. for what must have been the third or fourth time.

"Has to be. It's either Worthington or someone he knows. He's the one who sent me to that apartment." T.S. shook his head, still unsure. He had already explained his attendance at Worthington's party and his subsequent memory loss to Santos at the hospital while Auntie Lil was being bandaged. Neither spoke of the event in her presence. No sense giving Auntie Lil ammunition with which to shoot down T.S.'s new sense of equality.

"Think the kid will tell us who the big man is?" Santos asked hopefully.

"I doubt it." T.S. shook his head. "Little Pete won't stand up and say so, at least not in court. He's mad enough at Rodney to turn on him, but he's still too afraid of the man."

"That's okay. We probably won't need him anyway," Santos decided. "I've got enough to bluff it out. Rodney will roll over before the night is up. All it's going to take is Worthington's name and a reference to two counts of murder one. His lawyer will tell him to make a deal. He'll turn in the big man, whoever he is, before the sun is up. They always do. That's what those guys never figure out. They act so surprised when their people turn on them. But when you lie down with dogs, forget about the fleas. It's getting bit you ought to worry about."

As T.S. was untangling the detective's metaphor, they reached the precinct. The driver pulled up directly in front of the main door, leaving the car to block the entire sidewalk. It was one of the few perks that cops in NYC enjoyed. A small crowd stopped to see who was being brought in. The onlookers seemed disappointed that neither Auntie Lil nor T.S. was handcuffed and they walked away, grumbling. New Yorkers were hard to keep entertained.

2. Auntie Lil and T.S. were allowed to wait in a small room off the main floor. While additional detectives would question the other pier witnesses, Santos wanted to take their official statements personally. They had agreed to wait until after Leteisha/Rodney was questioned, though they'd been warned that it would be a long time.

The other witnesses were waiting a few blocks away at the Delicious Deli until they were notified that their turn to make a statement had arrived. Given the busy precinct, it was a good solution. It was far more pleasant to sit in the deli sipping coffee than to sit around the precinct watching drunks and wide-eyed crackheads being dragged in by angry and overworked officers. Unless, of course, you were Auntie Lil.

Even in her subdued state, she enjoyed the excellent view their small waiting room afforded. It was a good spot. They could see the front reception area, but were sheltered from the periodic chaos that inevitably afflicted Midtown North on a Friday night.

A few minutes later, a commotion in the reception area inspired Auntie Lil to limp to the door for a better look. A booming voice cut through the babble of apologetic police voices and roared, "Why didn't anyone call me in earlier?"

T.S. checked his watch. Detective Santos had managed a whole twenty minutes alone with Leteisha/Rodney before Lieutenant Abromowitz arrived. He hoped it had been enough time. A flash of movement at the door caught his eye. "What in the world are you doing?" T.S. stared at Auntie Lil incredulously. She had slipped behind the old-fashioned door and was cowering quietly behind the slab of massive oak.

"There is a time for discretion in everyone's life," she whispered.

Abromowitz's heavy footsteps approached the doorway and thundered past just as T.S. turned his back to examine an intriguing stain on the tabletop. Perhaps Auntie Lil was right. Having taken on a killer and a four-minute mile already that night, T.S. was in no mood to tangle with an angry lieutenant. He waited until the heavy footsteps stomped up the stairs and faded away in the distance. "You can come out now," he assured Auntie Lil, patting her chair with a smug smile. "The danger has passed."

She glared at him and sat down with aplomb. "I didn't see you rushing out to shake his hand."

"No," T.S. admitted. "But I am going to give Lilah and Herbert a call."

"*Herbert.*" Auntie Lil gave a faint sniff and it was clear that she was miffed at Herbert for being absent during their adventure. "He's probably still out whooping it up with that Adelle woman, who's no doubt into playing her party girl role tonight."

"Aunt Lil, Herbert can't always be there to untangle your messes. My God, the man is only human and you'd detest being followed around twenty-four hours a day. Which is what it would take to keep you out of trouble."

Herbert Wong was home and was so distraught at not being there to rescue Auntie Lil that it took a good three minutes for T.S. to convince him that she was safe and did not hold a grudge.

Herbert was relieved to know that she was safe, but unfooled about the grudge part.

"I should not have gone to have that cocktail with Miss Adelle and her friends. Lillian will be angry at me," Herbert predicted. "Her fear and pain will make her angrier."

"I can't contradict you there," T.S. admitted. "But I'm sure that she'll get over it."

"You are there all night?" Herbert asked. "At the police station?"

"At least for the next three or four hours," T.S. predicted. "They're taking everyone's story and you know Auntie Lil—she won't leave until the end."

"But of course. There are still many pieces missing from the puzzle," Herbert said. "And you know that Lillian's curiosity is a powerful force."

T.S. had to agree. It was a nice way of saying she was perpetually consumed with nosiness. "We'll call you tomorrow with details."

"Oh, no. I am coming down. Otherwise, it will be a year before Lillian forgives me for abandoning her. Besides, sleep will not come. This was to be my shift for watching Miss Emily's building."

There was no changing his mind, especially when T.S. couldn't put his heart into it. Herbert was right. Auntie Lil probably would hold it against him for a year. Or at least torture him with it for a good eleven months.

He checked the time again as he dialed Lilah's number. It was only half-past eleven and yet it felt like at least four o'clock in the morning. In fact, it seemed as if an entire year had passed since the day that Emily died.

Despite the late hour, Lilah was not home. With her servant, Deirdre, away for the week, only the answering machine was available to pick up. T.S. listened to the mechanical invitation to leave his name and number with a sinking feeling of acute disappointment. There was so much he wanted to say but so little that he could actually articulate, at least to a machine. He simply told her where he was and promised to explain in the morning.

T.S. was so absorbed in his misery that he nearly ran down a petite woman blocking his path back into their room. "Sorry," he mumbled, slipping past her. Auntie Lil still sat at the table, staring into her coffee. Until the caffeine kicked in, she'd have little energy for anything else. T.S. rejoined her without a word, consumed by frustration and despair over Lilah. He felt himself being watched and, after a moment, looked up to find the small woman still there. She was eyeing them curiously.

If she could forego manners so blatantly, so could he. T.S. stared back. She looked relatively normal but, for all he knew, she'd been brought to the precinct for pushing people in front of subway cars. She was about forty or forty-five years old, and just slightly overweight with a broad, round face and bright dark eyes anchored in a fine sea of laugh lines. Her medium-length black hair was touched with gray in spots and cut shoulder length. It flipped up in a smooth wave at her shoulders.

She looked familiar but he couldn't quite place her. "Do I know you?" he asked loudly.

The woman stepped into the room and sat down. "I'm Margo McGregor," she told him in a confident voice. "I'm a columnist for *Newsday*. I got a tip that someone was murdering old ladies around here. Is she involved?"

Of course. When she nodded toward Auntie Lil, T.S. recognized the slight smile from her newspaper photo. But other than the grin, it was obvious that the photograph was at least ten years out of date. That depressed T.S. even more. He'd had a crush on an illusion, a silly old man's crush.

"If I was involved, I wouldn't tell you," Auntie Lil said calmly. "You have no manners. I've called you at least a dozen times in the past two days with vital information and not once have you tried to call me back."

The columnist looked to T.S. for help, but he was too exhausted to come up with more than a halfhearted, "Now, Aunt Lil."

"Don't you Aunt Lil me," she said adamantly. "This young lady allowed herself to be used. She published inaccurate information about a fine man. And she didn't have the manners to call me back. She'll just have to dig out her own juicy details."

"I don't publish inaccurate information," Margo McGregor contested hotly. "I check out all my sources."

"You were duped," Auntie Lil told her slowly, relishing each word.

By this time, Margo McGregor was wild to find out which column Auntie Lil felt was inaccurate. She beseeched an implacable Auntie Lil for details and was rebuffed again and again. But T.S. knew quite well that Auntie Lil would eventually give in. She just wanted to be begged for a while to assuage her pride. He settled back and listened as the two women debated. Sure enough, a few minutes later, his judgment was confirmed when Auntie Lil's inherent taste for publicity overcame her stubbornness and she began to reveal selected details of what they had discovered. Once Margo McGregor realized that the recent deaths of two old ladies might somehow be related to her story on Bob Fleming and Homefront, she eagerly took notes and began to ask nearly as many questions as Detective Santos had on the ride to the hospital and back.

In fact, once she got the picture sketched out as they knew it, Margo McGregor had plenty of theories of her own. These she shared eagerly with Auntie Lil, who was highly impressed. Here was a woman capable of leaps of imagination, seasoned with suspicion and cunning unmatched by anyone but Auntie Lil herself. Soon, a bargain was struck: in exchange for an article on Emily's lack of identity, Auntie Lil would give the columnist exclusive rights to all the background information they had gathered and fill her in on what the police determined that night.

Not wasting any time, Auntie Lil launched into a highly fictionalized account of her adventures. Just as she was detailing some of the more heroic details of her mighty struggle against knife-wielding captors, a loud and exaggerated cough interrupted them. Detective Santos stood in the doorway. His gaze was a steady and unfriendly beacon directed at Margo McGregor. "You are?" he asked abruptly.

She introduced herself. He was not impressed. "Don't mind if I get to be the one to interview my own witnesses first, do you?" he demanded bluntly.

Margo McGregor was not a fool. She shut her notebook abruptly and rose. "Not at all. You must be Detective Santos."

The detective was unmoved. "Miss McGregor." He pointed toward the reception area and she took the hint. Mumbling something about interviewing some of the officers who'd been on the pier, she quickly left the room.

"It would be nice, Miss Hubbert, if you talked to the police before the press," Santos told her in a voice that hovered between sarcasm and graciousness. "Now, can I trust you to sit here and use a little discretion? I just came down to check on you. I'm not through with this Rodney guy and it's going to be a while now that the lieutenant is involved. Are you sure you wouldn't rather I call you in the morning?"

"We're not leaving until we find out who's behind this," Auntie Lil declared.

"Suit yourself. But, please . . ." His voice dipped and he stared steadily at her.

"All right," she agreed readily, afraid they'd end up on the side-walk if she didn't.

Less than half an hour later Herbert Wong appeared, bearing a bouquet of flowers along with several cups of cappuccino and profuse apologies.

"Forgive me, Lillian," he begged with a humble bow. "It is in-excusable. I was to have protected you."

T.S. thought Herbert was laying it on a little thick, but Auntie Lil lapped it up like a thirsty dog. So fervent was Herbert's regret, that she had no choice but to be gracious.

"Nonsense, Herbert, how could you have known my life would be placed in such dire jeopardy?" She sniffed at the flowers and brightened at the smell of cappuccino.

Herbert Wong was one smart man, T.S. thought with admira-tion. Within minutes, he had Auntie Lil relaxed in her seat and the flowers in an empty jar filled with water. He was soon gently pat-ting her hand and asking for details in a quiet and earnest voice. His presence alone served to calm her and T.S. was grateful for his help.

He was also, he admitted reluctantly, jealous. How wonderful to have someone like that who was so unafraid to show their affec-tion for you. For the first time in his life, T.S. wondered what Auntie Lil was like when she was alone with her admirers like Herbert. Surely, she was not brash and demanding. Perhaps, all of her exuberant energy became focused solely on her companion. If so, it would be quite an experience and would easily explain the utter devotion of her many friends.

3. Shortly after Herbert's arrival, an erratic parade of wit-nesses began to pass by the small doorway on their way to give their statements to waiting detectives. The first to be called was Little Pete, who was marched past firmly and held in tow by a determined-looking Nellie. A uniformed patrolman brought up the rear, but his presence was entirely superfluous.

"And to think Little Pete feared the police," T.S. remarked.

"Indeed," Herbert agreed. "It seems that Miss Nellie is the force to be feared."

"I wonder how much she knows about this whole thing?" Auntie Lil wondered out loud.

"I say nothing," T.S. said. "She just comes from another cul-ture. Minding her own business is practically a religion. She just didn't want to get involved."

Auntie Lil remained unconvinced. Her attention, however, was diverted by the arrival of Billy and Annie O'Day, accompanied by a pair of plainclothesmen.

"I didn't trust him," Auntie Lil admitted, nodding toward Billy. "And, come to think of it, I still don't know that I do."

"He's friends with Santos," T.S. complained.

"What better cover?" Herbert pointed out.

Half an hour later, Bob Fleming walked by. He looked exhausted, confused and just a little bit hopeful. It was his second trip to the precinct that night, but this one promised to clear him.

"He's clean," Auntie Lil declared firmly. "He's not the big man."

"Maybe," T.S. conceded, glad to return her favor. "Then again, maybe not. He could easily be in cahoots with Worthington. I'd like to hear what Timmy has to say."

"It may be days before the boy can speak." Herbert scrutinized the Homefront director. "It is my hope that he is innocent. But you know what I *really* wonder?"

They both stared at him, waiting.

"We keep seeing people come *in* to the precinct. Pray tell, where are they exiting?"

They contemplated this minor mystery in silence until, a few minutes later, they saw a determined-looking Fran and a tired Father Stebbins trudge past.

Auntie Lil rose from her chair when she saw the priest, but T.S. pulled her firmly back into place. "Forget it. We'll find out in a little while. We've interfered enough. Let's let Santos gather the rest of it together."

"No policeman is accompanying them," Herbert observed. "I think that, perhaps, Father Stebbins is here at the behest of Miss Fran."

"How could they have found out what happened to me?" Auntie Lil asked.

"Hard as it may seem, their presence here may have nothing to do with you," T.S. pointed out. "Perhaps they are here on their own."

But half an hour later, it became apparent that he could be wrong. A commotion at the front desk alerted the trio that Adelle and her followers had heard what had happened to Auntie Lil and were at the precinct, seeking information. Like Billy said—street talk was fast and it was often very accurate.

"We demand to know what's going on," Adelle was insisting in a rich stage voice. "I have heard rumors of an attack on one of us.

We may all be in danger here. Have they apprehended the culprit or do you intend to allow us to continue to be stalked like so many defenseless deer?"

A deer was not the animal analogy T.S. would have chosen for Adelle. "I'll handle this," he assured Auntie Lil. He walked to the door and shut it firmly, pulling the bolt lock shut before returning to his chair.

"Thank God," Auntie Lil said, putting her head on the desk.

"I do not think that they could see us," Herbert assured her, massaging the back of her neck gently.

An indignant cacophony of sound from the other side of the door signaled the eventual ejection of the actresses from the station house. Judging from the noise, a number of culprits waiting to be booked had decided to take sides and were heard encouraging the women to stand up for their rights. Unfortunately, enthusiastic support from the criminal underclass did nothing for their credibility and soon a relative silence descended on the precinct.

"They're gone," Herbert remarked. They all nodded and fell wearily silent again. The only sounds in the room were occasional gulps as they refueled their caffeine intake, and soft murmurings as Herbert reassured Auntie Lil.

T.S. felt miserably alone.

4. When the knock on the door came, T.S. expected either Santos or a minion calling for their presence in an interviewing room. He was unprepared to find Lilah waiting on the other side. His feelings zoomed from despair to elation in a single second. It was a wonder his heart survived the jolt.

"Lilah!" All other words left him in a stab of pure, unexpected pleasure.

"Theodore." She rushed toward him and he was enveloped in a cloud of faint gardenia perfume. "Your hand!" She touched the huge bandage gingerly and stared into his face. "What have they done to you, Theodore? You're not hiding in here, are you? Are you under arrest?"

"Good heavens, no." He quickly filled her in on the events of the evening.

"Oh, no," she said when he was done. She rushed over to Auntie Lil and fluttered over her until it became immediately plain that such treatment only annoyed the patient.

"I'm perfectly all right," Auntie Lil declared. "Go fuss over Theodore. He likes it."

"Since you're both okay, can they came in?" Lilah darted out the door without waiting for a further invitation. When she returned it was quite a procession that made its way into the room. A tall, coffee-colored man dressed in a neat sweater-and-slacks combination followed behind Lilah. The next member of her entourage was an enormously fat man in a brown-and-green plaid jacket and matching greasy brown pants. The rear was brought up by an immaculately groomed older man of miniature stature, whose regal bearing conveyed the illusion of far greater height. He walked extremely erectly, and his snow white hair was clipped in a neat but unpretentious style. He wore an expensive suit and silk necktie, despite the late hour, and a white handkerchief peeked from one pocket. The ostrichskin briefcase he gripped in his hands was worth more than T.S.'s entire outfit.

"I got your phone call," Lilah told T.S., sitting down next to Auntie Lil. "I came as soon as I could. I had no idea you'd been through such an ordeal."

The walking Whitman's Sampler of human beings behind her filed obediently to spots against the far wall and waited for Lilah to make the introductions. Even Herbert couldn't help but stare at the unusual trio.

"Let me introduce you," Lilah said sweetly and T.S. began to suspect that she was not above a little showboating herself. "This is George Scarborough," she explained, gesturing toward the tall black man. He bowed slightly. "You may not remember him, Theodore. He was your bartender last night."

T.S. colored slightly.

"Dewars and soda," George Scarborough announced solemnly. His deep, golden voice struck a buried chord in T.S.'s memory.

"You helped me to the car?" T.S. remembered and the bartender nodded.

"I'm afraid I'm just not very good at detecting," Lilah explained. "I figured that Worthington was too cheesy to be very original, so I spent the day calling every catering service in the latest issue of *New York* Magazine until I found the place that had supplied George for last night's party. They wouldn't tell me who he was, though. That's where Mr. Hermann comes in."

The fat man in the plaid jacket stepped forward, a hearty smile creasing his pudgy face. He produced a fistful of business cards as smoothly as a magician produces a bouquet of flowers from his fingertips. He pressed one apiece on T.S., Herbert and Auntie Lil. They examined their cards dutifully. It appeared that Mr. Hermann was a private investigator, or a "Marital Specialist" to be exact. One who promised "Discretion at Discount Prices."

"Yellow pages," Lilah whispered in T.S.'s ear. He nodded. "It would have taken me weeks to track down George," Lilah added graciously in a louder, more grateful tone of voice. "But Mr. Hermann was so ingenious. He found out his name within the hour."

The well-dressed third man coughed discreetly.

"And you are, sir?" Herbert inquired, catching his hint.

"Hamilton Prescott, Sr.," the gentleman intoned in a polished Boston accent. He, too, produced a small cache of business cards and bestowed them all around.

"Hamilton has been the family lawyer for ages," Lilah explained. "When you said you were at the police station, I didn't want to take any chances."

T.S. and Auntie Lil simultaneously thought of Lieutenant Abromowitz and nodded. It would be a good idea to have someone present when they gave their statements. They smiled gratefully at Lilah.

"Of course," T.S. said, gripping Hamilton Prescott's well-manicured hand. "We should have seen to such things ourselves." He was rewarded with an unmistakably firm handshake. Hamilton Prescott oozed confidence. Best of all, he did not look in the least inclined to yawn—which put him well ahead of the others in the room.

Auntie Lil was scrutinizing the new arrivals carefully. Finally, she turned back to Lilah. "It was lovely of you all to stop by," Auntie Lil began. "But why in the world is this man and this man here?" She pointed to the bartender and private investigator in turn. Both men shifted uneasily under her stare and Mr. Hermann managed to look downright guilty.

"Oh, dear. Of course. I told you I wasn't very good at this." Lilah hid her smile with her gloved hand. "George is here to make a statement."

"Statement?" T.S. stared at the bartender. "What on earth for?"

"They tried to poison you last night," Lilah declared. "That awful Worthington and his girlfriend tried to poison you."

"Knock you out, not poison you," George clarified in his deep voice. "I believe, sir, that they tried to slip you a mickey. That was why I interceded as I did. I did not quite understand what I had seen until you went down, sir."

"Went down?" Auntie Lil demanded, looking to T.S. for details.

T.S. was just as eager for details. Not, however, in front of a roomful of people. "Are you sure?" he asked the bartender.

George nodded. "I apologize for not realizing what was happening sooner. I should have known when I saw what kind of party it was. I was surprised to have the host request another Dewars and soda for you so soon after your first one." He cleared his throat in apology. "I knew it was for you, because you were the only one drinking Dewars. Yet you did not seem to be the type to guzzle his booze, as we bartenders say. If you'll pardon me for speaking so bluntly."

"Not at all." T.S. waved for him to continue. "What did he put in my drink?"

"I don't know for sure. He took your drink and turned his back to the bar and handed it to the woman with him. She, in turn, put the drink on a small shelf and took something from her pocketbook."

"And you stood by and did nothing?" Auntie Lil demanded.

George nodded. "I apologize. At the time, I thought it was a packet of sugar substitute. She had another glass with her and I convinced myself that she had gotten iced tea from the kitchen because she was tired of drinking. Wishful thinking on my part, of course. The woman in question did not tire of drinking all night. But it was not until later—when you could hardly walk and I could not figure out why—that I realized she may have poured something out of the packet into your drink."

"What was in the packet?" T.S. wondered.

"A mickey," Lilah pointed out triumphantly, relishing the slang. "Don't you see? George here says he isn't all that surprised. I suspect he has his finger on the pulse of rather seedy New York nightlife, don't you?"

"Unavoidable at times," George conceded.

"A mickey?" Auntie Lil demanded. "Why on earth would someone bother to dope poor Theodore? Surely, Worthington did not know that we suspected him of having anything to do with Emily's death?"

T.S. shook his head. "I'm sure he didn't know. I don't know why he would bother." The bartender's unusual voice had triggered buried memories. Disturbing shapes were taking form in his mind ... there was a hallway, shadows slipping past, a blur of distorted faces and voices. Oh, dear. He stared balefully at Lilah.

Lilah beamed at him and said loudly enough for the entire room to hear, "You were very sweet, Theodore. A perfect gentleman. We can discuss this later if you like."

"Let's do." T.S. loosened his collar and became conscious that the fat private investigator was beaming at him. He looked up and fairly snarled in return.

"Perhaps we should give these people their privacy," Lilah's lawyer smoothly intervened. "Gentlemen?" He graciously included Mr. Hermann in that group. "I suggest we speak to the desk sergeant about arranging for Mr. Scarborough to make an official statement. And, Mr. Hermann, you've been of great help but I'm sure we can release you for a well-earned rest. Grady will be glad to take you home. He'll be back just in time to accommodate Mr. Scarborough with the same." He hustled the two men smoothly out the door with a shower of murmured thanks. T.S. relaxed a bit. They were in good hands, indeed. Mr. Hamilton Prescott was a pro.

"Miss Hubbert?" Santos' voice filled the room with unexpected authority. Though tired, the detective looked well pleased with himself. T.S. suspected at once that Leteisha/Rodney was indeed talking. "I'm ready to take your statement now."

"You look optimistic," Auntie Lil said eagerly as she hurried to the door. "What did you find out? Tell me everything."

"Now, now, Miss Hubbert, it's your turn to do the talking, remember?" He smiled thinly. "And I'll have the whole truth this time, if you don't mind."

"Of course she doesn't mind," a commanding voice interrupted. Mr. Prescott was back and firmly in place at Auntie Lil's side. He had the unerring instincts of a highly successful counselor. "She'll answer anything I decide is appropriate with the utmost candor, won't you, Miss Hubbert?" His eyes held a warning that not even Auntie Lil would dare to ignore.

Detective Santos stared down at the lawyer. "You are?" he asked evenly.

"Her lawyer." His confident voice implied years of successful experience thrusting and parrying the finer points of law. His manner reeked of decades of research and millions of pages of knowledge at his fingertips. He saved his effort for when it counted, his demeanor made plain, and he knew clients' rights as surely as he knew his own name.

Santos knew he knew, too. He sighed and gestured for them both to follow. T.S. stood in the doorway and watched as they disappeared upstairs.

"I certainly didn't mean to interfere," Lilah told him. "But it's always wise to have representation on hand."

"Interfere?" T.S. pulled a chair close to her and took her hands in his. The bandage on his injured hand made him feel like he was wearing a baseball glove. "You are never an interference, Lilah. Never, ever think that you interfere in my—"

"Ahem." Herbert bowed politely and backed to the door. "I feel the need for a bit of fresh air. Please excuse me." He was gone in a flash.

"Terminally discreet," Lilah observed. She gave a merry, tinkling laugh. "Now do you want to know what you said to me last night?"

It was a dare he was not yet ready to confront. "No, no. That's quite all right. Though if it was good, I'm sure I meant it." He colored slightly. "But why does the name 'Albert' keep popping up in my head?"

Lilah shook her head and smiled. "Albert is an old friend of my husband's, Theodore. They went to Yale together, were both in banking and led pretty much parallel lives until Robert managed to get himself stabbed to death. You met Albert last night. He helped you to the car. But don't worry. He's just a friend."

"What was he doing at Worthington's party?" T.S. asked. "It seems a cut below him, if you know what I mean."

"I can't figure it out," Lilah admitted. "He spent our entire time together warning me not to invest."

"Warning you not to invest?"

"Yes. That was why he wanted to speak to me alone," Lilah explained.

T.S. had a sudden flash of memory and saw Lilah standing by a large potted palm, while a tuxedoed man hovered around her. "He was practically nibbling on your ear," T.S. pointed out with a lack of gentlemanly spirit. He couldn't help it. The memory had flooded back with sudden clarity and it hurt.

"No, Theodore." She kissed him lightly on one cheek. "Albert does not interest me in the least. He was bending my ear, not nibbling it. It was a very curious thing. Here he was investing tens of thousands of dollars in Worthington's play and all he could tell me was that it stank and not to put any money in and not to make the same mistake he was making."

"Let me get this straight," T.S. said. "Albert has invested tons of moolah in the play but seems desperate for you not to do the same?"

"Yes, I'd say that. Desperate."

"So why is _he_ investing?" T.S. asked.

Lilah shrugged. "I honestly can't say. He never let me ask any questions. I was confused even more because I know he was just as conservative an investor as my late husband was. Probably more so. Robert used to joke about it."

Something didn't fit. That much was clear. T.S. sipped at a cold cup of cappuccino, hoping the caffeine might clear his thoughts.

"I'll tell Santos about it and see what he thinks. Worthington is guilty of more than we think," he decided. Lilah nodded and patted his knee. "Why would he slip me a mickey? If he had tried to knock Auntie Lil out, it would have made sense. She is, after all, the nosiest human being this side of Jimmy Durante."

"Except Worthington doesn't even know that Auntie Lil exists," Lilah pointed out. She shivered delicately. "There's something about him, Theodore. I just don't like that man. He kept saying 'Live and let live' as if it meant something profound. What did it mean? What does he have to do with Emily?"

"And what possible profit could he get out of drugging me?" T.S. added. "I know that we're missing something." He stared at her for a moment. "What do you know about mickies anyway?" he teased. "You sounded like an expert a minute ago."

"You can knock someone out by putting plain old eyedrops in their drink," she said confidently. "Or any manner of drugs. Mr. Hermann told me." She continued to rub his hands with her thumbs.

If he had his way, they would sit like this forever, linked by Lilah's steady touch. He wanted to study her, quietly, without interruption. How had she known what he was thinking about Albert? He would never understand women, not ever. Especially since he had learned about them from Auntie Lil, who was not your usual female at all. She lacked the subtlety and the capacity for delightfully erratic behavior that he found so charming in Lilah. "What are you doing to my hand?" T.S. asked, stalling for time.

"I think it's shiatsu or kung fu or acupuncture or something Japanese. My daughter taught it to me. It's good for headaches. Which I'm sure you have now or will have before morning." She smiled at him.

Headache? He felt wonderful.

But their time together was interrupted by the sounds of deep sobbing. T.S. looked up and the pathetic sight framed in the doorway brought unexpected tears to his eyes. A thin man with a curtain of scraggly blond hair on each side of his face was being led past in handcuffs by two officers. He held a cheap, long blonde wig in his tethered hands and the strapless gown he wore was ripped up one side so that his pale white flesh peeked through. He lurched forward, sobbing, wedged between the two patrolmen.

"Oh, God. I know him," Theodore said sadly. "That must be the other prostitute. The one who wouldn't hurt Auntie Lil and got away. I've met him before."

"You know him?" Lilah's eyes followed his and took in the pitiful sight. The man had stopped, slumped against a grimy wall. A long scratch marred his bony shoulders and his black hose were ripped from the thigh to the toes. Sobbing louder, he proclaimed that he would never hurt anyone.

T.S. knew, from Auntie Lil's description, that he was telling the truth. He hoped Auntie Lil would tell Santos the same.

"You know him?" Lilah asked again.

"Yes. I have his card at home."

"What's his name?" Lilah was appalled but intrigued at this rare glimpse into a world usually kept so carefully hidden from her.

"I forget his real name. But I call him Peter Pan. Poor guy. He just wanted to be a star.

5. By the time Santos returned with Auntie Lil, Lilah had fallen asleep with her head slumped on T.S.'s shoulder. He could have slept himself, but it would have been a waste of the wonderful feeling that flooded his heart.

Auntie Lil slipped quietly back into place and gave T.S. a quick glance. "Thank God for that lawyer," was all she would say.

"Next," Santos announced, crooking a finger and beckoning T.S. to follow. "Don't worry. Your lawyer is waiting for you upstairs."

Even as T.S. followed Santos out the door, Herbert materialized and slipped back in his place at Auntie Lil's side.

An hour later, T.S. thanked Mr. Prescott and sent the lawyer on his way. He returned to the room to find all three of his companions fast asleep. Herbert was breathing quietly, sitting completely upright. But he was, without a doubt, deep in dreamland. Auntie Lil lay practically sprawled across his chest, her own lusty breathing just this side of an unladylike snore. Lilah had her head on the table and the silver glint of her hair against the dull brown of the cheap formica shone as finely as precious metal amidst mud.

"Thanks," Santos told T.S. quietly, patting his shoulder. "Why don't you folks call it a night? I'll tell you everything you want to know in the morning."

T.S. shook his head firmly. "We want to see it through to the end."

Santos nodded like he understood. "You won't have to wait much longer. Abromowitz made a phone call. Eight down and two more to go."

Twenty minutes later—with T.S. still the only occupant of the room left awake—he was rewarded for his vigilance with the satisfaction of seeing Lance Worthington brought into the precinct by four plainclothesmen. The producer wore his tan cashmere coat thrown over a pair of matching purple velour sweats and his hands were tightly linked by the metal bands of a pair of sturdy handcuffs.

"Try pulling on your stupid little ears now," T.S. thought with grim satisfaction. "Dope me, indeed."

Sally St. Claire trudged in behind Worthington, flanked by a pair of grim policewomen. Clearly, she, like Worthington, had been awakened from a sound sleep. Her hair was tangled and unkempt. Her pale face, devoid of makeup, gleamed with a plastic harshness beneath the precinct lights. Her inner hardness was emerging, T.S. thought to himself. One day, her facelift would give way and she'd crack, lines blossoming across her face until, within minutes, she'd shriveled up into an old hag.

He thought, unexpectedly, of Emily's tiny body, laid out on the autopsy table.

Discretion, he realized, was not always the better part of valor.

Having decided, T.S. walked firmly to the door and stuck his head out. His eyes met Worthington's and locked. He stared at the producer with contempt.

"You?" Worthington said incredulously, perplexed and dazed at his misfortune.

"Whatever happened to 'live and let live'?" T.S. asked him, turning away.

CHAPTER SEVENTEEN

1. It was light outside by the time Santos reappeared. Even T.S. had been asleep for several hours. They raised their groggy heads in response to his disgustingly cheerful greeting and tried without success to conceal yawns. Auntie Lil's curls were flattened on one side of her head but sprang out in clumps of wild disarray on the other side, making her look a bit deranged. Rather than alert her to this fact, T.S. surreptitiously ran his fingers through his own hair, forcing his thick locks back into place. Herbert and Lilah looked remarkably intact, though sleepy.

The first thing they all noticed was that Detective Santos held a thick sheath of notes in one hand. The second thing—at the moment, more important—was that Billy was right behind him bearing a box full of goodies from the Delicious Deli. He smiled and laid out fresh coffee, cappuccino and pastries on the table. Without a word, he nodded good morning and left to return to his work.

"Born and bred in Hell's Kitchen," Santos reminded them proudly. "People like him are the neighborhood, understand? Not these jerks." He threw his papers on the table and took his time selecting a large pineapple danish. Then he pried the top off a cup of steaming black coffee and sighed. "We don't know everything," he admitted. "But we know most of it. If I tell you, do you promise to go home and leave me alone?"

Auntie Lil ignored the question. "What don't you know?" she asked instead.

"We still don't know Emily's real name," the detective admitted sadly. "But I think we have enough to go on now. Trust us. It's just a matter of time."

Still no name for Emily? Auntie Lil was disappointed and her face showed it.

"Maybe the column will help," T.S. consoled her.

"Column?" Santos stared pointedly at Auntie Lil.

"Well, tell us what you *do* know," she demanded, ignoring his question and flapping a hand at him impatiently.

Santos took his time chewing his danish and surveyed her carefully. "You mean you want to know the whole story?" he asked idly, teasing her. At last, he held the upper hand. And he was going to make her pay.

Auntie Lil glared and Detective Santos pushed a cup of cappuccino across the table to her with a laugh. "Sit back and relax, Miss Hubbert," he told her. "This may take a while." Shuffling his notes, he cleared his throat with exaggerated care and began:

"For starters, 'The Eagle,' as you call him, is singing like a canary. But Lance Worthington is not. We can't even get Emily's real name out of him. If he knows it. However, like I say, that's just a matter of time. And we have been able to fill in some details, thanks to his girlfriend, Sally St. Claire. Who, surprisingly enough, really is named Sally St. Claire and appears to be a not very bright girl from Des Moines who came to the Big Apple and went bad. I would not want her for my girlfriend. Loyalty is not her strongest suit. Neither are hearts.

"Who is this man we call The Eagle, also known as the lovely Leteisha Swann?" Santos was enjoying his moment in the spotlight and milking it for everything he could get. "Apparently, he is Rodney Combs, a not very productive member of society who comes to New York via Los Angeles where, by the way, he left behind two dead friends, five outstanding felony warrants and a record as long as your nose, Miss Hubbert. Which is saying a lot. He is not a nice man and, apparently, an even nastier woman. He works for himself, so to speak, to pick up pocket change. He also does some very odd jobs for his landlord and part-time employer, Mr. Lance Worthington.

"Now, who is Lance Worthington?" The detective sipped at his coffee while he stared at some notes. "This is a more difficult question. He has no record and appears to be a legitimate, if marginally successful, producer of plays. He made a bit of money fifteen years ago on some *Oh, Calcutta!* rip-off that had actors disrobing all over the stage. He's spent the last decade or so trying to emulate his one success. From what we can piece together, he has lately turned to some very creative methods of financing."

"Blackmail," Herbert Wong interjected quietly.

Detective Santos confirmed this with a nod. "Very effective

blackmail, it appears. And, by the way, he is, indeed, 'the big man.' His methods were very simple. Once he identified a potential investor, he did his damndest to land the poor sucker in a compromising position. With some of his targets, particularly the married ones, his cooperative girlfriend and her highly acrobatic friends were enough. I will leave out the details of some of the adventures described to me by Miss St. Claire, as you would find them difficult to believe, anyway. Other marks were not so easy, but quite a few usually succumbed to the lure of the unknown and exotic. Specifically, a transvestite here and there. Or a young boy."

Lilah sputtered on her coffee and T.S. patted her gallantly on the back. "I wonder what he had in mind for me?" she asked.

"No telling," Santos answered drily. "But I can guarantee you that you'll never get the chance to find out." He shuffled his notes and continued. "People being as stupid as they are, his victims would apparently oblige him in his schemes by drinking so much that they could hardly see and were begging to be compromised. With their judgment drowned in booze and party drugs, it was an easy matter to gain evidence of some sort of sexual misconduct against them. Photographs were taken or, in the case of the apartment on West Forty-sixth, videotapes. Which he has probably turned around and copied for sale to voyeurs, if he's the kind of guy I think he is." The detective looked up. "He had the remarkable ability to sniff out investors with a penchant for these kinds of things. You, Mr. Hubbert, eluded his radar. According to Miss St. Claire, he couldn't quite figure out what you wanted."

"Thank God for that," T.S. interjected. The other stared at him curiously. *Well, that didn't quite come out right*, he thought.

"Once he had blackmail material," Santos explained, "he tightened the screws. Potential investors were told to put up a certain amount or risk exposure. The amount was carefully chosen to hurt, but not hurt too much. It was the perfect scam. Anxious to protect their reputations, investors would hand over tens of thousands of dollars. In return, Worthington kept quiet and, in some cases, kept feeding their nasty habits. Plus, the schmucks could always hold out the hope, however rare, that they might actually make some profits or, at least, get a few tax deductions. It wasn't a far-fetched scheme at all. In fact, Miss St. Claire maintains that he's financed three flops so far in this manner."

"Three?" T.S. asked incredulously.

"Yes." Santos consulted his notes. "A musical version of the McCarthy hearings, a drama based on Fatty Arbuckle's life and something entitled *Mr. Bojangles Goes to Washington*. Would you like to hear the details?"

"No!" they all chorused.

"At any rate, all three efforts bombed. But the financing was always there to try something new."

"Albert," Lilah said suddenly. She looked at T.S. and he shrugged. He didn't even want to speculate on what Lance Worthington might have on the illustrious Albert. As the victor, he could afford to be gracious.

"Can't help you there," Santos told her. "Though Mr. Hubbert here told me the story about Albert and it sounds like he is a victim. But I doubt your Albert or any of the other blackmail victims will be very forthcoming. To continue—Worthington does own the building on Forty-sixth Street. He bought it about three years ago. Some of his tenants were uninvolved in his activities, but about a year ago he started driving out as many of them as he could and replacing them with struggling actresses and actors who, in exchange for free or low-cost rent, performed small favors for him." He raised his eyebrows. "Details anyone?" They shook their heads vigorously. "Good. You don't want to know. One of the tenants, who calls himself Gregory Rogers, was involved in your kidnapping last night, Miss Hubbert. He has no prior record and your story matches his. He appears to be no more successful as a villain than he was as an actor."

"Please go easy on him. He didn't want to harm me," Auntie Lil pointed out again.

"He didn't particularly want to help you, either," the detective countered.

"What about Emily? Where does she come into it?" T.S. asked.

Santos sighed. "Here it gets sketchy, because Worthington isn't talking, but it seems that she first became involved simply through the misfortune of having rented an apartment in a building that was soon after bought by Worthington. First, she refused to move out when he embarked on his campaign to rid the building of anyone but his cronies. Then, when she noticed the activities taking place next door, she turned out to be a whole hell of a lot sharper than he had bargained for. She became particularly disturbed when she saw that children were involved. Being a decent woman, unlike so many others in this story, she still considered the two boys as children. She made friends with them, according to Little Pete, and tried to get them off the streets. When that failed, she caused Worthington trouble in some way and he ordered Rodney Combs to kill her in as anonymous a fashion as possible. We believe this was to deflect attention away from his building and to make it difficult for us to track her movements. Worthington was, in fact, hoping her death would be ascribed to a heart attack or stroke. And he felt sure that, without an identity, no family would ever step forward to ask for an autopsy or investigation. It was very important that Emily's identity be concealed, Miss St. Claire tells me. But she is vague as to why this is so. Rodney tells a similar story. Neither one of them seemed to care why Worthington wanted Emily dead. They just went along."

"Why do you think she had to die anonymously?" Herbert asked Detective Santos.

He drummed his fingers on the tabletop. "I think maybe your friend, Emily, started calling city agencies and complaining about the use of the young boys. She probably got ignored because our agencies are so overworked and the kids aren't in a home situation and enforcement is pretty much impossible. So maybe she went too far, tried to get photos or some other kind of evidence on Worthington. Or, she may have threatened him with an old law still on the books from the early 1900s that authorizes New York City to seize a building used for 'bawdy' purposes. I don't know for sure. But I suspect that she probably made the mistake of directly confronting Worthington or, even more foolishly, informing him that she had tried to turn him in to every department and official she could think of. She may even have said that she was going to start warning potential backers away."

"Or said she would go public," Auntie Lil chimed in. "We found clippings of Margo McGregor's columns in her pocketbook."

Santos stared at her. "In that case, I'll have to have a word with Miss McGregor." He did not sound entirely displeased at the prospect. "At any rate, any one of these reasons could have triggered the order for her death. Worthington had a lucrative gig going and he didn't want it threatened."

"She had to die without a name in case her name rang a bell with people in those city agencies. As may have happened if her name had been widely reported with her death," Auntie Lil realized. "That would have raised the possibility of a connection to him and the chance that her death was not entirely natural. That's why he had The Eagle remove all traces of her identity from her apartment—just in case they traced her back to there. And then, of course, he moved one of Sally's friends into her apartment as a cover. So far as they were concerned, Emily never existed."

"Probably," Santos agreed. "In fact, I don't think they had even counted on anyone knowing Emily's stage name, either. I don't think he realized that she had friends. She kept to herself so much, except for the soup kitchen. He underestimated her life. And her friends." He complimented them with a small nod of his head.

"I hope you're calling around the agencies, now," Auntie Lil pointed out. "She may have used her real name to report his activities."

"We're on it," Santos confirmed patiently. "Believe me, we're already on it."

"But how does Bob Fleming tie into Worthington?" T.S. asked.

"Well, frankly, that appears to be Miss Hubbert's fault." Santos looked at her sternly from over the top of his notes. "Worthington was already pretty pissed at Fleming because he sometimes took kids off the street that Worthington needed for his own purposes. But he was willing to live and let live, as I understand he loves to say, until he heard that Fleming was trying to make contact with Timmy and wanted to ask him some questions about Emily. That led him to believe that Fleming knew more than he did. He had to take him out of the picture so, instead of murdering him, he ruined his reputation."

"Pretty effectively, I'd say," T.S. added.

Santos nodded. "Worthington was smart about it, too. He had the kid go to a local priest about Fleming, and told Timmy to pretend to be confused and unsure of what to do. It would help establish his credibility, Worthington explained to the kid, if anyone questioned his story. Timmy did as he was told. And the priest, of course, did as he was taught to do and urged the boy to go to the police, never knowing the story was false."

"So Father Stebbins is only guilty of being gullible?" Auntie Lil said incredulously.

"So far as I can tell," Santos conceded.

"Father Stebbins told you about Timmy?" T.S. asked. "Whatever happened to the sanctity of the confessional?"

"He didn't tell me. He spoke in all sorts of cryptic mumbo jumbo clichés. But his, um, companion, filled us in on the details."

"Fran?" Herbert asked.

"I knew there was something going on between those two," Auntie Lil declared.

"Now, I didn't say that," Detective Santos protested. "In fact, I consider that definitely out of my jurisdiction. But I did get the feeling that she sticks pretty close to the padre. When she saw the boy, Timmy, approach him a couple of times, she made it a point to be around in case he came back. Without admitting it in so many words, I got this picture of her lurking behind the pews and by the confessional pretending to dust, if you know what I mean. But she was doing it for a good reason. She didn't trust the kid and thought he was a liar. She thought maybe he was setting Father Stebbins up for something. She came right out and told the priest so, but he didn't believe her. They had a falling out. And she still looks like she wants to wring his neck."

"But after Timmy went to Father Stebbins and lied about Bob Fleming, Annie O'Day found him and convinced him to change his mind?" Auntie Lil asked.

Santos nodded. "Timmy is a street kid. He'll blow with the wind. I think that when Annie reached him and made him feel bad about lying, he truly got confused and went back to see the same priest to sort it out. He doesn't sound like a bad kid at heart, just mixed up and frightened at Emily's death. He told the priest the truth and admitted that Worthington had put him up to lying about Fleming. Father Stebbins was pretty broken up about it— after all, he had counseled the kid to destroy a man's life—so he did his best to convince the kid that he had to retract his statements as soon as possible. He even had the kid halfway talked into ditching New York and going back to Texas. Timmy wouldn't agree to going home but he did agree to retract his accusations. That's when he went to Homefront."

"And said he would only talk to me," Auntie Lil added.

Santos shrugged. "Well, there's no accounting for taste, Miss Hubbert." His eyes twinkled and he located another piece of paper, checked his notes and finished his summary. "The kid was being followed, of course, by Rodney—who had been parading around exclusively as Leteisha ever since he'd poisoned Emily. Rodney puts two and two together when he sees Timmy heading for Homefront, calls Worthington, and gets his orders. As Leteisha, he tells Little Pete that the man has a way for them to make some really big money that night, but that he and Timmy will have to do a job together. Little Pete is sent to get Timmy at Homefront before he can retract the allegations against Fleming. They were told to meet Leteisha at the piano warehouse for instructions and part payment. But, of course, by the time the kids got there, Leteisha was back to being Rodney again and beat the crap out of Timmy to teach him a lesson. And, if you ask me, to kill him as well. But he lived and Rodney will probably eventually be sorry for that. Rodney didn't hurt Little Pete because they needed him that night for one of Worthington's investing scams." He eyed T.S. "The rest of the story, I think you know." He looked up at them expectantly.

"So even in the middle of all this, Worthington was still trying to get something on me?" T.S. asked. "That's why he doped me and tried to set me up with Little Pete?"

"You got it. Like I say, he found you hard to please."

"I should think so." T.S. sat back with great dignity. "How utterly sordid."

"Murder usually is," the detective reminded him.

"And Eva?" Herbert asked almost fearfully. "She was killed because of mistaken identity?"

Here, Santos softened. "Not really," he admitted with a kindly nod toward Auntie Lil. "Don't forget, as Leteisha, Rodney was a real working girl and had coworkers who were always happy to contribute information in exchange for a buck here and there. People, if you want to go so far as to call them that, had been telling The Eagle about you, Miss Hubbert, for a number of days. You'd been seen having dinner with Little Pete. And you apparently met the super of Worthington's building? Funny how that little detail slipped your mind when you gave your statement. Anyway, the descriptions of you weren't very exact. For one thing, they left out your big mouth—" He smiled again, loving every minute of his revenge. "All The Eagle knew was that an old lady was snooping around, and he might have mistaken Eva for you. But I think that Eva was probably killed because she'd put two and two together and had figured out that The Eagle was also Leteisha Swann. She'd been hanging around the stoop as a bag lady or something." He stared at the assembled group. "A curious fact that I'm sure you'll eventually enlighten me on. And she made the mistake of letting The Eagle know he'd been found. I think it was just a matter of hours for her after that."

"She should have told us right away," Auntie Lil protested. "Oh, those women. Always trying to upstage each other."

"Or you," Santos pointed out and she fell silent. "At any rate, after Eva was killed, Worthington figured out that there was more than one little old lady snooping around."

"Many more than one!" Herbert interjected, the memory of being trapped in a street opera still fresh in his mind.

"He was waiting with Sally St. Claire in his car outside Homefront today when Little Pete came for Timmy. He didn't want any more screw-ups and was personally supervising Timmy's removal. He saw you arrive and he saw Bob Fleming rush in after you.

Sally says that they went back to the super and asked for a better description of the old lady who'd been asking about Emily. That's when he realized you were the one who'd come around asking questions. And that you were still alive. When they saw you again at the hospital, it was easy to pick you up after that. Since you weren't paying attention like I had warned you to."

The constant undercurrent of jousting between Detective Santos and Auntie Lil was tactfully ignored by the others.

"And the ladies from the soup kitchen?" Herbert asked. "Were they involved in any way? I'm speaking of Miss Adelle and the others."

"The ladies from the soup kitchen are a royal pain in the ass and they turned this place into a zoo last night. But other than that, they are uninvolved. So far as we can tell."

Auntie Lil looked a bit disappointed. "What about Nellie?" she asked.

T.S. rolled his eyes. Auntie Lil loved conspiracy stories. Even when she had to make them up.

"Certainly she's involved," Santos said. "But only so far as the kid, Little Pete, is concerned. Seems she's had her eye on him for a while. Seen him around the streets. Wants to get him off them. Looks to me like she's going to do it by force, if necessary. She marched him in here and, by God, he told us just about everything. You would have, too, if you had seen the look on that woman's face."

"She's going to try and get custody of him?" Lilah asked.

Santos shook his head. "So far as I'm concerned, it's out of official channels. I have a feeling we should just let things take their course on their own."

"Well, what do you think? Is there enough to get Worthington?" T.S. knew the system and was not convinced. He'd seen worse people get off for more.

Santos nodded slowly. "Yeah, we'll get him. At least on blackmail and ordering Eva's death and endangering the welfare of minors and a handful of other charges."

"But what about Emily's death?" Auntie Lil said indignantly. "That's what started this whole thing."

Santos shrugged. "It's hard. There's not much to tie The Eagle into that murder, much less Worthington. And Rodney Combs knows the system. He hasn't come right out and said he did it. He probably never will. He knows we don't have much on him. I don't think we'll get him on Emily and we certainly won't get him to roll over on Worthington for Emily's murder. Not without a witness to hold over his head."

"Hey, Santos." The beefy desk sergeant stuck his head in the door and bellowed: "Some big black dude is here to see you. Says he's got someone with him you should meet." The sergeant rolled his eyes and twirled a finger by his head.

"It's Franklin." Auntie Lil knew at once.

"Send him in," Santos ordered. A few seconds later, Franklin entered the room, his enormous bulk dwarfing the slight figure of his companion—a funny old man with half a shaved head, uneven beard stubble and rummy eyes.

"I found him," Franklin declared with satisfaction. "Living under the Manhattan Bridge. He saw The Eagle put the poison in Miss Emily's chili. And he's all yours, Mr. Santos. Right?"

Franklin's companion fixed his unnaturally bright eyes on the detective and wheezed his way into speaking like a car getting started on a cold morning. "Yeah. Yeah. Yup. Yup. I seen it all right. And I don't mind saying so if you keep his evil eye away from me. You just point me to where I should stand."

Santos looked at T.S. skeptically.

"It's better than nothing," T.S. said with a shrug.

The detective looked at T.S. "You could be right," he finally admitted. "You have been right before." He gestured for the man to sit at the table and took out his pencil with a sigh. What was one more statement after an entire night of taking notes?

2. Margo McGregor kept her part of her bargain. Two days later, the following column appeared as the first in what would become a series of columns clearing Bob Fleming and detailing Emily's death. It ran across from the editorial pages of the Sunday edition of New York *Newsday*, landing in nearly three million homes throughout the metropolitan area:

It Is Time To Turn To Each Other

New York City is a city with invisible walls as insurmountable as any barrier the world has to offer. These walls separate the rich from the poor, pit black against white and, too often, turn the young against the old. Yet, sometimes we find ourselves breaching these walls in unexpected ways. Those are the times when I am proudest to be a New Yorker. A New Yorker like Emily Toujours.

Two weeks ago Emily died in a Manhattan soup kitchen. She was an old woman, maybe homeless and definitely hungry. In short, her death wasn't big news. Until you take a closer look at her life: after an absence of decades, Emily had returned to the city three years ago, hoping to live out her final years near the stage. She had enough money for a small apartment and, always, orchestra tickets. She did not always have enough money for food. It is probable that Emily found a Broadway much different from the Broadway she remembered. At least until the curtain went up. But even with the grime and the danger that had invaded its streets, her friends say that Emily never stopped loving New York—or the people who live here.

But it turned out that Emily had died as she had lived much of her life—under a stage name. And even then, no one was really quite sure that it was anything but "Emily." She had nothing on her to say who she really was or even to indicate where she lived. And her friends discovered that, among them, no one knew her real name. It appeared that her "Emily" identity would die with her. Despite the dismay of her friends, Emily was assigned a number and left to wait a week in a chilled city locker. Perhaps someone would step up to claim her. If not, there was potter's field.

Unexpectedly, someone did step up. Many someones, in fact. All of them New Yorkers like Emily. People who refused to forget. Her friends at the soup kitchen—more than two dozen in all—would not let Emily die unknown. "She has a family somewhere," they told each other. "She deserves to be mourned."

They mounted a campaign to find out her true identity. And if anyone among them doubted Emily's love for drama, they've stopped doubting now: though her real name remained a mystery, her friends discovered that Emily had been poisoned. Who would bother to murder an unknown, nearly penniless, old woman? It was a puzzle that our overburdened police force could not afford to solve. But her friends would not let it go. Young and old, black and white, and, yes, even rich and poor, they banded together to unravel why Emily had died.

They found that she died giving of herself to others. Emily Toujours, an old woman who only weighed 84 pounds at her autopsy, died because she tried to help two young runaway boys leave our streets. One boy was black and the other was white. Both of them called her "Grandma." There's nothing really special about either of these boys. They're the kind of kids the rest of us pass by every day. They smirk and make us uncomfortable. We, in turn, make them invisible.

But they weren't invisible to Emily. She turned to every agency, every hotline, every task force and every department in this city for help. Logs show she made more than 85 phone calls in all. What she wanted was someone, anyone, to show her a way to save two young boys from our streets. What she found instead was disinterest, apathy, discouragement and just plain exhaustion. And, like so many other New Yorkers, I am among the guilty ones.

Left to her own, Emily did what she could to encourage the boys to leave New York. She opened her home and what little money she had to two young men she hardly knew. For no apparent reason other than a belief that, even here in New York City, children should be allowed to be children.

Unfortunately for Emily, her plans threatened someone with money and power. That someone apparently paid to have her killed. But he made a classic mistake. He underestimated the determination of Emily's fellow New Yorkers. Thanks to their continued efforts and the help of a NYPD detective who can still find it in his heart to believe in justice, Emily's killers are now behind bars. In death, she beat the odds in New York City: her murder will be marked "solved."

In many ways, Emily triumphed. One of the boys is now off the streets. He has a home and someone to care for him. The other lies in a hospital bed, his future uncertain. But at least the hold of the streets has been broken, albeit along with his bones.

In other ways, Emily continues to fight. She still lies in a city locker on the East Side of Manhattan. And her friends still refuse to give up the search for her real name.

Whether "Emily Toujours" is a real name or not, Emily was definitely a real New Yorker. And her story is a real New York tale, with a moral that holds meaning for all of us: today, in what used to be the greatest city in the world, we often have no one to turn to but ourselves. If we're going to make it at all, we're going to make it by helping each other. So, for God's sake, tear those walls down.

Rest in peace, Emily. Whoever you are. And many thanks for the lesson.

3. New Yorkers are not a sentimental lot, especially about themselves. Response to the column was just a notch below the reaction that Margo McGregor had received for revealing that the fix was in at the last Madison Square Garden cat show. But, two days later, the column was picked up on the AP wire and landed in fifty million more homes all across America. Including a small clapboard farmhouse a few miles outside of Devils Lake, North Dakota.

Margo McGregor had just returned from a lunch date with Detective Santos when the telephone on her desk rang. Casting caution to the wind, she decided to answer. She was in a good mood—she could handle any kook in the world that day.

"Margo McGregor," she said crisply and was answered by an oddly important silence. The quiet gave way to what seemed at first to be static. Then the columnist realized that it was the sound of someone crying very far away.

"You found my mother," a muffled voice told her.

Margo McGregor broke unexpectedly into tears.

4. Exactly two weeks to the day after Emily's death, they held the funeral at St. Barnabas. Eva had been buried by the Franciscan sisters several days before. Now, it was time to tell Emily goodbye.

It was a true Indian-summer day. White clouds scuttled across the blue sky above the Hudson and private planes buzzed down the river corridor in enthusiastic confusion. The mournful toot of a liner pulling away from the dock signaled the hour before noon. The assembled mourners shifted on the front steps of St. Barnabas, unwilling to leave the bright day behind.

Among them were T.S. and Auntie Lil. They scanned the arrivals, looking for friends. As they waited, a small man dressed in tan with a huge bulbous nose hurried up the steps toward them. He tipped his hat to Auntie Lil and hurried by.

"Wait," she called after him. "I owe you a thank-you."

He shook his head, bowed deeply and disappeared inside.

"Who's that?" Auntie Lil asked, pointing to Eighth Avenue.

"If I didn't know better, I'd think it was Little Pete."

Nellie was hustling the small boy down the sidewalk, lecturing into his ear. She wore a voluminous flowered dress that flapped in the wind and she was desperately trying to keep her hat on with one hand while subduing her skirt with the other. Suddenly, a gust of wind sent her dress flying up to her waist and her hat tumbling down the sidewalk. Little Pete dashed forward and rescued the hat inches from the gutter. He ran back with his prize and they laughed together, heads thrown back, before slapping their palms in a gleeful high five.

"It's going to work," T.S. predicted.

"Thank God," Auntie Lil agreed.

Nellie and Little Pete stopped to shake hands with them before entering the church.

"You look exceptionally beautiful today," T.S. told her. "And Pete, my man, I have to say that you're absolutely stunning."

Little Pete eyed him carefully, trying to decide if he was being teased or not.

"He ought to look stunning," Nellie interrupted. "I figure this suit took me 843 meat pies worth of profit. Of course, Granny here ate about half of them." She looped an arm over Little Pete's shoulders and smiled at Auntie Lil. "You come in next week for my goat curry, okay?"

Auntie Lil agreed enthusiastically.

T.S. and Auntie Lil watched them enter the church together. "It's gonna work," T.S. predicted again. "Hey," T.S. elbowed Auntie Lil, but when she saw why, she didn't mind a bit. Detective Santos was trying to sneak in the far door of the church and it looked like he had Margo McGregor with him. "Is that a romantic first date or what?" T.S. asked. "He's taking her to a funeral."

"I don't think it's their first date, Theodore, dear. And let's just be grateful he didn't take her to the Westsider."

"That's funny. He looks like he's avoiding us."

"What's funny about that?" Auntie Lil admitted. "I find it quite sensible."

"I knew I'd see you here!" Billy Finnegan was the next to arrive and he had his entire family in tow. Megan looked like a miniature version of her mother, but clearly hated the full skirt of her dress. Billy's son, Michael, looked like a miniature version of his father, down to the hair still wet from a water combing.

"Don't you look like quite the little man," Auntie Lil ventured in a burst of goodwill toward the child.

Michael scowled and grabbed at his collar with a chubby fist. "Aarghh," he gargled as if he were choking.

His mother slapped his hand away from his collar with the speed of a rattlesnake striking. "Michael," she warned slowly. The single word was enough. The small boy stole a peek at Auntie Lil and stuck out his tongue.

"I'm going to be a detective when I grow up," Megan announced to Auntie Lil, unexpectedly slipping her tiny hand into hers. Auntie Lil found herself deeply touched. It was such a small and warm and trusting hand. My goodness, children were innocent.

"A detective?" Auntie Lil echoed.

Megan nodded. "Yes. I'm going to grow up and be just like you." She beamed up at Auntie Lil. Auntie Lil beamed back.

"Let's go, Megan," her mother ordered, and the small girl dutifully followed her family inside.

T.S. was staring at Auntie Lil strangely. "You were nice to that child," he said incredulously.

"She's an unusual child with unusually good taste for someone so young," Auntie Lil defended herself. "She wants to grow up to be me."

"Here comes Franklin." T.S. pointed out a huge figure headed up Eighth Avenue. "And it looks like he has someone with him."

Auntie Lil burst out laughing. "It has to be his brother."

Indeed it was. They were twin giants, as alike in size and coloring as two bears.

"Mr. Hubbert, Miss Hubbert," Franklin said when he reached their step. "I'd like you to meet my brother, Samuel. We'll be heading home to South Carolina tomorrow. I wanted the chance to tell Miss Emily and all of you goodbye."

"Franklin. Samuel—how nice to meet you." Auntie Lil grasped each of their hands in turn and T.S. could have sworn that she gulped. He even thought that he saw tears glistening on her eyelashes.

His thoughts were interrupted by the well-timed arrival of Adelle and her followers. The group swept past in a flurry of black silk and rustling, not unmindful of the handful of photographers who had arrived to capture the requisite heartwarming shot in case no sensational murders popped up that day.

"Black net is making a comeback," T.S. observed.

"With that crowd, it never left." Auntie Lil waved enthusiastically as a scurrying Herbert hurried up the steps to their side.

"I am not late?" he asked anxiously, straightening his tie and smoothing down his thinning hair with one palm.

"Not at all. And don't you look marvelous. Isn't that a wonderful suit, Theodore? Theodore? *Theodore*."

T.S. did not hear her. A long black limousine had pulled up to the curb and an elegant figure was unfolding from the back. Lilah wore a simple black knit dress and a strand of real pearls. Her hair shone in the sunlight.

"What on earth are you looking so green for, Theodore?" Auntie Lil demanded.

The answers to her question emerged from the car behind their mother. Two young ladies in their late teens, each dressed in navy, stood on the sidewalk clutching their purses and shyly eyeing T.S. He was acutely aware that Lilah must have described him to her daughters. He wondered what she had said.

Herbert tactfully hustled Auntie Lil inside the church, providing T.S. with privacy.

"Theodore." Lilah kissed him on each cheek and the familiar smell of her gardenia perfume gave him strength. "This is Alicia. And this is Isabel."

T.S. nodded and managed a smile. Alicia and Isabel ducked their heads together, giggling, and looked up at him from under long eyelashes.

Any nervousness he felt was erased a few seconds later when he distinctly heard one of the daughters whisper: "He looks kind of like an older version of that actor, Richard Gere."

"Yeah," said the other. "Except really, really old."

Well, he would take his compliments where he could get them. He straightened his tie and escorted Lilah inside.

Vase after vase of lilies and gladiolus lined the walls on either side of the church. The smell of flowers wafted through the pews and sunlight streamed through the stained-glass windows, sending tongues of red and purple and blue tumbling exuberantly across the marble floor. The front doors were propped open and fresh air and sunshine poured down the aisle, filling the church with the promise of the living. It seemed more of a beginning than a goodbye. It was appropriate for Emily.

"Look at all these flowers," T.S. said. "Who in the world paid for them?"

Lilah patted his hand discreetly. "Let's just say that a grateful friend of mine who no longer has to back a certain show about Davy Crockett decided that he'd like to make a small gesture of his appreciation."

T.S. stared at the rows of people filling the church. Many were neighborhood residents, some were nothing more than curiosity seekers. A few were strangers, but even more were his new friends. He recognized many of them from the soup kitchen and it was hard to tell the volunteers from the homeless. Everyone was well scrubbed, subdued and seemingly at peace. Bob Fleming sat stiffly in a shirt and tie in a front pew, next to a radiantly healthy Annie O'Day, who looked equally uncomfortable in her dress. T.S. smiled. They were perfect for one another. Bob would need someone like Annie to help him rebuild.

Emily's coffin gleamed in the filtered sunlight, its rich brown mahogany finish glowing with the reflected glory of the stained glass.

"Good Lord," T.S. whispered. "You really went all out on that thing. It's big enough to hold Orson Welles."

"It's my money, Theodore," Lilah reminded him sweetly. "I have scads of it and I intend to spend it however I like."

"Well, then why don't you throw a few handfuls at poor Bob Fleming?" T.S. whispered. "Homefront really needs it right now."

"I know. And I will." Lilah patted his hand and shot him a private smile.

They found their seats next to Auntie Lil and Herbert. T.S. was well content to sit between the two women he loved most.

Father Stebbins conducted the ceremony with a majestic and tasteful demeanor that surprised both T.S. and Auntie Lil. In his skillful hands, the sometimes ghoulish ceremony of wafting incense around the coffin was transformed into an ancient and vital farewell to the dead. His eulogy, of course, was peppered with cliché after cliché. After all, a leopard doesn't change his spots. But, somehow, it all seemed entirely appropriate. More to the point, he kept it short.

In fact, when he sat down after only a few minutes of speaking, T.S. stared at Auntie Lil in some puzzlement. This was not the Father Stebbins that they knew. But his reason for brevity soon presented itself.

A small woman had been sitting quietly in the front row. She was the kind of woman that was easy to overlook. She wore a simple blue dress and sensible shoes. Her face was plain and unadorned; her hair a dull brown cut in a functional bob.

No one, in fact, would have been likely to notice her had she not risen and walked to the podium when Father Stebbins was done.

"My name is Julia Hansen," the woman began. Her voice was hushed but it had great strength in it. "You don't know who I am, but I will be forever grateful to all of you for what you did for my mother. You were the most loyal and loving friends that she could ever have had and I see now that she was right about New York City.

"You have shown a great deal of love toward a woman you hardly knew. So I'd like to tell you a little about her. My mother was not alone in this world. She was, in fact, loved very much—by her husband and by me. She lived most of her life on a farm in North Dakota. And I think that she was very happy. But after my father died, there was nothing that my husband and I could do to stop her from moving back here to New York. I don't even think that I tried very hard to stop her. I remembered too well how, when I was a child, she would read about all the new plays on Broadway and how excited she would get when, sometimes, she even recognized the name of a friend. She would take me to every touring production that ever came through town. I knew that my mother had never, ever stopped loving the theater.

"And, I guess, she never stopped missing New York. One day, she told us that she was leaving and that was that. I guess she was afraid that we would try to stop her. Or that we would come and get her against her will. She would never even let me know where she lived. Her Social Security check went right into the bank. There were times when I couldn't understand her secrecy, but I think that I understand it now. She had a life here. She was Emily Toujours. She could come back and start over again. And, most of all, she could be near the theater she loved. I think of her sitting in the dark of the audience, dreaming of what might have been. She still loved us, I know. Every month, she would call me and tell me that she was okay. She always described the shows she had seen and her memory was so vivid—it was almost like being there with her."

She stopped for a moment to regain her composure. In the soft light of the church, there were many people who saw Emily in her daughter's determined face.

"My mother will be very much missed," she continued. "Not just by you, but by me and my family. When she didn't call last week, I knew that something was wrong. But I didn't know where to begin. You can't imagine the hurt that a person can go through in just a few hours of not knowing. I was lucky. A few days later, I found my answer in the newspaper.

"But if not for you, the police tell me, I might never have known what happened to her. It would have been too late, they say. She'd have been buried as a number. Instead, I've come to New York to bury my mother. And she will be buried here, because I know it's where she'd want to stay.

"But I've also come to New York to thank you for giving me my mother back. To thank you for giving my family the opportunity to grieve her. And, most of all, to thank you for caring what happened to my mother, both before and after she died."

The woman stopped and looked out over the church very

slowly, as if seeking to memorize all of their faces. She sighed and the sound was caught by the microphone. It moved through the church like a shadow.

T.S. reached for Auntie Lil's hand. He knew now that their latest journey was nearing its end.

"My mother's real name was Eleanor Perkins," Emily's daughter concluded. "And she was once a most extraordinary woman."